I0775623

Burden to Bear

BURDEN TO BEAR

SPEAR OF THE GODS
BOOK ONE

GREGORY AMATO

SED FERRO
PRESS

Published by Sed Ferro Press
Copyright © 2023

Cover design by James T. Egan of Bookfly Design
Illustration by Blane Bellerud
Edited by Jess Lawrence

Paperback ISBN: 979-8-9880613-0-4
Hardcover ISBN: 979-8-9880613-1-1

Sed Ferro Press
3439 NE Sandy Blvd, #484
Portland, OR 97232

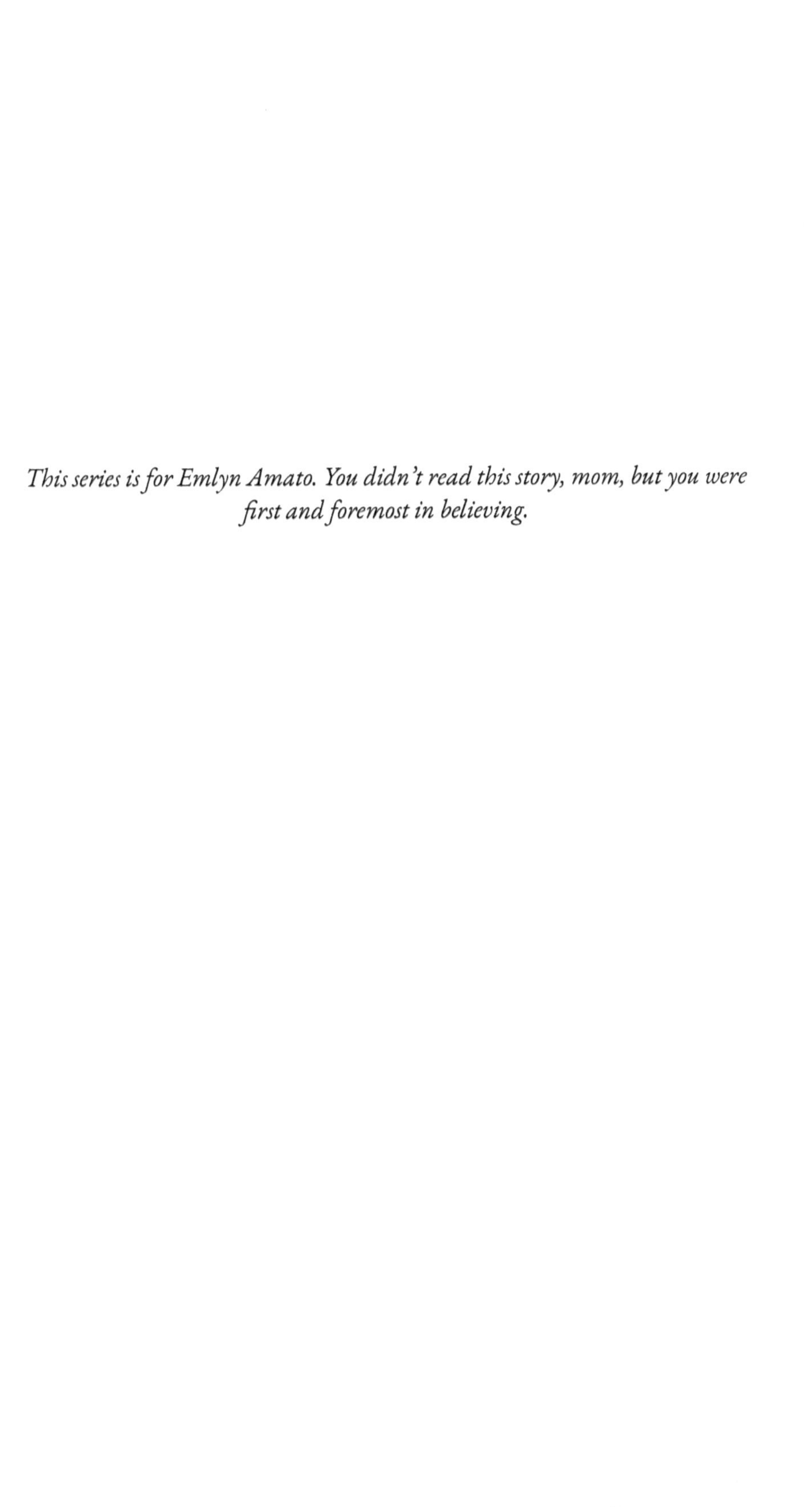

This series is for Emlyn Amato. You didn't read this story, mom, but you were first and foremost in believing.

Also By Gregory Amato

THE SPEAR OF THE GODS SAGA

Burden to Bear

Rune to Ruin

Fallen to Fury (forthcoming)

OTHER SPEAR OF THE GODS STORIES

Trollsbane

The Skald

The Sorcerer's Reward

STANDALONE STORIES

The Once and Future Sword

CONTENTS

Author's Note

Once upon a time, I wished somebody would write a Norse fantasy series.

I wanted it to feature the gods and legendary heroes I knew, treating magic and the supernatural in a way that would have been familiar to the people of the Viking Age. Or at least as well as could be reconstructed. And maybe, just maybe, the writer could try to have a sense of humor.

I picked up novels about vikings wherever I could find them. Harry Harrison's series, The Hammer and the Cross, co-written with the brilliant medievalist scholar Tom Shippey, was amazing. It focused on an alternate history of England though, and I was looking for something with more fantasy elements.

Eventually I realized I would need to write the series I wanted to read, if I ever wanted to read it. That series is Spear of the Gods.

This is a story about badasses like Beowulf, Hrolf Kraki, and Arrow-Odd. Like them, but not exactly as their written stories are known. Spear of the Gods harkens back to times when those stories really happened, when those stories were still just oral tellings. When they were a few hundred years away from coalescing into "canonical" written forms. It is set in a world where the Norse myths are real, where legendary heroes and monsters fight for ever-lasting word-fame.

Our protagonist is a skald. A storyteller. A poet finding his way to becoming a man and then a leader. Through his voice we hear echoes of familiar myths.

I take many liberties. Talking ravens trading stories as currency? My invention. But there's nothing in the myths that says they didn't trade stories. And how else do you think Odin's ravens give him news from all the world?

The world of Spear of the Gods is informed by modern scholarship, but it is not historical. It is fantasy based on sagas and myths, and that means adventure. Maybe these books will make you late to dinner. I certainly hope so.

-**Gregory Amato**, 13 January 2023

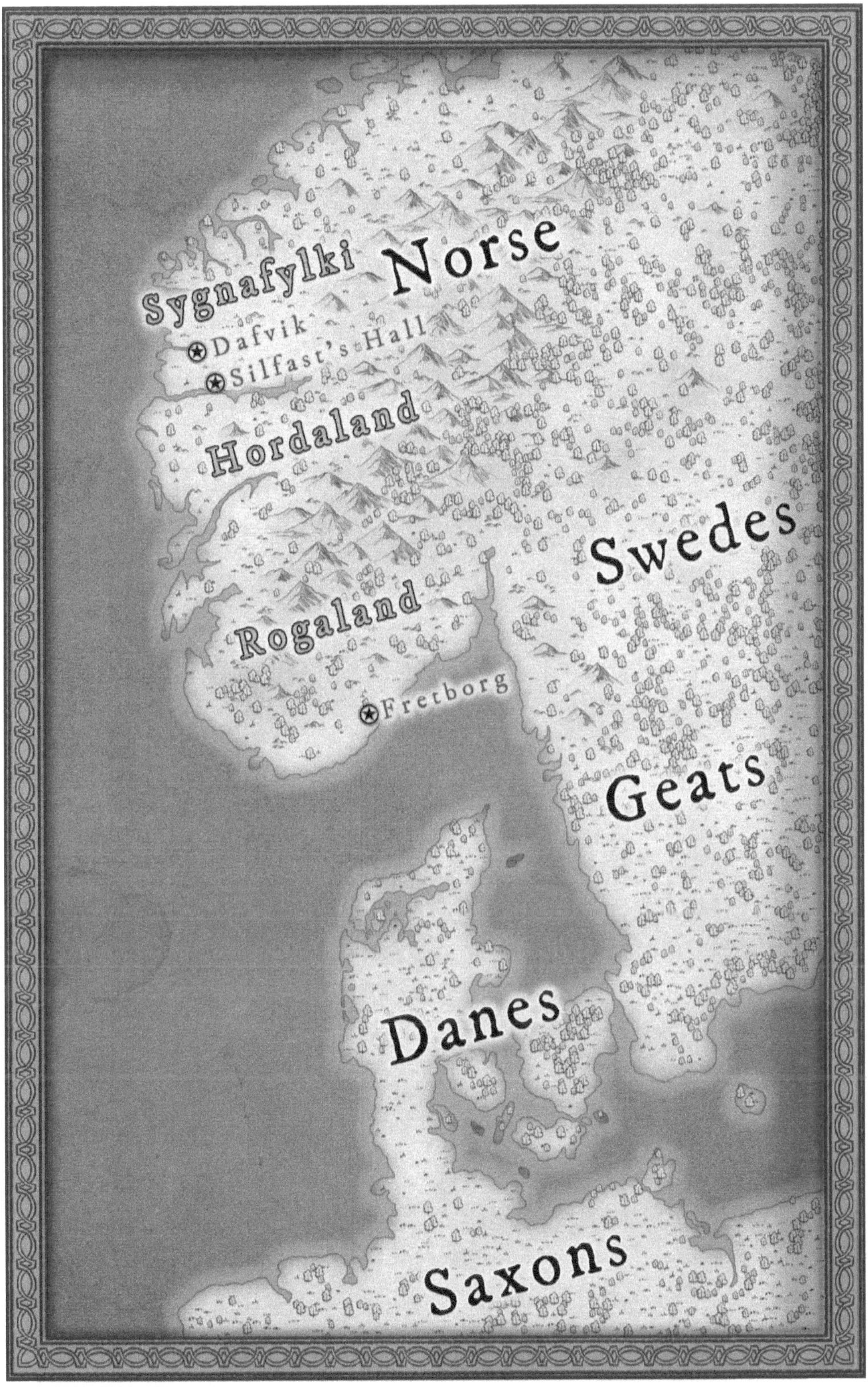

Sygnafylki
Norse
Dafvik
Silfast's Hall
Hordaland
Swedes
Rogaland
Fretborg
Geats
Danes
Saxons

Geats
Jutland
Danes
Fjon
Sjaelland
Roskilde
Lejre

Runes - The Elder Futhark (Pre-Viking Age Alphabet)

Rune	Name	Ideographic Meaning
ᚠ	fehu	wealth; cattle
ᚢ	uruz	aurochs; strength
ᚦ	þurisaz	þurs, jǫtunn
ᚨ	ansuz	god
ᚱ	raiðo	ride, journey
ᚲ	kaunan	ulcer, blister, boil
ᚷ	gebo	gift
ᚹ	wunjo	joy
ᚺ	hagalaz	hail
ᚾ	nauðiz	need
ᛁ	isaz	ice
ᛃ	jera	harvest; good year
ᛈ	perðo	pear tree or game piece
ᛇ	eihaz	yew tree
ᛉ	algiz	moose or elk
ᛊ	sowilo	sun
ᛏ	tiwaz	the god Tyr
ᛒ	berkana	birch tree
ᛖ	ehwaz	horse
ᛗ	mannaz	human
ᛚ	laguz	water
ᛜ	ingwaz	the god Frey
ᛞ	dagaz	day
ᛟ	oþala	inheritance

Burden to Bear

CHAPTER 1

ODIN, OUTSMARTED

WHEN I FIRST MET MAGNUS THE RED, HE WAS SOBER ENOUGH TO heckle me but too drunk to realize he was flirting with a witch. I didn't know his name at the time of the heckling. But even not knowing him, and even though he was heckling me, I knew I couldn't leave him to his fate.

The witch in question was young and beautiful and smiled as she looked into his eyes. She played half-shy by looking away and then back again. A golden band glowed along the top of her brown hair like the low embers in the middle of the longhouse we sat in. Her impression was of warmth and ease, with only the hint of something mysterious.

Warmth and ease were what we all wanted in Silfast's longhouse. A hot meal, some good ale. Stories and music in the low firelight while we kept the dark and cold of night at bay. Silfast was a generous host, so the stew had been good and the ale even better. Stories and music were largely left to me, however, owing to my particular skills. I was a simple delivery man looking to bring a sword to a customer and stay safe in the process.

Well, not all that simple. Maybe the other guests were friends of Silfast, or maybe they had exchanged gifts and favors already. Warmth and ease for us all, as well as safety. I was welcome to stay as long as I performed, and perform I did. Others could play the lyre a little, and some had a few good stories to tell. But I knew the best stories, those of heroes and monsters, and such entertainment was always welcome.

Monsters in the hall was not something I could stay comfortable with. Even wearing a necklace of protection from my foster mother. I wasn't sure how it protected me. Maybe my skin would resist the bite of a blade, or enemies would be less likely to notice me. She had never elaborated. She had elaborated on ideas like 'Looks are no mark of character,' however. This witch didn't look like a monster, of course. The worst ones never do.

Unless you knew how to find the truth in the details. And while she was smiling, keeping Magnus' attention toward her face, I could see her hands were far older than the rest of her. That was my first clue.

The box she carried was my next clue. What was that thing, and why was she carrying it? Just a box the size of a pair of shoes and carved out of an old ash tree. Maybe it depended on whose shoes, so the part about size was relative. I knew my wood, though, and ash it was. Clean but marked by the holding of many hands through the years, perhaps passed down from a relative that woman would never have known.

This was not a usual thing carried by the traveling merchants, mercenaries, and jarls passing through Silfast's longhouse. Ancient, bony hands grasped that box and held it like a dragon clawing at its hoard. The hands were a clue, and there had to be a reason they gripped the box so tight.

She was a full head taller than Magnus, a fact made obvious by his awkward reaching around her shoulder. Magnus was not a tall man and must have been used to things being out of his reach. When the woman didn't shy away, he grinned and drank more ale and listened as she whispered into his ear. A spell to muddle his senses, no doubt, as if the ale was not hard at work doing the same thing already.

One bony hand moved from the box to the silver armring Magnus wore with a caress that sent shivers down my spine. Shaped into two outward-facing axe heads, the armring's shine dulled as she stroked it.

Magnus looked only a little older than me, and I had just twenty winters then. Battle scars decorated his face and arms, marks of a warrior's life. Perhaps he was a mercenary, I thought at the time. Or perhaps he was of higher status. It could be some lord's champion was purring like a kitten under that spell.

Without the bright light of day, it can be a tricky thing to discern what is really there and what your mind makes up for you to see. There is a kind of clarity I get while trying to perform, the poetry of it cutting through whatever mist muddled my senses. I had a little of that feeling as I told my story and strummed my lyre, and my vision became sharper.

I couldn't cut that witch's glamour down with my poetry, but I could see those hands! The poetry of the story came to a head, and I improvised the tune on my lyre. It forced her attention away from Magnus just for a moment, and I saw her grimace.

Did I mention I was good? I was good. And the story I told—about Odin both up to some trickery and himself being tricked—was among my favorites. It had intrigue and magic, hospitality and violence. That was part of the story, at least. The bit about Odin bookended a long, poetic telling of the gods and other fantastic things in the world.

I was—still am, I suppose—a skald. And what is a skald other than lore's ledger, truth's triumph, history's hero? If I or someone like me didn't put it to verse, it probably never happened. We told stories of gods and heroes at night over warm cups of ale as long as there was an audience. There's a power there, in the poems that preserve memories of lives and deeds and ideas. There's a power in the poetic styles themselves, too, if you know how to use them.

Maybe not as much power as sorcerers like this witch had. And sorcerers can smell you trying to sniff them out. The grimace was a fleeting thing. When she looked up, that woman shot me a look like a valkyrie thinking how my entrails would make nice thread for weaving.

Imagine having all the smoke of a huge longhouse concentrated into space the size of a pea. Now imagine that pea shot from a heavy bow into your nostril and through the back of your skull, and that's what hit me. The evil eye just about knocked me off my bench.

Would have done, had Bolli Mossneck not been there to shove me back into place.

"Oy, Ansgar!" said my neckbearded friend. "Maybe something a little more exciting next." Bolli was the only man I knew to let his beard just grow. No shaving, no trimming like everyone else (everyone who didn't have invisible, wispy facial hair like me). That black chin-forest could have been residence to nesting birds if he ever stayed still long enough.

"What?" My own voice echoed in my head. The hall and its visitors came in and out of focus. I thrust down my lyre and grasped the table in front of me as my senses reeled. The hearth fire glowed like molten rock. Chatter from all sides shouted and muted at random. Banners, armor, and idols from unknown lands spoke in languages even I did not recognize while colors danced on the walls.

"Something more exciting," whispered Bolli. "That last story put Silfast to sleep!"

I knew the man well enough to know we should have called him Bolli the *Drengr*. The man had the cool courage and sense of fair play not all warriors possess. He didn't flaunt it either, I just knew it from how he had helped me out of a bad spot one time. Hence *drengr,* which was like calling him Bolli the Badass, as no real badass who ever existed felt the need to advertise it. So I trusted the man and took his suggestion as a surprise, phrased as if I had done something wrong.

My senses rocked slowly back into place and I could see that something was indeed wrong. Silfast, the hall's owner and my host on many occasions, sat chin-in-fist on his high seat, eyes shut.

"That was a terrible story!" shouted a drunken voice. "People stand around until one falls over dead. Where is the adventure, the excitement?"

All I knew at the time was the shouting came from a short but brawny man with fire-red hair. The curly locks framed a face not much older than mine but worn quite a bit more. It had weathered more than a few fights, judging from the scar above one eye. Yet whatever violence Magnus had seen, he was almost always smiling.

Standing up and spilling ale as he waved his cup for emphasis, he continued, "Standing around and naming things: What's intimidating about that? I think the skald has taken too much to drink with too little entertainment in return. Throw him out!"

That was Magnus. He would later blame the ale, and then the witch, and eventually claim that no man can overcome both evil magic and wit-dulling drink at the same time.

I would reply that wise men are more apt than the unwise to avoid that position entirely.

The blaming would come much later though. In the moment I had to win my night's hospitality or else risk my life sleeping under a tree. That part was not so uncomfortable—the issue was more with being robbed. I was carrying an important delivery, a sword my foster father forged. Had I hidden in the woods, perhaps I could stay there safely. But now my presence was known to everyone who had passed through the hall, and that marked me if I had to sleep outside and unprotected.

There was also the issue of things that walk at night and eat people sleeping under trees. I did not want to think too much about such possibilities. Nods and murmurs of assent warned my position was more precarious than I had thought, however, so I was nervous. Comfort and safety were high on my list of priorities. I had been on a few delivery runs already and thought myself a skilled traveler. I had overcome the dangers of night, after all.

But wouldn't a wise man avoid having to sleep outside in the first place? Yes, he would, and for good reason!

The look in Silfast's eyes when he opened them was reassuring. "I hear your request, Magnus," said the hall's owner. "The skald has made nights in this hall a merrier place more times than you have." Great news. "One dull story does not undo his reputation." Bad news.

"Let his fate hang on the next story then," said Magnus. "One more chance, but if this one is boring, he sleeps outside!" The murmurs were low but undeniably in his favor as he turned to me. "Let's hear a story about Thor."

"That's our heritage you're talking about," I protested. "I mean, the story I just told. That's one of the most important stories about Odin there is!" A wiser man might have made a joke and regained the audience. But I was hot about having my poetry attacked, and I had to explain why I was right and everyone else was wrong.

Magnus choked from drinking and laughing at the same time. "Nobody likes Odin," he said, "and nobody likes you!" The murmurs turned to laughter. Thralls scurried to bring more ale and then get out of sight as quickly as possible. Dozens of men and women were turning on me like sharks in bloody water, and the thralls did not want to share my bad luck.

He was half-right, at a minimum. The hard-drinking, hard-fighting Thor was far more relatable than the hard-drinking, hard-thinking Odin.

"Tell a story about Njord!" came a call from behind Magnus the Heckler.

"What better adventures than with that fine sea god?" added the man next to him.

They had been sitting near Magnus. Perhaps they were unknown to him. Or perhaps they were with him but edging away from Magnus' romantic interest. One was a bit fairer than the other, but even in the low firelight I could tell they must be brothers.

Murmurs became a general blur of indistinguishable voices at that. The first brother spoke up to add nonsense syllables. Soon his brother did the same, and it was clear the two meant only to raise the general volume to enjoy the chaos of the situation. Those two did not look inclined to get anywhere near Magnus' witch, who remained sitting, watching, holding her weird box.

Magnus hopped onto their table and motioned the audience to quiet down. "A story about Njord? I think I speak for us all in saying we've heard that one, and we don't need to hear any more about feet!" More laughter.

"It was a long trip to get here," I said, trying to change tack and get the audience back. "How about a story about wargs and witches and other things hiding in the forest? I can tell those from exp—"

Another look at the witch and I knew where I had gone wrong. I could blame her for my failure or adjust to my audience. Let her weave whatever magic she wanted; she would not outperform me in my natural element.

Like Odin in the story I had told, my audience just wanted to be well received with hospitality. Speaking riddles at them, even in nice poetic form, would only ruin their experience. There are two parts to that story, and the prose part is supposed to be the setup. It frames the second part, a long poetic telling about many mythical things. My audience was less interested in that forest of wonder painted by the poem than the trees of intrigue set up by the prose.

Or in other words: Focus on how Odin was set up, set on fire, and worst of all lost a bet to his wife.

Surely, that is not the grander part of the story. The poetry tells us how the universe was created, where the gods live, what creatures live in Yggdrasil, the world tree. It contains details like the names of the wolves that chase the sun and moon. And, as might be expected, it includes a few exploits involving Odin tricking people. Tricking and stealing from them, killing them, or otherwise taking advantage of them. Use your imagination.

Did I mention nobody likes Odin? No, that was Magnus. He was quite right about that. Odin was a god to be admired from afar, and only for a few select qualities. Emphasis on 'from afar.'

"Tell a story about Thor!" exclaimed Magnus again, slamming his fist down on the nearest table.

"I can tell something more exciting. I did not realize it would be redhead-themed story night." Right on the line of joke and insult, which is where my people like to be most of the time. It's also why so many of my people end up taking jokes as insults and killing each other. Improvising meant hoping for the best in more ways than one. "Maybe you missed the point of the story," I said, hoping he could not ignore the challenge. "I thought you would enjoy a story about gambling and good hospitality."

Again the nods and murmurs, which I hated. Perched away from the action was the easiest place of all to level criticism from. Murmuring compounded the cowardice of such criticism. Sweating, heart pounding, uncertain, I swallowed hard and hoped the murmurs wouldn't seize on my fear.

Confusion swirled in the crowd. Magnus, now responsible for speaking to the desire of the whole audience, had to take the bait. "What gambling?"

"And there are drinks involved in that story!" I continued, ignoring Magnus' question for now. I turned toward a woken Silfast and addressed him next. "No ale for a guest," I said, checking my hands as if there ought to be a cup full of ale in one of them. "Being ale-stingy is what gets the king killed, in case you missed that part!"

Laughter. If you want a crowd with you, get them to laugh on your behalf and not at your expense.

"Get him a horn before Silfast falls over dead!" yelled Bolli Mossneck.

A horn, he said. Not one of the ceramic cups so easily broken and so easily replaced, drinking horns were for special occasions or special people. Bolli held up his cup and banged the table with his fist, a sound now in my favor. Laughter and confederates in the audience: Once you have both, it is your audience to lose.

"There's no better advice for men in that one," I said as a young thrall handed me a horn of ale. Dozens of voices mingled. Some laughed, some expressed disbelief.

"And what advice is that?" said Silfast, his voice quieting all others.

I took a drink to stall for a moment's thought. No way could I give away the punchline up front. "Therein lies the magic of a story, Silfast! It is there, but you can't see it until you can see it. But the understanding only comes from the hearing of the—"

"GET ON WITH IT THEN."

I used a different tone to tell that same myth again without the poetry and cosmology included in my first telling. I just moved one key part to the end for a snappier conclusion:

"The gods were bored, as gods often are. Maybe Fire Hair is right about there being too much standing around. But standing around makes gods and men alike restless, and restlessness always breeds trouble.

"Odin and his wife Frigg, being bored, decided to make a bet. They saw a king with two children and argued over which child would make a better ruler. Frigg bet on Agnarr, and Odin bet on Geirroth, and they both gave advice to their chosen ones.

"Odin advised Geirroth to get rid of his brother. The boy listened! Put him on a boat and shoved it off headed toward an unknown fate. Agnarr landed up north of Halogaland where he scratched out a living among trolls and *jǫtnar*. Meanwhile, Geirroth became king upon his father's death. See? No standing around there.

"So Odin won the bet! At least up until that point, and at that point he lorded it over his wife Frigg because he was right and she was wrong." My voice rose in triumph with the last part of that sentence, sensing this would play well with the audience. The men banged their tables and cheered.

"But Frigg was not done. 'Geirroth is a stingy host,' she said. 'Some king you raised! He seized power only to torture his guests when they appeared too often.'"

"So she lied!" cried Magnus.

"She didn't care what the truth was in that case. She cared about telling her husband he was wrong." More banging, some laughing. This was not my intended direction, but it would do me well for the finale.

"Frigg had thrown down a challenge, and Odin had to show her she was wrong. So he set out on foot to prove it, blue-cloaked and hooded and calling himself Grimnir. The dogs in Geirroth's hall would not bark at him. That was suspicious! So was his refusal to give more of his background than a name. That earned him a hot seat in the hall. Geirroth placed him between two fires and chained him there, giving him nothing to eat or drink,"—and here I paused to take a gulp myself—"but still Grimnir said nothing.

"Now that's a hot bit of standing around! And not very hospitable.

"Well, this was many years since the original separation of the brothers, and Geirroth at that point had a son named in honor of his older brother Agnarr. Agnarr the Not-Troll-Raised was in his father's hall and didn't understand what was going on. Eight nights Geirroth demanded answers. Eight nights Grimnir gave him none. Agnarr had enough of that and braved those flames. He said he didn't approve of that sort of mistreatment and brought Grimnir a horn of mead.

"Always treat your guests well! They might be Odin in disguise. Once offered a drink, the god dropped his ruse and announced himself and a great deal more. Geirroth certainly changed his tone then! But Odin promised him misfortune, and that is not the mouth you want to hear about misfortune from. Geirroth got up and stumbled right down onto his own sword and died, and his son Agnarr became king." I drank again for pause, waiting for the question.

"So, what's the advice for men?" came the question, as I knew it would.

"Aha! Well, there is this other part of the story, the really important part, and therein lies the advice. You see, Geirroth was expecting Grimnir or someone like him. A woman had come to his hall and told him 'BEWARE! An evil old wizard has it in for you and is coming to your hall. You will know him by how your dogs refuse to bark in his presence!' And that old woman was none other than Frigg's handmaiden," I said, turning toward the witch and pointing at her. "*The witch Fulla.*"

Many a true word spoken in jest has gotten a skald into trouble, but I figured I was already on this witch's bad side. The dramatic flourish was rather ham-handed and therefore not my style, but subtle had not worked. Judging from the laughter when I pointed, and from the witch's thin expression, the current style was having an effect.

"Frigg had dispatched her with that message right away, before Odin set off. Fulla received very generous hospitality, by the way.

"Then there he went, wise man of the *Æsir*, Snatcher of Runes, Lord of the Gallows, right into Frigg's trap. And poor Geirroth! He had withheld hospitality from the Terrible One himself, snaring himself in the same trap.

"But remembering that story, you should always take heed of the good advice it has for men." I paused, sucked in my breath, even took a draught of my drink as the silent audience waited. "Never make bets with women."

Magnus' head fell. The howls of his two comrades echoed through the hall like war-whoops even before the rest of the audience erupted in cheers and applause. Silfast smiled and nodded. Bolli Mossneck's big hand fell on my shoulder in appreciation.

"That was worth the trip by itself!" he said.

I could not find the witch anywhere in the audience. Perhaps she had seen where things were going and taken to the night sky, or gone underground. Could witches do that? No matter. Magnus might still not see through her glamour, but he would have second thoughts about her, if just for a moment, because of my story. Whatever her purpose had been, she was gone from there.

Silfast called me to drink at his side after that. I told him stories of my travels, embellished with dirty jokes. He gifted me a fine blue cloak in appreciation. I thanked him dozens of times as the night wore on and my memory began to fail from too much alcohol. But why worry? Silfast's hall was my last stop before my destination. I could make my delivery and return in the same day even with a late start.

I had improved the mood under pressure, avoided bodily injury, and secured lasting hospitality. It was a good night that night. For the first time, I felt I knew something of what I was doing and could deal with whatever came about.

That was the beginning of this story as I see it. The beginning of high adventure and deadly intrigue, grand heroism and terrible tragedy. The beginning of going from boy to man in a way more important than growing older.

Next, I had a delivery to make, and though I could not see it at the time, that was no less part of the story.

CHAPTER 2

THOR-SOMETHINGS

THORGILS THORKELSSON HAD SIX SONS, I WOULD DISCOVER. I bet you can't guess which redheaded god they were all named after.

The day after I nearly had to find a tree to sleep under, I was feeling the effects of too much alcohol and self-congratulation. I had been drunk the night before—too drunk. It was understandable: I had been staring down long odds at singing for my supper once the heckler had begun his work, but in the end I had won over even him. That was a victory, victories deserved celebration, and celebration meant a headache the next day or you were doing it wrong. Or so went the understanding of the time.

My clothes were dry, my belly had been filled and emptied and filled again, and I had packed away my things before making for Thorgils' farm a few miles from the mead hall. A fine sword in its fine scabbard was bundled tight and strapped to my pack. Leaving it with our customer would make my load lighter and less precarious, and I hoped that would help cure my headache.

That headache told me I'd had enough excitement for one trip already. It made me eager to head home. Once I handed Thorgils the sword and he handed me the payment, I could do just that. Maybe linger for a good meal, if a good meal was in order.

Good food seemed like a fair bet when the house came into view. Thorgils was rich! If I hadn't deduced that by his purchase of an extremely fine sword, his house told me so. A roof that had seen little weather told me the house was built within the last year. Not a longhouse like Silfast's, meant for dozens of guests at a time, but a large house for a family. The smoke vent at the fatter end was carved such that it looked like a smoking dragon's head. The door was painted bright red, not that I got to it right away.

Instead, I met Thorkel Thorgilsson, the customer's son, who was outside stretching his legs. He breathed new life into my headache when he motioned for several unfriendly-looking servants to surround me, all of them holding sharp or pointy farm implements.

"I am Ansgar the Skald," I said, "and—"

"We don't need any skalds," said Thorkel.

"And I am here to deliver a sword to Thorgils."

Pleasantries took a bit more time to exchange than usual since they were anything but pleasant. Finally Thorkel dismissed his surly servants when I allowed him to examine the sword, his interest focused on the New Shiny Thing I had brought for his father.

"Seems too light," he said, pantomiming a crushing attack from above. Soft blonde hair wisped up and down like fine hay as he moved with mule-like grace. "My father may not be pleased. I can keep this for him and pay you. Half."

Too light, eh? Perhaps he meant me rather than the sword. He definitely didn't know a good weapon from an excellent one.

To accept the claim that Halstein's forge works were worth less than the agreed-to price would be unmanly. And foolish. Halstein was old, no question. The man was both my grandfather and foster father since my real father was ever away. But there was a good reason that old man's smithing was in demand for hundreds of miles around, at least by those who could pay.

Now, to indicate the deliverer was about to be robbed purely because he could be—well that was fine. As long as it was announced and not done in secret. I had heard that kind of drivel before though.

"I am to put this sword into your father's hands," I said. "The rest of the payment is due at that time. Word at Silfast's mead hall was your family was quite honorable. Especially when I told everyone there the errand I would be about today."

I knew little of this family other than they had bought this farm a few years ago. There was no need to know where they lived before—I was just the delivery man and a sometimes charcoal burner. The forge did not hold much interest for me, certainly not as much as the stories of heroes and gods and monsters Halstein and my foster mother Taika told me. Still, he had demanded some participation in the physical labor.

The dirtiest, least desirable physical labor around was burning charcoal, and that was largely what I had done. I doubted Thorkel had done much labor himself, but he also did not have the air of learning lore or music or languages—the things I bolted for as soon as my charcoal burning duties were finished.

That troll-wife lover Thorkel eyed me and nodded. He understood the implication of what I said, learned man or not. Pay in full, don't even think about negotiating down the price, and let me leave in peace or your family reputation will suffer over a few trifling silver coins. He did not like it one bit.

There was an intelligence to Thorkel I had to admit to as much as be wary of. He could size me up easily: Not much of a fighter. And he could threaten me. He could calculate angles and odds on what might get him the best result, paying or robbing. And about who was likely to find out if he robbed me, if anyone.

Thorkel was, as we would say then, a *níðingr*. A villain worthy of scorn, a man who knew how to win but had no sense of honorable play. Not a *drengr* who looked for the biggest and baddest challenges. A *níðingr* was a predator looking for easy, uncomplicated prey that would be unable to strike back. A useless, cowardly person.

Thorkel also didn't know a damned thing about how to swing a sword, and I couldn't stay away from that line of inquiry. One thing a *níðingr* can't stop doing is talking about himself and how important he is.

"Oh, I see it now," I said. "It was your father's purchase but intended for you as the firstborn. Am I right?"

Thorkel smirked and nodded. He was the important one. And the sword had to be perfect for the perfect son. He could tell I understood.

"You will receive a fine weapon then," I added. "Halstein is my foster father, the best smith in the west fjord lands and well beyond. You know Norse steel is not always the best, I take it? Sharp but brittle, or strong but can't take a good edge. His swords take a wicked edge, but are supple enough they don't break even in heavy battle. Nobody knows pattern-welded steel better than Halstein. Take a look—see the wavy patterns in the blade?"

I approached and took the liberty of tracing some with my finger, careful not to touch the side of the blade. "He takes different steels and folds them over each other again and again, giving the strength and the edge you want at the same time."

That had to appeal to him, I thought.

"The pommel could be more ornate." Declaring himself a halfwit would have been less pathetic than that statement.

I had to be patient and ginger. No gain in contradicting stupidity. I reached deep into the reservoir of patience in breathing my foster mother had taught me to keep my mouth shut.

I knew enough from my foster father's explanations what the pommel was for a sword. But as he had explained once, 'Sometimes the straight road is the journey with more fighting.' Better the indirect route in those cases.

The pommel was a counterweight to the blade. A pommel too light would make changing the line of attack slow. A pommel too heavy would weigh the sword down and make it difficult to cut or stab. A man testing a sword's balance by considering whether it was bejeweled rather than balanced was an idiot. I had to make sure this idiot was happy, or at best I would be explaining to Halstein why I had failed.

"Ornate with rubies and sapphires perhaps?" I asked.

"That would be a good start," he said.

"I can see you are very rich. Rich enough to throw jewels away, it seems."

That got his attention.

"What do you mean?"

"Well, stones inset into the pommel will come out or be broken. Imagine you need to strike an armored enemy with the pommel—those stones are going to collide with pure steel." I let this sink in for a moment. "Very good steel, if it's made by my grandfather. And that is in the heat of battle. You would never see those stones again."

Thorkel nodded, again examining the pommel. "If he is as good as you say, I can understand that."

Few men could afford swords and fewer still could afford Halstein's work. It was excellent, the result of long decades spent honing his craft. And it was rare, as he could not work as much as maybe he once did. He did not have all the energy of his youth, partly because of all the fighting and trading he had done decades ago and partly because he had given up some time and energy to foster such a difficult youth as me.

I was standoffish before I could stand, and while he was a good teacher, he did not have the warmth of his Sami wife Taika. I owed them much since my father was ever traveling and my mother had died of illness, too early for me to remember her. But I had never been an easy one to raise.

I had mitigated the difficulty of my existence, somewhat, by acting as a reliable long-distance delivery man for him. Fighting was never my desire or talent, but avoiding it I was somewhat an expert at. Running, climbing, swimming, skiing—I could do any of those for hours on end and easily outpace an enemy, assuming that enemy was human. As those humans germane to my home preferred to focus on the hardest strikes, the most powerful blows, they were usually poorer on the endurance side. A reliable delivery man for carrying valuable weapons and armor on one trip or carrying payment on the trip back was of considerable value to the old man.

He made use of me and I made my living without needing to insert myself into a shield wall. Few would seek to rob me as I traveled in the cold season, and as I preferred to take roads not traveled, it was unlikely anyone would watch for me. I enjoyed those quiet days and nights, unbothered and unworried.

And I enjoyed plying my trade as a skald, or at least most of the time. It was worth getting a real meal and a warmer place to sleep when I found my way to a hall. Singing for supper was not usually as contentious as it had been the previous night.

Then again, collecting payment was not usually as contentious as this errand had become, and I was losing patience.

"Perhaps it is not for you though, if it is not sufficiently pretty," I said. "I cannot say, I can only say I must deliver it to Thorgils in person. Perhaps it is a gift for someone else. A sibling perhaps. Maybe a gift for you is expected from another source."

"Hmph!" sniffed Thorkel. "I am the first son. Why would my father give a sword to one of the others?"

"How many brothers do you have?"

"My brothers? Thorstein, Thorleif, Thormod, Thorald, and Thorarin."

I blinked. Could he be joking?

"Ah, I know," he continued. "It could be part of a dowry for my sister Aslaug."

Not joking. Apparently, one sibling had the bad judgment to be born a woman, and so had been left out of the Thor-naming convention. Whatever this family was about, my sense of it was I had best get my business done and leave them be before I recited a poem about Thorgils not having enough arrows in his quiver for a seventh son.

"Better to keep it well oiled and unblemished," I said, taking the weapon back. "It is not particularly ornate to begin with, as you pointed out."

Past a few lazy guards and servants who were either well-treated thralls (less likely) or badly-treated freemen (more likely), Thorkel received me in his family's hall. There are responsibilities with hospitality, both on the giving and receiving ends. Thorkel had to offer even though he would have preferred I go back to town and wait.

I had to accept, even though I would have preferred the same thing. To do otherwise in either case would be an insult, insults meant damage to one's honor, and damage to one's honor meant either pay weregild or fight. Better for everyone to just endure the company at hand for a while.

As a guest at many halls, I was rather an expert at discerning the quality of the food and drink. The first few deliveries I had been wide-eyed and accepting of whatever was put in front of me. Later it became obvious when the host had brought out his good ale or mead or had simply tapped a poor brew.

In Thorkel's case, he made a show of calling his sister out to meet me and serve me rather than have my soup brought by a thrall. He was an imperious one, favored by his father and acting like it. Aslaug did as she was told and then disappeared to her weaving away from the main hall.

The soup and ale were both thin. Not as thin as the conversation, but still embarrassing for any decent host to offer. Especially a rich one. Thorkel finally asked for a story, and I gave him the previous night's attempt. The boring one, I mean. It put him to sleep, which I was very happy with.

Thorgils was not long in returning after that, and thank goodness, I thought, given the awkwardness of being there. To shed a few pounds of steel for less than a pound in silver was hardly the best part of the deal. I pined for the open air, with just myself for company for a few days before making it home.

Thorgils was not a man to be rushed, however. He wore a bright green cloak with gold embroidery and had many fine things on under that. After introducing himself there was to be no business conversation until he'd had a chance to change out of his muddy flared pants and shoes. Gray mane slicked back and tight, it was at first difficult to notice much about him other than his perpetual surprised and angry look, as if his scalp were pulling his forehead back.

"You have had good hospitality, yes?" he said, having finished his preparations. "My son has been good to you?"

Thorkel hovered just out of my peripheral vision. "Yes, he offered food and drink," I said, declining to use the word 'good.'

"I am pleased then. Sit." I did so and placed the sword and scabbard on the table. "No, no. No business yet. You have traveled far and it is not yet even summer. Tell us of your travels. I rode off right away this morning, looking for you. You are here, yet I did not see you on the road."

However awkward I had felt before was amplified by this hyper-vigilant lord. His words said everything of friendliness, but even by his fire I did not feel warm. Something was wrong, and I could not tell what. Unlike his son, he had an accent. I considered asking him where he was from but decided against it.

Perhaps I was the hyper-vigilant one, I thought. A second look at that face told me no. Not the only one, at least. I was being studied, but for what purpose?

"I found Silfast's hall yesterday evening, so I stayed there the night. Yes, you would not see me on the road. I tend to stay off roads. Wherever it seems no one else would go is my route, otherwise it is too easy for bandits to lie in wait."

"But by which way did you come to the hall? It is cold for sailing."

"I came on foot. Running and skiing mostly, a little climbing to skirt the west side of the lake to the north of here. It was easy, I did not even need to use my crampons. Then due south as the lake comes to a point, where a single yew tree sits atop an old barrow. It is only a three-day journey from Dafvik that way."

"Right by the barrow? And you cast no spells?"

"Spells? I am no sorcerer," I said, thinking this old man was very confused.

So I went by a barrow mound. So what? If you don't try to rob the dead of their possessions, they will leave you alone. Usually.

I always thought that mound might not be a grave site but a home for elves. Taika had advised me to offer a little blood there, but I had preferred to offer just quiet respect instead. "I give the mound a respectful distance and a nod of recognition as I go by, and find the dead are not anxious to share my company. I told stories for my supper and a bed of straw in the hall. They fed me then and this morning, and gave me directions to find your hall here."

"Hmm." He nodded.

Thorkel cut in, much to my surprise, in Greek. His gestures were friendly, inclusive, as if he was explaining something to his curmudgeonly father on my behalf. That cheery tone was a mask for his real intentions though.

"*He is clever,*" said Thorkel. "*His explanation makes sense. The seeress warned us of this. He could have sold the real sword and bought this one to take a profit, and then still be paid.*"

I traveled for a living and was fostered by a man who had traded around the world and back again. I hadn't placed Thorgils' accent at first, but Greek made sense now. He must have hired himself out in Miklagard. It was a profitable place to do so, if you didn't mind the long trip.

I spoke a handful of languages given my foster father's insistent tutoring. Greek was among them, so his words were obvious. I also knew Frankish, Latin, Sami, and even that mother of unintelligible languages, East Norse (ha!). But I digress.

A man selling himself as a mercenary to the Byzantines would do well to learn Greek. Halstein had done that and learned plenty of other languages. It seemed Thorgils had done the same, and that was probably where he had amassed his fortune.

"*Let him get far enough away first,*" replied Thorgils. "*Gather your brothers and ride north to that mound. On the road or not, he must break the edge of the forest there. No one will see, and you can give his body to the waves over the cliffs nearby.*"

They nodded and looked at me.

I nodded back, because what else do you do in a situation like that? Indicating I had any understanding of what had just been said would bring me a swifter end than either of these Thor-Somethings intended for me. I had to keep secret that I was in fear for my life.

During those times, everyone had cause to fear conflict from a neighbor. It could be that you bedded someone's wife or sister. Or it could be you disagreed with someone about money. Or it could mean that your father's father's uncle's grandfather looked at someone else's family member funny, and the two families have been murdering each other ever since.

It was an aspect of my people I learned early. I looked at someone funny and had taken a beating for it. I was never inclined to grab an axe in response, so I watched and listened. And I became very, very good at avoiding trouble and running away from it should it find me.

Away from other children, I had indeed listened to many lessons from my foster parents and learned many of the stories I knew from them. But I didn't spend all my time sitting; outside, I was on my own swimming, climbing, running, and generally making myself able to outpace the trouble I knew would find me again.

Trouble does indeed know how to find you. Even if you sent it packing the previous night with a good story.

The seeress! She had to be the witch from last night. And she had come here to spread ill rumors about me just prior to my arrival.

Hel's dragon! I had walked into the same trap as Odin had in my story.

"You like the sword?" I stated more than asked, more eager than ever to get away from that place. "I am pleased. But I have three days' journey ahead of me, so I should be off."

I smiled and nodded and gave even more thanks for their hospitality. Payment in hand, I left that place with a casual stride. What had they been on about? What was that about casting spells? One way or another, I had told them my route home, and that route was no longer safe. Better to overpay an eager boatman for a ride or think about a different route. Either case meant I needed time to think.

I headed back to Silfast's hall. It was still early, just past noon when I arrived. I sank into a glum stupor on ale still credited from the previous night's entertainment.

I had thought I might need to be wary of that witch who had disappeared, but it seemed she had done her part. Now all I had to worry about was being tracked down and murdered by a bunch of Thor-Somethings.

Deep I drank, and deep my mood became, until my dourness became sleep, and my foreboding became a nightmare.

CHAPTER 3

THE TROLL

THE DREAM WAS SO REAL, I COULD EVEN SMELL THE FOREST around me. Cool night air pricked up the hair on my arms and I suppressed a shiver.

I stood in the middle of a road through the forest. Not my usual way of things, and I had neither pack nor weapon, so I felt doubly exposed. Branches rattled and wind whistled through the trees. The path forward was narrow (although how could I tell which way was forward?) with the right side blocked by dense vegetation. Left looked even less appealing as I saw some open space between the trees, but also sensed something there, all the more disturbing that I could not see it.

Off the road was more the way I traveled. Not here, though. Off the road seemed like a bad idea.

"Burp," said the man-sized ram on my right. Or something like that.

Rams do not have the high pitch to their 'baaah's as sheep, and as a result, every one of their vocalizations sounds in its first part like a demand and in its second part like an insult. This one was even bigger and hoarser than most, his voice vibrating my guts as it sounded. He was standing on a rock to my side that left his height about even with mine. He was old, but with a fleece so bright white it illuminated the area right around us.

The edge of his fetid breath caught me and smelled like it had been chewing barley and iron in equal measure. I backed away to avoid more of that stink and to avoid being charged, just in case. Those horns curled completely around and then some, and rams were apt to butt heads first and figure things out later. This one stared at me for a few more seconds and then made his way down onto the path. As if I should follow, or so it seemed to me.

I followed, a feeling of warmth from his company against the chill surrounding us.

We walked what seemed like a long way in dream time. I saw nothing but felt much, as if that nothing were a great threat aimed right at me. A forest in the dark is never a place to be—you can't see a damned thing, and what you do see plays tricks on your mind. When I was very young, I had wondered if witches really had much magic they could use at all, or if they could just see in the dark like a cat and play on men's fears and bad vision.

It's both.

Nothing you see in the forest at night makes any sense in the light of day, but it can give you a strong impression at the time. That was what I was thinking as I looked over my left shoulder again and sensed something. Movement? No. Subtler than that. But *there*.

"What was that?" I asked my ram companion. But he was gone.

That chill wind drew up like it was one big frost *jǫtunn* taking in a slow breath. There was something in front of me on that path, just nothing I recognized. It was dressed, if you could call rags dressed, and held a gnarled iron staff pockmarked with solid white stones.

No, not stones. Those were teeth.

A great nose and chin protruded from under a tattered hood flanked by greasy black forelocks. It looked at me with those eyes glowing with hunger, and I knew I was in a bad place.

"Troll they call me," he said. His voice was like the raspy breath of a corpse. It carried on the wind as if the very forest around us spoke with him. Slow again, as if he had all the time in Midgard. If this was indeed still Midgard.

This troll had some power if it had vanished my friendly ram. The bigger and badder some monster was, the less likely we had a specific word to name it with. 'Troll' could have been anything or anybody, as long as they met a requisite level of malevolence and could be presumed to use magic to their end.

I would also add 'Ugly,' but I guess witches were trolls as well, and some of them weren't bad to look at. From a safe distance.

This was no beautiful witch, and I was not at a safe distance. My eyes were shut tight, and I tried to shake my head back and forth. Tried to open my mouth and yell a simple "No." Anything, if only my body would obey. A paralysis spread outward from my face and stopped, turned the screams in my mind to mere mumbles on my lips. I had to do something, anything, but I could not.

My mind flailing and that troll cackling in my ears, I fell backwards and writhed on the ground. I wanted to fight. Or I wanted myself to want to fight. That was how I pictured myself in the light, in the safety, where courage is easy: Bravely facing down such a threat. Not curled up and desperate for protection.

Here there was neither light nor courage, and whatever ideals I might think I held to, there was only one urge to overwhelm all others.

I wanted to get away.

Chapter 4

Jester Wanted

"Every man has his good nights and bad ones," said Silfast.

I stood on the docks outside his longhouse looking out at the fjord, afternoon sun glowing bright orange with a tapestry of clouds woven around it. Silfast had found me outside and this was his way of saying hello. Actually he was saying more than that, and I knew he would soon make his meaning clear.

"See the eagle carrying the fish?" he asked.

I nodded.

"I always wonder how many times they fail when trying to snatch one," he continued. "What do you think?"

Too much ale two nights in a row had left me with a monstrous nightmare and an even more monstrous hangover. I was not much for answering questions. But Silfast was my host, and he was not just some rich farmer. His influence extended up the many roads snaking inland and out into the water towards every port for miles. He saw trade of all types there and welcomed most of it. Even itinerant skalds asking to pay for their hospitality with story and song.

So I had to answer that question even though I was not much in the mood for talking.

"I think the eagle must have a good sense for those things," I said. "He must be successful most of the time."

"Most of the time, ah," said Silfast. He shifted in his stance beside me and crossed his arms. His next sentence he spoke slow and clear. "That seems a reasonable expectation. Or perhaps the eagle would need to try a different feeding ground, if his success was less than expected." He turned and went back into the longhouse then, leaving me alone with my thoughts.

I didn't need to be a poet to understand the man: He wasn't extending hospitality for me to get drunk and sit around the fire like some coalbiter. I received hospitality, and he was supposed to receive entertainment for the men in his hall. Break one part of the transaction, and you break the other. Tonight would either be a particularly good performance, or I should take my leave.

That left me with a choice I didn't care for. It was difficult to perform with such a dreary mindset. Getting home would also be difficult if I had to avoid the route those Thor-Somethings would be watching. To be safe, I might need to go four or five days out of my way. I knew vaguely how I might do it, but the question of why was what my mind kept coming back to.

Like King Geirroth, I had been Fulla-ed. For what possible reason? I was of no consequence to the gods or any *vættir* as far as I knew, and that was a fortunate thing.

My foster mother Taika would tell me to read the clouds to find such answers. Answers like which choice to make, maybe even answers to complex questions. The trouble was, I didn't know how to read clouds. That woman had shown me the greatest love and affection, taught me to speak Sami, and had spent a solid week yoiking on a mountain top while she carved bones to make me a necklace of protection.

I ran my hands over that necklace. I didn't understand the magic behind it any more than I understood the patterns in the clouds. At best I could look at the sky and know if rain was coming in the next hour or so.

No rain imminent. Very few clouds, in fact. Perhaps that was all the sign I would receive. If so, better to depart sooner rather than later, before the weather changed on me.

Low coals glowed in the central hearth as I went back inside. A few dozen guests sat on long benches. Most of them tended to their own business, checking supplies, mending clothes, sharpening weapons. A few spoke in low tones amongst each other or with Silfast. Lots of travelers meant lots of news, and news was business to a man like Silfast.

Thralls readied cooking pots full of stew for the evening meal and brought ale around for the thirsty. Food usually picked up my spirits, but I was in a dour mood. An encouraging hand on my back from Bolli Mossneck wasn't even enough to put me in the mood for poetry. I had made up my mind.

A voice intervened as I cinched my pack tight. Minds are there for changing, after all.

"Jester wanted," said the voice across the hall, on the other side of the hearth. I knew that voice. That was the voice of Magnus the Heckler. An enemy of good poetry. An agent of chaos. Might as well have been the mischievous god Loki himself. "*Jester wanted!*"

He couldn't be referring to me, could he?

"Hey you, skald! A story!"

"No stories," I said, looking at him through the smoky air. It was an awkward position, so I came around the hearth to face him more clearly. "I recall one not so well received the other night."

Magnus feigned surprise while his two friends shook their heads. They all shared a long table, a comfortable trio with cups full of ale and looking slightly bored.

The sandy-haired man sat next to Magnus, chin on fist, as he considered the game of *hnefatafl* in front of him. Black and white pieces were all over the board in what seemed to be the middle of the game. He moved a white piece, indicating he was trying to get his king to the board's edge to win.

Across from Magnus and his opponent sat the other man. He was darker haired, a little broader, a little taller, also sitting chin on fist. He considered both positions and waited for the move, hoping he could still surround the king to win.

The same men from the other night, and they had the look of brothers if I ever saw it.

"I told you he would remember that part," said the sandy-haired fellow without looking up.

"Not everyone carries a grudge as well as you do, brother," said the darker-haired one, also without looking away from the game.

He picked up one of his black attacking pieces, knocked over a white defender, and replaced it with his piece. He would trap the king and win soon if his opponent lost many more of his pieces.

The grudge-carrying brother growled. Those two took their *hnefatafl* seriously.

Magnus sat with his legs splayed out in front of him. "Not even for your friend Magnus the Red? I was hoping to get a story about myself soon enough! Unless you are still hungover, I suppose," he asked.

I shook my head in a bald-faced lie.

"Perhaps it is something else, then," continued Magnus. "Your ship can't be riding steady if such minor things grieve you."

"Minor?" I said, incredulous. "You tried to have me thrown out for the night!"

"But you won!" he said, taking a long draught from his cup.

"I won a night's rest. And if I recall rightly, which I do, I also won you free of that witch you were flirting with."

"*Aha!*" shouted the non-grudge-carrying brother, turning around to point at Magnus and then his opponent. "A witness testifies, she *was* a witch! I knew that was a good bet! Pay up!"

The snarling, grudge-carrying brother reached into a pocket and drew out a few pieces of hacksilver. He sorted those in his palm, picked out what I assumed was the smallest bit, and placed it in his opponent's palm.

"Shit!" said Magnus, shaking his head. "Good looks, battle-fame, and supposedly two friends nearby. And only some random skald looking out for me!"

"I was not looking out for you," I said.

Remembering that night's events, maybe I had been looking out for him. I wasn't keen on witches getting what they wanted, just as a general rule. An itinerant *vǫlva* taking payment for prophecy or for the odd spell was one thing, but those roof-riders that preyed on people in the night were something else. I had come too close to one in recent memory just to see another man taken in. Even if that man had a shit sense for poetry.

"Nevertheless," said Magnus, waving off my contradiction, "our ship could use a jester. And the 'Steins here think you're a good bet."

"Innstein," said the grudge-carrying brother, by way of introduction. "And no wager has been offered. What odds do I get?"

"Utstein," waved the darker-haired brother as he looked briefly from Innstein to me and back. "I think Magnus is offering long odds or none. They're the only odds my brother will take."

"Ansgar," I said. "Sorry to disappoint you. I need to return home before the weather turns."

"But the weather is already turning," said Magnus. "For the better! It is just about springtime right now, it's not as if you're about to be snowed in. Besides, what is so important at home? Now is the season for going out into the world."

"I don't see it's any business of yours," I said, gritting my teeth. The man was arrogant, self-important, haughty. I should have felt no need to answer him, but I did. "But if you must know, I am going back to Dafvik. I deliver weapons for Halstein the Smith, my grandfather." And I want to go home where it is comfortable and free of witches and Thor-Somethings. But that part is not the kind of thing you say.

"Halstein the Smith?" said Innstein.

"Father of Styrgrim the Bear?" said Utstein.

All three men picked their heads up at this, staring at me as if I were a rare species of dragon.

"You're Styrgrim's son?" asked Magnus. "Ymir's bones, his son is a skald?"

The conversation had been loud enough to attract attention from other guests, and a few snickered quietly at Magnus' last comment. With that, I was done, through, finished with sticking around to answer stupid questions. If there had been a sign about choosing, this was the sign to leave.

As I turned to grab my pack, three more men entered the hall. I only knew the one, but in knowing Thorkel Thorgilsson I knew the other two must be his brothers. I tried to play as though I had not noticed them at all. They noticed me though, and headed straight for me.

"You're not really leaving so soon, are you?" asked Magnus. "Come drink with us tonight! I can tell you stories of battle and glory, and you can tell the world."

It was at that moment I developed a very fluid sense of interpreting signs. I grabbed my pack and joined the three men, making sure to sit across the table, nearer to the wall. If there was going to be a fight, I wanted something solid between me and those sons of Thorgils. That left Magnus and Innstein on the other side, between table and hearth.

I had just settled into the seat and asked "Can I play next?" when Thorkel and his brothers strode up to make themselves known.

Thorkel cleared his throat, edging his cloak back on his left side. The new sword hung from his belt, his hand resting on the pommel as if long experienced with it.

Innstein grinned, his eyes glancing up at his brother for just a moment, and then he cleared his throat as well.

Utstein followed with an even longer throat clearing.

"Ansgar Styrgrimsson," said Thorkel, switching to words, "you will come with us."

"I was just with you," I said, "and our business was concluded. I see you wear Halstein's sword even now. If you wish to make another order—"

"You know why we are here," interrupted one of the brothers. I never learned their names properly. Let's call him number Two.

"We know you are up to something," said the brother we will call number Three. "What sorcery are you about?"

"Sorcery?" said Magnus, rocking back in mock-surprise. "Our friend is no sorcerer! He's barely even a decent skald!"

A little hurtful, even if it was meant to protect me. Skalds have feelings, too.

"We heard a different story," said Thorkel, his tone smooth and silky. The imperiousness of his demeanor would never have suggested an incompetence with weapons. Men with the most brash attitudes are least likely to know how to handle their own swords, take that to mean what you will.

"Stay here then," said Magnus. "There should be stories aplenty before the night is through, one of them sure to be more to your liking."

"I like my own story best," said Thorkel.

"Are you really a sorcerer?" Utstein whispered to me while Magnus conversed with the Thor-Somethings.

"Of course not!" I hissed back. "But that witch from the other night went and told them I was, so they're after me!"

"Hmm," said Utstein, a single eyebrow reaching for the sky.

Innstein gave the slightest nod and cleared his throat again.

The throat clearing interrupted Thorkel's next statement. He paused, gave Innstein a look with an inadvertent lip curl to it, and began again.

Innstein cleared his throat again. Only he took his time in this case and made a loud thing of it. Loud enough to get the attention of others in the hall. Long enough to make a nuisance of himself, and revel in that nuisance.

"Brother," said Innstein, still staring into the *hnefatafl* board and just short of shouting it, "my king finds the edge of the board in six moves."

"Only if they are the right moves," said Utstein, rising from his seat but looking squarely at the Thor-Somethings.

Innstein turned around to face Thorkel. "Of course. If I were to make a stupid move, I might have my king linger on the board too long. Then he would die. But why do that when he can get away as quickly as possible? That way,"—he paused, taking a deep breath and speaking his last words slowly—"he will live."

The challenge was implied but clear as day. Did Silfast have a rule against fighting in the hall? I couldn't remember just then. Probably. Lords hate fighting inside the halls. It is a bad look, and liable to spill a lot of perfectly good ale.

Magnus put his cup down and his hand on the axe at his belt. More clear than any of Silfast's potential rules was the willingness of these men to break them.

Two and Three fanned out beside Thorkel. Magnus and Innstein rose from their seats. No man took a step forward, however, but rather waited for a commotion outside the hall to resolve itself.

Commotion, not fighting. It sounded like cheering, in fact.

The main door opened wide, and in walked a giant of a man. He was nearly a full head taller than me, and I was tall. A wide midsection sloshed in time with his jowls as he walked. Axe in hand, battered shield strapped to his back, he walked ahead of similarly armed and armored men.

Cheers rose from those in the hall. The giant rounded the hearth fire, entreating those present to make some noise and kiss his ass.

"I know that man," I said, confused. "That's Svein Helgisson from my village! What is he doing here?"

Svein paused briefly as he found a horn full of ale and we locked eyes. After a long draught, he paused to breathe again.

"Tell any *stories* lately?" asked the smirking Svein. At that clever ribbing, Svein left our attention to find either a bigger horn or a pitcher to drink from.

"What do you mean, what's he doing here?" asked Magnus. "He's signed on to our crew, or at least he's sworn to Haldor so far."

Thorkel's smirk disappeared.

"Haldor?" I said, working the name through my memory. If Haldor was who I thought he was, Magnus was keeping legendary company indeed.

My eyes went to the main entrance once more. Slowly, another huge figure worked its way in. Almost as big as Svein, but with none of the rumbly midsection or jowls. He turned sideways to fit through with his baggage. His baggage being eight feet of dead warg unceremoniously tossed onto the long-house floor.

The giant wolf's tongue lolled across knife-like teeth, but the glassy-eyed stare gave the thing a confused look despite the formidable jaws. Fur so thick it looked like tiny strands of armor all along its back was caked with dry blood on one side. As the corpse flopped, I could see the foot-long gash just behind its left foreleg. A deep cut, likely deep enough to split its heart. Plenty of other wounds on the corpse, but that looked like the killing stroke.

At the man's hip was a broad axe, the weapon I guessed to have made that wound. Not the usual style in size or shape. The blade was angled in a rise from its mounting at the handle, giving it a horn he could stab with. From the toe at the top of its cutting edge down to its heel was a long way, only the backing at the handle supporting the middle of the blade. The butt was not the simple flat steel but was lengthened and shaped into a sharpened claw.

Most axes had straight edges rather than curved, and let the beard hang straight down rather than supporting it in the middle. Common bearded axes were as worms to this dragon. A custom design, and I knew the maker.

That axe was Halstein's work. Made when I was very young, but one of my foster father's proudest works. He had named it Silence.

"Silfast," called the behemoth, his voice rumbling the very walls, "your errand is done, and here is the proof."

He grabbed the monster by the scruff and hauled up its head to face our host. Having made mock greeting with its head, he let it flop back onto the floor.

"Haldor Skullsplitter," said Magnus. "The Great Geat. The Hero of Halogaland. Brother of the Brotherhood." At that last kenning, Magnus drew a sleeve back to reveal his armring. It was the same armring I had seen him wearing the other night, two axe heads of gleaming silver coming together. "Oy, Haldor! Come meet new friends!"

Thorkel's lip curled again. He fled that hall with his brothers in tow, not even bothering to try a parting insult.

"It seems the king won't linger on the board after all," said Utstein.

"Too bad," growled Innstein.

"There will be a story for certain," said Magnus as he grinned ear to ear. He slapped me hard on the shoulder. "Now aren't you glad you stayed to drink with us?"

CHAPTER 5

GOOD ENOUGH

THE AROMAS OF RICH STEW AND SPILLED ALE FILLED THE AIR. THE hall echoed with shouts and cheers until Haldor beckoned the guests quiet down. Then it was Ulf, one of Haldor's men and his *þulr*, who told what happened. Not a skald, the *þulr*, but still the group's speaker. Better with diplomacy, even if he didn't have much skill with verse or the craft of telling the tale.

Battle and loss, but ultimately victory. It had not been one big warg, but an entire cult holding this specimen up as its god. They had been taking travelers along the roads and offering sacrifices to Fenrir, the wolf that will devour Odin at *Ragnarǫk*. They must have felt unstoppable as they prowled the nights, taking people one or two at a time.

Haldor added they thought it fitting to leave the cultist bodies with their asses bared at the sky. Just in case their shitheel god was watching.

To celebrate the Brotherhood's success, Silfast ordered kegs of his best mead be brought up. Little of this was spilled. Mead was an expensive and therefore rare thing. I filled my horn and let the sweet scent of honey fill my nostrils. The first time, that is. I was soon imbibing as fast as those around me, only without the same tolerance.

I met Haldor Skullsplitter, the legendary warrior, and my head swam. Sigurd the Dragon Slayer, Arrow-Odd, Walking Hrolf—these were names of legend. And yet here was another man whose stories preceded him, only he stood right in front of me.

He gave me a solemn nod. It left me dumbstruck. Lucky for me, Magnus had taken it upon himself to bring me around to the entirety of the hall and introduce me as his new friend.

"And maybe our new jester!" he continued, every single time. "Angsar the skald!"

Mispronunciation of my name was different for every introduction, so I didn't believe it was slurring. Magnus had to be a heckler even when I wasn't performing.

The introductions were intimidating enough without needing to address my real name. The men of the Brotherhood were not as famous as Haldor, but to me they were just as much part of the legend. I compensated for the intimidation by drinking more.

There was Haldor of course, and we agreed Svein needed no introduction.

"Axe throwing contest," shouted Svein, who was busy anyway. His voice had all the grace of a drunken aurochs, an image I thought was maybe too on the nose to be a very poetic kenning. It was not a general call, but a callout of Haldor it seemed. Svein was aiming high despite—or maybe it was because of —his propensity to drink too much too fast.

Magnus pointed to the captain of the ship, an old man with spindly hair. That was Kraki Bentleg. The *Sea Squirrel* was his, and he decided where it went. Magnus decided I did not need to meet Kraki at the moment. A curious thing, such an old man in charge of where Haldor Skullsplitter's Brotherhood went.

The 'Steins I already knew but were new to the crew and had not yet earned their armrings. Ulf the *þulr* did most of the official speaking for the crew. No surprise that he was locked in conversation with Silfast, the most important person in the hall.

The tracker who had found the warg's lair was Hemming, but he disliked the indoors. He slept outside on all but the worst of nights.

Finally, Magnus led me back to the same table we began at, calling out to one more friend.

"Lose any toothpicks, Kari?" asked Magnus.

A dark-haired man turned around, shaking his head and patting the long quiver of short spears on his back. "Haven't lost a javelin yet," he said. "Despite the recent business."

Magnus nodded. "I was busy with important matters myself!" He laughed.

The two men clasped hands and embraced.

"No trouble then?" asked Magnus.

"We lost Hott," said Kari, shaking his head. "A good man, just got too eager for treasure. He broke ranks and got separated from the rest. We found his body in a pit after the fighting was over. And you? Tell me your important business didn't involve some trouble."

In the background, Innstein observed, loudly, that both Svein and Haldor were far too sober to start throwing axes around. After the competitors had both drained another horn each, he put to them a greater test than merely to sink their weapons into the opposite wall. First, they would need blindfolds. Thus encumbered, they would both spin in a circle five times before grabbing an axe from the nearest table. Then they could throw.

Accuracy counted in this contest, Utstein assured the crowd.

"Trouble, me?" asked Magnus. "Why, I even made a friend. He's a skald, too, Insgar the skald! Now he can sing about how tall I am."

I shook my head. There weren't that many more variations on how to mispronounce my name left. At least he wasn't calling me a jester anymore.

I took that as a good time to replenish my mead. As I did, an axe whirled end over end in front of my face.

That was Svein's throw, and way off target. I blinked as the top of my body struggled to move itself backwards as my lower half attempted to keep walking. I fell backwards and rolled to make it seem as if it was just a graceful dance I had just done. I was on the wrong side of the hall, so the axe must have slipped out of his hand as he wound up.

"The skald needs warding against trollshot," said Kari, as Haldor made a slower but far more accurate throw that didn't threaten to kill even one person.

"Perhaps I will watch the axes from down here," I said.

"Nonsense!" said Magnus, pouring himself more to drink. "You just need more mead."

So let it be done.

Kari reached out to help me up. He gripped my hand without any undue force. We were about equally tall, but his hand was so much bigger than mine

I felt enveloped. It was like shaking hands with a very old oak tree—no give whatsoever, despite its gentleness.

"Ansgar," I said.

"Well met. Ignore the redhead; he is good in a fight for being unpredictable. But sometimes unpredictable is not ideal."

"Pfah!" said Magnus, refilling his horn. "Fighting in a shield wall, blah blah blah. Most fighting doesn't involve walls! Unpredictable was why Styrgrim recruited me in the first place!"

"What's this?" I said. Better to downplay any surprise, but surprised I was. Also tipping over from slightly inebriated to definitely drunk. "You didn't mention this before."

"You didn't ask," said Magnus with a grin. "Oh, and there was that interruption. Who were those sons of goats, anyway?"

I waved off that last bit. "They're nobody!" I said. "What do you mean Styrgrim recruited you?"

"He means he was good at free-fighting," said Kari. "Which is why *I* recruited him after he sailed on the *Long Claw*."

"That was . . . five summers ago!" said Magnus.

"You left Styrgrim's ship to join this one?" I asked.

I had a better view of the second volley of axes, which was less dangerous to bystanders. Svein got his throw off first again but lost that round as well and nearly fell over. It was so far off target that it struck a ceramic jug that burst in a shower of golden liquid. Tragic waste, that.

Magnus shrugged. "Different kind of madmen," he said. "Styrgrim liked me well enough, even gave me my name. 'The Red!' But most of his crew were afraid of him. Never would admit it, but they were. If they had any sense."

"I never saw my father get angry," I said. It was the truth, or more accurately, the truth as I had seen and heard it from Halstein.

"Vicious training sessions," said Magnus, shaking his head. "Any man he thought was holding back got a beating worse than the beating he was already getting. But every man knew how to use seax and spear in a wedge, and I mean properly, not just thrusting hard. That must be familiar, eh?"

"Never had that happen to me," I murmured to myself. Then picking up and realizing I should talk to anyone but myself, I continued, "A good seax and sling are as much as I carry for traveling light."

"He trained you with just . . . a sling?" asked Kari.

I shrugged. What I knew of fighting I had learned from my foster parents. But I could tell this was a poor direction to take the conversation in, and so I turned it back around.

"He spent summers raiding and winters with jarls. Many a jarl hoped to see him pull up in the *Long Claw,* and host him and his crew. People flocked to towns all along the Nordfjorden when word was out that the raven banner was flying, and Styrgrim was taking on new crewmen for a raid."

What little I knew of fighting I knew from Halstein, since Styrgrim had not been around. Or when he had been around, had not been inclined to teach me. Certainly I never thought his own crew would be afraid of him.

"Exactly!" said Magnus. "New crewmen like me! Styrgrim had an eye for talent."

A jolt of something unpleasant ran through my body. I put it down to indigestion at the time, but it's pretty clear that was jealousy. Jealousy that my father had sought out and recruited Magnus, and shame that he had not deemed me worthy of training. Not even worthy of seeing for over two years. It was then that I realized Magnus' phrasing was off somehow.

"Why do you speak of him as he was?" I asked. "He still is out there. Probably in Miklagard, since he was headed that way."

Kari sighed. "Perhaps he is, but many sailed from there and headed north to the White Sea," he said. "Arrow-Odd was gathering another army to go that way, or so we heard. Since then, we have heard nothing. The White Sea is a dangerous place, even if he sailed past the trolls and dragons that live along the coast on the way there."

"Maybe he decided to stay," said Magnus, shrugging.

It sounds foolish, but I had never considered that my father might never return. Dead? Impossible. He was huge, bigger than life, more a product of my imagination than my senses. Not interested or able to come back? The concepts were so foreign I could feel my brain resist them like a man pushing on a door to keep out intruders. No, my father was a rare visitor, but never to be seen again? That could not be.

But if he had sailed north to the White Sea, that was something else. Arrow-Odd had done that before, twenty years ago in his war against the sorcerer Ogmund. Odd had a hundred ships at his command at the time. Only one returned, with few men aboard. My father had been one of those few. Why go there a second time?

"Stay among the Bjarmians and their sorcerer king?" said Kari, shaking his head. "I doubt that. They say King Harek turns himself into a dragon during battles, and that he only has such powerful magic through bloody sacrifice."

"Wouldn't be Styrgrim's first sorcerer," said Magnus. "I think he would rather be fighting such folk than not."

Without realizing it, Magnus' words gnawed at the back of my brain like the harts that gnaw at Yggdrasil's trunk. It was an unpretentious and honest appraisal of my father's motivations: He would rather be out in the world fighting a dragon-sorcerer than at home. Why would he want to go home?

Surely not to visit the son he was ashamed of.

A dead wife and a son not inclined to make his fame by fighting. No wonder he had so often been abroad. No wonder he had been angry and always looking for a brawl. Home was where he was most disappointed in life.

"You look ill," Magnus told me.

Alcohol and excitement are excellent intoxicants, and I was already full of both. Shame and the need for approval are no less powerful.

All the things I was good at, I thought they might make my father proud. Music, poetry, lore. But they did not make him proud, because he wanted a spear-son, an axe-son. A son who could learn languages and stories and ski and run well was no substitute. Even a random recruit sailing with him for one summer was able to say "He liked me."

I did not think I could say the same, and it was an ill feeling indeed.

Svein finished his next throw ahead of Haldor again but was in a bad state of it. Attempting to overcome his lack of skill by applying more force, the drunken giant had let his axe slip on drawing it back too long and with too much effort. It came loose in his hand on the windup, flying out of his grip up and behind him. The toe of the blade bit deep into a crossbeam and stuck there. Seconds later, Haldor's axe sailed by with a satisfying thunk into the same target as his others.

"That's a piece of silver for me!" yelled Utstein as Svein's unconscious body thudded to the floor.

I felt about as good as Svein looked at that point. Yet bad as his state was, he would not need to scratch or claw for acceptance. He had waddled his way into fame and adventure and brotherhood.

Down, down dropped my stomach to unfamiliar depths, until it found a bottom where shame turned to discontent and discontent turned to anger. In that pit was Svein, and he became the focus of my anger. Why should he live such adventures while I contented myself with a single night of acceptance?

Why should he earn the glory of an armring and call my father a peer while I ran from Thor-Somethings?

The way out of that pit seemed like a good idea at the time. I stood up, realized that would not be enough, and then climbed onto the table.

"Haldor!" I shouted, "I hear you need a jester for your ship." I glanced at Magnus, who nodded. Murmurs and laughter were mild, so I paused only briefly before continuing. "I am no jester, and some would say a poor skald!" I shouted straight at Magnus. "But a skald nonetheless, and one who knows many a language you might find useful while seafaring."

The hall was silent in anticipation. I took it for the gravity of the situation and not at all about how drunk I sounded.

"Hail to a great warrior!" I called out as I raised my horn, improvising on a verse I'd once heard. "A skald has come to his hall. Where should he sit? He is impatient standing at adventure's threshold, ready to try his luck." Better to be more straightforward, I decided. "I know you are in need of a skald, and I offer my services as such."

All else was near silence.

Haldor rose from his seat and raised his horn. "Ansgar Styrgrimsson, we are honored to accept you as one of our crew. Welcome, and count every crewman your friend."

In the ruckus that followed, Magnus suddenly came alive as a bonfire as he jumped onto the table with me. "And who recruited him, eh?" he shouted. "Just remember who found him sulking and befriended him!"

Kari fixed him with a look of annoyance before turning back to me. "What are you doing?" he said. "Now that you've joined us you'll be no more than part of the crew. No better and no worse than any other man."

"I wouldn't have it any other way," I said. With one statement, I was one of them. My father would never be able to downplay that. Not even the Thor-Somethings could do anything about it, even if they returned in force.

Magnus must have seen me smiling because he was already beckoning for more drink.

"Really?" continued Kari. "I would have thought you were an expert in asking questions, considering your profession."

"Well done, Ansgar!" beamed Magnus. "Do you know many stories about short fighters that kill enemies much larger than they are and then bed their wives? You should refresh your memory on those before we set sail tomorrow. You know, to keep Kari's spirit up."

"Questions would have been a good idea," said Kari.

"What do you mean?" I asked.

"You could have asked how long you were committing for. Or where we were going. Or if you would have to do any fighting, especially given your . . . choice of weapon." Kari was tilting his head back and forth and piling the examples like stones on top of me. "Or if you would have to row next to Magnus here."

"Ymir's bones! He could do far worse," said Magnus.

"Or"—and now Kari's eyes went wide, his smile broad and wicked—"you might have asked why we needed a skald in the first place!" He looked at Magnus, who burst into furious laughter. Kari slapped the table and downed the remaining contents of his horn. He had begun as serious, but had accepted the humor in the situation. Now he was laughing with Magnus.

"And why is that?" I asked, determined to sour their fun. But they merely looked at each other again, glanced at Haldor striding over, and laughed twice as hard as before. Magnus laughed at the silliness of the situation, while Kari shook his head as if making light of gallows humor. Magnus patted Haldor's side to get his attention while Kari got up to fill his horn.

"Hahahaha! Oh, our skald has a question!" The last words came out in shuddering cackles. Something was clearly funnier as we got closer to the answer. "He wants to know why we had a position open!"

Haldor, though most certainly not, seemed sober and looked me in the eye.

"What's done is done," said Haldor. "Though I am surprised to hear you join. I didn't take you as a danger-seeking type."

"Danger-seeking?" I asked. "Well, of course I understand the danger! There will be fights, and I will recount them!"

"You can recount from your own perspective," said Haldor. "Everyone fights. Don't worry, we will train you. And you look like a fast learner. Not like the others."

That dropping feeling returned to my stomach.

"Others?"

"Yes," said Kari. "The other skalds!"

"Did they do a bad job?"

"Their verse was just fine up until the points where they all stopped breathing," said Magnus. "How many have we gone through? Three?"

Haldor counted on his fingers. "Three since you joined," he said. "You missed the skald for a day, just before your time with us. I suppose he might still be alive."

"He didn't get out of that forest," said Kari. "No way. Followed directions even worse than Hott. Otherwise he would have maybe lasted longer."

"What happened to the other three?" I asked.

Haldor counted on his fingers one more time. "Axe to the head, spear to the guts, and went insane and drowned," he said.

"That last one is speculation," added Magnus. "I think he died an honorable death being eaten by a sea goblin."

Haldor shrugged. "He definitely went insane first though," he said. "I am confident you will learn fast. You will need to." And with that, the big man was done. He patted me on the shoulder, then turned to address the crew as a whole before leaving my company. "Early day tomorrow! We sail at dawn."

I turned to Kari, trying to think of something intelligent to say. If you've ever been drunk and tried to do this, you know how difficult it is. I came up with, "What did he mean I would need to learn fast? I thought I would stand back and observe, so I could compose about what happened."

"Oh, that's not how things work with us, skald," Kari replied. "You'll do the composing, that's for certain. But this is no great army that can spare a shield wall just to keep you protected. There's no more than three dozen at any time, and every man fights."

"But surely I will just . . ."

Kari shook his head and laughed. "Questions ahead of time might have been wise, but there's no sense worrying now."

I gulped, trying as I might to avoid it, my eyes wide with terror. I had survived this long by being an expert in avoiding combat, not facing it head-on.

"You probably won't need to fight the troll," said Magnus. "That will be Haldor's job."

"Probably," added Kari.

Magnus nodded. "You never can tell with those things."

"Troll?" My voice was a squeak at that point.

A troll could be a lot of different things. I was hoping this was on the small side.

"A huge one, apparently," said Kari. "Too big for the Danish king and his champions, at least."

"I hear it ate most of them," said Magnus.

Fighting? A troll? I thought I might need to carry a shield and whatnot, but only to stop an errant arrow coming my way. This was more involved than I had imagined in my mead-induced stupor. I hadn't even considered what Silfast had hired these men for. Haldor dropped the carcass of a monster wolf right in front of me, but that wasn't on my mind when I swore to join the crew.

This troll that even a king could not deal with sounded dangerous, frightening. Uncertain, even.

I scanned the room again, taking more detailed stock of the known crew of the *Sea Squirrel*. I looked at the other men. The softer, less scarred men were immediately distinguishable from the crew, even to my inebriated vision. The two giants Haldor and Svein towering over other men. The knotted muscles in Magnus' arms like taut ropes. Kari the javelin thrower. Kraki the wild old man, his leg only bent because he had been fighting for so many decades. The others looked just as hard.

This was not a ship full of summer raiders or men seeking to make some coin while their farms were tended to.

This was a collection of maniacs looking for the biggest, bloodiest, most dangerous things they could seek out to try their fame on. Hunters of the moon's minions. Night stalkers of things that stalked people in the night. Hardened killers who took the bounties no one else would take because those were the only ones to earn lasting word-fame.

And I had just signed on to be one of them, with the same rules and expectations laid upon me as every other man.

Magnus grinned at me. "Welcome and well met!"

Chapter 6

Burden

It took less than a day at sea for me to decide I would willingly convert to any religion that considered sea travel unholy. The daily routine was enough to make me hope the Midgard Serpent would swallow us whole and end the constant churning that turned my insides out. At least then all the discomfort involved would be condensed into a single moment rather than drawn out into that torturous journey.

And it would be two journeys, as Kraki had explained before any of us boarded.

"Gloryhounds," he spat, "we sail to Fretborg. There is no profit to be had there. A friend is in need. The sooner we get him out of that place, the sooner we then sail to Lejre in Denmark. Where, I am told, there is plenty of profit to be had."

The men had cheered at that, all but a few. Belatedly, I added my voice to the cheering. I had no idea what to expect, whatever our destination.

Then every man swore to uphold the rules, Haldor's and Kraki's, and boarded.

Some men walked away instead of boarding. Found a different path forward, or got the idea they didn't want to try their fame quite as much as expected, I guessed. I had my chance to back out, with all the dishonor that would entail, and I opted not to. Fear of shame was greater than fear of whatever lay ahead at the time, being that I didn't yet realize how many teeth and fangs lay ahead.

Sea travel is plenty unpleasant without teeth and fangs, mind you.

Rising early in the morning, there was little for breakfast. On most days, this was a blessing. Every other day was *hákarl* because it kept so long with minimal care. The taste is difficult to describe. *Hákarl* is the rotted flesh of an arctic shark and earns its own term beyond 'shark meat' because it is so much worse than 'shark meat' might suggest. Before being buried in the sand for six months, it is poisonous to humans. How any human would taste that rotted flesh and then declare it to no longer be poisonous is a mystery to me.

The texture is something between unchewable meat and potentially chewable cartilage a very hungry man might think to gnaw through. The only 'taste' is a burning sensation that burrows down into the windpipe and up into the brain at the same time.

Hákarl never went bad because it was never good in the first place. It was never in danger of being stolen by hungry shipmates or animals. Even carrion birds avoid it.

It was Kraki's pleasure to serve it to us as often as possible. He told us it was the best food for a ship. Even if we were stuck at sea, no one would be tempted to eat too much, and that would help make the rations last longer.

The rest of a typical day was spent shying away from a glaring sun and trying to keep the freezing surf and wind off my sensitive limbs. No tent or awning would they pitch on the ship to shield us from the freezing rain and wind. As if the physical exertion of constant rowing wasn't enough, the swaying of the ship and the sound of the ocean pounding the planks forced my insides out on many an occasion in the early days of our voyage. By the second instance, I had earned the title of 'Ansgar the Healthy.'

The stench of the crew was another force to contend with, though it was as nothing compared to the disadvantage of sitting behind Svein. When I complained about the smell, Haldor fastened a clothespin on my nose to the crew's great amusement.

Svein laughed, but for his own reasons.

"You look funny," he said, chuckle snort, chuckle snort, chuckle snort.

"Do you know why Haldor put this on my nose?" I asked, as inquiringly as I could given the circumstances.

"Nope!" he said, and laughed some more.

"It's because you stink, you filthy bastard."

"You stink!" came the standard response. The conversation continued as you might expect for some time.

Two more had joined our crew at our last stop along the fjord before finding the open sea. This was a strange pair—sworn brothers, they said, named Ingolf and Leif. They were amiable enough with everyone else but a terror to each other. Leif, the sociable but awkward one, ever enjoyed speaking his mind even when at great risk. His friend Ingolf kept more to himself and considered his words more carefully.

They came aboard only after the same swearing the rest of us had done. Men with armrings, like Magnus, had already sworn. For the rest of us, there were Haldor and Kraki standing like gods in judgment before Leif and Ingolf could board. First were Haldor's rules: No fighting amongst Brothers, and no unwilling sacrifices. If you wanted to sacrifice your own possessions, so be it. But otherwise, not so much as a mouse would be offered to any god.

Kraki's rule was not so much a rule as a challenge: No thralls on his ship. Therefore, anyone on his ship was not a thrall. And no disagreement about the status of such thralldom, or lack thereof, would be tolerated.

"What if a king disagrees with him about that?" I whispered to Magnus while the swearing took place.

"Some have," he said.

"And?"

"And I think he left them with little to say."

It soon became clear to me that Haldor did not defer captaincy to Kraki as a favor. The old man had the wispy hair and beard and the sagging skin of an old man. Yet his eyes showed no dullness, his gestures no torpor. A slight limp, yes, but other than that he was not slow. When he walked, men moved out of his way.

The *Sea Squirrel* had a strange name and a stranger captain. I was beginning to understand that I did not understand what I had joined into at all. Even the ship itself vexed me—I had expected a long, sleek dragon ship, cutting the waves at high speed. The *Sea Squirrel* was not a warship. Or at least, not a dedicated warship. It was wider about the middle and made for carrying both men and cargo, a versatile ocean-goer.

Able to go many places. Just none of them very fast, was my lamentation as the days dragged on.

The crew wanted singing and music, and I was not in a state to provide either. I preferred to tell stories huddled underneath a blanket whenever possible. Then at least I could get away from rowing and away from breathing Svein's poisonous air. I was a fair player with my lyre, but the rocking of the sea made me too dizzy to try.

We hugged the coast, but the waves were rougher than when we were surrounded by solid earth on both sides. I was no good at rowing. A short lifetime of avoiding people had left me with fair skills running, swimming, climbing, anything involving getting away from other people. Rowing involved being around other people for unfortunately long periods of time. It also involved muscles I had apparently failed to grow.

So I did what came naturally and tried to avoid the effort as much as possible, skimming the water only a bit as I rowed. It seemed the best I could manage.

"Dance for us!" yelled Magnus.

"I can hardly stand," I said, which was true.

"Sing then!" yelled Kari.

"I don't know any good rowing songs."

Based on the crew's reaction, this would be the most entertaining thing I would say on the entire trip.

"I'll compose a poem for our voyage," I said. Poetry was a strong suit of mine, or so I thought at the time. But there is a difference between delivering a poem accurately describing a situation while seated at a comfortable table and delivering said poem while confined in close quarters to men who could easily kill me.

So on the spot, I recited the following:

> "Ships sail the sea,
>> sorrowful their states.
> A morning meal
>> makes men mad
> When rotten meat
>> renders them ill.
> Who rows the reavers
>> when the raid is inside?"

And I thought that was pretty good for ten seconds of composition. There were murmurs among the crew, good and bad, as I left the front of the boat and returned to my rowing seat. I think they were murmuring just to murmur and see how each other man would react.

One did react.

Kraki rose up like the Midgard Serpent, his eyes fixed on me with death in them. And he did the scariest thing he could have done: He grinned, his eyes wide.

"Here it comes!" said Magnus. "Finally some proper entertainment!"

Kraki licked his lips and picked up a bucket full of *hákarl*. He made his way down the deck and left a bit of food (loosely speaking) for each man. Once he reached the front of the boat and left a bit for Hemming, who beat the rhythm of the oars, he turned round to face us and delivered his own recital.

> "Healthy Ansgar
>   heaves to starboard.
> The skald lovingly
>   lightens our load-
> Hardness of his heart
>   hardly matching
> that stiffness absent
>   about his breeches."

The crew roared with laughter. For reasons I did not understand at the time, they erupted a second time when I pointed out the poem didn't make sense because I was sitting to port.

That was the end of my poetry recitals on the ship. I was silent until landfall, but that took us a long time even once we saw the beach we would land on. I listened to what Innstein and Utstein said to Kraki to keep us headed in the right direction. This was the beginning of my sailing education.

Utstein and Innstein were traders part-time, shipwrights full-time, and gamblers all the time. And that's what sailing is—a gamble. You are betting the decisions you make based on the wind direction and the water direction are going to be more or less doable in combination, and that you can read said combination to make the correct decisions.

In this case, the water was moving one way and the wind another, with the wind pushing us toward the beach but the water pushing us away. So we did what I learned was tacking, or riding the wind at an angle into it. And this took quite a long time.

Venturing a question out of sheer boredom, I asked why we didn't just let the wind push us where we wanted to go against the direction of the water.

"Good way to capsize a ship," said Magnus. "Top half moving one direction, bottom half moving the other direction. You're not getting impatient, are you?"

Finally, we made landing. I fell off the ship into the shallow surf and stumbled onto the beach and kissed the sand for thanks that I might have a short reprieve from the horrid experience that is seafaring.

Then I had to spit out the sand. I looked up to Kraki standing over me, an immovable object, old and weathered and scowling at me with a look of half confusion and half disgust.

"I'm giving thanks to be back on land," was all I could think of to say.

"Hmm," Kraki replied, trudging up the beach past me. I shivered.

Something about his demeanor made me think '*Hmm*' could be interpreted as '*I wonder if you would be more useful if I used your skin for a blanket.*'

"Don't get too comfortable," said Magnus, never more cheery than when delivering bad news. "We are only here to camp for the night."

"We're not there yet?" I asked.

Several men laughed aloud at that.

We had only been two days at sea. Though there was solid ground and a fire for warmth, the atmosphere only became chillier to me. "Why's he with us?" I heard whispered, and "Maybe better to leave him here" among other things.

Magnus sat with me, the only one not put off by my presence. He was cheerful as ever, asking about stories of heroes and monsters. When I could think of nothing, I turned the question on him and asked about where he came from.

That was a sad story, but you would never have known it from the way Magnus told it. He focused on meeting my father, and then Kari, the happier parts. The Brotherhood was his family now, as he had been orphaned early. Most of the others had similar stories, he said. Lost all they had or never had much to lose. Extra sons unlikely to inherit much or with little to rely on other than their own might and main.

"So this is a new family!" he concluded with completely unjustified cheeriness.

It was not enough to improve my mood. I was miserable. My crewmates were annoyed. For all my will to make my father proud of me, it seemed I would be a burden for having joined up. I could see no way out, and no quick way of reversing my fortune. I cursed my own hurt feelings, cursed the Thor-Somethings, and cursed alcohol under my breath as I faded off to sleep.

What could be worse than this? I was about to find out.

CHAPTER 7

THE QUEEN OF STINKTOWN

It was one more day's sail to Fretborg, the kind of port town that made me want to be back out on the sea. For someone who threw up whenever the water rocked our ship, that was saying something.

I could see few people going about their business as we approached, and no lively trading center. Kraki steered us into the dock and let the 'Steins do the work of mooring the ship. The dock appeared to be solid even if the few ships attached to it did not, and there was plenty of room for mooring. There were no trading vessels to be seen and only a few fishing boats. Most of those looked like they were in a state to deliver the men to the fish rather than the other way around.

The wind whistled as if it threatened to rain but wasn't sure it could muster enough motivation. The crew disembarked under a cold, gray sky.

A raven flew overhead as we reached solid ground. It was circling and croaking, clearly excited even before we heard it speak.

"Traders!" she shouted, clear enough to be female. "And so early in the season! Perhaps you have interesting business to discuss?"

A collapsed cart lay off to the side of our path into the town proper, as appropriate a sign as any. The raven landed on it and tried to make conversation again. I knew her kind and her game. Ravens traffick in stories, and so while you might get good information out of them, you need to give them something yourself.

It was often a good trade, but might also get terrible information. Word has it this was why Olaf the Haughty (named posthumously) had met his end. Some raven had told him sharks could only bite you if they're upside-down, so he leaped off his ship onto one that was right side up. It bit him and he died. Olaf's men shook their heads, and the raven flew off telling the story of what had just happened. Truly, those are Odin's birds.

That is one reason I did not trust such a bird to send word of my new affiliation to my foster parents.

I had sent word back to them, along with the payment for the sword, with Bolli Mossneck. Not that he worked for free himself, but I had no fear of him lightening the purse any more than was agreed to. And he would tell what had happened as he heard and saw it. If I had sent a raven, I would have wondered whether the message would arrive as intended or mixed up with the details of three other stories picked up along the way.

Information from ravens could find you a treasure hoard or get you killed. Or both, depending on the raven's inclination and whose paths it had crossed. As for inclination, you would need to know the raven's name to even guess on that.

I was willing to give this one a try without giving too much away. "Ansgar Styrgrimsson. And our ship is the *Sea Squirrel*."

"Oh, I *see!*" said the raven, winking at all of us after that last word. "I understand completely. No worries, I am off!" In a few beats of her black wings, she was away.

That was not the expected reaction, and I called after the bird with some unflattering language. "What kind of raven are you anyway?" I demanded. She hadn't even given her name.

She croaked back at me. Laugh or apology, I could not tell. "Well met, son of Styrgrim!"

The crew walked on, no one interested in the raven besides me.

"Those birds are daft," growled Kraki to no one in particular.

"Are we not here because you had it from a raven that Finnr was in need?" asked Kari.

"Of course," said Kraki. "How else would I get word? They're still daft. Go chase that one for a conversation if you like. It's not as if they work for free."

"Who is Finnr?" I asked.

There were no walls to protect the town or much planning of the general layout, it seemed to me. The rocky beach turned to muddy before long, and here were the first buildings. Some abandoned, others in a state to be abandoned but apparently occupied, if the fires inside were any indication. Few inhabitants scuttled about, wary of our presence. A few ran toward the longhouse, splashing their way as they went.

The streets smelled of shit, the buildings smelled of rot, and the inhabitants smelled of both. Just my initial impressions.

"In due time," growled Kraki.

"You will like this, skald," said Kari. "Ever meet a dwarf before?"

It was no wonder Kraki had received word from Finnr that he needed passage out. This was a poor place and unlikely to ever be anything but poor, assuming it continued to exist. What business could a dwarf do here? There would be little he could create, few to appreciate what he could create, and little to inspire him. Why he was here was only one among many questions I had.

"Finnr is Kraki's friend," said Kari, "he is a dwarf. We won't leave until we secure his release."

"Can't he just get on the ship?" I asked.

Kari shook his head. "You might be surprised how much a dwarf looks like a man. But he is not a man of Midgard, he is a dwarf of the Down-Below. If he needs help, it will be more complicated than having him get on the ship. The message was we need to secure his release, not just pull him away from here."

"Secure it from who?" I asked.

"Enough questions," said Kraki as we approached the longhouse door. "We will have answers from the jarl, and until then there is no point in speculating."

Haldor nodded to the guards at the doors of the hall, such as they were. The scrawny men nodded back to indicate they got paid enough to stand and nod, but not enough to fight. One of them asked our names, and the other went inside to inquire if our names were good enough for entering.

It turned out that yes, our names were good enough for entering.

"Leave your weapons outside," said the guard who had gone to inquire about us.

Haldor stood stock straight and crossed his arms, staring at the man.

The quiet guard turned toward his colleague, eyes wide. It was enough to make his point without speaking.

"The, errm," stuttered the first guard. "Leave your weapons outside if you would like them oiled. It is damp outside, and we would not want our guests to see their axes rust."

Haldor patted Silence at his side and kept his hand there. He would not be handing that weapon over to anyone. Then he looked to the men behind him in a wordless request for takers.

"That's a fine thing to offer in a damp place," said Ulf, his voice rising as he eyed the crewmen behind him, "but I prefer to oil my own blade."

Haldor grinned as barely-contained laughter rose from our ranks and turned back to the guard. "Thank you for your generous offer."

We piled into the longhouse without another word.

It was a large hall, bigger than any I had grown up near. But there the sense of grandeur ended. The hall was large—too large to be kept up, at least. The fire in the main hearth was too small to heat the empty space. The ceiling sagged in so many places I thought the leaking roof would come down on top of us. Cracked wall boards spoke of construction spread too thin, maximizing size at the cost of sturdiness and insulation. The combination of poor construction and too little fire in the place led to mold in the walls, something I could smell before I could see it in the low light.

The thralls working inside had more energy than the guards. There was an effort to keep the place warm and well-lit, it just seemed doomed to failure due to too little fuel. Even for thralls, their clothing was minimal and thread-bare, their constant activity done as much to keep warm as to obey commands.

Perhaps it would be fine once the spring had properly thawed things out. That should mean more ships, more trade, and a less chilly hall. The lack of decent garments for the hall's servants was a bad sign, though. No jarl could be that poor and remain jarl for very long, but some could be that stingy and get away with it for years.

Stingy or poor, we still had to use the roundabout way of approaching our task by going to the jarl instead of straight to Finnr. We were an armed band of men, and so needed to make our peaceful disposition clear straight away, or else be assumed as hostile. We did not intend to invade or take anything (what was there to take in this place, I wondered), and so it was proper to stop by to offer our respect and our intentions.

In addition to not getting an arrow or knife in the back later, this was also the best way to get fed a decent meal. We could find the dwarf later. Not having a local armed host fall on us and filling our bellies were roughly equal priorities.

"Wait here," said the guard. "I will announce your presence to the queen."

"The queen?" Ulf mouthed to Haldor.

Haldor made no quizzical reaction the way I could not help but do. To do so would be to show surprise, and Norsemen are never surprised, at least according to the Norse Book of Manliness. Haldor did let a great meaty paw fall upon Kraki's shoulder as he pulled him away from the group and asked questions in a hushed tone.

Kraki showed no surprise either, staring at the huge man the entire conversation. When Haldor had finished, Kraki curled his lip and shrugged. "Word was, early in the season was better. That was all. I don't keep track of these people. So what if there's a queen?"

Except if that guard was going to the queen, where was the jarl? And why was his wife calling herself a queen? In those times just about anyone could call himself a king, as long as he was able to defend himself from his neighbors who might take exception to the title. I supposed that applied to queens as well, assuming they had the means to defend their titles.

But why anyone would think the overlord of this stinking burg merited high title I had no idea. Even the title of jarl seemed overdone for this place. Lacking the requisite sense of propriety to keep these questions unspoken, I opened my mouth to ask them. And would have done, had the queen's herald (still the same bedraggled guard, but now with more words) not stepped in.

"Haldor of the *Sea Squirrel*," said the guard, "Queen Gulldis is pleased to receive you and your men."

A woman emerged from behind him. Her presence would have commanded all attention in the hall, announced or not. Where to begin? Skin as white as snow and shining blonde hair glowed in the firelight. The bright red and white dress she wore and the fine furs atop it were impressively rich enough. Clothing colored and tailored that well did not come cheap.

Her jewelry matched her hair and there was plenty of it, including a woven circlet atop the circular braids that made it look like she wore two crowns. Gold rings, gold arm rings, gold necklaces inlaid with gems. Wearing an entire hoard, Gulldis pursed her lips as she eyed us each in turn.

"Welcome, Haldor. To what do I owe a visit from the renowned hero and his crew of . . .?"

"The *Sea Squirrel*," said Kraki.

The guard started to say something. I suspect that something was akin to "You should speak only when the queen speaks to you," but he swallowed his statement after Kraki looked his way.

"The *Sea Squirrel* is mine," clarified Kraki. "The crew is nobody's, but they follow Haldor on land. I had word from my friend Finnr to come here." A few low chuckles at this and Gulldis nodded in his direction, holding tight to that smile.

"Finnr is hard at work, as he always is. I do not know if he can be disturbed. And you are?"

He was Kraki. "I am," he said with finality, after a long pause. He was also picking his nose. "We will wait."

Gulldis wasn't so pleased to offer hospitality to guests, but she was quite pleased to have guests to show off to. As long as they were sufficiently impressed by her, which Kraki made a point of showing he was not. The silence would have been cold with malice in another hall, where warriors were more plentiful.

The handful of fighting men that remained in this place and the servants chilled to the bone were not going to enforce any particular manners. Some of them even looked like they might welcome some new blood for leadership, what with the lady keeping herself so warm while her servants shivered. A few errant nose diamonds Kraki decided to leave on the floor were the least of their concerns.

We were not in town to take over though. Indeed, why anyone would want to take over such a place I had no idea. But it had one thing we wanted, and we would get our dwarf more easily without inciting conflict.

"My lady, I am Ulf," said the ship's *þulr*. Negotiator, diplomat, translator, Ulf knew fewer languages than I did but far more about how to get things done.

His tone was deferential. He bowed low and dropped a knee near to the floor in a show of respect and borderline subservience. "If it pleases you, I would make a more suitable introduction. Kraki owns the ship and sets our course, but Haldor leads us by land and task. We intended to meet Jarl Gansi while en route to Denmark. If he is indisposed, we beg your hospitality—"

"I do not beg," Kraki said, too clear to be the muttering of a confused old man. By now he had turned away and was examining one of the old shields decorating the wall.

". . . during our time here, if you please," Ulf continued.

"Ah! Of course you meant to meet with Gansi," said the queen. "My husband went raiding last summer and did not return."

Did not return, not *has not yet returned.* Hmm.

There was no sadness in her voice, only the wonderful opportunity of Gansi's absence. "I rule. Until his return, I am certain," she added with a wry smile, and took her seat on her throne. A snap of her fingers (she was fond of this motion) brought out an old crone, who took charge of the thralls and organized them in preparation of more food.

"We recognize your authority, of course," said Ulf. "As it is you who speaks with authority, we then inquire—"

"Release my friend," said Kraki.

Gulldis put on her most vapid expression. "Who is this you speak of? We hold no prisoners here."

"*My friend,*" said Kraki, now striding towards her. "*Finnr!*"

"Oh," said Gulldis, a practiced understanding now dawning on her face. "Oh! But that is a different sort of thing. I think you must ask my husband, as Finnr is sworn to him. Of course, let me extend the hospitality of my hall!"

Things were not going well, and Ulf knew it. So he did what many a speaker does at such times, and he looked to the entertainer to lighten the mood.

"My queen, please excuse our abruptness. We thank you for your hospitality! And let us put our skald to work for you."

I was caught unaware, my skill in foresight not yet well developed. Once announced, I knew what was coming next even as I pleaded in silence for it not to be so.

"Perhaps he might favor you and your hall with a song to lighten the mood."

My improvised storytelling had gone well once. Improvised poetry was different—shorter, but more difficult due to the originality required. A good poem in this case would focus on at least one flattering aspect, but of what? I know what you're thinking: A flattering aspect of the queen. And you're wrong, because flattery may go wrong a dozen different ways that could be taken as insulting. As for complimenting the town itself this woman supposedly ruled over, there was nothing good I could see about it.

"Perhaps a tune on my lyre—"

"A poem would be most appropriate!" said Ulf the Asshole.

Gulldis looked at me with that icy smile and cocked her head. Kraki had insulted her, and I was supposed to make up for it by reciting a poem about how not-putrid her town smelled. This was a terrible position on top of my already terrible position with the crew. I knew immediately I had to stall, but with all eyes on me, even stalling would need to be done in verse form. In such cases, what comes through is humor. And the best humor has a bite.

> "Why so hasty, Ulf?
>   The high host
> finds hall guests
>   fumbling uninvited.
> Don't try her temper
>   with talks of trade
> before brandishing
>   a basic gift."

And in that way, I returned the onus to Ulf, forcing him to come up with something on the spot himself. Ha! Even without meaning to be, I was rather a shit.

Ulf snapped his fingers while he scowled at me. At the sound, Svein's great footsteps thudded one after another and the men parted to make way. The chest on his shoulder added even more weight to the considerable bulk landing with each step. He laid it down at Queen Gulldis' feet. "Please accept these small tokens, as we have come in peace."

The queen opened it and exclaimed her lack of enthusiasm. "Ah, amber," she said, unimpressed. "And a whalebone comb."

"That was mine," said Kraki, from across the hall and still not looking back as he spoke. "It is the best of combs," he added, stroking his white beard.

"Wait," said the queen, genuinely surprised at the next item. "A golden bracteate! Well, that is something!" She held up the thin pendant as if it might replace the sun in the sky. In her estimation, it just might—though more accurately she would sew it into one of her garments and display it as a badge of wealth. As if she needed another.

"I must have the dwarf look at this," said Gulldis. She snapped her fingers at the old crone, who bowed and shuffled out of the hall.

The crone looked none too happy to be ordered about, and the sigils and charms on her staff I took as a poor sign. This woman was no cook—she was a *volva*, probably more useful reading bones or making potions than preparing food or ordering thralls about. Perhaps that was the clue we needed, though. A *vǫlva* in a place like this seemed a likely suspect in how Finnr had been kept here.

I shivered. Call her a *vǫlva* without knowing any more about her, sure. Perhaps she was just a seeress traveling around speaking fortunes. But if she had any ill intent, that *vǫlva* would be more likely known as a roof-rider, a night-rider. A witch, and not the good kind.

"Oh yes, yes, yes," said the queen. Distracted by the gold, she waved us off, or for her servants to attend us, or both. "Please accept the hospitality of my hall, blah blah blah." She didn't say blah blah blah. I am taking a liberty there. I think you understand what she sounded like.

The thralls doing the cooking served us then. Rotten root vegetable and lichen stew. Which I suppose isn't poison, but also isn't far from it. Ale so thin I started to wonder if they had used any barley at all, or just the idea of barley. I almost pushed my stew away, but I imagined eating more *hákarl*, and that made finishing the meal easy enough.

Minutes after she had called for him, the main door on the side of the hall opened. The old woman stepped through and beckoned the dwarf in. Finally, we were getting somewhere.

Finnr looked older than most, though not nearly as old as Kraki, with long black-and-silver hair and a beard tucked into his belt. I could tell you about his eyes, his nose, and whatnot, but more than any of those individual features there was an overall impression he had about him.

If you took an axe, new and shiny and unmarred by battle, and then looked at that same axe after decades of use but good maintenance, that was Finnr. I could see it in the way his nose had been broken many times, and in the small but noticeable scars on his face.

"My lady calls," said the dwarf as he walked past our crew, "and I answer."

He was short, but still man-sized. His arms were long for his height and his hands were twice as thick as mine. These were the features that made him most distinguishable from a man of Midgard. Lithe limbs argued with a firm potbelly about whether he was skinny or fat. His eyebrows were so long they reached his ears. Speaking involved thick bushes of whiskers moving in time with his voice. I wondered if dwarves had such mustaches to conceal sharp teeth or forked tongue, as some claimed.

Gulldis held up the bracteate for Finnr, both proud of the gift and curious at its true value. "What do you think?" she asked.

"From our last battle," said Haldor. "The inscription is meant to convey protection."

Too quiet for Gulldis to hear, the 'Steins had their own analysis.

"Didn't he take that off a man he killed?" whispered Innstein to his brother.

"Maybe it only protects the person not wearing it," Utstein replied.

Which sounds like a joke, and was, but at the same time was entirely serious. This is why carving runes for magical means was a bad idea for all but the most expert on such things. A novice or (especially) intermediate at carving runes might have the effect right and the direction reversed.

So Haldor was honest in what he said, but it was probably a good gift to give to someone you didn't like.

"Ah, yes," said Finnr. "Quite valuable. Red gold, unadulterated. And the runes! An adornment quite beyond me, as I am more of a steel worker."

"Ha!" screeched Gulldis, snatching the golden disc away. "I have heard this tune before, dwarf! Always the lowering of expectations. Did the dwarves not make Freya's necklace and Odin's ring? Things of *value*," she said, scrunching up her nose at the last word. "The world does not need more weapons."

Finnr hooked his thumbs into his belt and took a deep breath before he spoke. "As always, my lady is wise."

I noticed he did not tell her what those runes said. Either he didn't know or he didn't want her to know, and I didn't need the gambling ability of the 'Steins to know which of those I would bet on.

"Well then!" the queen continued, cheerier now. "Off with you then! You have plenty of gold and silver and gems to work with. Mark this as an example, and make something to remember!" She snapped for the crone to attend her in the back rooms while Finnr marched back out the way he had come.

As he exited, I saw him pointing. Not at the queen, but at the crone. *The volva!* he mouthed, and something else besides. He was gone before any of the hall's more regular visitors could see.

It was night by then, and I had more questions than answers. The men spoke in hushed, conspiratorial tones. Ulf and Kari spoke to Haldor, his two main advisors. Others chimed in at times, and I found they had the same questions I had.

"Where is Gansi?"

"She didn't sound too keen on finding out."

"That crone keeping the dwarf here?"

"Maybe wait for the jarl?"

"The less time we spend here, the better."

I listened, but no one included me in the conversation. I had already screwed up the business at hand.

"You've screwed up our business here," said Kraki as he took a seat beside me on the bench in between slurps of a second helping of stew. "Those gifts were to get the dwarf out of here. Now they're just an introduction. We will probably need to fight his way out now, probably need to kill every man that queen has got."

"Wouldn't that be doing them a favor?" I asked. "I mean to say, then they wouldn't have to live in this miserable place anymore."

It took him a few seconds to realize I had made a joke. Soon I saw the most frightening thing in my life, and that was Kraki's sun-pinched lips pulled back across yellowing teeth in a great, homicidal grin. "Maybe it would be!" he said.

My joke got a few grins, but not enough to improve my standing. I had been called on for a flattering poem and had responded with my characteristic contrarianism. It had not helped us, and I felt ashamed for failing at the one thing I might do well. I wanted to curl into a ball in a hole in the ground and wait until my misadventure was over to crawl out. Seeing no holes nearby, I headed for the door.

"Skald, where are you going?" demanded Kari.

"Out, uh, to pee," I said.

"Well get it done and then go find Hemming at the ship," he said, rising from his seat. "Magnus and I will have a look around the town. You and Hemming do the same. The rest will stay here to not arouse suspicion."

"Look around, right," I said. "For what?"

"For that witch!" said Ulf. "She is binding the dwarf here, no doubt. Find her if you can, and don't cause any trouble doing it."

I succeeded at one of those, at least.

CHAPTER 8

ROUGH STUFF

IF YOU'VE EVER NEEDED TO SNEAK UP ON AND SUBDUE AN OLD woman, you know it's a lot more complicated than it sounds.

To Hemming, it was a simple task. Find the old vǫlva and get her to tell us how to free Finnr the dwarf. The task at least gave me something to focus on, even if I had to focus on finding my way through a rainy night in an unfamiliar and unfriendly place. And maybe on putting my knife to an old woman's throat to make her do our bidding.

The wind didn't sing so much as whine, humming in the background of everything I thought and did. My wool cloak was heavy enough to stay on, but could not stay in place with each gust of wind. My head and the patchwork I called a beard were moist and then wet and then soaked.

Magnus and Kari went one way as I headed down to the Sea Squirrel. Hemming was there under a tent and looking reasonably comfortable. A few minutes later, Hemming still looked just as comfortable as we approached the hall again, and I pointed out which way Magnus and Kari had gone. Hemming split the two of us up and told me to double back once I reached the edge of town, and not to attract attention.

I didn't like it, but I wasn't exactly in a position to contradict anyone. Especially the crew's most expert tracker.

A few dim lights from hearth fires inside houses hinted at where I might look. I tripped a few times from the uneven pathways playing at being roads and cursed myself. Each time I looked up to see if I had attracted any attention. Every time, it was just darkness and silence.

It was getting me nowhere, so I stopped. A technique I had learned was to stop and picture myself looking at myself from someone else's perspective. I would ask myself from that point of view, 'What should I tell him to say or do?' And something, however general, would come to me as the beginning of the solution.

So I closed my eyes and imagined myself standing about ten feet away, staring at myself with my eyes shut. What should I tell him to do?

I opened my eyes because I heard something or someone, jolting me from my out-of-body thought. Feet moving quick and then slow—not the cadence of a friend. It was the shuffle of a predator moving into position. In the dark, not knowing where I was or where I was going, the fear that I would need to fight for my life blossomed and spread like a flood through my veins. I drew my seax and crouched, eyes swiveling back and forth.

It was just a pebble, half the size of my thumbnail at most, that hit me in the back of my head. But it rattled my brain as nothing had before. Half-blind with surprise and madness, I pivoted and slashed once, twice, three times, then held my seax straight out in front of me and shuffled backwards trying to find the attacker, hoping the long knife would be enough.

"Fierce, that was fierce!" exclaimed Hemming in between heaving laughter. "Oh, the look on your face!"

I was furious. I had been given a serious task, and here was Hemming, casual as could be about it and making fun of me. How did he even see my face in the dark, anyway, I wondered.

"Just a joke," he said. "All I could see were those wild knife slashes! We need to teach you how to fight properly."

I sheathed my knife. "And are you the one to do that?" I spat, venom in my voice. "Will you teach me to fight with that limp wrist, or just how to find something to hide behind?"

The woodsman winced. It was one of those comments that people make now and say 'brutal but honest' to justify their verbal brutality. I, at least, had the excuse of inexperienced youth at the time. It was a little bit of an attack on his manliness since he'd just had a laugh at my expense.

Maybe more than a little bit. His hand slipped down to his knife as I was putting mine away. For a tense moment, I realized I really had been stalked by a predator.

"If you two are trying to hide, you're doing a poor job of it." The voice came from my left, Hemming's right, and shook both of us. It was the vǫlva, basket in hand, cloaked and weather-readied far better than I had been. Quick as she had appeared, she disappeared into a hut nearby.

Hemming and I stared at each other. He sheathed his knife. We followed her into the hut. Could it be this easy after all?

Ha! Of course not.

She fed the embers of a dying fire in a corner of the hut and glanced at me as I walked in behind Hemming. I could see well enough, even in the dim light. Though she had been serving in the hall, her clothing and other items marked her as a vǫlva, if we hadn't known already.

"Ah, you were looking for me," she said with an appraising look for each of us. "I have other things to do at the moment, things other than whatever it is you need. Find your own seats by the fire if you like. I won't deny wet fools hospitality. But I have work to do first."

She wore a gray cloak that had straps decorated with stones down to the hem. Around her neck was a string of glass beads and on her head a black lambskin hood lined with white catskin, all of which she removed and put down before getting to work on some mushrooms.

Around her waist was a strange belt I could not identify the source of, but it was not leather. On her belt, she kept a large leather pouch that clinked and crackled when she walked. Hairy calfskin shoes with long, sturdy laces kept her feet warm, and knobs of tin or brass decorated them. Her gloves were furry and white inside, and looked extremely comfortable.

Hemming looked at me and craned his head toward the vǫlva. I looked at Hemming and shrugged. We traded more idiotic looks without understanding, and that was the problem: An advantage of numbers isn't always an advantage if those numbers have never worked together and don't know what the other numbers are doing.

You can have long experience working with another man where each knows how the other is going to move, or you can rehearse a plan beforehand. We hadn't known each other long enough for the former and hadn't bothered to do the latter, other than trading insults only minutes ago.

Magnus and Kari could work as a single unit, far more effective than two other men together. The 'Steins had this same connection. I had no connection to anyone, least of all Hemming, perhaps the only man aboard the Sea Squirrel less likely to win a straight fight than I was.

The vǫlva prepared something on a table and worked with her back to us. The fire found new fuel and new flames began to bring warmth and light into the hut. But instead of finding a seat at that hearth, I was inching toward her in utter stealth, goaded by Hemming's nonverbal suggestion to grab her.

You might be wondering, "Why didn't you just talk to her?" And I would need to write you a treatise on how we Norse understood manliness. The summary would be: When in doubt, use more force than necessary because looking weak by failing is the worst possible outcome in the world. I was never good at using force. But force appeared to be the plan, and I was trying to go with the plan and be a part of the crew, and so I intended to grab the old woman from behind, put my knife to her throat, and demand the information we needed so she would see we wanted to be friends.

However badly you think this is about to go, it will be worse.

I crept up behind the vǫlva and unsheathed my knife in dead silence. A cat could not have heard my footfalls. I would hold her around the chest and pin her arms with my left while my knife went to her throat. Hemming could then question her and determine how to release the dwarf from being bound here with her spell.

I got just within reach when she whirled on me. I saw her pivot, but never saw the iron pan that followed her turning shoulders. The side of my head felt it, though, and I staggered back in a daze. Did I drop my knife then? Probably. Did it matter at that point? Not whatsoever.

Quick as she had turned on me, Hemming was on her and had his hand pressing the side of her face, driving her back against the table she had been working at. I thought Hemming was in control of the struggle until I heard him yelp like a kicked puppy.

She had slipped his grip, but only a little. She was not trying to get away. She had simply squirmed into position to bite the webbing of his hand between his thumb and index finger. He freed himself by threatening an eye gouge, but she was a step ahead and kicked the side of his knee as he did it. Now it was Hemming's turn to stagger back.

Shocked we could still be failing at this, I lunged at her, wrapping my arms around her and tried to lift her off the ground. I had seen this move when other boys in town had wrestling competitions, though I had never tried it. Why practice wrestling when I could just outrun someone trying to wrestle me? But I was a good student of observation, and I saw that when you did this, it was very difficult for the person being held to do any further harm to you as long as their arms were pinned.

The thing with fighting is there are always subtleties to what's being done, or what's not being done. And what I had not observed was how someone who knows this is about to happen might counter that bear hug.

I lunged, I pinned, and I lifted.

The vǫlva saw this coming and turned away from me. I thought this would make it easier, and that she would kick wildly upward in frustration. That's what I had seen women do before—flail wildly and to no effect. Instead, she moved her left heel backwards in between my feet and used her right foot to hook my right calf.

I lifted and found I was trying to lift myself up along with her, which was never going to work. When I realized this and shifted my weight to adjust, she kicked her hooked foot forward and drove her shoulders back into me.

My top half went one direction and my bottom half the other like a badly-sailed ship. I fell hard on the ground, my neck snapping backwards and delivering me a second blow to the head. Before I could open my eyes there was a bony old knee scraping down into my groin. I tried to sit up, as you might try to do when your balls are being crushed, but that was her plan. Her forehead slammed into my nose with a loud, wet crunch. Everything—sight, sound, smell, taste—was red with pain.

Having spent so much time brutalizing me, the vǫlva was not ready for Hemming's counterattack. He grabbed her hair from behind and jerked her back before delivering a nasty blow to her stomach. It knocked the wind out of her and gave him a fighting chance, though I didn't see the rest of the fight.

I lay there reminding myself that this was what I had signed up for when I pledged to join the crew. Honor, glory, and maybe treasure had been on my mind at the time. Screwing up plans, trading insults with the crew's worst fighter, and taking a beating from an old woman was what it was turning out to be.

That was the last thought I remember having that night. The end of the night though? Hardly. That was just the end of my waking hours, when the world of men was making my life miserable. As I fell unconscious, some unseen raven was carrying a message to the gods of Asgard to let them know: Time to play in Ansgar's dreams.

CHAPTER 9

THE ROAD TO ASGARD IS PAVED WITH HEAD INJURIES

THE WOMAN SHOUTING AT ME IN MY DREAM WAS A PICTURE OF feminine beauty at a glance. If she had been standing tall and smiling, she would have rivaled any queen for grace and bearing. The contours of her face showed youth but sophistication at the same time. Her golden locks fell at her shoulder and waved like rows of barley. She didn't even have any crooked or missing teeth, they were perfect.

But she was not standing tall, and not smiling.

"Get your dingleberry-sprouting beard away from my apples!"

I knew her teeth were perfect because she was snarling at me, shoulders hunched, arms swinging as if in need of a weapon to wield. Her gait as she headed toward me looked a lot like a coming attack, but I was not worried. I realized I was reaching for an apple, on an apple tree. Splotches of matte red and green on each ripe fruit, their surfaces unmarred by worms or insects or bruises. It only seemed natural to eat one.

"STOP!" The voice pierced my ears such that I winced and recoiled from the apple. The woman slapped my hand and stuck her face right in front of mine in challenge. "Those . . . are . . . not . . . for . . . you!" she enunciated at length. It was as if she thought I couldn't hear her. I could hear her and her suggestions. I was in no pain, had no worries. That apple looked so good, it was the only thing I could think about enough to care about.

Those apples looked like other apples but inspired a desire no real apple could. The beautiful, vicious woman in front of me, I realized, was just as desirable. Locks of blonde hair shimmered in the sunlight, and I noticed her scent was of fruit and something else, something I had never known before but that I wanted more of. As long as she wasn't talking.

"Like a dog in heat," she said. "Well, I didn't bring you, dog, so go find your friend, whoever it is." She stepped back and gestured away from the tree, towards a great hall with ornate carvings all along the walls and doors. They were pictures telling a story, I thought, but I couldn't keep my attention focused long enough to think about it very hard.

I think she shoved me by the butt to get me moving and muttered something about 'first-timers.'

I didn't care, I was enjoying the view of the hall as I tried to take it all in. The doors had swung wide and could have welcomed six abreast, but it was so bright outside that I couldn't see anything inside. As I entered, my eyes began to adjust and my sense of awe was tempered. It was less like floating through some fantastic story and more as if I had come to a place of importance, though I couldn't say why.

Great fires down the length of it cooked various meats and stocks. Pig boiled and elk roasted. Mutton stewed and mackerel smoked. Tables were being scrubbed, floors being swept, all in what appeared to be preparation for an event of some import. I tried to ask some of the people at work, but they ignored me. I felt no motivation to bother them. All the men looked mostly the same, as did all the women, and they all wore simple but clean clothing of linen and wool.

If I had thrown a rock with my sling at one end, I was not sure it would reach the other. I walked farther down what seemed to be an impossibly long hall given its exterior dimensions. The longer I walked, the more cooks and cleaners there were. I dodged an energetic sweeper and thought I would collide with a cook, but she was ready for me with a sample of the richest, most delicious broth I had ever tasted.

She stared at me until I nodded, then smiled and went back to work.

Voices ahead at the only occupied table I had seen drew me onward. Three men sat together conversing about something I could not quite make out. I heard 'children' and 'luck' and 'not my idea' and a few other words and phrases. As I approached, the taller, paler one with strange eyes flicked his finger in my direction, alerting the others to my presence. It was a lazy gesture, as if he had been bored with the conversation and was glad to have a distraction.

"Welcome, skald," said the closest of the men. He had a full but neat beard the color of harvest barley and was dressed in bright green and gold. His cloak was of fine wool and his shirt showed a stag with many-pointed antlers. "What brings you here?"

"He doesn't know that," said the pale one. "He doesn't know anything." I fixed my eyes on this one, but he was difficult to focus on. Some strange quality about him made it a distraction whenever I tried to scry a bit of him at a time.

"Don't care what he knows," said the third. And looking at this one, there was no confusion as to his identity. He took a swallow of ale that would have been an entire pint for a man of Midgard. Immediately he put out his horn for another fill. "He shouldn't be here." He was slouched over, trying to hide the girth of his massive shoulders. There was no hiding the fire-red beard and hair, though, or the insatiable appetite.

That was Thor, without question. The Thunderer. The protector of gods and mankind. Drinker of oceans, slayer of *jǫtnar*. Strongest of the gods, even without wearing that girdle of strength. Rather fat and slovenly for a god, I thought.

"Where should he be then, if not here?" asked the pale one. His identity was less obvious, but the ram's head embossed on his thick leather cuirass told me this was Heimdall. The watchman of the gods and guardian of Bifrost, the bridge between Midgard and Asgard. Who in nine realms wore a leather cuirass, though?

Thor's belch shook the room. He gave a nod to acknowledge this would indeed be his only answer.

"I'm not certain of his presence either," said the first one.

"I thought you said I was welcome, Frey." All eyes turned towards me. Frey's eyes showed he was glad of the recognition. Thor with his mouth hanging open so he could breathe. Heimdall showed no reaction at all, maintaining a thin, noncommittal smile.

Frey did not hesitate. "And so you are. But that doesn't explain *why* you are here."

"I was hit on the head," I offered. "Three times. Wait!" I stopped, terrified I'd had everything wrong until that point. "Am I dead?"

"Not yet," said Thor. "But the way you fight, it won't be long."

Frey and Heimdall showed strong agreement by making no reaction whatsoever.

"Idunn, that was Idunn outside," I said. "The apples of immortality, they're real, and she really is the keeper of their tree! She said she hadn't brought me though, so who did?"

"Maybe you brought yourself," said Heimdall, gesturing at a raven-haired servant to bring me a horn of mead. "If so, it must have been out of need. Is there something you would ask of us?"

I thought about this for a moment, and my mind was blank. I would ask so many things if only I could straighten them out in my head. But gods are tricksy, even these three who were known for being more straightforward than most others I knew of. I was making so many mistakes that one question alone could not cover my need for wisdom. The servant brought me the horn and I stared into it as if the answer swam in the suds. Finally, I decided.

"The crew thinks I'm useless. I can't fight. I can't row. I screw up plans and it's obvious I shouldn't be there. How do I make myself of some use and make my father proud?"

"Learn to fight," said Thor.

I took a sip of mead. It was rich and powerful. Too much though, and I coughed after swallowing.

"You cannot make anyone else anything," said Frey. "So stop trying and give yourself time to grow." Time, patience, harvest. No surprise from the fertility god.

I took a second sip of mead, and it warmed my throat.

The watchman turned his gaze my way and his eyes flashed bright blue for a moment. The one who could hear the grass grow and see a hundred leagues at night as if it were a few feet in broad daylight. There were no stories of Heimdall fighting giants or tromping around Midgard to have adventures like Thor. But that look from those eyes froze me with the cold certainty this one was just as dangerous.

The kind of dangerous that went about its business unseen and unheard. He just watched, and waited, and let my imagination fill in the mental picture of what happened when the watchman was done watching.

"Your use is that which no one else will do," said Heimdall. "You think you cannot do the difficult things they do, but for them those things are easy. Do the things they find difficult. Go where they will not. Cross strange thresholds and dare their wardens to deny you passage. Grow stronger through each one."

I took a third sip of mead. It was so good I closed my eyes to savor it. I opened my eyes and the hall was spinning, my balance unsteady. Someone grabbed the horn from my hand as I lost my balance entirely.

On the long way to the ground, I thought I heard a woman's voice say, "And stop complaining so much."

As soon as I realized what that voice had said, I woke up, the taste of fermented honey receding as the pain in my head increased.

CHAPTER 10

THE HIDDEN WOLF

"Stop complaining so much," I mumbled as I sat upright to a blurred vision of confusion and pain. Even breathing hurt.

"No complaints here," said the *vǫlva*. She sat on a bed of straw while some horrid concoction smoldered in a clay bowl. Holding it up, she inhaled the fumes through her mouth and held it there a moment. Then white smoke was billowing out her nostrils as if from an oversexed fire drake, and I felt none the more relaxed for it. "Your friend was very forthcoming with details after I put a knife to his throat. I haven't had that much excitement in years!"

I remembered walking into the hut, and then everything was a blur of apples and pain. My head ached and my balls throbbed, both sensations bringing back more specific memories. There was advice I should take. Later, do that later. A glimpse of morning light outside told me how long I had been out.

"Where is Hemming?" I managed to ask, the least stupid of the questions occurring to me.

"At the hall making up some story about how he overpowered me and got all the information he needed," she said as she rose and went to her work-bench. "And how he made me agree to heal you after casting a spell to throttle your mind."

"How do you know all those details?"

The *vǫlva* exhaled another stream of smoke and I was able to place the bowl's contents. Dried dandelions and wet socks, it smelled like. Assuming the socks were very, very dirty.

"I am old, and I know men," she said with less mirth than before. "Although what possessed you to attack me in the first place is still puzzling. Your friend is a moron, so I can understand him coming to the conclusion that was the best way forward. Were you acting on his orders, or are you also a moron?"

Getting to my feet was a challenge, but I did so on my own. It seemed to me I had been following Hemming's direction, but evidence appeared to be mounting that I was, indeed, a moron. "The first for certain, and maybe the second," I whispered, each word a hammer in my ears.

"Good answer," said the *vǫlva*. "Now give me your name, and I'll trade you for something to ease your pain."

I almost did, but her wording was strange. '*Give me your name*' was not to be taken lightly when spoken by a sorcerer of any kind. My foster mother had been a seeress from the Sami and not a practitioner of *seiðr* the same way this woman would be. But *giving* my name was not the same as saying it, and I wasn't about to make such a trade lightly, even in my addled state.

"I'll tell you my name, but won't give it to you or anyone," I said. "If you tell me yours. And then I have business easing my pain elsewhere."

"Huld is my name," she said, all a smile. "And take this with you to your business." She tossed a dried ball of herbs at my chest. It knocked against me. My hand, thankfully acting on its own, lifted to catch it while the rest of me was still slow and groggy. "Henbane leaf," she said. "Hold it in your mouth until the pain is gone, then spit it out. It will help with your head. If you don't swallow it."

"What if I do swallow it? And how do I know it's not something more lethal than henbane?"

"If you swallow it you will hallucinate, convulse, and if you're lucky you die quickly after that. And you don't know if it is more than henbane. But Finnr is my friend, and though I am not impressed by you lot, I accept you are the ones who came to free him."

I had gathered henbane, something my foster mother had many uses for. I had never consumed it. Herbal lore I knew was more about what I could forage and eat and what might kill me if I ate it. Henbane could kill you, but you would be very hungry indeed before trying to eat any given the bitter taste. I waved my thanks and almost forgot my part of the bargain as I tucked the ball into the side of my mouth.

"Ansgar," I announced. "We thought you were the one who bound Finnr to this place. But you are his friend?"

"None better," said Huld. "Who do you think sent the raven telling about how he needed help?"

"Could have done with more details," I said, leaning up against a wall.

"Ah, men lamenting lack of detail," said Huld. "They lament the lack of detail, yet never their own failure to ask simple questions."

I rubbed my temples and groaned. My head throbbed, but my testicles were worse. I mumbled something incoherent, probably about not being cut out for this sort of work. I shook my head, realized that made it hurt more, and righted myself. "If you are not the one who binds Finnr here, why can't he just leave?"

"Answered once already to that lackwit," said Huld, "but I suppose you may hear it from me as well. Finnr swore an oath to the Jarl of Fretborg. Not by name, but by title. And that was a mistake, as the title was passed on. So you have plied the queen with treasure, but that is a mistake twice over. She will never have enough, and will always want Finnr to make more. She would not release him even if she could."

"But that means we need Gansi," I said. "And he's probably dead!"

Huld shrugged. "I foresaw as much before he left on that raid, and told him. It's a rare thing for men to take the advice of women, though, so off he went!"

I stood there eyeing Huld with slightly better balance than a few minutes ago, turning over all this new knowledge in my mind. We weren't leaving without the dwarf. To get the dwarf we needed Gansi. Gansi was probably dead.

"Shit," I said.

"Yes," said Huld.

"There's nothing we can do then! We're stuck here!"

"Oh, I doubt that very much. Power never tolerates a void for long. Why, one of you could probably marry Gulldis right now, take the title of jarl, and be done with it!"

That sounded at once like the easiest and most painful solution. And, oh gods, there was the fear that if the crew had to vote on someone to leave behind in this place, it would be me.

"I don't want to stay here!" I whispered, a plea to myself.

"*Neither do I*," said Huld. "That is why I am going to help you and your crew of idiots, and then you are going to take me with you."

"I'm not sure—"

"I am certain enough for the both of us. I've given you medicine for pain and information for aid. Now out with you."

There was no witty retort to that. I nodded and stumbled into the morning light, glad to be rid of the *vǫlva*'s presence. Just as I thought she was closing the door behind me, I heard her once more.

"One last thing," she said, standing in the doorway. "I cannot see clear enough to a good end to tell you what to do, but I know the raven is involved. Find her and make friends." The door thumped shut with the sound of finality.

The mid-morning sun shone dull through the clouds. A cheery day in Fretborg, since at least it wasn't raining. Huld's hut was a short walk to the hall, where I saw some of the men were already out and about. A very late wakeup for me, as I was usually up before the dawn.

One good thing about a small crew rather than a full warband of hundreds of men is the ability to organize them on shorter notice and with less confusion. Confusion as to when to be ready and where to go and, more importantly, where to take a piss.

They never mention this in the sagas. People shitting over the sides of ships or in the middle of streets or just wherever, as if heroes in stories don't need to relieve themselves. Well, we did. And the business of easing my pain I had mentioned to Huld involved me taking a piss, perhaps the only relief I would have that day.

Not knowing where exactly to relieve myself and not wanting to start any more fights that trip, or ever, I honed in on Magnus whom I saw just outside the hall. What's the proper way to do things? The way you see others doing them, or at least that's what we assume whenever the need arises.

So I walked up next to him and, with great relief, peed in the same direction. He fixed me a sideways stare of disgust but said nothing, and I knew I had chosen my spot poorly. This was Magnus' Spot. Not A Spot for Anyone Who Needs to Pee.

The awkward silence was broken by the 'Steins laughing as they came up the street. Innstein stopped when he saw us, backhanded his brother's chest to make him pause, and on the spot offered a verse:

"Early hour it is
    to offer ale's answer.
Blood brothers
    without blood
Share steaming,
    smelling showers.
Tell us soon what they share
    together next!"

Humorous, I suppose, but technically speaking, it was terrible. Too many stressed syllables, too much alliteration in the wrong places. Sometimes poetry doesn't need technical purity for appreciation, though.

"Haha!" added a pleased Utstein. "You're piss-pals!"

"Well done, skald," muttered Magnus.

Sometimes what you see others doing is just what others are doing and not what or where you ought to be doing the same. For such a reticent culture, the wisdom offered by observation ought to have gone farther than it did. But cultures are idiosyncratic, not logical, even though they claim the opposite is true. That lesson would take me a longer time to learn, hence the inappropriate peeing.

Magnus grunted his disapproval and left me there. I wondered if I needed to compose a counter-verse midstream. Before I could complete that thought, both he and the brothers had already headed back into the hall. Doubtless, I should follow, and doubtless, I had already earned myself another byname.

I chewed my henbane until I could feel the effect for certain, bringing a numbness to the pain and all my senses. Then I gave it another minute or so for good measure, spit it out, and headed into the hall. My knees were only a little bit wobbly.

In high spirits from Innstein's poem and the sight that inspired it, the brothers were the only ones grinning. Most of the crew were left to their own devices, but those men with Brotherhood armrings, and a few others, sat at a long table in the hall. The 'Steins were crew who had not earned Brotherhood armrings yet, but they were included anyway.

I hung back a bit, finding myself a bowl and a pot of loose porridge, and listened.

"Nobody knows where he is," said Ulf. "Look at this place. Would you stay here?"

"Hemming says he's dead though," said Kari.

"The *vǫlva* says he must be," said Hemming. "She says so, but who knows!" His tone threatened to spiral into a babble of semi-coherent mutterings.

Haldor held up a hand and the group went silent. "Jarl Gansi went raiding last summer. Correct?"

"Correct," said Utstein.

"As far as we heard around town," added Innstein.

Haldor nodded and continued, "And he was headed for Frisia, to join his half-brother Halfdan, correct?"

"Correct," said Ulf. "Gulldis confirmed this."

"Halfdan is also a jarl, for whatever that means," said Kari. "He is not much, though. Surprising he has lasted this long with so few men and so many attacks on his holdings."

"So he would have been glad of support from another jarl, maybe," said Ulf. "Maybe offered that Gansi and his men should winter with them."

"He would have accepted support," said Kari. "Halfdan is a *niðingr*, and everyone knows it. Takes without giving. Not to be trusted. Gansi would have been a fool to accept an invitation to winter there."

"He may have had no choice," said Ulf. "If he had to make ship repairs too late in the season, or if the waters were particularly rough, he might have stayed. Could be on his way back here right now. Assuming the *vǫlva* is wrong and he is still alive."

"How does she know that he is dead though?" asked Haldor.

"*Seiðr!*" said Hemming. "Tricksy women's magic! I saw her use it on Ansgar, and he barely survived. Look—even now his brain is addled. I was lucky and took her down between spells."

He pointed at me as I was aiming another spoonful of porridge at my mouth and obviously uncertain it would get there.

"See that?" continued Hemming. "That's what happens when a *vǫlva* doesn't like you."

Even in my addled state I knew I was wobbly from the henbane. I had taken three hard shots to the skull though. Regardless of cause, it was better to look the part of an addled skald than admit I had been beaten up in a straight fight by an old woman. I decided it was better to change the subject.

"Or she just . . ." I stammered, unsure where exactly my tongue was in my mouth. "Or she just knew Halfdan better than Gansi did."

Haldor turned my way. "What does she say comes next then?"

"Someone . . . else becomes jarl?" Thinking was difficult. I took a deep breath and managed it with all my effort. "The raven is the key. I mean the jarl. But the raven too. And Huld said she would come with us."

"Clear as mud," said Ulf, shaking his head. "Healthy Skald, I think you should rest a bit. You look pale, even for you."

I shook my head. This was not going well.

"The *volva* wants to join the crew?" asked Magnus, this being the first point in the conversation that interested him.

"I think we are not likely to have her," said Ulf, grinning. "Maybe if she were forty years younger and better looking!"

Magnus shrugged. "If she swears the same oaths, I am not afraid of an old woman on a ship."

Which was a genius way to say Ulf was a coward if he kept her off the ship. A skald-worthy insult in fact. I grinned like an idiot while Ulf's smile became razor-thin.

"She can ask and swear same as anyone," said Haldor, waving the subject off. "Assuming she hasn't already lied to us about Finnr's binding here."

"The question is, what do we do now?" said Ulf, audibly irritated. "We can take the dwarf by force. What other option is there?"

"We wait," said Kari. "Wait for the Jarl of Fretborg to appear. Or for word of his death to reach here, for Gulldis to marry, and to ply the new jarl."

"Tedious and unnecessary waste of time," said Ulf.

"We must wait," said Kraki.

"The man who is always ready to fight does not want to fight?" said Ulf.

"We can fight if you like," said Kraki. "It will make no difference. Finnr is bound by an oath. That is not the same as for you. Dwarves are flesh and bone, but oaths bind them fast. I know, I lived with them in the Down-Below. Even if we put him on the ship and sailed away, he would be pulled right back here. I could sense the binding as soon as I saw him last night, or he would not have been half so deferential to the queen. My ship goes nowhere until we secure a release from that oath."

Haldor nodded at the statement. "This *volva*," he said, addressing me, "does she want to help, or is this a game?"

I cleared my throat. "Just . . . probably the former," I said. The men laughed.

Haldor ignored the jests. His expression did not change as he eyed me. "Why?"

"She sent the raven," I said. "The one to get Kraki's attention. And she thinks the raven here has a part to play. If she meant harm, she could have done it already." My voice was small and more high-pitched than normal. Effects of henbane or just anxiety, who knows, but the result was obvious.

"I'm not cleaning his pants when he shits himself," shouted Svein through the murmurs, to even more laughter. "Better he should stay with the ship and stick to rowing if need be."

"Guard it with him," said Haldor, one hand up to silence the crowd.

It was not just the side comments that were cut off, but the tone of the morning had changed. Haldor was in little mood for jokes and was not making one himself. Svein needed reminding he was not a maker of decisions for the crew.

"Kari and Ulf, keep eyes on the queen and see if you can gain her favor. Magnus, find this *volva* and see what you think. Hemming, pick a man or two and scout the area nearby just in case. And you two . . ." Haldor stood to his full height and loomed over the 'Steins, who had been playing *hnefatafl* for nearly the entire meeting. "Ship repairs?"

"Because they have such good materials for that here?" asked an incredulous Innstein.

"I wouldn't recommend it," added Utstein.

"You're not paid to play games all day," said Haldor.

"Game playing is underrated," said Innstein. "We can teach you if you like."

"Well hold on, brother, he wants us to be productive in a different way," said Utstein. "What if we make friends with the *volva* ourselves? We are good judges of character."

"Find some tar for the ship," said Haldor, his tone implying an absence of patience, "or we will find some for the two of you."

That was enough for the 'Steins to stop their game.

Whatever Haldor would do himself he had not said. I think he just wanted to be done with the talking. And it was done, because that voice carried a weight behind it you could not ignore.

Soon the men were filing out of the hall except for Kraki, who walked straight towards me, and Svein right past me. Afraid to be where I was and afraid to get back on the ship, I stood my ground and waited for whatever might be coming.

"Runt," Kraki said, a complete sentence in one word. "You were bewitched, were you?"

I wondered if the crazy old cook would carve me up and boil me without Haldor's mitigating presence.

"I, um—"

"'Overpowered her between spells.' There's no one dumb enough in the world to believe that coward's word," he interrupted. "I don't know what happened to you, but I never heard of a spell for breaking noses. Tell me no lies about it unless you want your head bashed down so far it comes out your ass."

No idle threat, that. But he paused, and I realized the old man wanted something of me, not just to deliver insults.

"I need a man of some lore. So listen: I had a dream," he continued, looking away at nothing in particular, his attention clearly on his mind's eye.

Just what is the proper response to that kind of statement after first being threatened with death? I guessed none, and let the urgency of the situation help sober me up.

"What was the dream about?" I asked.

"A wolf," he said. "A wolf like a man, or a man like a wolf. Hard to say. But smiling like some bastard wolf stroking his cock and lying in wait for us."

I had never met a man with the gift of prophetic dreams. If I had expected to meet one, I am certain it would not have sounded like this. If anyone else had described a predator as being more dangerous for masturbating while waiting to bite someone, I would have laughed at him. But anything Kraki said was to be taken seriously. Not because he had some ability to portend the future, just because he might kill me if I didn't.

"Hmm, I, uh, that's bad," I said, or something equally stupid.

"You know what it means?" he asked, wide-eyed, grabbing my shoulders. "You know any stories that would hint at what it portends?" It was the first glimmer I had seen in him of hope that I could be useful for something.

"Kraki, I know you want me to do something because of your dream, but I have no idea what a wolf with its cock in its paws means. Or what I'm supposed to do about it. I can tell it as a story if you want. But I have no lore to tell you about it."

The hope in his eyes faded. He let go of me and sighed a snarling sigh. I was a skald, not a wizard or a seer. As he turned to walk away, he added, "Just one paw." As if that cleared it all up.

Kraki's dream did disturb me. Some say dreams are how the gods really communicate, not through runes or bones or battle outcomes. I'd had weird dreams and dismissed them before, only to see them have some kind of strange meaning later. What I had experienced after being hit in the head too many times was different and felt more real. And had actual gods in it. But even so, it was difficult to take much meaning from it, that much more so a dream about a masturbating wolf.

I pondered this on my way to the ship, following well behind the old man to avoid further conversation until I could think of something useful to say. Kraki was an old and experienced warrior who would have had many dreams, some right on the battlefield. Anything worthy of bothering him was either a sign the man had finally lost his wits or something to be heeded.

I considered the former possibility as I boarded the *Sea Squirrel*, and was reminded of where Kraki stood to deliver his counter-poem on the spot. A counter-taunt in poetic form was not a sign of a man losing his wits. No, Kraki's mind was clear, just very inclined towards violence.

That left a vague and unidentified lethal threat lurking somewhere unseen and unidentifiable. Was Jarl Gansi the wolf? Perhaps he was known for strange sexual proclivities before battle. Maybe he had spies in town and knew we were there already. Maybe his ship had a wolf's head for a prow. Or maybe there were hungry wolves in the forest.

It was none of those, but we'll get to that.

The problem bothered and energized me at the same time. Riddles, word plays, hidden things—those I could get lost in and I enjoyed finding my way out. I had never tried to find my way through the mystery of a dream when my life was at stake before. My mind was on the predatory nature of wolves. How they were stealthy. How they would strike only when confident of success without injury.

I heard Svein shouting from our ship, his face doubtless wolfing down whatever extra rations he could find. I dismissed it as an annoyance but took notice after Kraki called me forward. The shouting was accompanied by pointing toward the water, and it was plain to see why.

Two dragon ships had appeared, and they were headed straight for us.

CHAPTER 11

BAD TO VERSE

"What do I do?" I asked Kraki.

I think he mouthed the word 'die' before shrugging. "Take a hard look at the sails. They are different, but I can't make out the details."

We stood on the pier gazing out over the open sea. Two ships hugged the coastline, creeping towards Fretborg. Ships that close to shore were looking to make landfall, not to continue on, especially at the snail's pace they were cutting the water.

"One is a bigger ship but its sail is defaced. A white field with something on it. A boar, I think, in blue. But a crude black line down the middle."

"Gansi's ship. But Gansi is no longer its master."

"The other sail shows red teeth set on a white field. There's nothing defaced about that one."

"Halfdan's sigil," said Kraki, his voice grinding the name out. "Jaws of the wolf." If there was anything to guess about Kraki's disposition towards the occupants of those ships, it was gone when I saw he had already deployed his weapon.

It was a club, technically crude and not that effective compared to something made of steel. This one was made from the femur of a *jotunn* Kraki had slain. A real giant, not some man-sized *jotunn*. And it was supposedly magical as a result. Magic or not, that thing struck like a hammer when Kraki swung it. A spike was sharpened into the lower handle, and the woven leather grip was stained with old blood.

Facing the jaws of the wolf and having had a dream about a wolf, the old man was preparing for a fight. Who could blame him? But that was not my inclination.

"Your dream was not about the wolf's jaws," I said.

"What else could it be? We have our enemy right in front of us."

"That's the point!" I said, caught between exasperation and fear of the man right in front of me. "Your dream was telling you about a hidden danger, of being stalked. This lot is rowing right for us. We don't even know they're an enemy."

"Boy, you are greener than the spring forest. Two warships are rowing our way: They are the enemy until shown otherwise. Gansi is an enemy—he held my friend here in this shithole against his will. And one of the ships is flying the sail of Halfdan the Toothless, the only one intact."

"The Toothless?" I said, mostly to myself. Sometimes such names had meanings, but often enough they were ironic. No viking would keep his status by actually being toothless, literally or figuratively. "How did he get that name?" I had to ask.

"Bit through his brother's throat," said Kraki. That was not good. "Some say he never spit it out." And thus, what seemed like it could not have been worse was, indeed, worse.

Svein harumphed and fingered his axe. "His brother was probably weak."

"Maybe he will want to trade," I offered, hoping this was to be the case, however strong his brother might have been. I could feel myself beginning to shake. Battle seemed inevitable, and with the numbers that much against us, a mere twenty-odd men against what might be over two hundred, we would lose.

"He is a viking, not a trader," said Kraki, which I took as confirmation. "But he will like it if you flatter him. He is that type."

"Flattery seems a better option than the three of us fighting two hundred men right here and now. What do we do if I am not sufficiently flattering?"

The response came back as a growl. "I could teach you to fight right now, for the few minutes we have. If the training doesn't kill you, the three of us can fight two dragon ships worth of men." He paused, palming the business end of his bone club, and then looked at me. "Shall I teach, or will you make it a good poem?"

Fast lesson indeed. Thor's advice or not, that would likely end with my skull cracked. I tried to think of a poem. All I could think was: I hope Halfdan feels he has enough ships already and doesn't need one more.

When the dragon ships docked, I thought I could pick out which one was Halfdan. There were bigger men, darker men, and more handsome men. But all of them moved with a sense of urgency or even unease, as if they had to accomplish something as simple as docking the ship and disembarking at peril to their lives.

One had no such sense of urgency and moved with the ease of a man on the verge of boredom. He had dark blonde hair and a thick beard that failed to hide multiple scars on the left side of his face. He gave no commands and said nothing to his crew, just waited for them to be ready. A wool cloak hid most of the rest of him from view, but not the spearhead-shaped pendant he wore around his neck, marking him as a devotee of Odin.

So far I hadn't needed to compose a real poem, just single stanzas which were good enough in the moment. A single stanza for a newly conquering lord might be considered overly short. Two stanzas would do well, assuming I didn't forget my alliteration and compose myself into a corner.

Three of Halfdan's biggest men disembarked and didn't spend much time looking the three of us up and down. They must have rightly surmised we posed little threat.

The man I pegged as Halfdan then rose and stretched as if tired from so much sailing. The stretch opened his cloak and revealed his real intention of showing us a bright coat of ring armor, a seax with a carved walrus tusk handle, and a sword with a silver-wrought hilt.

I wasn't certain if he was showing us he was dangerous or wealthy or both. I assumed both.

So now you know everything I was working with for those two important stanzas on the spot. For the first time on our journey, I felt less pressure. A poor poem could get me a knife in the belly, sure, but from what I had seen I was likely to get a knife in the belly later anyway. If it happened now at least I wouldn't need to eat any more *hákarl*. So when Halfdan silently demanded who we were and Kraki named us, here is what I spoke:

> "Ships wandering far
>   from familiar shores
> Weathered winter's fangs

> well away from the berg.
> But the boar's bloody spears
> battered and broke, and
> The wolf's sword
> severed Gansi's head."

Right, I only got the one stanza. What was Halfdan going to do, kill me for lack of poetic volume? If he didn't like the one stanza, I wasn't likely to save myself with a second. Also, I was too nervous to think of more than one.

Halfdan stared at me eye to eye as if confused. "How did you know I cut off his head?" he asked.

"I didn't," I admitted. And given further silence, I added, "Poetry isn't supposed to be that accurate."

Halfdan threw back his head and roared, hand over his belly. That was a deep, dark laugh, the kind one might hear in a nightmare. His men, including the ones who didn't hear any of it, laughed with him.

Halfdan slapped a hand on my shoulder and shook me, and looking at Kraki proclaimed, "I like this one! You could screw everything up and he'd still know to tell about how well everything went. These men drink with us in celebration!"

A cheer went up among the crew. Perhaps because they knew they were supposed to make one. The second ships' crew made shouts of loud approval of whatever it was they were supposed to approve of.

That had gone off well insofar as Halfdan hadn't ordered us killed. But we were stuck with him, with our crew scattered. I would probably be called upon for more bloody poetry, likely on the spot. It was in Halfdan's last comment at the docks and the following happenings that I learned my next important lesson in life, a lesson that all good people know but whose subtleties take years, if not decades, to truly appreciate and master:

Flattery solves problems, but it's a lot more effective if you combine it with ale.

CHAPTER 12

PROBLEM SOLVING

I KEPT FLATTERING HALFDAN ALL THE WAY TO THE LONGHOUSE. It was a slow walk, the attention of Halfdan's men wandering away from me as they eyed the scenery with a mix of hope and disbelief. Disbelief at what they saw, hope that it would look better as they kept walking.

Gulldis welcomed Halfdan as 'husband' before even knowing his name. She was happy to introduce our crew, as semi-famous visitors reflected well on her as a hostess. More important, she was ready with plenty of not very good ale for Halfdan and his crew. Not very good ale is still ale, however, and compared to no ale might be considered quite good indeed.

Some of them thanked the gods for that drink. Others banged on the tables for some food. The crew was a hungry-looking lot, all jagged cheekbones and slim waistlines. I got the impression the voyage had not been easy.

Less difficult for twelve of them, the biggest of the lot carrying the biggest weapons and using the biggest voices. They seemed fine, if bored, and sat down by Gulldis' place at the table uninvited. I took it these were Halfdan's champions, perhaps better fed than the rest of the crew. They didn't have very good manners for champions, though, more like a pack of semi-tame wolves loosely tethered to Halfdan.

Gulldis set the thralls to firing up more cauldrons of stew right away, but she was more of a pointer at things that needed doing than a doer of them. It was Huld who ran things in the longhouse, and she began preparations for what would be a great feast that night. I wondered if Gulldis had any idea that her main cook was a *vǫlva*.

Formal introductions were in order. Haldor said he'd heard of Halfdan, and Halfdan said he'd heard of Haldor. Neither indicated what they had heard, so it was up to interpreting their tones of voice and total guesswork to decide what each man meant when he said it. To break the tension, Ulf asked the new jarl for his personal invitation to stay at the hall, a deference Halfdan toasted to.

Flattering as I had been with poetry on the way in, Ulf knew this game far better than I. A different way of speaking, a different calculation. And the *þulr* was good. So good, I wondered if the crew really needed a skald.

Ulf was a great flatterer without making it obvious he was flattering. The man knew fewer languages than I did, but had a kind of magic in his conversation I did not. He did not talk as much as get others to talk, and talk about themselves. Thus primed and comfortable, they quickly considered him a friend and let on what they might not have otherwise.

So it was with Halfdan. I think Ulf used me as a distraction to ask the more probing questions he was really interested in that night, namely why Halfdan had killed Gansi and what else had happened.

To hear Halfdan tell it, raiding together had been profitable the previous summer, but the seas were rough after he and Gansi returned to his hall. It was late in the season anyway, owing to the great deal of plunder they had taken. Gansi requested to winter there instead of sailing back in harsh weather, and Halfdan obliged him as a good host should.

They'd all had a bit much to drink one evening in the middle of winter and Gansi had become surly. One comment led to another, another comment led to a perceived slight, and the slight led to Halfdan challenging Gansi in a *holmganga* for everything he had. Which was a little strange, since a *holmganga* was a one-on-one duel, and that made me wonder: If Gansi lost, shouldn't all his men still be here? What sort of *holmganga* was this?

I'd seen the quick and nasty sort, where the two participants have one wrist tied each to the other and then go at it with knives. A more graceful version involves a sword, if you can afford one, or more probably an axe. Then up to three shields per man, where shield destruction might mean the end of the argument. Or you can fight to the death in a more free-form style. Personal preference.

The one Halfdan described was going in the direction of sword and shields. But some of Gansi's men spoke up for their jarl and wanted to be involved, at which point Halfdan suggested that all of them grab a weapon and shield each and have it out outside. The *holmganga* quickly turned into a full-on battle. The two shield walls lined up, engaged, and Gansi's broke down. Halfdan fought Gansi in single combat, cutting off his head, and the rest of the men fought on with no quarter asked or given.

Halfdan had sustained some losses, even winning the engagement so completely. With two ships, he now needed to fill out his crews. That and see what finery Gansi had left behind. Seeing the shape the town was in, Halfdan guessed there wasn't much, and that he'd be keener on using two ships to go raiding that summer than he would be sitting in his new hall.

A casual question from Halfdan snatched my attention when Ulf said we would not be in Fretborg long: "Headed north to see what Ogmund will pay?"

There were stories and there were legends and there were myths, and Ogmund the sorcerer had a bit of each to him. Raised on foul magic in the far northeast by Bjarmians, his first well-known act was to betray his closest kinsman. Some said Ogmund was half-demon, attracting followers interested in that very magic he had been brought up with. He was also the sworn enemy of Arrow-Odd, who my father had fought for over twenty years ago. I thought Ogmund had died in that last battle, but apparently not.

Since the answer was no, Halfdan suggested we swear service to him and go raiding with three ships "rather than do errands for that coalbiter King Ragnvald in Denmark."

I held my breath for a moment until Ulf politely declined.

"How would it look if we said we would do something, and then we did not do it?" said Ulf. "It would be a poor showing at best, more like the act of a *niðingr*."

Something about the statement had poked Halfdan, and his smile faded as he sipped his ale. Maybe it was just the poor quality of ale, but I thought not.

"It would be, indeed," Halfdan said through his teeth. Then, regaining his grin, Halfdan stood up and addressed his men. "Well then! How about we see more details of what's ours now?"

They gave a great cheer and downed the rest of their drinks before filing out.

The rest of that day involved Halfdan and his lieutenants arguing. A lot.

Having killed all of Gansi's men along with Gansi, there were some differences of opinion on which men now owned which dilapidated huts, bone-skinny animals, and broken or rusted pieces of junk. Some of these disagreements looked as though they might come down to single combat themselves, but ultimately the realization that nothing in Fretborg was very good and certainly not worth fighting over won out in most cases.

One exception was two men killing each other over one of the few healthy pigs. Halfdan claimed the swine himself after the mutual slaying, "to forestall any further infighting." I don't know what Halfdan and his men were saying to each other, but there was a lot of shaking of heads. Perhaps the worse fate for Gansi would have been to come back and live in this miserable town.

Halfdan did not seem so disappointed as I thought he might be. Or he might have been quite disappointed but knew enough not to show it. Something about the way he walked and talked made me think this was a viking who knew what he was up to.

Whatever Halfdan was up to, there was plotting afoot by our crew as well. You could see it if you watched for men leaning in to whisper, or just give knowing nods at who knows what. Something was going on, and nobody thought it all that important to include me in the plans.

That was alright, I reasoned. Better not to have too many expectations on my shoulders.

It was a bad sign, I knew deeper down. It meant the crew did not think of me as one of them.

I kept up a cheery face despite my trepidation and spent my time watching and listening. It was during that time watching and listening outside that I heard the raven's hoarse croaking and remembered something Huld had said.

The raven has a part to play. Find her and make friends.

Easier said than done! Ravens did not have friends as I understood them. They might favor you for a while if you gave them a very good story, but only if. And soon they would want another, and then another, or they would seek their stories elsewhere.

But I had nothing else to do and a god who had suggested I do things others found difficult, so I decided to follow the raven's call. Where would it lead me? A building with a trap door leading to secret tunnels? A cave away from town where the dwarf kept his workshop? Maybe something completely unexpected!

It led me back to Huld's little hut. The raven was perched above the door, looking down at me in every sense of the phrase.

"Already afternoon. You are very careful," said the raven, which I suppose was her way of telling me I was slow or late or both.

"Not as careful as someone else I know," I said. "You haven't even told me your name yet." I paused, staring at her without knowing what I was trying to do or if I was trying to get something specific.

"Subtlety," she said.

I continued to stare while considering this.

"Did you expect my name to be Ansgar?" she asked. "You should know how raven names work, skald. What are the names of Odin's ravens?"

"Huginn and Muninn," I responded without thinking. "Thought and Memory. Yes, nevermind. Makes perfect sense." Which it kind of did not.

I shook my head and walked inside. No one was home. No surprise, Huld would still be busy with the feast preparations. Subtlety hopped in after me and flapped up to the workbench.

"Why are you here, anyway?" I asked.

The raven blinked at me but said nothing.

"A raven might frequent likely trade routes and battlefields, or lonely passes where adventurous travelers roam," I continued. "But this place is none of those."

"You're here," said Subtlety.

"I don't want to be here either," I said. "But I could use a favor. Or so I'm told."

"Favor?" she croaked, her voice suddenly becoming hoarse with surprise. "You want a story?"

"Nevermind what I want," I said, since I had no idea what I wanted.

"Trade for trade!" she said. Then, a little disappointed, "Huld said you would have good stories."

"Plenty," I said, my mind suddenly blanking on all of them.

Then I realized the raven had not been in the hall to hear of Gansi's end. I told her the story as Halfdan had related it. The *holmganga* that had turned into a battle, the beheading of the former jarl, and thus the winning of Fretborg. I added a little to say Halfdan had considered taking his ships north to fight for Ogmund, but decided to come here anyway.

Thus pleased with myself, I crossed my arms and awaited the raven's response.

"That doesn't make any sense," she said.

"Well, I don't know for sure about Ogmund," I said, "but that's a good, bloody story."

"I don't mind a little exaggeration," said Subtlety, "but that story is aurochs-shit! Why did you make it up?"

"I didn't! I heard it direct from Halfdan."

"Oh," said Subtlety, stretching her wings. "You are not as smart as Huld said, then. Did you not notice that crew was all starving?"

"They were hungry from the voyage, of c—"

And I stopped myself right there, realizing that I had seen but not paid any attention.

Two crews worth of ships wintering in one hall. One crew no longer around for about half the winter. That would mean twice as many rations for those left alive. That would mean those left alive would be fat and happy, even on a long voyage back to Fretborg.

But they were not fat and happy. Their pants were falling down from weight loss. Their cheekbones were poking through emaciated faces. They were even fighting over the potential food.

"There was no *holmganga*," I said, half to myself. "Halfdan must have realized the provisions would never get them all through the winter and killed off Gansi and his men. Probably in their sleep, which is why he lost so few of his own men. Food must have been stretched a long way even with one crew, given how skinny they all are. Halfdan is a *níðingr* to murder men secretly in the night."

"There is no one left alive to dispute his story, though," said Subtlety.

I gulped, then tried to stop so the raven did not see it. "If things don't go his way," I said, "Halfdan will not want any of us alive, either. He'll just tell a story convenient to his ends."

"If it doesn't go his way," said the raven.

"That's the way we want it to go!"

Subtlety shrugged. "If you die here, I'll tell others about it."

Which was a raven's version of a comforting statement.

It also gave me an idea. Huld had said the raven had a part to play but had no other details to give me. I still wasn't sure how to interpret that, but I realized that if Gansi had a raven around to tell his death story, maybe Halfdan would not be able to spin his own version of it so far from the truth.

"A favor then," I said, "because I don't intend to die here. I want to make sure Halfdan doesn't try with us what he did with Gansi. I need you to stick around and watch what happens from my shoulder."

"There might be better places to watch from."

"I need you with me. And I need you to fly away and make a big show that you are taking the story you just witnessed to other places. That way Halfdan may not be so quick to think he can cover up another dishonorable act with a false story."

Subtlety cocked her head. "Trade for trade."

And we were back to that.

Subtlety hopped and spread her wings in excitement, blowing some of the desiccated flora off the table. A dozen or more dried herbs and mushrooms were laid out, neatly separated, most of them tied off to keep their bundles together, but those did not move. Up the wall from here hung more plants, one of them a veiny flower I recognized as henbane. Or maybe I would need to call it 'Huld's Relief.'

A high chair sat by the workbench, perhaps the *vǫlva's* most important tool. It was important to practice *seiðr* from a high vantage point, the higher the better. Why that was, I could not even guess, but I knew that much of the *vǫlur. Vǫlur* if you liked them, I suppose. Roof-riders or Night-Hags if you didn't like them. My insides were all still inside me, so I was confident Huld was the former.

A memory came to me of running into a witch who was very much one of the latter. It happened on a delivery run I was making that put me far afield from my home in Dafvik. Up into the mountains, down into the forest, and then, it seemed to me, I passed through a Myrkwood and wasn't exactly sure what realm I was in. And that wasn't half the story.

"I can tell you a story I lived," I said. "It even begins with a raven, or I like to think of it beginning there. I was lost and had to win a battle of wits against the bird just to find my way. Then my way was not safe, just slightly less dangerous. I won another battle of wits against a sorcerer, conversed with the dead, and killed some goats."

If there were two things to hook any raven, they were magic and bloodletting. Subtlety stared at me wide-eyed. Which, for a bird, is hard to achieve.

"Why did you kill the goats?" she asked.

"The explanation would take the whole story," I said. And so I told her.

"That's a fine story," she said after I was finished. "Very witty!"

"Thank you," I said.

"Wit is not enough to get you through though," she added. "Did you notice that for all your wittiness, you still had to fight your way out?"

I rubbed the stubble on my chin in contemplation. Yes, I had noticed that. For all the wit in the world, it can never be the only tool even a skald carries. Some say violence does not solve problems. Those people are probably just causing problems, and they don't want you to kill them for it.

CHAPTER 13

BERSERKIR

WHEN ALCOHOL AND FLATTERY DON'T SOLVE YOUR PROBLEM, violence is usually the next best thing. Assuming you are the one controlling the violence. And it seemed the crew of the *Sea Squirrel* was confident of doing just that. When I returned to the hall, I saw the feast had begun. Despite the feast, the tone had changed from spilling ale together to threatening to spill blood.

"You don't look like traders to me," roared Halfdan. The conversation was no longer conversation. It was the exchange of fighting words that precedes a real fight. "You don't look much like anything with such a small ship!"

"We trade in steel," said Haldor, to a low chorus of angry murmurs behind him. "And we trade with people who are awake."

The hum rose to a roar. Men slapped tables and stomped their feet. Ulf was egging the men on rather than speaking honeyed words into Halfdan's ear. It would be Haldor's version of diplomacy from here on in.

"I am awake! And my *berserkir* are awake!" yelled Halfdan, gesturing towards his twelve huge, fur-clad, mouthbreathing warriors. "And all the rest of my men are awake! Perhaps you can ask them if they want to sell this dwarf so cheaply."

Grumbling rose from Halfdan's men. Not really words, just grunts of displeasure and disapproval. This was escalating to become a general melee, which did not bode well. A duel was one thing, but the chaos of free-fighting over a hundred men was not part of the plan. At least, I assumed it was not part of the plan because I really did not want that to be the plan.

No doubt Haldor and Halfdan in single combat would be in our favor, but the rest of us would be fighting four men each. Some of the crew could take those odds and more, easily, but others would be overwhelmed right away. Then the better fighters would have maybe eight men rushing them, some unexpected and unseen. If the fight were one after another though, long odds might work. They often worked in the sagas, I told myself.

"Innstein," I asked, "how many of Halfdan's men do you think Haldor can beat in single combat?"

"Just Haldor?" Innstein eyed Halfdan's warriors and sized them up. If I could compose a poem insinuating Halfdan was afraid of single combat, he might need to respond to protect his honor in front of the people in town. "Hard to say. Some of them might be tough. Are you worried? We have a plan."

"What is the plan?" I asked.

"Don't worry," said Utstein. "It's a fluid plan. Just try to insult Halfdan a little bit if you can. Maybe make him challenge you."

"Make him challenge me?"

"Ah, don't worry so much," said Innstein. "You wouldn't fight. You would choose a champion to fight for you."

"Then you choose Haldor," said Utstein. "And then Halfdan either backs down or dies fighting. See? Good plan."

I declined to tell the brothers this was the worst plan I had ever heard. Most especially since it had been developed without me, and without my even knowing about it, and had the distinct possibility of not working out at all the way it was designed.

The plan left me more ill at ease than I had been when I greeted Halfdan in the first place. Now I could hardly think of any composing. Or rather, I could, but poetry is a subtle art. The insult would need to be strong enough it could not be ignored, but not so strong as to legally allow him to kill me on the spot.

How to do that? Tell him he's fat and stupid? He was clearly neither, and would laugh those insults off. I had to put him in a position where he didn't have to fight, but if he chose not to he would lose face.

I thought about this as the louder war of words rang through the hall.

"Time is not unlimited," said Subtlety, whispering from my shoulder.

My composition to insult Halfdan wasn't coming up quite right. My timing was uncertain. The verse I meant as a subtle dig kept forming in my head as what would be a massive insult. If I did that, I might get myself killed. Context and delivery can change a thing from failure to success, however. If I had learned even one lesson from the night I met Magnus, I at least had learned that.

And from there, the idea blossomed. I needed an introduction. I could see it play out in my head but I needed someone else to create the context for what I planned to deliver.

"Hey, you two," I said to the 'Steins. "I have an idea, but I need you to set the tone."

"What kind of tone?" asked Innstein.

"Seems like the tone here is largely decided," said Utstein.

I shook my head. "It involves betting."

I explained more about what I wanted them to do, but they were both sold from that instant.

The brothers looked at each other in silent conversation, the way only those two could. Then they nodded and moved into the ring of men that had centered around Halfdan and Haldor.

Innstein cleared his throat.

"It sounds like Halfdan could beat us all with one hand behind his back," yelled Innstein over the din.

Quiet began to descend. That sounded like a challenge, and challenges were serious business.

"Maybe with no hands," added Utstein. "But we should set fair odds on a fair fight."

Even quieter.

"Can Halfdan the Toothless win against Haldor Skullsplitter by himself?" screamed Innstein.

Silence.

"You have big mouths for so few spears," said Halfdan.

"We have large purses," said Utstein, thrusting his hips forward to some low laughter. "But little patience to spend."

"How much longer were you going to trade veiled threats before we could set some terms on a real fight?" asked Innstein.

"I see no such purses!" hissed Halfdan. "And I see one man of yours to six of mine, one little cargo vessel to two dragon ships!"

"A good ship though!" said Utstein, ignoring Halfdan's suspect arithmetic on the number of his men. "And not just for cargo. Worth two of yours, probably. Would you care to wager ships for ship?"

"Odds are quite favorable for you," added Innstein. "Being that our ship has a better history and a better name than either of yours."

I am certain I did not know the names of either of Halfdan's ships, and confident that Innstein did not either. The sheer arrogance was delicious to take in. It also set the stage for the real offer.

"Or here's a better idea," said Utstein. "Our ship for your dwarf. We could use one of those! But not your stinky, smelly ships."

Halfdan sneered and shook his head. The air seemed to leave the area as everyone held their breath, waiting, and I got the reaction I wanted from Halfdan. The mention of the dwarf, as I had told them to do, attracted the attention of a previously quiet spectator.

"No!" shouted Gulldis, pushing through the ring. "He is *mine!* And he is not for betting!"

"You mean he is *mine*," growled Halfdan, reaching out for the woman and putting his hand around the back of her neck. The gesture turned from gentle to rough in an instant. "Tell me," he repeated.

Gulldis' back arched and she tried to throw her head back to resist Halfdan's grip. The more she did this, the tighter he squeezed, smiling as his look bored into her eyes. She kept up her composure under that pressure but could not resist long.

"Yours, he is yours," she said. "My jarl."

Halfdan loosened his grip on her neck but did not let go.

"I would tell you more of the dwarf—" said Gulldis, before she was cut off.

"Be silent," said Halfdan. Then, turning to address the general assembly, he continued, "Where is this dwarf, anyway?"

"Here I am," said Finnr, appearing through the ranks of the *Sea Squirrel* crew as if emerging from the ground itself. "The Jarl of Fretborg calls, and I answer."

Gulldis pulled away from Halfdan's now-distracted hand. Not that he was the only one distracted. All eyes were on the dwarf. His rolling potbelly.

His belt-tucked beard. But most noticeable to me, his easy grin, despite the high stakes at hand.

"Hmm," said Halfdan. "I expected you to be shorter."

Finnr's eyebrows perked up. "What is there to life but to defy expectations?"

Halfdan snarled. "I will do just that," he said. "Maybe I would rather care to have all my men kill all of you and be done with it," he continued, turning to Haldor.

The newer men, Ingolf and Leif foremost among them, drew their weapons. It was not chance that two sworn brothers had found it profitable to join such a crew—they had their own story and I imagined it included little luck. But they were a reliable pair, and more than loyal enough to our crew they would not shirk their duty once the fighting started.

Those new men, however, were less privy to the plan than those in the know. Or those, in the case of the brothers, I had conspired with.

And so I spoke a verse in *ljóðaháttr*, not the meter of narrative like my others. The meter of wisdom, more like. I thought it most appropriate to the situation:

> "Feeders of ravens
>   rarely refuse
> spreading of the spear-din.
>
> Half a Dane,
>   half a *drengr*;
> Shy of shield walls Halfdan shows."

And that was my verse, to seal in the minds of everyone hearing it that Halfdan would either fight our way or be called half a man for the rest of his time as jarl. It wasn't a perfect verse. It had too many stresses in the last line. And even though the alliteration between the two long lines was not supposed to be connected, there was something discordant about how I'd phrased it. But it was good enough to get a message across. I would let Halfdan make his criticisms if he wanted to.

He did not point out the imperfect composition, but his face did turn bright red.

The silence that followed was heavy with threat, and I knew I had done my part. Halfdan would challenge me, I would use Haldor as a proxy.

But plans rarely survive the first spear thrust. Thus it was with my idea, as Magnus' sharp, derisive laughter pierced the night air.

Magnus had stepped forward to become the center of attention. He had it, and took his time making a show of it, pointing, guffawing, leaning on a table for support. Making a spectacle of himself, and making a spectacle of Halfdan in the process.

Suddenly gaining control, he stood up smiling and said, "Here is my challenge, take it or leave it: I don't think you have a single *berserkr* who can beat me, and we will wager our ship for your dwarf on it. Enough with the boasts, take the bet or slink away!"

It was the right bet but the wrong person. What was Magnus doing?

The challenge must have appealed to Halfdan. He was already short on men, so even though he could murder us all right there, he would take heavy losses to do it. Perhaps too many losses to defend his ships and hall. A single fight would satisfy the need for bloodshed and make a demonstration he was in control without risking many men. It would also show he was adhering to the rules of a *holmganga*.

A good rebuttal to any accusations of treachery against Gansi, should they ever arise. All in all, a good choice for him to make especially when presented with a small, hotheaded challenger like Magnus.

It wasn't what I had intended. I knew Haldor could cut down Halfdan without difficulty. He was nearly as big as Svein and nearly as quick a Kari. But the challenge had already been thrown down, and Haldor would be a spectator only. His expression did not change as Halfdan's turned a wicked, wolfish grin.

"I have twelve *berserkir*," said Halfdan slow and clear, "and if you think not one can beat you, we will have to test that boast on them all! Let me see what they think." Halfdan turned to address his men, and called out, "Well, men, it seems we have run into a big challenge. It will be a tall order should you accept it"—he paused here for the laughter to start—"and I can't guarantee a massive reward for victory."

"Perhaps an anthill of a reward rather than a mountain," added a nameless, faceless lieutenant who nobody gave a shit about.

The men's laughter got louder.

"They won't need to use smaller weapons will they?" added another, to an even greater uproar.

"No, but we will need a very short gallows!" screamed Halfdan suddenly over the laughter of his men. "Because we will offer his body to the Gallows Lord strung up by his intestines! Who accepts his challenge, step forward!"

His smile gone, Halfdan's face looked every part an angry wolf, and even his men looked ill at ease at the bitter anger in his voice. I thought of Kraki's dream and swallowed hard, hoping my plan hadn't dropped Magnus straight into the trap that dream warned us of. I looked for Kraki in the crowd and found him sitting on a barrel. He clutched his bone club, looking frustrated.

Twelve men, if you could call them that, stepped forward.

A word about *berserkir* for context: The only criteria for being a *berserkr*, other than calling yourself one, were to be generally smelly and unkempt and to enjoy killing people. You didn't need to be very good at killing if you chose to attack only weak people. But howling while you did it was expected.

Maybe once, in ancient days, *berserkir* were the frenzied warriors who fought their best outside a shield wall and without armor. That's probably more true of stories than of history, which also cast them as hard against steel and immune to fire. They are usually imposing presences, most of them near the size of Haldor or Svein, saying little, doing as they please. '*Berserkir*' are literally 'bear shirts' or 'bare shirts.' Whether that means 'without a shirt' or 'wearing only a bear's skin for a shirt' was subject to the interpretation of the *berserkr*, even during my time.

In the sagas, they almost always appear in packs of twelve. I don't know why, it's just one of those things. Keeping twelve around was likely Halfdan's nod to the old stories. If I had been part of his crew I would have advised him to do otherwise. We'll get to why in just a moment.

This lot was particularly scruffy-looking. Big men holding big axes, the kind you wouldn't want knocking on your door at night. Or at all.

They all moved in much the same way, too. Shoulders up to their ears, their heads hardly swiveling without the entirety of their chests moving as well. The animal skins they wore hung loosely about them, probably more for style than warmth, and they began taking those off.

Magnus nodded at Kari, who was already on his way over. Kari bade some of the other men fetch a few shields and others extra weapons. He knew how this would go, as did Magnus. I knew how it would go insofar as I knew the basic rules, but I was seized up inside.

All I wanted to do was tell Magnus I was sorry I had blundered him into such a mess and that I hadn't meant to get him killed. But you don't say those things in my culture, and you don't acknowledge them from Magnus' side either. He had the look of a man who simply had a lot of work to do rather than a man who was about to die. He stretched as Kari laid out spare shields and weapons.

I had to say something to Magnus. He had hardly stopped insulting me since we first met, but I didn't want this to be his last fight. Or at least, I didn't want it to be my fault he died because I had already made enough mistakes. Before I could get to him, Kraki intercepted me and got right up in my face.

"Was that your shitty plan?" he asked. "And you didn't think it would be a good idea to tell me so I could do the fighting?"

Haldor's hand slammed into the back of Kraki's neck before I could admit I had no response. It would have been enough to knock the wind out of me, but for Kraki it was barely enough to get his attention.

"Don't be so greedy for glory," Haldor said. "You have plenty of it already. And I don't think our skald's plan was quite as calculated as you think."

"I was . . ." I stammered. "I thought . . ." I looked Haldor in the eye but was too distracted by Kraki and Magnus to be coherent. Shaking it off, I got it out: "I thought you wanted to fight Halfdan man to man and the poem would force him away from a melee and into a duel."

"Plans," spat Kraki. "Plans and plans and more plans." He stalked off, muttering to himself and swinging his bone club in frustration.

Haldor shrugged. "Pay no attention to Kraki. He wanted to fight because he has the itch."

"That's not an itch I relate to," I said. "They have four or five times our number and I am not the best in a fight. I thought I had to do something."

"You did," said Haldor. "Played into what we intended completely."

"But I thought—"

"Forget it," continued Haldor. "This way is much better. If I made that challenge and killed Halfdan, I would be the jarl of this shitty place when I inherited everything he left behind. Your way, Halfdan is stuck with it, a suitable punishment. And Magnus gets to earn some extra fame."

"But he needs to fight twelve *berserkir*," I said. "They're huge! They'll kill him!"

Haldor grinned and gestured towards Halfdan's men. "Take a look at those *berserkir*. What do you see?"

I saw twelve men, all much bigger than me, all with arms far thicker than mine, all holding huge axes. They were bare-chested and readying themselves for a fight. One pair was taking turns pounding on each other's chests and screaming into each other's faces. One was slapping himself in the face and muttering. Some were supplicating themselves to Odin.

The one that caught my attention was doing exercises with his axe. With both hands on the handle, he straightened his arms in front of him and lifted the axe above his head. Except he couldn't do that with his arms straight. He bent his elbows at about eye height and then lifted the handle only to about his forehead before coming down again.

The *berserkr* was strong, no doubt. But his range of motion was poor. If he tried to swim or climb rocks or trees like I was used to doing, he would not do well. What if he had to attack or defend at an odd angle, or suddenly change direction?

And what were the others doing? The veneer of intimidation pierced, I saw them differently. They were not preparing. They were posturing, hoping their enemy would freeze in fear.

Magnus started on his shoulder rotation exercises. Those done, Kari turned his back and Magnus put one ankle on Kari's shoulder and leaned into it to stretch. Magnus had incredible range of motion with that flexibility, and had certainly done this warmup before.

Both crews moved outside, where the fight would take place. Thralls carried out torches and set them high so we could see. There were more formalities and an announcing of the rules. There was a good bit of banging on shields and yelling. A fighting area was marked off with four poles, and all combatants swore oaths over their weapons.

When all that was done, Magnus pointed his axe at me and said, "A good poem, or you stay here."

I didn't know how to answer that at the time and Magnus didn't wait for one. He stepped out to what still looked to me like certain death against the first of Halfdan's *berserkir*. The *berserkr* charged and brought his axe down with both hands, looking like he would split Magnus in half from head to toe.

The *berserkr's* axe buried itself into the ground because Magnus was not there.

At the same time, Magnus' axe had cleaved into the back of the *berserkr's* neck and stuck there, briefly, until the weight of the man pulled away. The body hit the ground face-first while Magnus let his axe hang in the air, dripping.

The body spasmed in death throes after a moment, or perhaps it was inadvertent movement while still briefly alive from having the spine severed. Nobody was going to check. Nobody even spoke until the silence was broken by Magnus tapping his bloodied axe on his shield. No loud bangs, only the gentlest taps.

"PAY UP!" yelled Utstein. While some had been concerned with formalities, the 'Steins had been busy taking side bets. Bets with long odds in their favor they would now collect on. Long odds were Innstein's game, and taking money from the ignorant was Utstein's favorite activity, making this event the perfect venture for them.

What Haldor had known all along was finally clear to me: Despite his short stature, Magnus was not one of the lesser warriors on our crew. He was among the most dangerous—pound for pound, the best fighter we had.

The next *berserkr's* axe came so close it sheared off some of Magnus' beard as he pivoted out of the way. There was no time for a follow-up stroke because Magnus was already so far inside the *berserkr's* range, whirling his axe in a wide arc. He was loose, relaxed, and quiet; a contrast to the loud posturing of his opponents.

They couldn't touch him. After three fights, Halfdan's men were noticeably quieter in their cheering. After six, there were cries of confusion and someone shouting, "Wear him down!"

I mentioned advising Halfdan against being poetic about having twelve *berserkir*. It's true they often appear in groups of twelve in the sagas. But those groups of twelve never end well. In almost every story they suffer the same fate: All twelve slain one after another by a single hero.

Number seven took the 'wear him down' idea to heart by swinging left to right and not committing fully, forcing Magnus to hop out of the way. After one such hop where Magnus drew back three more paces, the *berserkr* stuck out his chest, threw his arms wide, and howled. There was a roar of challenge from Halfdan's side.

I blinked and Magnus' axe flew sideways through the air to stick deep in the *berserkr's* throat. For a moment the cheers, ignorant of the sudden change in events, drowned out the gurgling noises the *berserkr* made as he tried to breathe through an axe head. In a final, desperate effort, the *berserkr* staggered a few steps on his last breath and then pitched forward before he could swing.

In a loud, clear voice, Magnus called out, "They wore down my axe." He paused for effect. "New axe!"

Kari was already there with three choices. Magnus tested the balance of each while the *berserkir* tried to decide who would be next.

Magnus wiped away a splash of blood that had reddened his hand before choosing a new weapon, and then it dawned on me. So obvious, and yet I had let my assumption do my thinking: My father had not named him Magnus the Red for his hair color.

My blood ran with elation such that I almost lost sight of the most critical part of my plan.

"It will be important to tell how this went," I told Subtlety, still perched on my shoulder. "You will need to make a big show of carrying the story away with you when this is finished. A story that Magnus won this challenge, and that the dwarf is ours."

The raven rolled her eyes at me. "Not very subtle at all, skald! You are lucky this is turning into such a good story."

"And you are lucky as the only raven to be able to tell it," I countered.

She took the hint and made no more complaint.

After the tenth fell, the last two came out at the same time.

"Hold, hold," said Utstein. "This affects the betting, and we don't want bad blood from bets lost due to a sudden change in rules."

"There's no reason we can't work out terms, though," added Innstein.

These sounded like friendly and honest gestures, but both brothers did it with axe in one hand and long seax in the other. Terms were clear: Agree to terms, or there will be a bigger fight with your crew already ten down.

"Can your man not handle two at once?" yelled Halfdan. "He's been sure enough about his business. Why not make it more interesting?"

"A fair question!" offered Innstein from the edge of the crowd. "But Magnus might need a new weapon quite suddenly while fighting two, and right now he would need to get back to Kari for another. We will be right here with extra weapons and shields. Then he can fight two at once. Fair?"

The crew of the *Sea Squirrel* moved and shifted, several men offering equipment. Utstein was still in the fighting area making it as clear as possible he was ready to fight if need be without actually making a challenge.

There was something strange and needlessly busy about the crew's movement, with most men carrying a single extra weapon or shield, milling about, and only then finding a new place to stand to watch the fight. Haldor stood unmoved during the entire process, staring down the middle of the fight area with Halfdan at the other end.

Halfdan pulled at his beard. "Fair. Get on with it."

Utstein stepped back and Magnus stepped forward and banged his shield twice. The *berserkir* smiled and spread out in their approach. The one closer to me was the taller and leaner of the two. His reach was much greater than Magnus' reach, especially with that two-handed axe. Having come a few steps forward, Magnus stopped and dug his heels in while watching both opponents out of the corners of his eyes.

I knew Magnus could throw his axe if he wanted, but I was surprised when he did just that. He attacked the tall one, the one nearer to me, with an overhand throw while circling away from the other *berserkr*. His position put him almost in between Kari and the tall *berserkr*.

Almost, but not quite. Kari quietly slipped a hand to his quiver. Magnus' throw surprised the *berserkr*, who used his own weapon to deflect it. He smiled, taking that to mean the rest of his task would be easy.

Magnus stared straight at Kari. "Weapon!" he yelled as he reached nearer into that space between Kari and the *berserkr*.

In the time between the beginning and end of that one-word request, Kari unsheathed and threw a javelin, one of his 'toothpicks' as Magnus called them. It struck the still-smiling tall *berserkr* in his right eye, the tip punching through the back of his skull. His body stopped working mid-stride, and he collapsed still grinning the smile of a man who thinks he has just won a fight.

Magnus pivoted and caught the axe Utstein tossed across the fighting space with barely a look. New weapon in hand, he charged the other *berserkr* who was momentarily confused by our crew's interpretation of the new rules.

The berserkr roared and advanced, slashing diagonally one way and then another as Magnus dodged left and right, putting more and more space between them.

Enraged, the *berserkr* came back at Magnus at full speed, his axe held aloft. He was ready for Magnus to dodge again, unlike his comrades, and knew that just a bit of delay on his stroke would allow him to redirect it. He never got the chance.

As he looked like he was positioning himself to dodge, Magnus hopped forward at the last possible moment to put himself inside the *berserkr's* range.

The big man was in no position for infighting, and the toe of Magnus' axeblade punched upward into the *berserkr's* throat.

Shocked, the *berserkr* hammered down his axe with a single hand. It caught a glancing blow off Magnus' shield. Magnus dodged around the side to chop into one hamstring. The *berserkr* whirled to counterattack, but his slash hit Magnus' shield boss and turned the blade. A slash to the other hamstring and the big man fell to his knees.

As he leaned on his huge axe to prop himself up, Magnus cleaved the back of his skull. The *berserkr's* eyes rolled white, his hands fell from his axe, and his jaw went slack.

Magnus pried back his weapon with a sudden jerk and let the body flop down face first. Gore dripped from Magnus' red beard as he looked around for other potential challengers.

Halfdan's expression was unchanged. I could see him weighing his options at the outcome. It was a big loss of men and face, but did he realize how overmatched he was? Or would his anger dictate he had to fight, even if it meant risking most of the rest of his crew?

In that tense moment, Haldor stepped forward. He said nothing for a long time and did not smile or gloat. Halfdan looked in my direction. Then back at Haldor. A silent conversation was occurring between the two, a favorite of my people, the type of thing I never understood.

I had my knife and sling, only the former much good in close quarters. If we were about to fight Halfdan's entire crew, well, let me be honest: No weapon would have helped me very much back then. I held that knife as if a talisman against battle.

"Who knew you had a *berserkr* of your own," said Halfdan. "And in such a small package."

"But he's just a young little—" Kraki yelled from behind Haldor and was cut off as Haldor turned around.

Shirtless, Kraki gestured with his bone club and paced back and forth to make it as clear as possible he wanted to fight, too.

Haldor faced Halfdan again. "He's not our *berserkr*," he said.

"But he's a favorite of Loki it seems," said Halfdan. "A bit of trickery to win. Did you see that fight, bird? Stick with me, and you will see more of the like."

And I realized Halfdan had not been looking at me. He had been looking at Subtlety, and he was trying to bribe her. *Tell the story my way, say I was cheated,* he seemed to say, *and I will give you a better one later.*

I couldn't let that happen. It was time to call in my favor with Subtlety and make it clear Halfdan would not control the narrative of the night's events.

Halfdan fancied himself wise even in defeat, but he was outmatched here. I had spoken to more ravens during my travels than he had likely ever seen. And I knew there was only one thing they liked more than a story about bloody battle: A story about bloody battle in verse form.

So I interrupted and spoke two verses to solidify the telling of the story:

> "Halfdan's twelve
>   heaved mightily,
> one after another
>   wondering what
> mist had vanished
>   the man before them:
> Magnus' axe
>   their only answer.

> Felling foes
>   fiercely in the fray,
> Haldor's man
>   held his ground.
> Two last, desperate,
>   looked for advantage,
> found more iron
>   than otherwise expected."

THE TENSION WAS like a bowstring pulled overly taut, and I knew it was time. "And you heard our wager with Halfdan. The dwarf is ours," I shouted to the raven. "Now go!"

"Caw!" said Subtlety in her excitement as she flapped into the air. "Twelve to one, well done!"

The implication was there before her black feathers disappeared into the night sky. Word of what had happened would spread, and Halfdan would not have the ability to silence all the witnesses before that story was told.

Now Halfdan had been outsmarted twice in one night. I wondered if my desire to make our story right was about to guarantee the battle I had tried to prevent in the first place.

Haldor spoke first, in what sounded like a concession but was really a demand, saying, "There was no trickery. Before or during the fight. The challenge was that not one of your *berserkir* could beat him. Not one has beaten him. And I do not think any of them will make another attempt. Still, it was not Magnus' hand that felled the eleventh man. That was an accident. So it seems to me he cannot collect that one's goods and treasure."

Halfdan paused in a half snarl before speaking. "Unfortunately for your man," he said, "that was the richest of the twelve. A big loss of treasure indeed. Unless you care to take issue."

Gulldis strode over to Halfdan then and whispered in his ear. He changed nothing about his expression other than to indicate he was listening. Gulldis finished whispering and looked each of the *Sea Squirrel*'s crew in the eye, smiling. Only after she had done so and taken a few careful, ladylike steps forward did she speak aloud.

"In one day I find I am a widow, and then there is bloodshed on my doorstep. Surely no more is necessary?"

"No more delay of payment is necessary either," said Kraki, in a hoarse voice to cancel Gulldis's sweetness. "We require only the word of the jarl that Finnr is free."

Halfdan took a long time in speaking, perhaps weighing the magic that might come back at him if he held his tongue. Eventually, practical consideration won out, and he spoke the simplest thing: "The dwarf is free."

The air popped in my ears as if I were skiing fast down a mountainside. Whatever invisible thing had bound the dwarf had burst in a way we could feel but not see. He smiled then, and embraced his friend Kraki.

Other warriors from Halfdan's crew brought the belongings of eleven dead *berserkir*. Magnus looked them over and nodded in approval, despite the paucity of the items. The last two bodies were taken away to the same place as the rest, along with a weapon from each pile. And I realized Magnus was not validating the treasure, but consenting to give up a weapon from each pile so they could be included with the funeral rites.

Halfdan invited us into the hall, stating he would not be called an ungracious host even to his enemies. The moon was high at that point, and there was no other real option unless you think setting sail without being able to see what's in front of you is a good idea. It was to be an uneasy night, accepting the jarl's hospitality but not trusting to it.

The others headed into the longhouse as I pondered this. I followed, disliking this idea. But what else to do was not clear at all, and so I was confused when Finnr pulled me out of my own thoughts.

"You are not done for the evening," said the dwarf.

I stopped in my tracks. Was he talking to me?

"Oy! Skald!"

He was.

"What do you mean 'not done'? You are free now, are you not?"

"Free and surrounded by enemies is a special kind of free: The kind I would like to pass on with great haste. Did you think the night would involve sleeping?"

"In shifts, of course."

"We don't need shifts to get us through the night. We need the *volva*'s art. Go see her and do everything—EVERYTHING—she says."

I started to reply but Finnr cut me off. Why Huld? Why me? What would we do? There was no explanation or time to prepare. The dwarf had no patience for questions and soon I was being shoved and halfway thrown by hands that felt like they were made of solid rock.

It had been a long day. It would be a longer night.

CHAPTER 14

SEIÐR

"Put this chair on the roof of the hall," said Huld.

"Put this chair on the roof of the hall?" I asked.

Huld had gestured toward the chair in a corner of the hut. It was not so much a chair as a high seat, to be climbed upon when needed. Lighter than I expected when I picked it up. Stronger, too.

"There is indeed a magic in repetition," Huld continued. "But that does not include repeating my words back to me as if you did not understand them."

"How would I ever get this thing to the roof of the hall?" I asked. "And whatever for?"

"By standing on one of the eaves and lifting, I would guess," she said without looking up. "Perhaps followed by walking up to the top of the roof!" Huld was filling the pouch at her belt with what I could not rightly identify. I figured they were charms for various spells, and I did not care to know any more about them. "And it is for me to sit *seiðr* on. I will also need this," she continued, handing me a feather pillow.

Seiðr, the same magic Odin the evil-worker uses, learned from the goddess Freya. I knew it was primarily women's magic despite being used by Odin. I heard it was sex magic and not for men to be involved in, though some of the older stories I knew contradicted that. Whatever it was, I did not want to be involved in it. Too many ways it could go to places I had no intention of going.

"Why is the chair necessary?"

"It is not," she said, "but I don't want to be grounded to the earth while I sit *seiðr*. Too many things from the Down-Below can hear or smell the magic, and I don't want to be within reach of them when I sit."

The Down-Below were those realms beneath Midgard. Dwarves lived there, and some *jǫtnar*, and other things I did not know about and did not want to meet. Go deep enough and you'd end up in the realms of the dead. I shuddered at the thought they might have such a long reach upward.

"Why the pillow?" I asked, wondering if it provided further protection from malevolent spirits.

"So my arse doesn't get sore!"

I took the pillow and shook my head. "Why me?"

This got the *vǫlva*'s attention. "What do you mean?" she demanded, the hint of urgency evident on her breath.

"Why did Finnr tell me to come here and help you with this? You need someone to take directions without asking questions. How is that something I was chosen for? It doesn't make any sense. I always ask questions!"

Huld's shoulders relaxed and she let out the breath she had been holding. "Ah," she said, "you do not see the need yet. But you will. You are a skald, are you not?"

"I try to be," I responded, feeling as lame as I sounded.

"Then you can chant, and chanting, you will aid me." Huld fixed me with a look that she might have used on a dog born with only two legs. I said nothing, but my face told her all. "You're a skald and you don't know how to chant. Or is it that you are afraid to aid me in the *seiðr*?"

Why not both? I thought. My heart raced, my palms went cold and sweaty. The appropriately manly response I gave was "*Seiðr* is 'women's magic,'" though inside I was terrified of what it might call upon us. Conjuring foul beings and tempting the valkyrie-like *dísir* to take notice of you was not my idea of a comfortable night.

"I know *seiðr* as I know the herbs that woke you and helped your pains. That is my domain. Chanting a few *galdr* ought not to prick your pride, although if you knew your magic you would know *seiðr* is Odin's art, even if learned from Freya."

"Odin is a lot of things, few of them good to emulate."

"Then bugger Odin and just do the chanting!" Huld snapped, annoyed at my propensity to take a conversation down the wrong path. "It is simple, so it may take you a while to get it. Now take the high seat to the high place, and don't forget my pillow or I'll cut off your buttocks!"

I believed her.

The high seat was light for its size, but unwieldy. I carried it out of Huld's abode and hoped no one would see me carrying it. The moon was high at that point and my only source of light as I crept close to the hall. Huld was right about the eaves—they dropped low and at a steep angle. I set the chair down, vaulted myself up, and then pulled that great chair up after me.

Then came the difficult part. It was not that the chair was heavy, but the roof was so slanted the added weight made me almost fall backwards twice. Then there was the matter of making too much noise and calling attention to myself. That part did not trouble me. I was already in such an absurd position, I decided that if anyone spotted me, I would claim to have been bewitched.

I reached the ridge and sat down, panting from the slow but steady exertion. The chair I dragged upright and set it down. A well-made piece of furniture carved from solid birch. Not at all made for roofs, but it balanced solidly in place without my even trying.

How would Huld get up here? I wondered. And in that instant I hoped she would not, because I had forgotten her pillow in my haste.

On she came though, a slow, three-legged gait with her staff in hand. Its knob was ornamented in brass, now dulled with time and use. Stones below the knob glowed low in the darkness. The effect was eerie as those stones seemed to breathe light in and out. Huld halted ten feet from the base of the hall, and I wondered if our plan—her plan—had been discovered. The glowing stones on her staff breathed out a long sigh and left her to the surrounding darkness.

What came next I only know because I looked on so intently: Huld held the knob of her staff up close to her mouth and whispered something I could not discern. She turned so that her side was to the hall and hunched over, grasping her staff with one hand. She then walked backwards, one step after another, dragging her staff behind her so that it traced a line in the ground. At each step, she rasped something unintelligible under her breath, but only as she breathed in.

I thought for certain she would be seen as she rounded the main entrance, but no guards stood sentinel there. The hour was late and attention was no doubt high, but only within and not without. Huld passed unheard and unseen and completed her circuit. Then she hopped up to the roof as if a series of low steps had been laid out before her.

"Women's magic," she said, shaking her head as she climbed the unseen stairs to meet me. "And where is my pillow? Hel's dragon, you may be less useful than I thought. You will learn though. You will learn."

"I can go fetch the pillow," I said. "Be right down and bring it up to you. Or throw it up, and give you privacy for your work here, now that you have the chair."

"Keep your seat, skald. Your buttocks are safe for now. I have spells to cast, and I do not intend to lose myself in the casting of them. You will chant, and keep chanting until I leave my seat."

Now it occurred to me sometime before this conversation, which was not quiet, that we were being rather loud and foolhardy for a supposedly secret thing we were doing. At that point, it bothered me beyond endurance, and I had to ask: "How are we not found out?"

"You were watching, were you not? You should have seen me draw the circle below."

"Yes, you traced something with your staff. So?"

"So! I drew the circle, and inside it only those I wish to hear me can do so."

"What about all the noise I made walking on the roof before you did that? Did you have another spell cast already?"

"No, I told Finnr to make a lot of noise inside the hall. Claim other dwarves were afoot if he had to. Halfdan is suspicious and also knows nothing but his own little world. He will be easy to manipulate."

I sighed. Whatever that manipulation entailed, I did not understand it, and, not understanding it, I did not like it.

"Why would you have me chant? Perched up here like the eagle atop Odin's hall, only confused and wanting to get down. A skald doesn't sing with no purpose in mind. Share your manipulations," I said, my tone growing more aggressive until the *vǫlva* sneered. "I mean, if you would."

"I suppose there is no harm in knowing the what, though I won't teach you the how," she said. "I will sing one song to entice a spirit to me first. It is when you hear my song change that you need to begin chanting. The second song will be one of binding, and bound to me, I will have the spirit do our work. You will chant to ground me. In the case of the spirit being over strong and able to entice me back with it, your chanting will keep me here."

Wide-eyed I searched her for irony or some play on words. "Bind the spirit to you?" I asked. "Are you not casting out your *hugr* to do such work?"

"I can do that as well," she said, "but that is not what we need here, now. We will have those in the hall sleep, and sleeping, Halfdan will not enact his plan to kill all your friends."

"But this will affect everyone in the hall, even Haldor?"

"Cannot be helped. But we do not need an advantage to attack, only to pass through the night without incident. Before dawn, you can rouse your own and we will be off. Now ready yourself! You know the runes and their sounds?"

"Which ones?" I asked, perhaps with a higher pitch than I intended. I was unsure of myself in helping Huld and not entirely certain she wouldn't head-butt me again. For a skald though, my question was valid.

Runes were letters my people used to set words into wood or stone. We used sixteen, and I was quite familiar with them. But runes were also an older alphabet used in ancient times no longer known by many. The two runic alphabets are similar, but the older system has twenty-four runes instead of sixteen. The twenty-four elder runes are what you would use if you wanted to carve if you needed a spell cast. I knew them, more or less, since they were not entirely different from the younger runes.

There are also runes referred to in Odin's death song. The runes he died to find and bring back with him from some terrible place. I always imagined these to be the twenty-four runes of the elder alphabet, full of magic and mystery, as dangerous to know as Odin himself. Or so my foster mother Taika had told me.

To my foster father Halstein, they were just old letters fallen out of use. The Greeks use one alphabet and the Romans another. Why should there not be change over time as well as over geography? No story I ever heard said the old runes were the same as those Odin snatched up. In any case, no one ever heard of Odin sharing his hard-won knowledge with people of Midgard. He sought wisdom, but kept it to himself when he found it.

Nobody knows anything about the origins of our letters or Odin's story. It was widely known that casting spells was extremely dangerous for any casual student of magic. By the look of Huld's many stocked herbs and other strange substances, it was clear to me she was not a casual practitioner. She was not just an old woman who knew what roots to harvest from the forest. She was a powerful *volva*, a seeress, a sorceress if you want her title to remain mysterious. Or if you didn't like her, you could call her a witch or a troll.

Managing great patience, Huld clarified it was the old ones she spoke of. "Tell me how you pronounce the alphabet first."

I recited the twenty-four runes as asked, and Huld nodded. "Not as bad as some, but not right either. There is no time to correct them all right now. You will focus on chanting *wunjo*."

Then came a short but frustrating lesson in chanting the rune correctly. Imagine the letters you know, and now imagine focusing on one in particular. What is its name? What are its sounds? What is its essence? If you were to sing that letter in a deep voice or a high one, how would it sound?

Now imagine answering all those questions wrong while being yelled at by a witch on a lonely rooftop in the middle of the night. That was my first lesson in magic.

Once I had it good enough, I began the low rumble for the rune *wunjo*. "Good enough. Wait for the second song, then begin. Plug your ears first."

She ascended her chair and sat with her staff across her knees. Much to do about staffs, especially those of *volur*. '*Volva*' just meant 'staff-bearer,' but what was behind the significance of the title was the real mystery.

"To stop from hearing your chant?"

"To stop a spirit from entering you. Since you only have two hands, better hold your arsehole tight by itself."

I fingered my necklace, suddenly hoping it was a necklace of protective clenching.

"They have ways of getting in."

"I get the idea!"

Huld closed her eyes and sang low and slow. I puzzled over her song, this first one of enticement. It would not have made me want to get a closer look at the singer, but then I was not a spirit roaming the night.

A sharp breath in and Huld yawned wider and longer than should have been possible, and I froze. Huld's eyes rolled into the back of her head, showing only the whites.

Then began the second song, high-pitched and sweet. The dissonance between the friendly sounds she made and the possession I saw chilled me. But I had a task to do, and so I began my chant. In a few minutes, Huld's second song ended and she, or whatever it was she had bound to her, turned around and fixed an eerie gaze on me. As I continued my chant, a conversation between the *vǫlva* and the spirit began.

"Who have you brought us?" I heard not-Huld's voice ask of Huld. I wanted no part of that conversation. I concentrated on chanting louder and thinking about the rune *wunjo* and nothing else. Soon the conversation turned away from me and Huld looked out across the town, the backs of her eyes staring at nothing in particular. Conversation slowed and then stopped.

Huld let out a breath so great it sounded like the wind off a mountainside. Her eyes rolled back into place and her posture straightened. She blinked a few times and, regaining herself, waved me off of my chanting. "It is done," she said, climbing down from the chair. "Now put this thing back where you found it."

The old woman stumbled on her way down, but I caught her arm. She snatched it back away as soon as she was able, but I could tell the spell had taken a toll on her. "Just out of practice," she wheezed.

"It seems to me you are in no shape for cutting off a man's buttocks," I said. "More the better for me." She laughed at that, an inadvertent, natural sound, and continued down the roof with only her staff as an aid.

Taking that troll-cursed chair down was more difficult than on the way up. Always the thing threatened to draw my weight down the slope and pitch me forward, but I kept my balance. I made it back to Huld's hut safely where she was finishing her preparations.

"They will sleep until noon," she said

"And all wake up at once?"

"If left alone, more or less. You will be up at dawn to rouse your friends. Drag each one out of the hall and outside the border I drew. They will wake then, with Halfdan none the wiser. Mead?"

I accepted the offered drink. It was plenty good and strong, and I suspected Huld had a better grasp on making mead than most. She raised her cup in a toast, a wry, tired smile on her face.

"And then we will be off, and never return to this shithole."

Chapter 15

How to Start Fights

I dragged the men out and roused them early, before even a hint of light to brighten the sky. They were groggy but none could argue that an early start was a good idea. Then sunrise and easy conditions on the sea soothed our tired spirits. A blood-red sun bloomed in the morning sky well after we were already at sea again. Even I thought it all a good sign as the *Sea Squirrel* cut eastward through the water like a knife through cold butter.

Not the fastest ship in the world, but fast enough.

Soon we turned south. This was a shortcut through blue water, and sailing on blue water carried a new sense of danger. Water is water, maybe you think. Try sailing when you can see land, even if it's just for comfort. Then try sailing when you can't see anything for orientation, and your belly can feel the unseen depths below you plummet. It's a small feeling, indeed, a sense that maybe you're so small in this world, maybe you don't matter so much as you thought.

Hugging the coast through the north and following it as it curved back south was the safer option. It would have taken us longer to get down south to Denmark going that way though, and Kraki was restless.

Rougher water it was, then. But less time spent on the ship since the trip would be shorter. Soon we passed into waters where no land would be visible, and that would be the worst part. Danes to the west and south and Geats and Swedes to the east—they were there, even if we could not see their lands.

Some of the men may not have cared much or even preferred the sense of adventure that comes when all you can see is water and sky. I was not one of them. Kari was not either; I could see the muscles on his neck tighten like ropes.

I was pretending to row better and better by the hour. Svein shot me a look once, but I just shrugged and went back to daydreaming. Or so I tried. The dream I had of the gods pulled at my brain now that my mind was idle. I had been called there. Or so said Idunn, the keeper of the *Æsir's* apples of immortality. She was angrier and more vulgar than expected. From the stories I had heard, she was a delicate and naive thing needing the protection of Asgard's walls. I liked better what I had seen of her.

Who had called me? There were three gods in the hall, though I wasn't certain whose hall it had been. You could argue it would be Thor, to protect the tree. Or Frey to keep the tree healthy. Or Heimdall, watching who came to the tree.

The dream left me confused. Should I even pay it any attention? I had taken those hard hits to the head before that dream. If the dream was just a result of Huld smashing her forehead into my nose, there was little point in thinking about it. But if not . . . I still could not wrap my head around what that would mean.

Heimdall had suggested I brought myself there. If so, I had no idea how and was interested in repeating the process. I asked a question, and they all answered it. Thor's advice seemed most pertinent: I needed to learn to fight. Hopefully not from Kraki since he might kill me in the process.

The respite from having to think on my feet was welcome as far as time went. But between my balls aching and my head throbbing, it was difficult to not meditate on my pain and how much I wished I had not signed on with the crew.

Svein treated my unease as a cause for taunting until I looked him in the eye. My face was bruised, one eye bulging purple, and my pale expression must have projected the state of my insides. Svein took the hint and told me to make myself comfortable. Taunting the tauntable is a traditional habit of my people, but not having a nearby crewmate throw up on you is an even stronger tradition.

My head cleared a bit later in the day after we turned south, and I realized there was a natural advantage to the quicker route: soon there would be real food again. No more of what barely qualified as food like Kraki made us eat. I mean real food, like salted meat and dried fish. Cheese, even. My mind conjured memories and possibilities alike. Fresh flatbread with honey. Smoked mackerel. Boiled pig. The possibilities made my mouth water.

"What are you smiling at?" accused Svein. "If you can smile, you can row better than that."

"That is sound logic, Svein," I countered, moving the oar into the actual water instead of just skimming it. "Not very poetic, but have you considered becoming a philosopher?"

"Do philosophers fight much?" he asked without a hint of irony.

"They fight with words."

I had just been thinking about how to fight, or rather how not to fight, and specifically the mistakes I made against Huld. This old woman had taken down a fit, if not particularly muscular, young man. When I grabbed her from behind, she prevented me from lifting her so that I was essentially trying to lift my own self. Then she did exactly what Magnus described us trying not to do with the ship: She pushed hard on my top half one way while pulling on my bottom half in the opposite direction.

And down I had gone—hard. This seemed an important connection to make. I wondered if there was a further sailing metaphor for the part where she raked her bony knee down into my balls, and immediately winced at the memory. One insight a day was plenty.

Svein's upper lip curled into a snarl as he pulled back again. "You can't kill a man with words," he said.

"Cattle die, kinsmen die, but word-fame lives on," I said, roughly quoting part of Odin's advice. "A man can be made immortal with words. If he can live by words, he can die from them as well."

Svein snorted. I could not tell if it was a sudden comprehension he was reacting to or a rebuke of my explanation. I imagine it was the latter. Abstraction to him was weak, and whatever was weak was for others. Svein was strong, and that was all there was to his world. Articulation to him was a snort, of which I heard many.

"You think too much," said Svein. I took his comment to be closer to 'You row too little' but I could see how the two might be intertwined. Svein was without a doubt the dumbest sentient being I have ever encountered, including every animal and every reanimated corpse I have spoken to. As such, I felt it my responsibility to make sure he knew how dumb he was.

"Maybe you think too little," I shot back on reflex.

"Odin says thinking is bad for you," he continued.

His appeal to authority was fair. Odin would be the last word on wisdom, even if people were a lot more likely to invoke Thor when they needed help. There were different poems where Odin described general advice for men. Some for women, though it mostly consists of being wary of men. The advice quickly gives way to boasts about women Odin has raped, *jǫtnar* he has tricked, and treasures he has won.

The advice about wisdom is not 'too much thinking is bad for you,' but that wisdom in middle measure makes a man happier than if he were to know everything.

If you're dumb as a rock, it is a fair justification for being dumb as a rock. And nobody can argue with you. They would be arguing with Odin after all, the wisest and most miserable of all the gods.

But if you weren't dumb as a rock, you knew more than one story about Odin. There were many even then, and they painted a complex picture. And these were early days, before the god's ascendancy into something like the chieftain of the *Æsir*. He wasn't understood as much more than a god of grim wisdom and death back then. And a lot of those stories describe him as a psychopathic shitheel with a penchant for breaking his word.

"Odin tore out his eye for a drink from Mimir's well and offered himself as a sacrifice. He did both for knowledge. He also risked his life to drink the mead of poetry."

"Well he would know, then."

This was the kind of argument that I participated in during my youth. It served no purpose other than to frustrate me that someone would be so willfully stupid. This time though, I was ready for Svein's aggravation. I knew he would ignore anything indicating he was wrong. So I left logic behind and decided to insult his patron god instead.

"He also knows Thor is a moron," I said with as much casual tone as I could.

"Thor is middle-wise!" said Svein's voice plus one octave.

"I mean, just dumb as a rock," I continued. "And scared of *jǫtnar* bigger than him. That's what Odin said."

It is indeed what Odin said, although it wasn't exactly what happened. Odin was not the god of truth-telling.

"That's not true!" Svein bellowed. As if that mattered.

It hadn't been long and I already had Svein near ready to attack me. But the next thing said sent him right over the edge, and it wasn't from me. It was the most damaging thing I could have imagined. An insult as bad as being called a mare. A haunting sound as derisive as it was untouchable.

Huld's cackle was at once wordless and unmistakable in its derision.

In the next moment, the butt end of Svein's oar flew across the middle of the ship like one of Kari's javelins. He stood up and stomped toward Huld.

The *vǫlva* unsheathed a knife with a wicked, forward curving blade and stood up, staring the giant down.

All rowing came to chaos as oars clanked on each other out of time. Some of the crew made half-hearted attempts to assuage Svein's anger. Svein roared as one of his massive arms swept three crewmates out of the way at once while cocking his other arm up for a hammer fist.

Finnr placed himself between the two, hammer in hand.

"It's my ship," growled Kraki as he left the steering oar to step past Huld and Finnr.

The statement froze Svein two steps away from the old man. Not everyone froze, but everyone went silent. Kraki stood, bone club in hand. The unmistakable message was unsaid but understood. Kraki could and would fight an entire crew if there was disorder on the ship. Or if the fancy took him. He would certainly fight Svein. And nobody wanted to find out how dangerous the old man still was.

"There is no fighting amongst Brothers," shouted Haldor, near the prow.

Huld had assented to the rules and clasped Haldor's arm. She might be a not-crewmate in Svein's eyes, but they were not Svein's rules to interpret.

If Svein had been willing to face Kraki and his bone club or Haldor and his axe alone, even he was not stupid enough to take on both men at the same time. But how to save face at that point? Fighting a fight he could not win was a consideration. He would not be the first to die of pride. He would not be the last.

"Mealtime," said Kraki.

We knew it wasn't. It was a command to take our seats and shut up. And we could follow his commands, or he could drive that club's sharpened handle right through our skulls.

Svein, jaw set as if ready to crush rock, waited to be the last seated. True to his word, Kraki did give us an extra small ration of *hákarl*.

"Land," said Kraki, pointing off the starboard bow. "Not our land. That will be the east coast of Jutland. But we are close. Another day, at most. So we have extra food. I don't want it to spoil."

We took the joke in knowing silence. No one wanted to laugh, but everyone understood.

Minutes went by and we waited patiently for our *hákarl*. Kraki was slow in its dispersal. Eventually, the brothers broke the silence on the ship in their usual fashion.

"I bet you Ansgar starts another fight before we get to shore," said Utstein, looking to his brother for confirmation.

Innstein took a deep, thoughtful breath and squinted up at the sky, looking for wisdom. He took his time thinking, and it seemed the entire crew listened for his answer as if a simple yes or no would determine some significant outcome for all of us. But like every other betting proposition put to Innstein, he had his usual answer:

"I want odds."

It was safe to laugh out loud again.

"Ansgar!" roared Haldor from the front row on the port side. "Stop talking about making word-fame and make us some!"

The shock of Haldor's voice was a thing to feel as much as to hear. Svein could not make his voice do that even though he was physically larger than Haldor. Svein's voice was lower and doubtless, he could be just as loud. But Svein was an idiot, and everything he said was either tinged with half-brained confusion or so child-like in content that no one wanted to listen.

Haldor's tone had something I did not understand at the time. Something that demanded attention the same way Kraki grabbing you by the throat would demand attention, but invisible and gone as suddenly as it occurred. Haldor did not speak often. He spoke when something needed saying, and that meant when he spoke we were wise to listen.

I wanted to compose but was still a poor hand at anything on the spot, especially with no inspiration. Left to my thoughts I tended toward satire. Nobody was in the mood for that.

"No word-fame from rowing," I answered. "What about a topic I can work from? Give me a start and I will take it from there."

"The Midgard Serpent!" Hemming called out, high-pitched as ever. Jormungand, one of three monstrous spawn of the trickster Loki and his mistress Angrboda, was the dragon coiled around the whole of Midgard. So big he encircled the world ocean completely and bit his own tail.

"Plenty of stories about him," I called back. "Although he does not need me to tell his stories to be immortal. Do we have any ox heads? The best story is about when Thor put one on a hook and went fishing and—"

Shouts of confusion cut me off. The sea was calm and quiet, but some of my shipmates were standing wide-eyed off to the stern. The rowing stopped and each moment saw more men ignoring commands in the ship to make sounds I did not decipher but understood to have an urgency behind them. Haldor was shouting across the ship to Kraki at the rudder and Kraki was shouting back, but I could not focus on any one conversation still sitting down. So I stood and looked out around and above the other heads and shoulders.

Every part of my body hurt at that point, and I saw nothing at first. Then I saw what I assumed was a ship cutting the water at high speed. It was distant, but was that really the size of its wake? And then I realized it was not a ship, and as it became clearer what I saw covered my pain with a thick coat of fear.

Shouts came into focus. I heard Hemming's voice above the din for its clarity of pure panic. "It's him!" he screeched. "Jormungand is coming for us!"

Chapter 16

The Chase is Better than Being Caught

Far west of my home Dafvik, out in the middle of the Encircling Sea, a ship can be lost for days or weeks. At some point, you see no indication of where you've come from, where you are, or where you are headed. The sun is invisible, hidden behind overcast skies so thick they must be made of granite. There is nothing to navigate off of, nothing to tell you even general direction.

That's where you encounter sea monsters. Or maybe further on, if you are foolish enough to lose yourself in the massive sea that encircles Midgard. You might find great serpents to devour ships, or nameless tentacled monstrosities to pull them down, or those horrific sharks with the white bellies waiting for a ship to cast off a hapless sailor. You go out into the beyond, you may not come back. Everyone knew that.

But here where you can hardly leave the sight of land on one side before you see another shore appear in the direction you're going? None of the sea there is very isolated, even if coast travel is safer. No sea monsters here, so close to land, so near civilization.

And yet, the upturned head breaking the water heading straight for us told me otherwise. Behind it trailed a horrid serpentine motion, kicking up waves big enough to devour longships whole. There was at least one exception to what everyone knew, and it was heading right for us with teeth the size of our mast.

"Row!" Haldor's roar cut through the confusion and the men heeded his command.

Kraki was already working the rudder with the energy of a much younger man, turning us toward the land at our starboard side. There was no sense in anything but rowing as hard as I could. The trick is, that is not how you get a ship up to speed. Having every man row as hard as he can will clank oars, create confusion, and slow progress to a crawl. Having every man row exactly in time is how you get a vessel to fly across the water. Try doing this with a crew in panic for its life, though.

We turned to starboard and picked up speed as Haldor's commands steadied our pacing. I had to fight the mesmerizing sight to stay on task and turned for a moment to see where we were going. Shore was in sight, and the serpent would not have the space to follow us far. Certainly not if we made it to the mouth of the river I could see. Assuming we could keep the discipline of rowing in time.

Hemming beat his drum just slightly faster than normal, and we put our backs in to pick up more water each stroke with a faster pace at the same time. The effort would not last us long, but it was our best chance.

It was difficult to estimate Jormungand's size, but we could see him a long way off. Coiled all around Midgard? I doubted it. What if an enterprising (or perhaps just ill-natured) fisherman found part of the serpent's body a few thousand miles away from his head and decided to cut it open and take a peek inside? It would take hours or days for Jormungand to respond to such an insult.

Hyperbole aside, he was big. Head as big as a dragon ship at least and a body drifting an unknown distance behind. I could not see if he had two front legs for walking or burrowing on land as other lindworms had. I did not wish to get close enough to find out. His head was horrible enough—much like a large snake's, but narrower. Powerful jaws full of jagged teeth opened and shut in what looked to me like a smacking of his lips. If the stories were true, his very breath was poison.

The wind was all wrong for us, which is why we turned farther away from the shore in the first place. As we heaved, I heard Huld chanting something. It did not seem to me the magic of an old witch could do much for us against one of the gods' greatest enemies. Then I thought: But neither will my rowing ability.

Suddenly whatever Huld was doing seemed much more important and I was glad she was on the ship. A knee to the groin and head to the face seemed for better fates than what was coming. Sometimes one misfortune is overcome by being in fear of another one.

Jormungand swam steadily on toward us and let out a low roar that chilled my spine. Is that what a dragon sounded like? His massive body swished left and right behind him in a slow, irresistible cadence. That unhurried air to his movements threatened to destroy even my smallest amount of hope.

"Unfurl the sail!" shouted Huld, as if we had not thought of this already. The wind was wrong, and we had no time to tack this way and that.

"The witch is daft," said Ulf. "Maybe she is what the serpent smells. Can't you make us invisible?"

"No more than I can make you less foolish," Huld shouted back at him. "Now unfurl the sail if you want to live." Annoyed at being distracted from her chanting, she began again.

The argument continued and I could not understand why either of them would waste time on this. Or why Haldor did not tell them to shut up. But I was facing away from him, so I saw only the aft of the ship. And that is where Finnr was, nodding back across the ship towards Kari and then Haldor.

Finnr could move fast when he needed to. In one lithe movement, he unsheathed his knife, charged the mast, and cut the rope holding the sail up.

"Oars up!" came the sudden command from Haldor.

From anyone else, the unexpected nature of the command would have caused half the crew to look around first before they considered obeying. Not at that voice. Almost as soon as oars were up the wind took the sail and sent us gliding along the sea faster than we could have done by rowing.

"Oars in!" And we obeyed.

What more was there to do? Nothing, and that is the point at which the worst ideas make themselves manifest, drawn to idle minds to do their work as valkyries to battlefields. We sat there having done what we could, all staring out at the monster coming to eat us. Spears would be useless against him and commotion on the ship would only slow us down.

There was nothing but the waiting on an uncertain bet about how shallow we could get the ship before the serpent was upon us. That silent waiting is the most unpleasant state imaginable for men of action. The warrior mind cannot accept that nothing can be done. Even when about to die, at least die doing something. Thoughts form about insane actions and seem credible because at least they are something.

That draw of feeling better by doing something, anything, even when it is better not to, I would learn is a great killer of men.

"Throw the witch overboard!" yelled Ulf.

It was not unexpected. Men are suspicious of *vǫlur* even when they address them properly and bring them gifts and ask them for wisdom. They know *seiðr*, the same magic Odin the evil-worker uses. Their knowledge is esoteric and untrusted just because it is known by few. Bad luck to kill a *vǫlva*, bad luck sometimes just to be around them, which is what Ulf was getting at. Until you needed one, of course. It was a stupid thing to suggest, but it was something to break away from that terrible waiting.

"Shut your mouth, Ulf!" growled Kraki. He was holding the rudder above the water to avoid slowing us down but had to dip it back in to keep us on the straightest possible course. "We will outrun this thing or not, that is the only question. When I die it will not be as a coward."

There were some murmurs of assent. Stoic embrace of one's fate is a strong impulse in my people, even if I am not the best example of it.

"A question we could improve the answer to by leaving the witch behind," implored Ulf. The murmurs of assent were louder for Ulf. The will to survive and the inability to sit still are even stronger impulses in my people, and these were winning.

Huld continued chanting, her eyes closed, her face turned skyward. She was not in a position to defend herself. Despite Kraki's warning, I wondered if he would leave the control of the rudder to fight a mob if the crew backed Ulf's idea.

And I was not sure whose side I was on. Looking back, sitting in a comfortable chair, feeling warm and maybe covered in a blanket, you might think Ulf was a coward for his suggestion. It would be an easy thing to do.

If you have never seen your death creeping towards you, leaving you unable to do anything but wait to see what would happen, you cannot understand what it does to a man. Throwing the bad luck to the sea seemed a reasonable thing to improve our lot. Men are apt to be stupid where women are concerned during the best of times, myself included. Panicking men are apt to take that stupidity several levels higher.

Panicking a bit myself, I was not so quick to judge Ulf as a coward, though I thought he was wrong.

Magnus, perhaps sensing misdirection was better than contradiction, stopped the murmurs with a question. "What says the skald in our last moments?"

I had no side. I had as much uncertainty about it as anyone else, including Ulf. In my uncertainty, I could only see one thing clearly, and that was Kraki's desire to die as he lived. I was no hero and could not pretend stoicism should be the way I conducted my last moments. I was a skald, and a skald should not die without a verse on his lips.

The verse I spoke came without conscious thought, the words effortless and unknown to me until the moment they left my lips. And in that moment, I found where I fell after all, because the verse was of instructive rather than narrative form:

> "Caprice of the Norns
>   crazes men's minds
> when the water-worm advances.
>
> Clear-headed Heroes
>   harken and heed
> the wind-bringer's word."

All heads turned toward Huld, taking my meaning right away. *The wind-bringer's word.* They forgot themselves in that instant. Haldor's voice brought them back and gave them the action they needed. He pitched his voice low and sang the same chant as Huld.

Innstein and Utstein looked at each other and joined the chant almost immediately, missing the pitch at first but adjusting after a moment.

One after another the men of the *Sea Squirrel* sang the same chant. The ocean wind sang with us and Huld's voice rose in volume as her hands reached to the sky. The water turned from calm to rough, and we sang.

Jormungand's monstrous head was perhaps a few hundred yards away. He flicked his tongue out, tasting the air.

We sang. The waves came up and down, but the wind changed. It pushed us toward land while a cross-wind tore the sea and pushed the serpent away from us.

Jormungand growled, and the vibration of it sent a rattle through the wooden strakes of the ship and up into my spine. The voice felt as if a challenge to me specifically, arrogant or paranoid as that sounds. If the others felt the same thing, they did not falter for it. We rode the waves faster and faster, as if the sea god Njord ferried us from danger.

With the roar, Jormungand ceased his swimming and reared his head further up and out of the water. Teeth like swords flashed in the daylight, with vicious front fangs framing his vile forked tongue. Green plumes of noxious vapor erupted from the creature's nostrils.

In the story about Thor's final battle with the serpent, Thor kills him but falls dead after nine steps, a victim of the serpent's poisonous breath. I doubted we would last one step if we got that close.

Jormungand's head crashed down in a fury, not simply dropping to the sea but smashing it with all the force of his great body behind him. It seemed to be an act of frustration as we headed into water too shallow and rocky for a creature of that size to follow.

Jormungand crawled back the way he had come, having run out of deep enough water to support his bulk. We had not seen the last of his presence, however. The force of his head coming down all of a sudden had created a huge wave coming at us.

The shallows were not safe for our ship either, and the serpent's parting statement had set the water behind us rushing forward. Whitecaps already tossed us back and forth and grew in size as we neared the shore. Still we sang, uncertain what to do otherwise.

Only Kraki knew his definite purpose as he worked the till furiously to keep us away from exposed rocks. He knew the great wave coming upon us would be barely navigable, looking fore to aft and back, calculating a course to put us on that might not involve watery graves for us all.

Kraki's eyes opened wide and his teeth clenched in defiant concentration. No enemy would intimidate him. If he had to fight the entire ocean, so be it.

With the wave only a spear's throw behind us, Haldor's voice called out above the dins of sea and men, ordering us to hold fast. The chanting faded then. Huld opened her eyes and Finnr beckoned her to hold on to the gunwale by him. She dove into the side of the ship and braced herself with a look that did not brace my confidence.

I held onto the gunwale with one hand and my seat with the other and scrambled to wrap my feet around something, anything. If I could have held on to something with my teeth as well, I would have done so.

I knew nothing I did could make the next moments more bearable—the rhythm of the sea as we crossed it in good weather was unpleasant enough. At best we would ride too high and too fast for comfort, to be deposited roughly on a sandy shore. We could easily be rammed into a large rock at speed, or have the wave take us fast in one direction while the wind caught our sail to take us in another, turning us over completely. Or the wave could just break on top of the ship. It was easy to see how things could go wrong.

Kraki shouted with a battle glee I would come to expect from the man. He was smiling as the wave hit us, his sagging, sun-beaten skin drawn taut over stony muscles. Feet braced against the gunwale, the old man had made his decision about how to handle the wave, and he pulled the rudder hard to take us suddenly to port.

We turned. And then we were flying.

The ship rode the crest of the wave just before it broke. At speed, the ship seemed to leave the water completely for a brief instant. In that instant was the first time I experienced what I would later turn into the kenning 'the stain of lost honor.' I was not the only one. At least I did not throw up.

Riding down the back of the wave was still horrific, but an anticlimax to nearly being eaten and then nearly being drowned. We plunged downward and the trough behind the wave found a brief moment of calm. The next waves were not nearly as large, and Kraki turned us again, this time pointing the ship straight at the shore. The ship rose again and was pushed ever forward in that direction.

Kraki had aimed us true, but could not see an outcropping of rocks just below the surface. The ship's port side banged and scraped against it. We were lucky to not be caught and stuck there, but the brothers still gasped as if they themselves had been wounded along with the ship. The *Sea Squirrel* took on water, and we bailed as best we could.

It was rough going to the river's mouth even without the bailing. Wet and cold, we beached without further incident on a sandy bank with much fatigue but far from any sea monsters. The ship came to a halt and Haldor began barking orders to fold the sail and then pull the ship further inland. We had stared down one of the greatest monsters of Midgard and lived to tell about it, but no one mentioned it. Practical matters and ship repairs were everything in conversation.

I used to think this was something to do with getting over the great fear just experienced but later changed my mind. Men like those faced fear often. Their great embarrassment was not that they felt fear but that they might not be stoic in its presence. Everyone ignored anyone cleaning his britches out with seawater, and even I knew enough not to talk about the smell.

If you've never been chased by a sea dragon the length of a thousand longships, you don't get to judge.

CHAPTER 17

FIRST SIGHT

THE 'STEINS MADE WHAT REPAIRS THEY COULD, BUT THEY WOULD need more space, time, and materials to put the ship right again. That took the rest of the day, which was just as well since no one was eager to test the waters so soon after encountering that monster. We spent a cold night on shore.

When we took to the sea the next day, we rowed fast, took turns bailing, and hugged the coast as much as possible.

I did not start any more fights on the way to Lejre, but it did little to improve my standing with the crew. No one asked for any stories, poems, or songs. So far my talking had gotten me almost entirely the opposite of what I had intended it to. This is a problem for a skald, enough to make one feel unlucky. As bad as that feeling is, it is worse to have the feeling that your crew-mates think you are unlucky.

A man deemed unlucky might be left alone before he infects others with his bad luck. And by 'left alone' I mean 'thrown overboard to be left alone in the sea.' I hoped I might be considered merely incompetent rather than unlucky.

We made landfall in Denmark later the next day at the port town of Roskilde, on the island of Sjaelland. Lejre was miles off and on a great hill, but the Danes kept a watch on the coast for vikings and so Haldor, Ulf, and Kraki made introductions to say that we were there with peaceful intentions. The rest of us pulled the *Sea Squirrel* farther inland. The 'Steins directed most of us to chop logs for propping up the ship. With enough wood, the brothers would be able to build proper supports to get in under the hull and do their work.

Declaring peaceful intentions when beaching a ship full of heavily armed men was a good idea, the kind intended to avoid preemptive defensive attacks. Even small towns might be suspicious enough to decide a preemptive attack was a good idea if the citizens thought those heavily armed men might be coming for their lives and goods. A few clear words prevented a lot of unnecessary fighting.

But Roskilde was small, while Lejre was not. Haldor soon headed up to see the king with Ulf and Svein at the invitation of our Danish guard.

Why Svein? Because he would look impressive when only three men showed up.

Why not Kraki? Because he would not leave his injured ship just yet and because, as he had already demonstrated once on that journey, he hated royalty.

Meanwhile, the rest of us worked, including Kari as Haldor's unspoken proxy. Finnr pulled me with him to the furthest tree out but did not explain other than to hand me an axe. I glanced back at some of the other men and it was the same thing all around; two men to a tree, one on each side, swinging in a rhythm one after another. Finnr decided on a suitable tree and we began chopping.

The axe Finnr handed me was a broad-bearded two-hander. Too heavy for battle, but perfect if your enemy was standing still and made of wood. It seemed simple enough, but every time I swung it, something was wrong with the stroke. I was either off my intended mark or the blade bit at the wrong angle. Meanwhile, my arms were getting tired and I saw no sign of Finnr slowing or even breathing heavily. He was shorter than me but probably weighed half again as much, his potbelly jiggling at every swing like a half-filled wineskin.

How did a pudgy old dwarf with arms too long and feet too small move with that kind of grace and certainty while I was young and athletic and couldn't keep up?

Where I was overextending and trying to use my arms too much, which threw me off balance, Finnr looked as if it was a lazy activity, not even looking where he would swing but still chopping away exactly as intended. "Loosen your shoulders and swing from your hips," he said, giving a wry smile. "I'm so old—can't you keep up with an old dwarf?"

I tried to correct my problem by swinging harder. It did not correct the problem.

A tree behind us fell a few hundred feet away. Finnr eyed the result and stopped his work. "Fast work is good for felling the tree, but not for smoothing the trunk," he said. "I'm going over there to make sure they take their time. This tree is yours now, your responsibility."

"But I don't know how to—"

"Ansgar, Ansgar, Ansgar," he said in a soft, soothing voice, still smiling. He paused a moment to let the calming effect sink in. "By the burning balls of Surt, just do it." He clapped me on the shoulder with a hand that felt like it could crush rock and then was off to the felled tree. At least I would be considered incompetent and not unlucky if he had to come back.

Or so I thought. You can be unlucky in the chopping of trees, and I don't mean the tree falling on top of you. That would be stupidity. After a few minutes of random hacking by myself I stopped, closed my eyes, and took a deep breath. I visualized Finnr's movements and how I was wasting time and muscle by doing it my way. Finally, I breathed out, envisioning the same grace and ease Finnr moved with, as my own.

I opened my eyes to find a spear staring me in the face.

"Who are you to be chopping down our trees?" asked the spear's owner.

I didn't have an immediate answer. My mouth moved, but it was inadvertent while I recalculated my situation with a few unexpected facts. One involved the spear: Not one like Kari's javelins. This was long and stout, a weapon for thrusting out of a shield wall or felling a wild boar. Another was the spear's owner: Beardless with long red hair and soft facial features and no helmet. A woman.

"You're a woman," I said, for no good reason in particular.

"You're an idiot," she said in reply. "Now explain yourself before I run you through and disappear without your friend ever knowing I was here." She was beautiful but unattainable, which only increased my attraction to her.

"I'm the skald of the *Sea Squirrel*," I said, trying to sound important. "We're felling trees for repairs."

"Goat's breath and cat piss!" she said, though I couldn't see what made her so frustrated. "Why are you here in the first place?"

"Oh!" I said, just realizing I had answered her question without telling her anything of use. "We're here to kill the troll. Or whatever it is. I mean, Haldor is here to kill it. Finnr is here to make sure weapons and armor are in good repair and not live in a miserable town anymore. Kraki is here because he owns the ship, and also because he wants to feed us all rotten food. I'm not sure why Magnus is here but I think it's to kill *berserkir* because he's good at that. Kari is here to keep people from doing dumb things and the brothers are here to get people to do dumb things and also to repair the ship, and I'm here to compose poems about it all."

She stared at me, expression unchanged. "Is that all?" she asked after a long moment.

"No, there's more," I said, every minute a fervent hope I would marry this woman. "I am Ansgar."

She rolled her eyes but took her spear out of my face.

"Do you know King Ragnvald?" I continued. "We sent an entourage ahead to announce ourselves. The rest of us are just securing the ship."

"I am a handmaiden of Queen Alfhild," she shot back. "You would do well to ingratiate yourself to her."

"I'll start the ingratiation process by chopping down this tree."

"That doesn't make any sense."

It didn't, and wouldn't. Words came automatically, without filter or any sort of consideration when I was anxious. She glared at me as if her eyes would burn my face, but I couldn't look away. She wore a brown tunic and britches with no underdress, preferring a setup closer to a man's than a woman's.

Her spear was sharpened but well-worn from tip to handle, and she moved more like a hunter than a queen's handmaiden, with her hair kept in a single tight braid behind her. I wondered if she had taken the wolf fur she wore on her back from the wolf itself.

"Is the queen behind you?" I asked. She made no reply. "I'll assume no. So the only way I can ingratiate myself to her is to get up to that hall you've got. And to get ourselves to the hall, we first need to get our ship set up for repair. And to build a support structure, we need logs. And in contribution to said logs, I need to chop down this tree."

She looked confused but waved me off when I tried to continue and pointed her spear at something behind me. "I think your friend has a better chance of felling this tree than you do."

The gesture and statement induced me to turn around and look, expecting to see Finnr on his way back. He was not, and I saw nothing. When I turned back around I saw and heard the rustle of some bushes nearby, and that was all. Soon I wondered if she had been there at all or if I had dreamed her.

Who could say? But this might be as good a time as any to mention my worst quality at that point in my life: Virginity. I started hitting that tree with a fervor only a giant blue sack could inspire. I felled the tree and had half of it smoothed out before Finnr returned.

He gave me a sideways glance that might have said 'I know something happened but I don't know what,' or 'You are terrible at this and I'm never handing you an axe again.'

Moving the *Sea Squirrel* and packing up was of little note, although Huld was more interested in me than normal. She said nothing at first. There was no hall at Roskilde, just a few houses and open-air structures. Some of the men spoke eagerly about what we might find at the hall, some about the monster, and some had never-ending conversations about weapons as we worked. Once this pattern was in full swing, which is to say I had no one to talk to, Huld approached me.

"Who'd you fall in love with in the forest, boy?"

What is any man supposed to answer that with, even ignoring being called a boy? It seemed to me there would be no good outcome from that conversation, so I played dumb and said nothing.

"Be careful, boy," said the *vǫlva*, "it's the prettiest things that are often the most dangerous."

CHAPTER 18

UNSPOKEN RULES

OUR WORK WAS SOON FINISHED, THOUGH IT TOOK INNSTEIN AND Utstein some effort to convince Kraki to leave the ship for the time being and come back to make repairs later. They would stay for repairs.

Hemming would also stay, as he did not get on well in cities. He would build a shelter by the ship and remain comfortable there. Indeed, he had almost finished with it by the time we were ready to make the trudge up from the landing.

That was a long, wet march in the rain from Roskilde to Lejre. Between Huld's smug look and Magnus' unjustifiable cheeriness, I kept to myself.

"We were chased by the *Midgard Serpent!*" said the short warrior. "And we survived!"

Some of the other men were like to take on the same attitude. Leif joined the boasts. "And now a mere troll!" he added. "Riches and glory!"

Ingolf may have been his sworn brother, but he did not add his voice to this and was as taciturn as I while we walked.

The road was wet and cold, but at least there was a road. Unchecked forest thinned-out about halfway there. After that we could see the outline of Lejre's hall on the city's famed hill because the air was open. Acres of farmland swept across my view, thralls and freemen sowing the many fields that surrounded the city. It took a lot to feed the city's inhabitants, even if they were less numerous than some years ago.

We arrived at the main gate on Lejre's north side. An impressive structure by my experience, though I had never lived in a walled city. A great deal of what had to once be far more forest made for great, pointed posts along the perimeter. The sheer number of trees required to create that wall made me wonder if every inch of the flat, open ground that was most of Denmark had once been forest. A guard calling out from the palisade beckoned the gate to open at Kari's introduction. We were expected, much to his relief.

Inside the gate was a great open area where a few hundred people could congregate, but only one stood there waiting to escort us. A more conical helmet than I had seen before and a flowing linen shirt edged with black and yellow patterns marked him as either a foreigner or a connoisseur of foreign dress.

The notion of borders was a bit looser back then, so 'foreigner' to me was anyone I didn't recognize. I am trying to translate into modern terms, so bear with me on the anachronisms. 'Foreigner' really meant more like 'anybody who talks funny.'

Our escort was pale even by my standards, and that is saying something. His pants were flowier than ours, which was also saying something. He wore no armor I could see. Probably because, like me, he could not afford it. Chain shirts did not grow on trees.

Also, I hate wearing armor, but that is just me.

"King Ragnvald and Queen Alfhild await you. Follow me to the hall," he said through a thick accent I did not recognize. Perhaps from the east, one of the Balts, or even beyond there.

I wondered if I had just met a man from a place new to even Halstein. Then I wondered if I would live long enough to tell him the story of it.

More exciting than a new story was the prospect of fire and food. Heimdall's teeth, probably *hot* food! It sped us on faster than the wind at our backs.

The guards posted at the hall entrance did not attempt to have us leave our weapons outside as might have normally been required. A good thing too, since I could not imagine Kraki setting down his club unless it was to kill a man with his bare hands. A simple nod from our escort was enough to get us through. Both guards wore similar conical helmets, and I had hoped our escort might be of a mind to speak to them in their own language. No such luck, but I was more than content with what luck we already had.

This was no thinly-built structure, but thick and solid and full of life. My bones warmed in the soft orange glow of fires that lit a visage of legend:

Tattered banners, rent chain shirts, and split helmets decorated the high walls, all monuments to King Ragnvald's conquests. The beams were carved with ornate, stylized animals. Bodies and limbs of looping tendrils, huge round eyes, and curled snouts crawled up and down the supports and sideways on the crossbeams.

Two champions, marked as such by being the only men fully dressed for war in a hall full of mirth. Chain shirts, helmets, and expressions that strongly suggested violent tendencies. They approached and looked every one of us up and down without a word. They might have been taken for neighboring jarls for their swords, but their dress was too practical and not showy enough.

"Beigadh!" called the king. "Hromund! Are you welcoming our guests or harassing them?"

Who was who, I could not tell, nor were the champions about to let on. "Welcome," they both growled in unison, and turned to take up positions near the king.

A third man, similarly clad, sat to the queen's left. He was of brighter disposition and stupider haircut. Cropped short in the back, it was allowed to grow long in the front and covered half his face like a wispy blonde curtain. He was not the only one. I hoped that style would not catch on enough that I would need to adopt it.

There was one interesting thing about Stupid Haircut that I wanted to know more about, as he held a curious weapon. He held it as a club, its carven grip the only part with any stylized parts. That grip gave way to a square hunk of wood without any decoration at all. It might have been a club in another life, but the strange part was the short bow affixed to its front in horizontal fashion.

You might take seeing a crossbow for granted, but I had never even heard of one at the time.

Men jostled and joked and drank, while on high seats the king and queen listened to counselors. Savory stew was in the air, but at the center of it all, a whole pig roasted above hot embers while thralls took it in turns to rotate it. At those sights and smells, I lost all focus and calculation alike to listening for languages. I was starving.

The king raised a toast to the crew of the *Sea Squirrel* and finally we could eat. My joints ached as I sat down. A cup appeared in my hand out of nowhere, and its contents eased the day's exertion. The ale was surprisingly young and over-sweet. Wouldn't a celebration for the arrival of a great warrior call for mead? This was less impressive stuff. For that matter, were there no other skalds to make music or tell stories?

"Welcome indeed to our new guests," said the king. "It is now long since we had the hall so full and so merry. Eat and drink your fill, I will not stand in the way of a man's stomach, and then we must have a story from such a famous crew!"

Shit.

"Hold on!" I called back to the girl who had poured my ale.

Unresponsive, I grabbed her shoulder and she started.

Hands up in apology, I tried to explain, "I mean no harm, it is only that I have just discovered a great need of a great quantity of ale. Either it will help loosen my tongue or will help me forget the drivel I am about to compose."

There was no understanding in her eyes. A mute perhaps? Or simple? She did not look so—quite the opposite, and less of a girl than a woman. "More . . . ale?" she asked, offering another pour. And here was the second strange accent of the night, though this one I knew. She was a Frank, and she had not understood me, but got the idea. Had I said just 'More ale,' that was close enough to be intelligible, but instead I had gone on and on and confused her.

The ale poured, I watched her fade into the background and toward a gaunt young man. He was similarly clothed and similarly unwashed. There was no reason to follow her and even less reason to take notice of the other thrall. I did so anyway, following the scent of curiosity, and found cause to pretend distraction just inside earshot.

Unlike the Thor-Somethings, these two were not planning my demise. They spoke enough Norse to serve, but it was limited and accented. I overheard Frankish between them in hushed and hurried tones. I knew that language well.

Never, never, *never* let them know you speak the language before you have to. Knowing languages is not for impressing people or showing off. It is for nodding when a bunch of Thor-Somethings are plotting to murder you so you can walk away and join a crew of monster-killers.

They seemed long-traveled from where their previous masters had been. Perhaps those had been killed and their land taken. Or perhaps they had been children of a great lord there, only to beg for scraps where they could in the wake of being related to the loser of a great battle. Who could say? After faring that far, there was little to do but offer their lives to a jarl who would at least feed and lodge them.

"No, he is just dumb," said the young woman who could not possibly be talking about me.

"Did no one tell him to avoid looking directly at the queen?" said the other, no longer a boy but not quite a man.

"They just arrived, no one has told them anything."

At which point I realized I had been pretending not to listen to their conversation by casting my gaze out in a different direction. It happened the queen was in that direction, and it happened I only realized that after hearing the last of their conversation.

Why avoid looking directly at the queen? Her hair and skin shone as if lit by the sun even as we all had to manage by firelight. The silky streaming dress fitted her form in a way that may have been more alluring than if she were naked. That form could hold a man's attention and then some. Soon I was lost in the dark caverns of her eyes and against all advice I knew, I was staring straight into her.

"How do you find our hall's hospitality, Ansgar Styrgrimsson?" said Alfhild, her eyes not leaving mine. She drank deep from a golden goblet. "Is your stay so far worth as much as your previous story?"

Previous story? I hadn't told anything yet.

"These three"—she gestured at Haldor only, though she meant to include Ulf and Svein—"told us much. Such adventures! And only here and now you arrive for your real task." Her tone turned colder then. "But they are not skalds. Surely you might grace us with the gifts you alone can bring to bear."

"Yes, a story!" shouted one ill-advised freeman.

The hall became very quiet very quickly, and the queen's gaze drifted shark-like to the man who had spoken. He raised his horn and looked around, confused as to the lack of general cheering. Most others looked at the ground.

"Who is this, who interrupts the queen?" she said, her voice soft and sweet.

No one was fooled by the sweetness of the tone. Eyes dropped to the floor or shifted to the unlucky speaker. He would not be able to hide.

"Sigfus is my name, Queen Alfhild. I, uh, I meant no offense."

The man wore decent enough clothes as far as tailoring, but all in the drab browns and tans that marked him as no rich man. Perhaps he had a small plot of land, but it would not be much. He would be in that hall, at that time, to ingratiate himself to the king and perhaps win himself some reputation or treasure. There was little to win just by farming a small plot, and much to gain from a king who had few friends of late.

Doubtless emboldened by Haldor's arrival, I think he imagined joining the hero on a hunt of Lejre's troll and coming out of it with the kind of favor that could improve his fortune. And so eager was he, that he had called out for the same thing the queen had asked, only too soon.

"Shackle him," said Alfhild with a sigh.

The words had not even left her lips before the man who had been our escort and two others launched themselves and grabbed Sigfus by the throat and both shoulders. Sigfus, henceforward Sigfus the Unlucky, had his drink knocked out of his hand and the wind knocked out of his lungs before he could protest the decision. In short order, he was dragged outside, though not before taking a few more blows to the stomach.

Ragnvald looked away as if to avoid noticing an inopportune fart. Heads shook, but all heads that shook kept eyes aimed downward. Those heads that belonged to the men of the *Sea Squirrel* looked on with curiosity. One in particular bobbed up and took a closer position to the king and queen. Kraki's half-bald head was aimed anywhere but at the ground.

As he started to speak, Ulf shot up from his seat and headed my way. "Now is a good time for a poem," he croaked, half choking on his ale as he wiped his beard. "Now!" he hissed, in the face of my dumb look.

"Why now?"

"He can't speak to this queen as if she were the one in Fretborg. If he speaks out of turn with Alfhild as that man just did, we will be fighting the entire city!"

Several thoughts occurred. One, mustering the whole city would take a long time. Two, running away downhill is much easier than running away uphill. And three, we could just run to the ship . . . which was raised for repairs and, in its current condition, maybe not even seaworthy.

I decided Ulf was giving very good advice.

"You have heard stories of Haldor," I shouted across the hall, "but what do you know of the captain of the *Sea Squirrel*?"

It was a naked change of subject from what she had asked, which was undoubtedly to compare our stories of the journey to Denmark, but it was also a naked challenge. And no one, not even a queen, could ignore a challenge.

"Is Haldor not your captain then?" quipped the queen. "I have heard of an old man whose mother was a rock, who took to the seas in a ship that might sink any time. A lover of thralls and far-flung peasants and elves of ill repute. A relic of primitive culture and weapons."

"Thank you for all such compliments," said Kraki.

There was a tense moment when he spoke. Would it be laughter, or more brooding silence before we were seized? Would any of the freemen dare laugh?

The crew of the *Sea Squirrel* cared not. Huld cackled, a sound that had already made men nearly come to blows. Haldor laughed deep and loud, and the rest of the men did as well. I followed that crack in the air's icy atmosphere and counted how it cleaved the room: Men I might recognize as Spear-Danes by dress or disposition hesitated but smiled along with those of the *Sea Squirrel*. Some covered faces or turned but did little else to hide their humor.

The king was not among the amused, and yet his two champions grinned with bared teeth. Alfhild's champion stood with no expression beyond his stupid hair but gave a flicker of notice at the building tension. The men I found less recognizable shuffled without murmuring, and that set my senses on edge. I may have been a fool, but I was not dumb enough to miss the rift in that room between the amused and very much not amused.

"No doubt your captain has many stories," said the queen, whose voice quieted the hall once again. "I will hear the one of your journey here." Eyes all on me, it was time to acquiesce. What could I do but give in? And yet every fiber in my body wove a contrarian idea in me such that giving Alfhild what she wanted was the one thing I could not do. Not even if I wanted to, which I did not.

I had to make an answer, and she would weigh it against Haldor's, though for what purpose I knew not. Alfhild stared me down and dared me to deny her. I could have tried that or a change in subject again, but neither seemed like good options. Something about the demand told me that acquiescence would mean we were there for her. We were not, but I could not give a flat refusal.

What would a *drengr* do? Something bold. And in that thought, I had my answer, though it would be a stretch to perform well enough to work.

I shoved Ulf aside and leaped onto the table. There I turned away from the queen and addressed the rest of the hall, though not in verse form yet. I danced all along that table and others, not bothering to tell our story of Fretborg and winning Finnr's freedom from Halfdan.

From our setting sail, I wove in a tattered tale of Thor going fishing for the Midgard Serpent, a story most would surely have heard. Only I weaved it into our own, to make it clear I was telling of our exploits but not in the way Alfhild had wished it. There was more though, and that was how this version of the story would end. Near that time, my antics having secured the attention of the hall, I switched to verse:

> "Across the froth
>   flew the serpent!
> Sea-thunder
>   threatened our Squirrel;
> Round us it reared
>   roaring poison
> to devour our crew
>   and claim our lives.
>
> Looking down
>   on Loki's spawn,
> the dauntless crew
>   considered their champion.
> No steel at hand
>   had the skipper
> but scorned the beast
>   while bare of skin.
>
> Pantless he pursued
>   the piss-worm.
> Rising to the occasion,
>   too close it came
> when he let it rear
>   and raise its head,
> and then down crashed
>   Kraki's club!"

In that last stanza, I made a great show of grabbing my crotch and waving around. There would be no wondering what I meant by the kenning 'Kraki's club.'

Fists thundered on the tables and feet stomped on the floor. Cheers filled the hall and cups were raised. There was life in the Spear-Danes yet! Their sleepy king even came alive at that ruckus, though he was less impressed by my poem than most.

"That must be an impressive club," said Ragnvald, too tired or bored to move chin from fist. "And an impressive story. Indeed, it has already left an impression, I think, though for good or ill . . ." And there he shrugged. "It is not the captain of your ship who sought out my hall, however. And should we presume, Haldor Skullsplitter, you intend to fight the monster vexing my hall, my city, my very country, by bashing it with your member?"

The last words rose in volume to a shout as the king's voice heaved itself hoarse. Little had he moved of late, but the man who decorated his walls with the broken sigils of his enemies still stirred there.

Haldor stood, invisible waves washed outward from his towering figure like a giant rising out of the sea. He was a large man, as I've said, but he was more than that. Nearly as big as Svein, only leaner and faster, and with a reputation to match Kraki's for willingness to fight.

Had Haldor been ugly of face and living deep in the forest, we would call him a troll. Instead, he was fair of face, other than for the scars, and those perhaps existed only to speak silent truth to the stories about him. The hall hastened to silence in anticipation as he drained his cup and looked longingly at its emptiness.

"This is some troll you have," said Haldor, voice booming without any effort to raise it. "Has it conjured more than imagined insults or disappeared more than your store of mead?"

This was not a way one might talk to a king unless one was very much needed by that king. And Haldor had no doubt already answered some of his questions. He wanted those questions answered in front of all, however, and I hoped an end to the interrogation of his poor skald.

The king stood up at that. "If leaving glory for others is what you desire, I will bid you and your crew goodbye tomorrow. I should not think anyone a coward to do so, but there is hard work ahead for those remaining under my roof. That demon came under cover of night and mangled good men before making off with my mead. Again and again it came. Iron would not bite it, and always it stole my alcohol! Only the thinnest ale we brew is safe from its thirst.

"I had twelve good champions then. Nine sought the thing out where it might shelter, and none have returned. I forbade these three who remained to do the same. Many a freeholder found his hospitality elsewhere since then. My hall became as thin as my ale, and only my queen's call to her folk in Gardariki has given me enough men to hold my outlying lands."

Rus! Halstein had told of men called Rus who were from Gardariki, a place to the north of Miklagard and the Byzantines. A wild place, Gardariki, on the edge of the Ironwood where Loki's spawn dwelt. Somewhere north of Gardariki was Bjarmaland and the White Sea, but to the east was the end of human civilization. Further east was the Ironwood, where the weather was as cold as on the mountains but stretched across untold miles of dense forest. Only Loki's demon spawn lived in that place. Those were hard people to have lived bordering such monsters.

Or less charitably, you could call the Rus a bunch of miserable Swedes who went too far east and got even more miserable than they were before. Some of this lot definitely looked like this was the more apt description.

"Tonight marks more than a few fast friends appearing," continued the king, scorching the room with his gaze. "Fair-weather friends, perhaps. But I will make no pretense of it: I am *old*. I cannot defeat this troll by the steel I used before,"—and here the king's voice rose, surely this the tone that spurred on so many Danes to win the battles attested on the walls—"but I will bring its death with gold if nothing else! I will weigh the thing down with treasure buying force of arms, and spend my last if need be, but I will see it done!"

Ragnvald's words echoed in the hall, though I thought the ring had a hollow quality. I dismissed that as too much ale in my belly, for the king had spoken with force and was willing to put all of what he had behind his words.

"Every man of our crew who dies shall be sent off with honor. Every other man—" Haldor stopped, cut off by Huld clearing her throat and banging her staff. He gave her a look before returning to address the king. "Any man or woman who swears our oath and abides by our rules shall have that. And among those living when it is finished, you shall reward us all the same, to the degree you deem fit. We will not haggle on the price of hunting monsters."

"Hmph!" said Huld, placated at her potential inclusion, but disappointed in the lack of haggling.

Haldor ignored her. "Brew your mead and make it rich: No troll will have it but to go through me."

So it was, and so it would be. Not to be ignored, or perhaps having seen our *volva* and wanting to preempt any ritual done, the queen announced she would prepare a blessing for our mission. That was all, other than we would be called down on the next day to attend it in Lejre's most holy of spaces, just outside the city. Ragnvald nodded with great enthusiasm that his wife would lend us her magic. We would need it, he said.

It seemed to me Haldor alone knew what we needed. That thought I left unspoken as I ran a gauntlet of men with commentary on my performance to find the door. Most loved the poem. It had a dragon and a penis joke—how could they not? Whatever praise to be piled on though, I had a stronger desire to deliver ale's answer than to bask in the glory of a good performance.

The chill outside was bracing, as it was still colder than expected for the season. There was a sobering effect to it that comforted me, however. Who knew what the next day's ritual would bring? I had no need for Huld to read runes or prophecy about what was about to come but thought even less of having Alfhild in charge of such a conjuring. Whatever that was, best to just endure it. After all, we had already come through outwitting a jarl, besting far better numbers than ours, and outracing the Midgard Serpent.

That was the last happy thought that night before I turned to notice a silent announcement posted just minutes ago. An old spear thrust butt-first into the ground dripped its warning. Sigfus' head sat atop the spearpoint, his expression pleading. Had he been still alive at the start of my performance? Had I taken a different turn, could I have called out the queen's capriciousness? I did not hear the man speak out of turn or counter to the queen's wishes. But insults are more like spirits than men in that they are greater for what they might be imagined as, and given power only as far as they are acknowledged.

Like spirits, or perhaps trolls, I would need to navigate what unseen things had already woven their way through Lejre. I decided I'd had enough of that sobering feeling and wondered if the danger was really in front of me or lurking somewhere behind.

CHAPTER 19

RAGNVALD'S WAGER

"Aha," crowed Huld. "Your look tells all."

"Does it tell you to be quiet?" I hissed back, as loud as I dared.

There was an implied suggestion of quietude in the grove we stood in. Not of silence, just a calm and peace. You would understand that just standing there, even without the prohibitions against violence in sacred places and rules about weapons being left outside.

Manicured hedges marked the grove's periphery, and even now local freemen of import filed in, their heads bowed slightly as they crossed that threshold. Down from Lejre's great hall, the grove was well away from the noise of the city and off the path between city and coast.

Lone trees here and there stood sentinel out from this place, having grown up without the same community of other plants for protection and mutual aid. These would have been fair game for cutting down, technically. But no one had taken these as timber. That suggested a reverence that extended outward from the grove of more tightly packed trees.

It was so green was what I kept thinking about. From outside, it looked like a concentration of trees. From inside, it was as if we stood in a domed hall of nature. The smells were fresh and floral, of leaves and flowers and healthy bark. The canopy softened the sunlight streaming in, making the whole place glow. Gentle sounds of birdsong played in the background while farmers, crafters, and merchants whispered in hushed tones.

No one was likely to have heard me hissing at Huld because no one particularly wanted to be near Huld. Scattered conversations were kept low, and none of them were close to us. We were in a sacred grove, after all, just awaiting some manner of ritual. Dozens had come down from the city. The volume of voices seemed to be encapsulated within the boundaries set by that low hedge. Our crew, the king, two champions, a few picked men, and the queen's handmaidens waited while others gossiped about what would come next.

Three handmaidens, any one of which could steal a man's breath with a look. One after another they struck a silent chord in me that still rang minutes later. Beauty, yes, but there was more. They each moved with the lithe grace of a warrior, their eyes telling of elfin mysteriousness. Perhaps they were elves of a sort. I had just met a dwarf and been chased by the Midgard Serpent, so why not elves?

The last one, the one with fire-red hair and freckles down her face and chest, she was the one I had met in the forest. Despite the dramatic change in visage, I knew her right away. Before she had been garbed in the clothing of a hunter, all wool and leather, armed with a spear. Now she had on a flowing underdress that sparkled a white so entrancing I would have sworn it was woven by the Norns themselves. Her hair was re-braided around her head, allowing some of it to flow freely down and cover the freckles on her shoulders and chest. I stared, transfixed.

"It tells me you saw but did not see," Huld answered. "Beauty is no mark of character. If you want to learn *seiðr*, there are better sources."

"Who said I wanted to learn *seiðr*?"

"You will. Or you will find some other pretense. One way or another, you will try to find yourself beside that one." Huld nodded in the general direction of the handmaidens, but I knew which one she meant. "If you are a skald, what is she?"

I looked around to see if this ridiculous conversation was being overheard. Satisfied well enough, I answered, "Maybe she is a *dísir*, come to witness a ritual in her honor."

It was the wrong time of the year for a *dísablót*, but I supposed the local *dísir* would not have rejected extra offerings. Whatever the local guardian spirits might be, and it seemed they were always women, I hoped they were half as beautiful as those three.

"HA! Idiot!" Huld hissed, shaking her leathery face. "They are witches."

"So are you."

"If you insist," she spat. "But don't come to me for help calling me that. I had you under my knife, yet off you went with herbs to heal your hurts. Imagine yourself in that position with a sorceress bent on doing you harm. She will lock your limbs at best and let that queen bitch ride you at worst."

"Fine, you're a *vǫlva*. Perhaps you should perform the ritual instead of the queen."

Most likely Thor's name would be invoked if the ritual were all about good hunting for Haldor and the rest of us monster-slayers. Perhaps Frey if they wanted a fertile season ahead. It could have been anything, as the exact details of beliefs and ceremonies started changing as soon as you crossed the nearest hill. We had gone much farther than the nearest hill, so I wondered what these Spear-Danes might have in store for us.

"You are the least dangerous thing in this grove, boy. You would do well to seek better friends."

"Like you, I guess you mean."

"You would be lucky to have me as one," she replied through her teeth.

That statement could have told me a lot if only I had been listening for anything beyond insult. I bridled and considered her to be looking down upon me. She, an ugly old hag, telling me *I* would be lucky. What arrogance! I was indeed still enamored of the beauty around me and did not think as far as what it might mean that a seer of the future did not want me around. Like most of my conversations with Huld, this one involved her insulting me in at least three different ways followed by friendly advice.

"You think you see, but you see what they want you to see," she said. "The glamour is a mild one. But I saw greater magic at work in the hall last night. You should be wary."

Wary of the overly sweet ale? Perhaps. But the boar had been plentiful. It had been a good night when the bulk of us arrived in Lejre. We were well received and in a mood to make friends, as long as those friends were offering food and drink. Easier to make friends when the queen doesn't have someone killed, I thought.

"What greater magic?" I had to ask.

Huld shook her head. "There are things you can know if you are told, and things you can only know if you come about them without help."

"Which kind of knowable is this greater magic then?"

"As long as you are so easily entranced by breasts, it is beyond your ken," she snapped, which was neither entirely fair nor entirely unfair. "That charm you wear around your neck," she said, "you should focus more on that." At least she found this a fitting statement to finish speaking on and left my company to find the dwarf.

Strong magic was suspicious to most of my people. Whatever kind it might be, *seiðr, galdr,* something else. But what of it? The lure of esoteric knowledge was strong, and the mystery of what Huld had alluded to pulled at my attention as I fingered the carved bone pieces of the charm given to me by Taika. It was 'for protection' she had said, without explanation, and I was always to wear it as I traveled. That had been enough for me, the assumption being I might not want to know too much about her magic.

Receiving that gift seemed a long time ago now, and I wished I had asked her more about her art. I was no sorcerer, but now I wanted to know what sorcery was happening and why. A survey of those around me was no help, it was all just low conversation. Huld and Finnr, Magnus and Kari, Haldor and Kraki. My attention lingered on the last pair. They were the only ones looking unhappy.

A hand fell on my shoulder. "A weighty ceremony," said Ulf. "Have you prepared a poem for the occasion?"

"Perhaps later," I said. I should have felt warmed to the core to receive any words of encouragement, but I felt Ulf's presence unwelcome. "This is not a place for poetry."

"It is a place for magic," said Ulf. "And poetry is your magic. Like that spell you cast on the ship—a spell of influence. You even got your way."

Ulf had a presence, a charm. He had traveled far and seen much, the only other crew member who knew more languages than Norse. Premature gray peppered his otherwise black beard as he gave a broad smile. Something was different to my eyes though. I pondered this as I fingered the charm, as if to focus more easily.

You even got your way. What a strange way to describe it! He had wanted to throw Huld overboard and I countered him, only to have Huld save us all.

"I compose poetry," I said. "I describe people and deeds in a way to be remembered. What is a skald other than that? And of those here, I know few."

"Hmmm," said Ulf. "A good impression here and now is important. Especially after last night's insulting of the queen." Another pat on my shoulder. "You know the king and queen, and you can sing their praises by whatever means. And you can name Haldor, but you should also have some local knowledge. See that one?"

Ulf motioned toward a group of four men, but I knew who he meant and nodded. Three of the four were much younger and neatly if not expensively dressed. Browns and grays, well-made but undyed clothing. The fourth man was older—older than Haldor, not ancient like Kraki. Deep reds, muted blues, silver jewelry—this one had money. Thick silver hair fell to his shoulders and shrouded a thin but long mustache. It was an unusual style to not keep a beard, but he must have been particular about it. Whatever his choice of facial hair though, he spoke, they listened.

"Gorm Tin-Whisker, a jarl loyal to Ragnvald," continued Ulf.

"Never heard of him. Tin-Whisker?"

"You've never heard of him because you're not from Fjon. But all the men on that island know him and know him much better than they know Ragnvald. And Ragnvald knows very well where Fjon is because it's practically the back door to this island for any would-be invaders. Gorm got his name fighting for Ragnvald when they were both much younger. Supposed to be that the other men liked having young Gorm in a shield wall with them, but that he chewed so loud at mealtime it was like every hair on his face rattled together like tin."

"Not a very dramatic name for a jarl. I'm not even sure it makes sense. Chewing food doesn't sound like tin."

"Other names may be less desirable," said a scowling Ulf, and turned to go.

In Old Norse, we had many ways to express certain ideas. None of these ways is very close to saying 'Don't be pedantic' in modern English. Ulf's last statement was about as close as you might get, with most of that meaning implied or taken from his facial expression.

That was often how my people liked their meanings—implied. A means of poetic understatement and at the same time a maddening idiosyncrasy if you just wanted to know what was going on. Otherwise, the closest thing Old Norse had to 'Don't be pedantic' was a punch in the face.

I paced the clover-cushioned ground, a moving object among an otherwise patiently stationary group. I feared standing still might garner me yet more cryptic advice, and I wanted no more. Being a poet gave me leave to be a bit more eccentric and less social on account of my need to compose, and I took full advantage of it.

Greater magic afoot. The charm around my neck. Expect to be called upon. Not a damned thing connected any of these as far as I could see, and I was relieved to focus on something other than myself when Queen Alfhild made her entrance.

The king had left her one of his champions as an escort while he had kept two others with him. They remained behind a great rock at the other end of the grove and took no heed of the anticipation running through the crowd.

The handmaidens also took their places behind the rock, which I took to be the center of attention for the ceremony. Two carried large bowls and laid them down on opposite sides of the rock while the last carried a large bag and placed it behind. The king smiled widely at the handmaidens, who bowed and smiled back.

The two champions, Hromund and Beigadh, remained unmoved, never more comfortable than when wearing their grim expressions. Bored and sleepy? Angry and wanting to fight? Impossible to tell.

Frothi, the last champion, entered the grove well in advance of the queen, scanning every face. He handed his strange weapon back over the threshold, not relinquishing it fully until he had taken the measure of the crowd. Moppy blonde hair jerked with every movement of his head. Eyes darted with the suspicion of a commander induced to a parlay he did not trust.

This was as safe a place as the queen could be, and I knew of no reason for her to hesitate, so I put Frothi's efforts down to a man making it clear he took his task seriously. Even if it was not much of a task. Satisfied, the champion turned back to the queen and her retinue of servants and nodded.

The white-robed lady was as radiant as if lit by the sun itself even while standing in full shade. Beautiful, imperial, she did not draw attention so much as command it with nothing but a gentle presence. Voices quieted as her bare feet glided over the soft greenery to cross the threshold. Her platinum hair was wrapped in gold adornments and draped across her shoulder and over her chest.

Queen Alfhild ushered two thralls forward, a boy and girl, their invitation to the ritual an unexpected gift. Their bearing and wide eyes at the warriors around them told of surprise and hesitant jubilation. The linen finery they were dressed in was plain but good quality—those were borrowed clothes.

Those two thralls had poured ale the night before, and I had marked them as Frankish but as no more than that. Were they thralls of conquest, or escapees who found a hall to feed them while they worked? Today they were wearing long, white shirts instead of dull brown rags, their hair combed, their faces clean as new snow.

Two thralls suddenly cleaned and dressed up. Two bowls. They had no idea what was in store for them, but I could see it. The queen glanced my way, her lips upturned in a smile, and she could see that I saw. My heart thudded in my chest, beating so loud I could no longer hear the soft footsteps or the birds around us. Breathe, I had to breathe, but my hands were going numb as they twitched. It was wrong, the place was wrong. The impression of tranquility was a false one. What else was false? What had we walked into?

Wide-eyed, I froze with a panic unnatural even for me. A greater magic, Huld had said. Was this it? Arms crossed, eyes locked, feet stock-still. My limbs were indeed locked.

Whatever Alfhild was, she was more than a seeress and Huld had warned me. "Beauty is no mark of character," she had said, familiar advice. I had called Huld a witch only moments before, and now here was the real thing. We had many words for witches, some nastier than others, none ever clear as to whether they described a specific trait or a general predilection for visiting ill upon people. Most of them were just insults about how ugly or amorous witches were.

I had no defense against that art other than luck. And my luck happened to be an old, warty *vǫlva* who had crept up behind me while I was being paralyzed. Thank the gods she waited until Alfhild had passed by, drawing the gazes of the others further away from me. Huld grabbed a handful of my hair and yanked my head down hard. A harsh whisper pierced my ear and I winced, unable to make it out clearly.

A few blinks later I could move again.

"That was my magic," she spat into my ear. Letting go of my hair, she glanced at the walking sacrifices and then to Haldor. "What is yours?"

The *vǫlva* had freed me only to lay down a challenge. I had no idea how I would meet it, but this was my responsibility. Fighting was prohibited in sacred spaces like the grove. Or at least, non-ritual violence was prohibited there. Alfhild would make her sacrifices and Haldor would . . . I was not sure. How deep did his prohibition against sacrifice run? Would he intervene? Would he spit on this place and take us raiding for the summer instead of earning King Ragnvald's favor?

The answers looked irrelevant as I saw Kraki tighten the grip on his club. His prohibition against taking thralls evidently extended beyond the planks of the *Sea Squirrel*, and foolishly nobody had identified that bone as a weapon. I needed that magic Huld had described. There was some magic inherent to what I did, but I was limited in my knowledge of how to take that further than simple influence.

Or I could focus on breaking a rhythm. A plan sprouted in my mind. I would need a confederate, though.

I found Magnus at the edge of the crowd. He was more surprised than put off when I shouldered into him hard to get his attention. "Ask annoying questions," I hissed at him.

"How many old women have you lost fights against?"

"No, not at me! When it is time."

"When is it time?"

There was no time to explain. "Just figure it out after I start talking!"

I left Magnus on the edge of the group and made my way past our crew and into the midst of Gorm Tin-Whisker's group. Alfhild stood on a stool behind the rock and prepared to begin. Magnus and I were in position in different parts of the crowd. Now all I had to do was guess the right thing at the right time, every time.

There is no sense in trying to run through options at a time like that. Your practice has either been sufficient or it has not. I closed my eyes, tried to clear my mind.

Alfhild began with generic welcomes and thanks and compliments. "How grateful we are to feed a bunch of hired killers our thin ale." Okay, she did not say that, but that was the thrust of it.

Come on, what god will you invoke? What themes will you use? Until I knew one or the other, I would flounder. I needed something substantial to play off of.

The second part of Alfhild's address recounted some of the terrible things the troll had done and why Haldor's success was so important. Many warriors trying their fame, even some of the king's champions, had gone off to find and fight the thing only to never be seen again. As a result, the hall had thinned in its number of guests. Lambi the brewer had been dragged off to a terrible fate while walking the road to the coast alone. The troll had crushed his body so badly they had to bring it back to town in a cart. And still the monster raided for ale and mead wherever else it was being made.

Who hasn't heard of a monster that stalks at night and drags off the help-less? That story might be older than the gods. But who ever heard of *this* version? For all the stories I had heard of trolls, whatever form they took, I never heard of a troll whose primary purpose was to steal all the good drink. They were too busy skulking about or casting spells or murdering people. All of those at once, if they could manage it.

"The Spear-Danes have suffered too much and for too long," said Alfhild. "And from when did that suffering come? We owe the gods thanks for our prosperity. Here we will offer them our thanks and ask their aid."

She snapped her fingers on both hands and the children were brought forward. That sounds so passive, doesn't it? People brought those children forward, toward their certain end. On Alfhild's left, her tallest and brightest-haired handmaiden forwarded the girl. On Alfhild's right the other, dark-haired and no less lovely, shoved the boy. Aldis and Valborg, respectively.

Frothi the champion stepped forward and handed a cloth-wrapped knife to Alfhild. That would be the only blade in the grove, I figured. He was, then, as much involved as the queen's handmaidens, and as invested in the sacrifice as those who performed it. Looks might be no mark of character, according to Huld, but I decided a man with a stupid haircut was wearing part of his nature on his head.

A glance between Alfhild and the king had the look of asking permission, but the feel of command. When I saw Ragnvald's eyes, I understood. If this was the greater magic Huld had warned me about, it was no great mystery. Bewitched or smitten, there was little need to determine which.

The king sat on his bench, comfortable to remain seated and defer to Alfhild in such matters. She was a seeress, after all. She would know what was best for the Spear-Danes. She would ease the burden of his old age.

One day years ago, Ragnvald had decided he'd had enough of cold feet and wet clothes and sore wounds after battle, and had decided to stay inside to keep warm. This was the coal-biting Halfdan had spoken of. It was rare for Ragnvald to venture out with Alfhild taking care of things for him.

The girl, maybe the elder of the two, could not catch my eye. She looked elsewhere with a pained expression, looking very much as vulnerable as she was. I caught the eye of the boy. Did he recognize me from the previous night? I don't know what he saw as he looked, his expression set in grim determination to face his fate without complaint.

But I knew he understood something was up when I winked.

The rich air filled his lungs again and he stood up to his full height, an energy unknown radiating from his expression. In fairness, I didn't know what was about to happen, so how could he? That was no excuse for failing to act, however.

"Are they warriors?" I called out.

Faces fell. Eyes scrunched up. Men shook their heads. Some turned my way, confused, angry, surprised. Most people assume awkward statements in awkward tones are both inadvertent. It seems a fair assumption because it sounds embarrassing for the speaker. And it is! But if the speaker is willing to fully commit, awkwardness is just another arrow in the skald's lyrical quiver.

East Norse was the dialect common to Danes. It was mutually intelligible with the western version, or what I spoke, enough so that I could speak in West Norse while they answered in East Norse. Which is what I did, keeping it clear the question was from a relative outsider.

The differences between East and West are understood and ignored during such exchanges. One wonders how or why they developed in the first place. The Danes said West Norse sounded like East Norse if you tried to speak it with rocks in your mouth. My foster father said East Norse sounded like West Norse if you tried to speak it while chewing porridge. Maybe we devised the differences just to have more reasons to insult each other.

Alfhild's fake smile remained unbroken even as she locked eyes with me again. Not going to fall for that trick again, I looked away and searched out the king's gaze. Aha! He could not sit idle if I called him out.

"I was wondering about their general battle-prowess and distinction, you know," I said, fully committed. "You had promised an offering for our success and, well, our success could be determined by whether this is a good one, and if they are just thralls—"

"What are their names?" demanded Magnus.

I let the audience murmur a moment. The plan was hatching.

"Hey, you!" I called out, still intelligible to my audience. "What are your names?"

No response. How surprising! The men looked around and said what I needed them to say: The thralls could not speak our language, unless in response to a demand for more ale or roast pork. And then I was able to use my magic, the kind Alfhild had no business with.

"*What are your names?*" I shouted in Frankish to a silenced audience.

"*Ulfberht!*" called the boy. "*And my sister is Nanthild!*"

"He says his name is Ulfberht and his sister is Nanthild," I said, pausing to let the vicious murmurs build.

"Ulfberht Bloodaxe and Nanthild the Raven Feeder?" asked Magnus. That got a chuckle. We were well on our way to screwing up this ritual right good. "Have they even killed anyone?"

"Wait, I can find out. *How many men have you killed?*"

"*We only killed seven or eight!*" said Ulfberht. "*They were Martel's men. They killed our father and tried to rape my sister. I locked them in our house and set it on fire, and I would do it again!*"

I thought about this for almost an entire second.

"He says they haven't killed anyone and don't know what's going on!"

"Ha!" laughed Ulf, shaking his head.

"Thor will take these two as meaningful sacrifices," said Alfhild, now floundering against the general sentiment. "He will aid us in—"

"Your aid stands here before you," said Haldor, his voice unhurried and yet thundering through the grove. Suddenly no one was laughing. No birds sang. No squirrels chittered. The trees leaned in to listen and the earth held its breath while all eyes shifted to him. "Send Thor on your quest if you like. Our errand will not be sped by the deaths of children."

The king rose at that, unable to allow strife in the grove unchecked, or just too embarrassed to sit still. He offered what he could of wisdom. "You risk much by not sacrificing to the gods," said Ragnvald. His tone was deep and grim. This was no trifling matter. He had led the Spear-Danes through good times and bad, shouldering the burden of whatever ill events had come about. War, famine, disease, now a troll that would persist until they were all gone. "What if Thor rides against you because of it? Such a simple thing, two thralls of no consequence, and such a great risk to not offer them. For all of us! We do not wish these attacks to continue. It is a foolish thing to bet."

The 'Steins laughed openly at such betting advice.

"What will ride against us?" repeated Haldor. "Who else has ridden against us before? Scores and more, man and beast." He paused, dropping his voice in pitch and raising it in volume. "Where are they now?" The statement rumbled out slowly, and indeed it was a statement, a threat even, and not a question.

There in that grove, something changed. Not my magic—I had spoken no verse. And not Huld's or Alfhild's that I could sense. Did it change every man I had sailed with or only my perception of them? As I looked out over the crowd for reaction, there I thought I saw every man grown larger, as if having hidden their true size before. Fists clenched and teeth ground.

Kari was tall and stout as an oak, Magnus as swift as a gyrfalcon as he moved amongst the crowd. Haldor and Svein towered over other men like mountains. Ulf's ears pointed and grew, his mouth a sneer of glowing white teeth to dare any challenge. The brothers' ever-glad expressions hardened to steel, standing by Finnr whose skin had turned to living stone. Hemming was just a shimmer, stalking behind the treeline and out of sight. And Kraki just looked like Kraki, which was to say like old, simmering rage made manifest. If it was magic, it was Haldor's voice spurring it on.

And Ymir's bones! Gorm did have a face of tin whiskers at that moment.

"Ragnvald!" Haldor called, Silence held high, though I was certain he had laid it down at the entrance with the other weapons. "I have faith in my axe, the one you were glad at seeing! It has proven faithful to me. I did not see Thor at my shoulder when battle was at hand. And if he watched me, he knows who earned glory on those red days and why I boast of my deeds. What boasts for killing thralls? We all march forward to our fates—will you march with such a stain, or keep your load light of it?"

Turning towards the gathered men, he held out his arms in question.

Did they really think this was an appropriate offering? Some looked around or at each other, or at the king. Gorm held his arms crossed and his expression unmoved. Others were questioning. Haldor had their attention, but the king was the authority, and the queen's magic was a powerful thing.

I had no authority, but I had my own magic readied, and I spoke the killing blows for that fool's ritual:

> "A prophecy comes
>   about killing the weak
> to gain favor against the strong.
>
> Cast to capture
>   caprice of the Norns:
> Working to change their weave.
>
> On the *Sea Squirrel*
>   no supplicants sail:
> That ship shuns sacrifice.
>
> A weak thrall

           can work a forge;
      What can a dead man do?"

The stillness of the moment that followed broke by the slightest movement of Tin-Whisker's head. He nodded and others followed, and I knew I had them. Would they rely on superstition, on vague threats whispered on the wind? Or on the might and main of Haldor's men right in front of them?

The Spear-Danes were weary of losing, but what they saw in front of them was undeniable. I had never been in battle but if it were Haldor's voice commanding me, I would follow it as well. He was not the only one with such a skill, however.

"Take them to the forge then," boomed back Alfhild's voice. I felt the shock of it in my knees and it almost knocked me off balance. She spoke with a sound in triplicate, her head lolling to the side, her body suspended by the unseen.

I had seen something like this before, but never so strong. Stripped of her planned-on ritual, Alfhild was entering a trance. If she was acting and not really a seeress, I had never seen a more convincing act. She was the real thing, and no wonder the king deferred to her. Prophecies are not just predictions. A spirit, or spirits, had entered Alfhild and would speak a prophecy through her. Three voices at three pitches was something new to me. It made sense as to speak for the three Norns at once. At least that was my interpretation. The effect was disconcerting, and there was nothing to do but wait for the prophecy now.

"Work the forge till the night sky's sword crosses the clouds and quench a weapon under the darkness. Two lives given, but the gods are jealous. You have taken their gifts, and they will take in return."

The voices, the movements, the power I could feel all made it seem so real. And yet: That was the worst prophecy I had ever heard. What was the night sky's sword, and why should I care? We had a dwarf to work the forge. Weapon making and weapon quenching would be done as he saw their need and not based on the blatherings of spirits. I had picked enough of a fight for the day though, so I followed Haldor's lead and nodded gravely as he approached. Kraki strode forward and took Ulfberht and Nanthild by their wrists, jolting them forward in shock. To my further surprise, he brought them to me.

"It is settled then," said Ragnvald, standing to address the crowd. "The dwarf must make a sword to kill this troll."

Which is not how I would interpret that prophecy at all, but at least Alfhild was done with her ritual, the thralls still alive.

"You must tell them," said Kraki. "We take no thralls. They are free." There was a hurriedness in his manner and voice, even urgency.

The two former thralls were more confused than ever.

"*What is happening?*" asked Ulfberht.

"*The witch was going to sacrifice you, but we did not like that idea.*"

"*Do we run or fight?*" asked Nanthild, with as much matter-of-factness as Magnus might have asked 'Do we fight now or later?' She eyed Kraki with suspicion, not liking his looks or his manner. I liked her right away.

"*The dwarf will take you both in for work at the forge. Or you may leave if you wish. You are free to choose where you go.*" Still, the two eyed the maniacal form of Kraki holding them tight. "*You do not need to fight.*"

"*He is dangerous,*" said Nanthild, eyes still on Kraki.

"*He scares everyone here. That is why he is the safest one to be around.*"

"What are you saying?" demanded Kraki. "It should be simple enough."

"They are afraid you mean them harm," I said. "If they are free, let go of their wrists!"

The old warrior grimaced at that and let them go. He was embarrassed at scaring them and then embarrassed at his failure to understand, and ultimately embarrassed to be embarrassed in a never-ending cycle of masculine self-flagellation.

Kraki's departure coincided with the rest of the men beginning to leave the grove. The ritual had ended and most wanted to see the light of day again, and perhaps forget that tripartite voice and its disturbance of this peaceful place.

Finnr found me before I found him, and his introduction to the two Franks was considerably warmer than his friend Kraki's. The dwarf had a subtle but easy cheeriness to him, and also a facility for languages. Soon he was introducing himself in their tongue and they were responding in ours. Basic phrases only, but enough to calm Ulfberht's anxiety and let Nanthild feel less need to fight her way free.

They departed together, and I thought it prudent to follow and put some distance between myself and the queen. And the king. And the witches. And perhaps especially the king's champions, all of whom looked like wolves who were somewhere between hungry and starving. I took one step before Ulf caught my attention and waved me over. A strange thing, and one I did not wish to acquiesce to but had no excuse.

The brothers had kind words for me on their way out. "You know they call skalds 'Odin's thought-smiths.'" said Innstein.

"That's a fair description from what we just heard," said Utstein. "But we want to know what you think about something."

That was strange enough a request until I saw I was holding court with some of the other men of the *Sea Squirrel*. Most were gathered round clear enough and interested to hear what came next, whatever it might be. Haldor himself lingered in the background with Ulf and Kari, just enough to seem that they were not listening. Somehow his axe was gone again, as I had seen at the outset.

"What do you think of Ragnvald's wager?" asked Innstein.

"He makes a fair point, even if Haldor might disagree," prodded Utstein.

"Ragnvald's wager is a sucker's bet!" The words were out of my mouth before I knew what was happening, and not spoken quietly. What was I thinking? If the king or his champions heard me say that it could be my head. We were honored guests to be sure, but kings had limited patience.

The two brothers smiled as the hulking, shaggy form of Haldor Skullplitter lumbered over to the group. I stood awaiting public judgment for the over-candid statement. A skald's job may be to speak, but speaking too much is worse than not enough.

"That way is a way to follow fear," said the giant, almost a full head taller than even the tallest man gathered there. "Any man is free to do so. But he must leave our crew then and declare himself Ragnvald's man."

Heads nodded and looks were exchanged. None of the crew was about to do that publicly. Some might leave later, but Haldor knew the core of his crew would be stronger for it. Others seeking to put their faith in the might and main of the men at their shoulder would take up with us. We would never want for brothers in arms.

Ulf chuckled and stroked his chin. Haldor was a man of few words, and he had already said more than intended. He nodded to Kari, and the two were off, peeling away the crowd. The brothers smiled at me and then followed themselves. Only Ulf lingered behind a bit.

"Haldor thinks you are good," Ulf said, smiling and nodding. "I think you are lucky." Then he leaned in and whispered a familiar phrasing. I knew it from somewhere, part of a proverb that might be taken one way or another, interpreted as needs be. What got my attention was the language he spoke it in and the fluency of his speech:

> *"Better to be alive,*
> *no matter what, than dead—*
> *only the living enjoy anything."*

He winked, gave a knowing nod, and was gone from there.

I could not tell if his statement about luck had been intended to diminish me or to give me the highest compliment he knew of. I would come to know Ulf well later. But even in retrospect, I could not guess which meaning he intended.

Chapter 20

Frank Discussions

though? Maybe it was just as simple as he described—avoiding the stain of dishonor.

Whatever it was, the men were in high spirits the rest of that day and night. It did not hurt that Ragnvald had continued the feast for us. Food and drink were plentiful. The mood in the hall appeared to be on a course to return to its former glory.

I didn't drink to excess that night, and I rose early the next morning. It was time to do some exploring, maybe even find a few thresholds to cross, as Heimdall had suggested.

My morning ritual involved less beard-grooming than the others, seeing as I had little beard to groom. It made me apt to leave the hall early before someone could make fun of the thin, wispy hairs on my face. It did not warrant a brushing, unlike Haldor's chestnut mane or Ulf's pointed black beard. The others took their time combing and trimming and commenting. It is indeed good to go out preened and dressed and with a meal in your belly, but it is also good to avoid being the butt of jokes.

As I finished up washing, I thought I caught sight of a large bird flying high over the far end of the hall. A raven maybe? No, a hawk. Circling the hall, then breaking off to fly high over the city.

Lejre emerged from the mist in the low light as I headed down a path toward nowhere in particular. I intended to go where the others were not likely to explore, wherever that might be. Explore long enough and the *land-vættir* will whisper to you, assuming you are a guest with manners. I wondered if those land-spirits had equivalents for large settlements, or if the nature of cities was too anathema for spirits of any type to settle into comfortably.

Halfway down the hill, I found I was not the earliest riser after all. Two men on horseback trotted my way, already awake and comfortable on their mounts. The forward rider, an older man, eyed me and gave a curt nod while I stood aside.

The second was younger, maybe my age, but more harshly worn than I was. "Duck," he said, before I could take in much more than that.

The rush of air beneath beating wings clued me in better than the man's warning, and I ducked. Just over my head ripped the screeching '*Ack-ack-ack-ack*' of a goshawk. The bird stopped short of the second rider, flapped a few more times, and settled onto the man's forearm where he wore a thick glove. Long talons dug into the leather, and the bird stretched out, showing its finely barred chest and long legs. The bird's blood-red eyes traced my every movement, its beak open as if to shout a warning.

"That is some hawk," I said, with the tone *your bird is crazy*.

"The best of hawks," he replied, with the tone *go away*.

The riders continued apace on their mounts, straight up toward the hall. Perhaps the arrival of the *Sea Squirrel* had emboldened some new would-be heroes come to Ragnvald's hall.

I took the implied advice and continued down to the city to explore. There was something strange about this place. Perhaps it was just the result of years of raiding by a troll, but that did not seem quite right to me. As the way forward became a little clearer, so did my status as an outsider. Sideways looks from some. Outright stares from others. Smiles were rarer than cut gems in that place.

Lejre was supposed to be a rich trading city, but commerce meant noise. Wheels rolling, animals squawking and squealing, men and women talking or shouting, coins clinking. I heard none of those things. The middle of town sounded more like Fretborg on a good day, if Fretborg had any good days. The mist was burning off in the morning sun, but the suspicion hung heavier and would not disperse.

Any time I saw someone staring, I stared back and stopped cold. I can't help it. If there's nothing to be gained from conversation, the only thing left is to win the battle of awkwardness. I won those battles so easily, I soon had to move on from each one.

The main path led me nowhere interesting. I had plied my trade enough mornings to know that morning was the wrong time of day to ply my trade. Drowsy, hungover, or just starting to work, few people want a song or a story first thing in the morning. So I kept quiet and made a few polite inquiries.

Soon I found my way to the forge Finnr had been set up with. Doubtless, he was displacing another craftsman, but who could resist the lure of dwarf-made trinkets? They were the stuff of legend, and often not cursed at all.

Forges can be strange places, a little like sacred groves, though lacking in a grove's subtlety. There is a magic there. You can feel it even if you don't have a feel for anything mysterious. It is the kind of magic that hits you in the face with a sudden breath of hot air. A smith brings a new order to raw material, and there is a lot of energy involved in doing it.

You know hot air maybe. The kind that gently nudges your cold feet to come closer at night. The heat from a red-hot piece of steel is more like a wild boar hitting your leg at full speed. It is no small thing to shape that sort of material. Even as the steel turns from red to black and becomes too cool to bang on, make no mistake: That metal is still burning hot, just not hot enough to shape well with a hammer.

Heat and hammering were what I expected as I opened the door to the forge. But there was no heat, no energy. And no hammering. Wall shelves hung bowed in the middle or cracked if they hung at all. An anvil stood near the hearth, its face so beaten there was no more flat area to it. The bellows feeding the hearth was torn, and its lever was broken. This was no displacement of another smith. No one had worked this forge, or even been in this building, in years.

Ulfberht sat half-asleep in a corner. Finnr tossed tools of varying quality into various piles while muttering various curses.

"Good morning," I said to the both of them, hoping Ulfberht would understand well enough.

"It is?" said Finnr, pricking up in surprise, a worn smith's hammer with a cracked handle dropping straight onto the ground. "Seems just the same as most other mornings. The sun is in about the right spot. I hope that is quite average and not particularly good."

"You have two new assistants. That should be a good morning, at least."

"Are they the ones making it morning? I don't think they had anything to do with it." This was not the dwarf's normal tone. He picked up one shank of a pair of tongs and watched the other fall to the ground, the boss rusted through. "The morning is just the morning. And in any case, I only have the one assistant."

The unchanged expression on Ulfberht's face told me he had not understood.

"Where is the girl then?"

"Off brewing or somesuch. One of the king's lackeys came by yesterday just as I was being understood. Said this was men's work. Hmph!" The dwarf shook his head. "'And women should tend to women's work,' or so says this king. He took her off to help brew more ale, and with her all progress I had made on teaching her to speak Norse. Now I need to teach the slower apprentice your language just to get him to burn charcoal so we can begin work."

"Too bad for him. I hated burning charcoal." I knew my mistake as soon as it left my lips.

Finnr whirled on me like a predator, which in the frame of a portly but agile dwarf is a frightening image. Eyes blazing, belly jiggling, beard flapping like a raven banner flying over a battlefield.

"You know how to burn charcoal?" he asked, not really asking. "And you know his language . . ."

Burning charcoal is dirty, tedious, thankless work. I knew that from doing it for my foster father, and it was the source of initial insight into my offering of delivery service. So miserable at standing around burning charcoal, I decided it would be better to risk my neck out in the wilderness on delivery errands. Halstein had agreed, and so I was done with that hated work. I thought.

"I have other places to be!" I said, uncertain what those places were, but certain they existed somewhere.

"Wherever you have to be, here you are," replied the dwarf. "Now good on you for intervening. And I suppose good on you for getting me an assistant, though that remains to be seen. But that has brought some attention to us, and now they want to replace one ritual with another. Which is their way of saying, 'Get the dwarf to make a valuable dwarf thing.' Like a sword that will kill any troll."

"Who is 'they' in this case?"

Finnr raised his voice. "They! The They! Whoever They are! Who cares?

Doesn't matter if it is the gods or the king or the wind, but now that is the expectation. I need to make a sword, and not just any sword, before Haldor can kill that troll. By decree or by divination, I have heard this kind of thing before, and I know when it rings true. And they leave me no raw materials, rusted tools, and a forge falling in on itself! Do they think dwarves just shit ingots of good steel?"

"I assumed it was pig iron."

Finnr's massive whiskers curled up in a smile. The belly laugh that followed was so full I saw his teeth for the first time. They were not sharp, which was one folk tale demystified. His teeth were still a frightening shade of yellow, though.

"Well, skald," he said, tossing me two old wood axes, "it is indeed a good morning after all. Now take this lump and show him how to make charcoal. Between the smelting and the smithing, I will need quite a bit."

"*Do you know where they took my sister?*" asked Ulfberht, finally piping up. I considered the young Frank, putting him at twelve or thirteen years perhaps. Strong for his age, but the contours of his face spoke to his youth.

"*Yes, and we can go see her,*" I said, not quite ready to commit to the long process that was burning charcoal.

There was a question I had myself, one that had been in my mind since meeting the dwarf but I had assumed was not to be asked. Well, by the burning balls of Surt, I was going to ask it anyway. I was supposed to be going where others would not go, and now I was relegated to the worst job I could think of. So I asked.

"As I have heard it, you ought to be stone from being in the sun. What is a dwarf doing above ground, sun or no?"

"Some of my kin and others I know might turn to stone if they got caught by the sun. Only those who would not countenance leaving the Down-Below very long, though," said Finnr as he looked away from his task. "Fools don't know much about dwarves. Or anything else, though they will speak about whatever they can. As for what I am doing above ground: I am cleaning out this troll-ridden forge."

Expert as I was in telling stories, getting others to tell me their own stories was a skill I was still working on. Not because I did not want to, but because I did not know how. It was my job to learn such stories so I could tell them later. One day, around a campfire or in a great hall, or perhaps out at sea needing distraction, I might be the only living memory of some of our crew.

Who else would tell their stories and help them live on? Who else would cause cheer to go up at the mention of their names? I was to burn his charcoal rather than learn his story as the ship's skald, and that made me angry and heedless, as was my verse in response.

> "Some day
>   die memories
> but for the skald's
>   skill at stories.
> Both hero
>   and history lost
> when a poet
>   practices elsewhere."

The dwarf's eyes came around slowly, and a chill ran up my spine. I had not seen him displeased in such a way before. Any question as to his patience left was answered with the white, hairy knuckles of his right hand squeezing the life out of a thick hammer handle. It snapped under the pressure, and the head fell to the floor with a thump that might be taken as a warning. If only there was still time for a warning.

I had expected to speak and steal away, but Finnr had taken that verse as a challenge, and thus it was his turn in the battle of wits. Gaze steady, the dwarf replied in kind:

> "A stripling claims
>   to carve memories
> into men's minds,
>   marking past deeds.
> The dabbler's words
>   do no work:
> They warm no metal;
>   win no matches."

The dwarf's stare was so hot it could have smelted iron.

I nodded and left that place, grateful the only audience had been someone who could not understand. At least he would not know how badly I had just lost that battle of wits. Or so I thought.

"Did the dwarf say something nasty to you?" asked Ulfberht.

"No," I lied.

"He sounded angry."

"We have work to do. Follow me."

And so I left that place, wondering if declaring it a good morning had been a hasty thing.

The city had come fully awake by that time, though the sounds of it still seemed muted by something I could not see. There was less movement than I expected as well as less noise. Where were the chickens squawking as they were dragged from one end of town to the other? Where was a fishmonger smoking mackerel? Few wagons were set up along the streets, with people opting to do business from house to house. By then I had walked much of the city, the largest settlement I had ever visited. It spread out in a ring around the hill Ragnvald's great hall was perched on.

That splendid building loomed at the top of the highest hill to be seen, overlooking the landscape for miles. This was my first time seeing it in the clear light of day, its outline drawn bold against the blue sky. No wonder Ragnvald was king despite his disinclination to go out into the wide world. He was old and could live off his reputation and off that glorious structure on high.

The hall was longer than any I had seen before, but it was more than that —the lines of architecture were sharper, the wood stouter. Some of the carven figures above the doors I could see even from a distance. Those ravens and eagles and boars stood sentinel watching the city. The impression given by size and art together might stand as a challenge to the halls of the *Æsir*.

"I think the brewer is this way," said Ulfberht, pointing ahead of us.

I followed and caught the smell that had put him on the right track. That was the sweet aroma of malted barley in the air. Few things have such a pleasant fragrance. Sometimes I wondered if that was more enjoyable than the ale itself. Briefly, of course. What is better than good ale? Mead was the more expensive and kingly drink, but give me good ale any day.

For all the sophistication my nose had to offer, Ulfberht already had the scent tracked like an elkhound. Soon we were at the right building and the other scents in the air told of the other ingredients this particular batch would use. Juniper and fir were there to balance the sweetness of the malt.

I was thirsty and the smell of ale being brewed was a stronger draw. The brewhouse sat aside from most of the other buildings in town, neither much up nor downslope from the rest. A semi-covered well was off from a side door, visible as we approached from the front of the structure. It made sense the brewhouse would have its own well, as it would require so much water.

I licked my lips in anticipation that a few friendly words to the brewer might get me a sweet sample. Instead, Nanthild came out to embrace her brother, and half (the easy half) of my promised errand was done.

A woman followed her out, taking her time to look around and apprise herself of anyone else at the door. Much of her blonde hair had gone white and she wiped gnarled hands on an apron that might have been older than she was. She eyed me with a smile that curled her lips but left her eyes watchful.

"And now that she has begun, you come to take her somewhere else?" asked the old woman, massive spoon clutched tight. But for my previous bad result in an old-lady fight, I might not have noticed that her posture holding the spoon cut an image suspiciously like Huld holding her staff. Or Kraki holding his club.

"No taking on my part," I said. "That was the king's decision. I am but a humble charcoal burner, according to my latest task."

"We have one of those already," said Inga. "And since when are you *not* one of the king's men, here to do his bidding? Your company says you are here at his pleasure."

"What company says that?" said a curious voice behind me.

Making my way through forest and mountain for some years, I had developed a keen sense for when something—anything—was nearby. My hearing was acute and I was rarely surprised. So I was quite surprised when I turned around to see the man who had spoken.

Here was a fellow with an amiable expression, white-bearded and mail-shirted, and he had come upon me unawares. There was not a trace of stealth about him with all those metal bits clinking and a cloak of red wool about his shoulders, yet he had surprised me.

"You lot!" said the spoon-wielder, and spat in the dirt.

The newcomer looked at me and shrugged. "I am your company, it appears. Well met then, skald. I am Gudbrand. I see you have met Inga, our finest brewer."

"Trolls take you!" spat Inga.

"It is good you stopped by now," he continued, "as she is most pleasant mid-mornings and becomes less so as the day goes on. These are the Franks, I take it?"

Ulfberht and Nanthild had been busy speaking quietly and still heeded none of our conversation. Shifting my attention, I caught the end of a sentence only that went *"and then the dwarf growled at him and we left."*

Hel's dragon, it might be better to not teach Ulfberht any Norse after all.

"So you've come to take her instead of this skinny rat?" asked Inga. "I just got this one. Made herself useful right away, and I won't lose her just because some coalbiter king changed his whimsy."

"I came only for questions," said Gudbrand, hands upraised. "You have both the advantage and that deadly spoon! I have been away and am only now meeting many new guests. One of whom left the hall quite early."

"I was staring at the people staring at me," I said. "It seemed like the only thing to do."

"Or nodding at people nodding at you," he said.

"You were riding up to the hall this morning," I said, recalling the two men I had seen. "Two more champions of the king? I thought he had only three left, and we met them all."

"Oh, no champion is this one," said Inga. "Here is Ragnvald's errand-boy."

No amount of vitriol could break Gudbrand's smile. "Please, woman! Ragnvald's errand-man, at least." Then he turned to address me. "He keeps his champions for fighting. I merely take care of the horses."

"You are the staller then," I said, believing the title but not the role. "Quite the mail shirt you have for someone who fetches oats and mucks stalls."

'Staller' meant he kept the king's horses in good order, but that was just a title. His real job would be as the king's general problem solver. As the general problem solver, he knew everyone who lived in town. What their business was. Who their relations were. And whether they liked the king or not.

Gudbrand shrugged. "I also take care of the things that require the riding of the horses. Could be to bring the war-arrow around Denmark to muster fighting men. Could be to escort the king's nephew Hrolf."

"That was who rode with you this morning?" I asked. "The one with the hawk?"

"I saw you meet both Hrolf and High Pants," he said, grinning. "You can tell Hrolf is better-liked than most because I mentioned his name and Inga did not even spit!"

Inga glared at him, but the man had an easy charm unbreakable by evil eyes. He winked at her, and she snarled back. Turning slowly my way, he changed the subject. "I heard there was to be a sacrifice," he said. "And I heard it was dissuaded by some well-timed verse."

Had I been credited as such? Doubtless, I had something to do with it, but I had seen the real influence as Haldor's doing. If others were speaking of me in those terms, perhaps there was some hope for me on this journey after all. I may have blushed.

"By this one with the soft hands and pink face?" said Inga, pointing her war spoon at me. "He said he was a charcoal burner."

"I am not a—" and realized I had said I was, only in jest. I shook my head, trying to right my brain as to why I should even be in that place anymore. "The dwarf will have me instruct Ulfberht in the art of charcoal burning."

"I told him we had one already," said Inga.

"The young Frank burning charcoal or you doing it, either way, we do have one already," agreed Gudbrand. "He is . . . temperamental."

"Does that mean I should let him do the teaching or that I should avoid him?"

"Complicated," said Gudbrand, stroking his beard.

"Ha!" added Inga, and spat again.

"If our fair brew-maiden would make use of these two," said Gudbrand, gesturing toward Ulfberht and Nanthild, "perhaps I can take the skald around and explain."

Inga took the hint. I think she was done with the both of us one way or another, and ready to get back to work. She called the two Franks back in, and whatever confusion Ulfberht had was outdone by the ease he felt at his sister's side.

Soon I was off on a path to nowhere with a newfound friend. He liked to talk. I would humor him, I thought, and hope his friendship might somehow get me out of burning charcoal. It would get me far more than I had bargained for.

CHAPTER 21

THE STALLER'S STORY

GUDBRAND TURNED IN THE OPPOSITE DIRECTION OF INGA'S house and started walking. No gesture to follow, no invitation. He headed up a well-trod dirt path towards the hall, then turned and began to circle around the hill to the south over soft grass.

I caught up with him quickly and matched his pace.

"Inga really doesn't like you," I said.

The staller grinned. "She doesn't like the Rus. The Rus and I both answer to different people," he said pointing at the great hall. "From Inga's perspective though, those people are no different. But if you think Inga is tough, wait until you meet the charcoal burner. He is not the easiest to deal with."

"What can you tell me about him?"

"Other than he is surly and drives a hard bargain? Very little. His name is Ketill."

"How do I find him?"

Gudbrand shook his head. "He lives in the forest and appears in town here when he feels the need. I would not know how to find him."

At the staller's quick pace, we were soon away from any of the worn paths or buildings. Our only listeners were among a flock of sheep we passed through on our way. There was plenty of grazing area for the few animals, but no shepherd I could see. Soon I realized why.

A ram picked up his head as he chewed his grass. His gray fleece was unshorn and longer than the others. His horns curled over themselves twice, but on one side a piece had broken off. Nobody took shears to this beast, and whoever or whatever had fought him was probably dead. He would be as good a shepherd as any human, and he stared me down as I looked at him.

I let him win that staring competition. Not a good idea to get on the wrong side of a ram. Some animals were stubborn, like donkeys and goats. A ram who takes you as a threat is not stubborn so much as iron-willed in his desire to break all your bones.

"Where in the forest?" I asked after a long pause. It seemed like a rather important detail if I was going to find him.

"Couldn't say," said Gudbrand. "He shows up with a cart of the stuff once in a while and trades for what he needs."

"That can't be enough charcoal for the city!" I said.

Gudbrand shrugged. "The city needs far less of everything these last few years. Most make whatever they need for themselves, but not much more."

"Is that why the old forge was so worn down?"

"Ah," he said, "you must mean Skallagrim's old forge."

"If it's the one falling in on itself, full of broken tools, yes," I said. "Why they would give that to Finnr, I can't understand."

"The dwarf?" He paused for a few moments as we came to the west wall and turned left. "You mean you can't see the why of it?"

"Can you? Finnr is a master smith. He could be making things as legendary as the sword Tyrfing, or Volund's wings, or the Brisings necklace! Why give him shoddy tools to work with?"

"If I were to speculate," said Gudbrand, tugging gently on his gray beard, "I might speculate that the person who made that decision does not like your crew very much. Maybe someone your crew's skald poked at. Twice."

My chin fell to my chest. I had been brash with verse in Lejre and the queen had taken offense. So obvious, too, and I had not put it together myself.

"I did not mean to put the crew in a difficult position."

Gudbrand waved that comment off with one hand and pointed with the other. The sleeve of his mail shirt pulled back from near his elbow to reveal two armrings.

My eyes widened at them, and at recognizing one, but I shook it off to look at what he was pointing me toward. About a hundred yards away, a mirror image of the gate we had come through stood facing south.

"No Rus guarding that gate," I said. "Men more loyal to Ragnvald than to Alfhild. And most have chosen one allegiance or the other."

"Ah, see? You are not so slow as you just thought. I did not really want you away from Inga to talk about burning charcoal, more to show you this. A man who likes to kick hornet nests ought to know where to run when hornets are chasing him."

"So you're Ragnvald's man," I said. "My thanks to you, in case I ever need to run from the queen's people. But I need to ask about something else."

"More about the charcoal burner?" he said, sounding disappointed. "I would not—"

"Did you fight for Arrow-Odd?"

One of those armrings was no doubt Ragnvald's. He used a hart for his heraldry, and one armring branched into a pattern of what looked like antlers. It was the other armring I was interested in, the one shaped like an arrow-fletching on one side and point on the other. I knew that design from my father. He had fought for Odd twenty years ago and still wore the armring.

Not many men who wore those armrings twenty years ago had come back with them.

Gudbrand's ambivalent smile said at once he was serious, but still playing a game, whatever the game was.

"That is what you want to ask me? Not about how to bed Fanya the witch?"

Heimdall's teeth, he was good. Not quite as good as he knew, however. Now I knew her name without having to ask it.

I wondered what else he had heard, and who had been talking to him. A staller might be a king's right hand, or the best of the king's champions, or perhaps the king's closest confidant. This one had the tone of a jester but felt more like the king's spymaster. And wearing mail just to come down for a walk and conversation? There was more to him and to what he knew than he let on.

"So did you know my father or not?" I demanded, using a tone I had no business using. That was the real question, because fighting for Arrow-Odd, while interesting, was nowhere near as interesting as fighting alongside my father. "Yes, I think you know who. You asked about me before coming down that hill, and you knew I met Fanya. You know I'm Styrgrim's son, I think, or you might not even be here right now."

"Hmph." Gudbrand gave me a half-look and cocked his head, indicating I should follow.

Once I realized standing still would not get me an answer, I hopped after him and waited for further clarification. His reticence annoyed me, but we were in a contest of who would stay silent longer. I had no choice but to match his quickened pace and follow wherever he was going.

"What do you know about your father?" Gudbrand finally asked, as much in his own memories as in the present. We were headed closer to the city's center of commerce, what little there was. The quiet had lifted a bit. At least there were people socializing and haggling now.

"He preferred the sea to the land," I said. "Always out raiding or trading and rarely even back for a winter." But that didn't describe his personality. "He was quiet and diligent in his work, and rarely stopped to rest or play. A serious man."

"Interesting," said Gudbrand. "You describe him as you remember him from being a child. And you speak of him in the past tense. I wonder if you have a sense of him, even far away."

Had I spoken of him as if he were in the past? I had. I wanted to dismiss that as irrelevant, but I knew it was not. A pang of aggravation coursed through me and I had to shake my head. "I am remembering him from my past, so yes, I speak about him that way. I do not know when I will see him again."

"Fair enough. But you remember only what a child recalls. He is a great warrior."

"I know that."

"You know but you do not understand. You have never been in battle. You have certainly never been in battle with Styrgrim Halsteinsson."

"Have you then?"

"Once." Gudbrand's chattiness disappeared into a single word so deep, I thought he might fall into it. Crossed eyebrows and a near snarl screwed up his face, which had been relaxed and unhurried for the rest of the time I had known him. Some memory must have had a powerful effect to change his demeanor so quickly, and that made me want to know what it was even more. At the same time, I knew he would resist saying more.

"You have a great advantage then," I said. "Tell me about this battle. It would be a time unlike any I spent with my father."

"I could tell you, but you would not understand."

"Better to hear it than not."

Gudbrand stopped, drew a deep breath, and fell at ease as he looked at me. "That is not a good time for remembering," he said. "And you may think you understand when I tell you, but some stories must be lived to be understood. I will tell you this: Your father does not love the sea as much as you think he does, and his preferences are not to travel or to be particularly quiet. He has done those things out of necessity, or what he believes is necessity. A great warrior only begins to describe him. More than that, it is not my place to tell."

Naturally, I thought of how I might get him to tell me more as soon as I heard him say this. But I would need to be careful. A straight question asking for more information would not work, and might even get me a hard cuff on the side of the head. But a challenge . . . my people cannot avoid challenges. Like milk for cats, they can't resist. I nodded thoughtfully as I considered this, and then the obvious came to me.

"A greater warrior even than Haldor?" I asked.

"I would not want to fight either one," said Gudbrand. "Haldor is bigger and stronger, yes. So what?"

"So what could my father do against a giant like that?"

Gudbrand eyed me with a confused look. "The real measure of a warrior, the real test of his might and main, is what happens when he is nearly dead," he explained. "Dead from wounds. Dead from exhaustion. Dead from no hope. Surrounded by dead friends and burning ships. What happens then?

"I saw your father when hope fled from me in just that state. I was ready to fall down and never get up. This was in Arrow-Odd's war against the sorcerer Ogmund. Twenty years ago, but it is burned into my memory and will not fade until I do.

"We had been fighting at sea for three days. He had a hundred wounds and a dozen burns. How many broken bones he had, I can only guess at based on his labored breathing. His left hand had the only fingers left pointing the way they ought to have. Part of his scalp flapped over his left ear like a gruesome banner in the wind. He had taken an arrow through his balls. I know—I am the one who cut the fletching and removed it.

"All that and he was still in better shape than most still living in our last ship of that last battle. Our sail was aflame, the smell of smoke and dead men's entrails drowned out the salt of the sea on the air. The ravens circled us, considering how our eyes would taste.

"I felt myself about to fall, but I saw him rise up and snarl. For an instant I saw a giant polar bear like mist around him, and so I kept looking. He stripped down and took nothing but a long axe with him before he dove off our starboard side into the half-frozen sea. He swam toward the sole surviving ship of Ogmund's forces. The Bjarmians on board, out of the thousands who had sailed to war, were the only ones we saw left other than Odd and Ogmund doing battle just beyond.

"Their crew watched while Arrow-Odd attacked. Ogmund coiled and struck back like a great hairy snake, leaving strange blurs in his wake to confuse the eye. And meanwhile, that shitheel crew of Bjarmians that had done us in watched the two battle from as close as they would dare.

"Then it was your father I saw again, his axe emerging from the sea like the hand of some mad god, and with it he hooked the gunwale and hoisted himself up.

"The Bjarmians wasted no time when they noticed their ship rocking. They tried for him before he could get his legs, but they were too late. The first took the toe of 'Grim's axe in his throat. Two swings later, two more were down. Still 'Grim was surrounded. Yet it was the Bjarmians who were afraid.

"'Grim's roar split the sky in two. It was no word, only a single sound. And yet we knew! We knew what it meant. It was defiance. It was negation. It was no mere resistance, it was—" Here he stopped and stared skyward. Whatever he was describing could not be described. It had to be lived, and yet he would do his best to make it clear. "It was as if mind and axe wove a counterthread that opposed in every possible way every thread the Norns had weaved for him. That weave rippled through his body, changing his *hamr*, his very skin. He became a machine of murderous armor apart from men or gods.

"We turned then, many of us who had accepted death. We rejected it, and rejected our fates, and we too howled. In pale imitation, but howl we did. And we followed him, staggering swimmers as we were in that state, axes in our teeth, ready to do battle one final time.

"I was the first of us to board the Bjarmians' ship. There I saw another man, bigger and stronger than your father, big as Haldor I am certain. He was cleaved from forehead to teeth, and set up straight, surrounded by a pile of dead men as an offering. 'Grim had not just won against those odds but had also straightened up before we could aid him.

"That is what your father could do while half-dead or worse. He did more than that in the days leading up. Is he alive? I have no idea. But I have yet to encounter a thing, man or beast, that I thought might kill a man like that. And I would not wish to."

PEARLS BEFORE RUS

GUDBRAND HAD SURELY TOLD MORE THAN HE HAD INTENDED. I wasn't sure if I should feel accomplishment or confusion as a result of that. One seemed to always to accompany the other. He must have felt the same because he took his leave after that story with an excuse about needing to tend to matters with the king.

That was quite the story to take in. I wanted a drink but didn't want to walk with Gudbrand back to the hall. Nor did I want to return to Inga the brewer to be assaulted with a spoon. There had to be at least one place to drink somewhere in town. Perhaps I could even ply my trade, tell a story for some amusement, and lighten the heaviness of my previous conversation. Maybe even get a few reactions and gauge the mood of some of the townsfolk.

A place with a few benches and some ale would be best, but it was not the time or the place, and ale was only for guests to be received at this point. I ran through the dynamics of the entertainment I would be providing and considered what I was trying to do: Nothing in particular. Since I was looking for reactions and familiarization, a long story with lots of killing would be best. Positioning was next, and the area next to the baker would allow me to address a large crowd.

The bread smelled delicious. A good story often needs food to go with it, so my performance would bring the baker business and her baking would help ensure a happy audience. I even bargained my way to a free loaf, and that bought some time to hone the details of the telling.

This was good. Things were going well. I was ready to perform. And then a saw a shock of red hair in the gathering audience and froze.

You could say I was bewitched with a little smirk perhaps. That would be a sly way of indicating Fanya was working some kind of intent upon me at the time though. A more accurate way of describing the scene was that I was totally infatuated, and did not know what to do with that feeling. I was lucky a small crowd had already started gathering, demanding I follow through. Luckier still, I had already decided on a story to tell and did not need to do anything but recall what I knew very well.

"Who knows the story of Tyrfing?" I asked.

A few nods in the crowd, mostly glances exchanged or shrugs. Of the few people listening.

"The story of the evilest sword in history!" I shouted. "Kingmaker and kinslayer! Tyrfing killed more people than death! Come around to hear the story!"

That got a bit more attention.

I'm not going to recount the story in its entirety. It is strong on genealogical details and short on gods and giants. But that's the nature of the story of the cursed sword Tyrfing because it is a desirable object to new, stupid generations. There are opportunities for embellishment from its dwarven origin to its last known use as a cleaver of Huns.

I thought about that as a few Rus joined the crowd, and I got that luck-pushing feeling I sometimes (as in always) have.

"It was a dwarf-made sword, and that means magic," I began. "Good enough to cut through stone and steel as easily as cloth, though it carried a curse. More than one, in fact."

Dwarves are spiteful little shits when they want to be. They made great weapons for gods, like Odin's spear and Thor's hammer, but those were gods who could have visited untold nastiness on said dwarves if their wares were not as expected. Humans are not so dangerous, so dwarves are freer to curse items falling into the hands of mortals. In this case, the mortal took the sword by coercion.

"But it was not cursed at its making," I said. "Oh no. It was made good by two young dwarves. Then King Svafrlami of Gardariki caught the dwarves and stole their sword." I paused and nodded to the Rus, as if to lay the fault with them as much as their legendary king. "Only after its theft did the dwarves curse it. Cursed it in thorough fashion!

"As soon as Svafrlami had it in hand, the dwarves made it clear it would do him little good. It would kill its owner for sure, whoever owned it. Once drawn, it could not be re-sheathed without first killing someone. Anyone taking even the slightest cut from it would die of the wound. And just in case the sword's owner was very, very careful, three evil deeds by this sword were guaranteed."

That is the setup for the story, involving multiple generations of people ignoring the curses laid upon the sword. Why use such a thing? It was powerful, and both men and women in this story craved power, regardless of the cost.

You would think a man carrying such a sword would not carelessly draw it to show his brother when no one else was around, but that turns up as the second evil deed. The first evil deed involves a *berserkr* with his eleven *berserkr* brothers (I told you they traveled in twelves) killing a brave, if somewhat arrogant, friend of Arrow-Odd.

I was always more interested in the sword's owner in between evil deeds one and two. That would be Hervor the shieldmaiden, daughter of Angantyr the *berserkr*. There are three Angantyrs in this story, by the way, the first of whom is the *berserkr* and the last of whom is the one who kills all the Huns with Tyrfing. But I digress. Hervor claimed the sword from her father's burial mound, which is a story all by itself. Then she used it to lead profitable raids, retire rich, and marry well before settling down to become a mother.

What a woman!

But the stories I know don't talk much about her or why she lacked the trait of being an idiot held by her male family members. The last we hear of her, she passes on the sword to her son Heidrek. Heidrek being the careless one who unsheathes it to show his brother, Angantyr number two, the Short-Lived.

By the time I got to the third evil deed, the audience was caught up in the excitement of the battle of the Goths against the Huns. There Angantyr the third wades out into the thick of the Hunnish troops and makes such a great slaughter of them that the bodies clogged up a river. That's an important detail to remember—it always gets a cheer. Unless you have a Hunnic audience.

When you get down to details of lineage and everyone having the same name, it gets hard to tell that story without it dragging on too long. That was as intended because I wanted a story I could make some pauses in and take stock of my audience. I tried to keep track of Fanya's reactions, but she was here one moment and somewhere else when I next looked, even though I only ever saw her standing still. Some people stopped and listened for a few minutes, some for longer. Some cheered the violent scenes, so I drew those out with a bit of creative license.

The more important creative license I took was that I didn't mention Huns at all, but changed them to Rus. Maybe I was feeling saucy after talking back to the queen two nights in a row, and it made me want to turn the Big Losers in this story into Rus. Or maybe I felt like kicking a hornet's nest, since Gudbrand had advised me on where to run. It wasn't premeditated, it just happened.

I told you I sometimes had that pushing-my-luck feeling.

Goths against Rus is a bit problematic if you know their history, which I knew my audience would not. Also, who cares? I wondered what effect that might have on the Rus in the audience. Based on their reactions, they understood enough Norse to know in general what I was talking about.

I finished and bit by bit the crowd dispersed. Some of the children made to play as characters in the story, crying "I'm Angantyr!" (probably not the second) or "I'm Heidrek!" and making that reason enough to hit their friends with sticks.

I had lost track of Fanya; she must have left before the end. Women moved off smiling and remarking on Hervor's strength and tenacity, and men nodded approvingly. Except for four men, who did not move and gave no expression except to stare at me while I looked for Fanya, who I could not find.

It seemed a safe assumption these men understood west Norse well enough, but were probably more familiar with East Norse by now. To seem more familiar, I bought a loaf of bread from the baker, bit off a big hunk, and spoke while still chewing, asking them, "How did you like the story?"

I was rather pleased with my cheeky question following my impromptu performance. I expected the next few moments would involve me getting some compliments and perhaps a mild heckle. I expected this because I was an idiot. But I was not so much an idiot as to not know what it meant when the closest of the four Rus to me drew a very long knife and started in my direction.

And then I was running. I was not thinking, just running, spitting out a big hunk of bread as I ran because I knew I needed to breathe deep for this run, or it might be my life.

My pursuers were shorter than me, and I was long-legged for my height. A burst of speed, and then I had them by four or five strides. I looked back and was confident they would not catch me. I smiled at the angry frontrunner, who seemed to realize the same thing. Good news.

And then I slammed shoulder-first into Fanya, knocking her down, and causing me to stumble and lose almost all of my speed. Maybe some dwarves had cursed me to make dangerous mistakes. Mistake number one must have been changing a story about a bunch of dead Huns to a bunch of dead Rus. This would be mistake number two. Who knew if there would be a third; there was a third mistake in the story of Tyrfing, but at least the people doing the evil deeds got the benefit of a magic sword in the meantime.

As I struggled to regain my balance, mistake number two was compounded as I went down and took a fist-sized rock to the side of my right leg. It was no ankle sprain that would have done me in right there, but it hurt, a lot, when I could not afford delays.

I scrambled to my feet and could feel the leg was not injured. It was not quite right either, certainly not right enough to get me to full speed. It would take some time to shrug off the bruise, and I had no time because I was surrounded. The three Rus to my sides and in the direction I had been running, and the one with the knife drawn behind me. If only I had that magic sword in exchange for my ill deeds, I thought, I would probably be fine.

With no magic sword, I had to rely on my command of many languages. Or in the case of the Rus' language, a guess at what else they might speak. I tried speaking Sami slow and careful, but this did not get the desired response.

It got a few chuckles, and I tried to laugh back. In response, the Rus with the knife said something I did not understand as far as words went, but that I took the meaning of anyway: He spoke slow and careful right back and at the same time he said it he made an unmistakable gesture with his knife plunging through a gap in between a circle made by his thumb and middle finger.

I didn't need to be a skald to take his meaning.

Behind him, I saw Fanya staring at the ground at my feet and murmuring something I could not hear. She gripped her spear with white-knuckled concentration, and murmurs came louder and faster. The Rus were closing their circle around me when they stopped and looked wide-eyed at my feet. I didn't want to take my eyes off them, but I had to see what would distract them from their quarry. I only noticed the thin columns of air because of their wide-eyed reactions.

The first vortex crossed my line of sight and continued around me as if directed to do so. Which it was, as were the other two, all making their rounds to protect me at their center. They were small eddies, not of any notice other than too convenient and too coordinated to be natural. They grew in size as they circled me, and as much as I was alarmed the Rus were far more put off.

A final shouted syllable from Fanya sent each little whirlwind out at my pursuers at lightning speed, not enough to knock them down but more than enough to be disconcerting. The butt-stabbing Rus wheeled around and shielded his face with his arm. I leaped between him and the man to his left with just enough time and space to avoid being slashed.

And then it was a footrace again.

The running part was easy. I could out-sprint them and then slow to match their fastest pace for however long they could run and then some. I described before how I focused on getting away from things, but that is not the reason it worked. It worked because Norsemen do not care how long you can endure and do not run anywhere if they can ski or sail or ride. They focus on the greatest amount of strength behind a single blow or throw or shove rather than repetition, so while I was weak compared to them, I could also outlast them at anything, except for rowing, which I hated. As I heard the heavy breathing of the one closest to me, I knew the short, fur-clad Rus were no different.

But there was also the difficult part, the part I had not yet figured out. Where was I going? At first it was a series of easy decisions about going over, under, or around people and objects. Then it was a realization that I was going the wrong way. The right way might have been towards the hall. That would be an uphill run even more difficult for them, with my shipmates to help take up the matter if they made it all that way. But the over/under/aside series had cast me off towards the city's south gate. I could keep going without trouble but could not very well change direction against a fanned-out pursuit.

Soon I was out of the city entirely and trying to plant my footfalls outside of planted crops. I ignored the road and lit out across open fields to the east. Acres of open farmland led to a dense treeline that seemed reasonably easy to lose pursuers in. The forest would slow me down but would slow them down more if they lost sight of me. I sprinted the rest of the way and hit the forest with a good lead on them, then got as deep into the woods as I could before turning further south.

I slowed to a walk less to catch my breath than to get my bearing. The big oaks were comforting, as if crooked walls between myself and the Rus, but I knew it would be the underbrush that concealed my location. Looking back, I could make out two of them entering the treeline, pointing in anger and hopefully in confusion. They would not know what direction I had taken unless they were skilled hunters, which I then realized was not only possible but probable.

I could double back perhaps, then try to outrun them to the hall. Tiring, yes, but doable. That assumed these were the only pursuers and no others had been called to assist them. If I ran into a trap, I was done for. Better to keep going and lose them completely. I kept going, driven by whatever parts of the forest looked thickest, occasionally needing to change course a bit in impassible parts. None of this would help me when I returned to town, but by then Haldor and the crew would have heard their skald had been attacked by four Rus. As long as I didn't get myself killed in the meantime, I would be safe.

Some miles into the forest I became confident I was no longer being followed. It was a good time to head back west then, instead of backtracking the way I had come, and then go north until I cleared the treeline. Simple as that.

Only this deep in the forest the trees were so tall and thick together, I couldn't tell which way was west. The friendly oaks I had come through had given way to a sea of white birch with no obvious end. I looked back at the way I had come, only none of my surroundings were familiar. I did not know the way forward or the way back, and the forest sounded very quiet all of a sudden. Much too quiet for a wood undisturbed by men.

And I felt the kind of alone you can only feel when you know you are not alone, but you don't know who or what your company is.

CHAPTER 23

THE REAL REASON ODIN WEARS A WIDE-BRIMMED HAT

I SAT DOWN, STOOD UP, TURNED AROUND IN CIRCLES, AND HAD A spasm of panic every time I heard something. This was not a forest with a familiar feel to it.

Moving off in any direction threatened to get me more lost than I already was. If I stayed put, I reasoned, I might remember something about my path to that point and be able to retrace part of it. Or perhaps I would hear one of my pursuers and, staying out of sight, follow him out of the forest.

Fate answered me with paranoia and a crushing sense that felt like I was drowning on dry land.

An oak I could probably climb for a different view, or at least for the security of not being vulnerable on the ground. The birches were like rough spear-shafts though, with no limbs to speak of until high above me.

Having looked around me for perhaps the hundredth time and checking that I at least still had my knife for the same number of times, I had to do something, anything. So I found the biggest tree nearby and started up it. I was a few feet into this endeavor before a voice startled me.

"You talk too much," it said. The voice was coarse but musical. I couldn't place it as male or female, or even human in particular. I was half-expecting it to be a dwarf who would explain why he and his brother had decided to curse me.

I clung to the tree, uncertain whether I should keep going up or get down. It seemed a lot like a choice between avoidance and confrontation, so I chose the former.

"Where are you going? You won't find anything in that tree."

I kept shimmying up the tree, heedless of the advice. At about fifteen feet off the ground. The trunk swayed a bit but held fast. I was better at climbing rocks than trees, but I could hold myself in position without too much effort.

"That's a good, defensible position there," the voice said, softening to emphasize the irony. "Since you are making so many good decisions, I will leave you with some advice: Run away from the men and towards the bird."

My eyes had been closed, but they exploded open with fear at the implication. I hadn't even realized I was keeping my eyes shut until then, but as soon as I let myself see, there was movement between the trees. And there I was, fifteen feet in the air, not hidden and not protected. I cursed my stupidity as I slid down the trunk and hoped I could remain undetected doing so.

No such luck. A shout from one of the Rus alerted the others to my position before I was down, and then they were closing the space between us while I continued my descent.

I hit the ground and it took a few steps to regain my sense of balance. The voice was right about the men, I would run away from those. Turning around as I sped off, a raven croaked and swooped low in between a set of trees. 'Follow the bird' was as good as any other advice I had heard that day.

You may imagine several armed men speeding through the forest with grace and power, intentions of violence writ large on their faces. The truth was we were all tired at that point, the Rus could hardly breathe, and the bird was leading us up a steep hill. None of us was moving fast or with much grace. The face of the closest Rus looked like it was an overfilled wineskin about to burst.

The ground flattened out a bit and the trees started to get thinner, but we were not approaching the edge of the forest. I could make out a mound, no not a mound, an earthen structure. The raven had made right for it. I was almost down to a fast walk, but I kept going, thinking I only had to reach this little hut and then the Rus would leave me alone for some reason. Stumbling to the door, I leaned and banged on it and looked back.

The Rus had stopped. A few hundred feet away, they had stopped and would not come any closer. They exchanged looks, and one kept repeating a word I could not translate. And then they left.

"Are you going in or not?" said the voice above the door. It was the raven, the same voice that had told me to get down.

That seemed as good an invitation as any, so I opened the door to a face full of stale air. There was smoke and ale in there, and a good bit of the smell of a man who needed to bathe more often. Like Silfast's mead hall! But unlike Silfast's mead hall, the dank odor gave a distinct impression any guest would be better off turning around and seeking shelter elsewhere.

The raven laughed as I crossed the threshold.

Blue flame flickered at the hearth in the middle of the house as if too shy to be seen by unfamiliar eyes. Something above the fire simmered in a small cauldron. It and the fire looked far friendlier than the occupant sitting behind the hearth, regarding me with a stare cold enough to freeze the room in contrast.

He was old, maybe as old as Kraki, and had a similar look in his eye.

"Come on then," the man beckoned, sounding more than a little annoyed.

The smoky smell I had noticed was stronger as I stepped onto the smooth stone surrounding the hearth and took a seat on an ancient wooden stool. My first impression was that he was sitting down to ease his old muscles, preferring to not move much.

As I sat, I noticed the crouched position he was in and the knife he held. This was no small utility knife, it was a long seax with a broken back, a good shape for stabbing. He was not aching to move less, but coiled to spring in case I turned out to be a poor guest.

Wall candles inside illuminated runes, carved or drawn into the house itself, as well as some dried herbs hanging and other desiccated flora on a table next to the man. The only thing I recognized for certain was the fresh fly agaric, the large mushroom with the speckled red cap. Runes carved in bone were cast about on the floor at his feet. I wondered where they had come from. Then I realized the more appropriate question might well be 'Who' did they come from, and I swallowed and kept my mouth shut about it.

"The raven said I should come in," I said. "I did not mean to intrude on you."

"The raven didn't say any such thing," he said. The old man coughed, bringing the knife hand to his face to cover his mouth. "He asked you if you were going in."

"Should I leave then?"

"That depends what you want," he said after some further hacking and coughing. "I have few guests here, so I want to know who you are and why that bird thought it right to bring you here."

"I wanted to get away from some men pursuing me. As for the bird, you would need to ask him."

"Are you an outlaw?" he asked with casual indifference to the possibility that I was. Outlaws were vigilant or dead, since anyone could legally kill them without punishment. I am certain some of those lone wanderers I caught wind of during my travels had been outlaws, and I turned around to go nowhere near them as a result. That much vigilance against that many threats makes men desperate and dangerous.

"No, nothing like that. I told a story some Rus did not like. They meant to do me harm in return, so I ran. There were four of them." He stared at me as if to squeeze the rest of the details out of me, but I was still on edge from being chased. "I am Ansgar Styrgrimsson, skald of the *Sea Squirrel*."

"More wanderers in the forest than usual as of late. Most looking like they had no protection other than remaining unseen. But a skald!" he said in a tone I could not tell if it was surprise or mockery. "Maybe you should tell me a story, but alter it to insult me and then wonder why I would do you harm."

I was already beyond tired of mystery. And I was physically drained to the point where I could not play mind games. "Do you kill men over mild jests then?" I asked, my tone losing its polite air. "You seem to know much more than you let on. I think you sent that raven to lead me here in the first place. And I think you are no charcoal burner."

He half-smiled as if amused at a dog that has figured out you are only making the motion of throwing a stick. But he also sheathed that wicked-looking knife, and I felt just a bit safer. "I am a charcoal burner, so you are wrong on that count. What more useful thing can a man do than to provide the fires of creation and cooking?" he said. "For someone who uses words as his trade, you seem to lack a certain command of them. And word does travel fast if you have the right friends."

"You are Ketill then. But if you are the charcoal burner I was told of, why did the Rus stop following me so close to your house?" I asked.

"Because they are not my friends, and they have heard stories you have not."

"What stories are those?"

"About incantations of evil intent. About songs that make men insane.

About *draugar* wandering at night to torment the living and beasts no one can describe roaming the forest, devouring anyone wandering too deep here. About an old man who would as soon use your parts for spells as look at you." Ketill sucked at his teeth in emphasis. "Only one of those is not true."

"So they are afraid of you," I said after a sufficiently smoky pause.

Ketill stopped mid-breath and arched an eyebrow at me. "That is well-stated and too obvious for words at the same time," he said. "Would you further offer that the fire from my hearth is hot, or that I am old, or that I live deep in the forest? Please share your further insights with flowery verse."

Rus mercenaries do not scare easy any more than Norsemen do, but a reputation for danger was something to be heeded for any but the short-lived. This man had a reputation, and further, no one lived like this.

Maybe you have heard stories of weird old codgers or witches living in houses on chickens' feet. They don't. Nobody does. Food is scarce, winters are harsh, sickness is near unbearable alone, and everyone needs to trade something for something else. Community is essential to survival. Except this man was living out in the woods, alone, apparently self-sufficient.

A terrible thought occurred to me: What if the raven had brought me here to be his next meal? Or his next parts for a spell? He didn't look like much; perhaps I could beat him in a straight fight if I kept my knife at the ready. I sensed something else at work though, and figuring nothing I said was likely to make my situation worse, I decided to say something deliberately stupid.

"You don't scare me, old man."

"We have moved to the entertaining part of the conversation," said Ketill, grinning with the wide eyes of a madman. "At last!"

I hadn't anticipated that, but I hadn't anticipated any other answer either. So I did the thing that has reliably gotten me into more trouble than anything else: I started saying whatever came to mind.

"People are afraid of things they don't understand, and they have no idea who you are. They must conjure up all manner of horrible ideas, more than you could ever put into action. Meanwhile, you still need to eat. Little do they know that while they imagine you cutting men's balls off and throwing them in a fire while you chant some curse, you are just growing vegetables or hunting for mushrooms so you don't starve here. And chopping wood for your fires so you don't freeze. And making your charcoal to buy what you can't otherwise take from the forest.

"Or maybe you do spend a lot of time with men's balls, perhaps as much as they give you credit for. So what? I know men far scarier than you. Just days ago I saw a man half my size murder one *berserkr* after another until twelve had fallen, but he is at least sane and of good cheer.

"But one of our crew, a man named Kraki, is as old as you or older. He fights with a bone club and is like to murder everyone around him at any given time. He says he wants to teach me to fight as a pretense to hit me in the head with his club. He makes us all eat putrid food so we won't want to eat too much. The best interaction between us was when he described a dream he had involving a masturbating wolf.

"That is the absolute best I can hope for from our journey: Poisonous food, insane ramblings, and head injuries. So you be scary, scary old man. I would be afraid of encountering you in these scary woods, but I know what waits for me when I get back, and it is a bunch of Rus trying to gut me and an insane crewman who might teach me literally to death. It is scarier than you are here, surrounded by *draugar* or beasts or not."

Ketill stared at me wide-eyed as if he had never seen the like. He finished with a coughing laugh and grabbed his stomach as he doubled over with long, crowing laughter. "Teach you to death! Ha!" He slapped the table. "I like him already."

It seemed like a long time I waited for him to stop. He did not stop, but slowed down enough that I heard something else, something outside. Upon listening more closely, it was the raven. I knew what a raven's song sounded like but this was different. This also sounded like laughter.

"That's an interesting lot you describe," said Ketill, recovering himself somewhat. "Maybe you aren't the coward I took you for. Here, have some stew and be welcome." And that is what he did, he spooned out a bowl filled with mushroomy broth and then did a thing I was not expecting at all: He opened a barrel nearby and scooped out a horn of ale each.

"You have ale," I said.

"Back to obvious statements?" he said. "You were doing so much better when you got away from those. I like ale and mead, but they are not free. So I burn enough of the hated charcoal to trade with the hated merchants in town."

"I mean to say," I said, shaking my head in frustration, "there is a troll stealing all the alcohol in Lejre. Anything sitting for more than a few days or two he snatches right up. The king's champions have tried to confront it and it got away. Powerful enough to wrap its arms around a man and crush him to death. How do you have half a barrel of ale here, just sitting around?"

"You make a lot of assumptions, and they make your questions stupid," he said, spooning some too-hot stew into his mouth, chewing once, and then spitting it back into his bowl before cooling off with some ale. "I want to hear more about crazy old Kraki and maybe the rest of your crew. I think they must have good stories." His demands made, he returned to the stew and waited for me to produce another entertaining monologue.

I could not argue. He had received me as a guest and provided food and drink. That was after saving me from the Rus who would have provided me only a knife to my guts. Still, I had managed to find the elusive forest hermit only to have him deny my ability to ask all the questions I needed answers to. I spoke with a frustrated tone, I am sure, though he did not chide me for it. Perhaps he wanted company as much as I wanted information.

So I described the men of the *Sea Squirrel*, or as many as I knew by name, and our general mission to kill this troll. And I went on to describe the king, or as much of him as I knew, and the queen's suspicious behavior, and Gudbrand taking me around earlier that day. I recounted the story about Tyrfing and how I changed it, and how this offended the Rus who then came after me with ill intent.

Ketill stopped eating to laugh again, shaking the thick wisps of white hair that dangled in front of his face. I was a guest in a house that probably accepted few people, and so I made a good telling of it all. Except for Fanya. I wasn't going to open myself to ridicule on that front with so many others available.

"You have a good sense for storytelling," he said with a mouth full of food once I was done. "Even if it's not true, you make me want it to be true. But there's one thing outstanding, whatever the truth of the rest of it."

He finished chewing and eyed me with a long pause. I was certain he'd seen through what I had left out and wondered what to say about it. Should I admit I had never been with a woman before? Or just that I was enamored of Fanya? I waited along with the old man and didn't answer, though I felt certain my face betrayed me.

Ketill leaned in close before he spoke. "You told why you joined the crew and why you regretted it later, though not in so many words. You left out what you intend to do now."

My secret was safe. For now. Not that I knew how to answer Ketill's question. Silence had just saved me from serious embarrassment, so I tried it again.

"You want things, but you don't want to admit what you want," Ketill said, his tone curt at answering his own question. "You wanted to find me. Here I am. Old as I am, my patience is not infinite. More distinctly finite than ever, I think, or why else would I be here, so far from needing to be around people? Why are you here?"

"I needed to escape the Rus," I said. "Your raven led me here."

"That's no answer!" said Ketill, rolling his eyes. "What kind of shit answer is that? You might as well say 'I am breathing' or 'I am eating your food and saying stupid things in your house.'"

"Fine, I came to ask you about the troll," I said.

"Who cares about the troll?" Ketill's eyes widened in exasperation. "He is not stupid enough to come around my house at least. And your crew does not likely expect you to fight it. Why are you here?"

Anger boiled in me. I felt as though a drill were slowly boring into my core, one slow but unstoppable turn at a time. And I was angrier for not understanding why this old man was making me so angry. My mind seemed out of my control, and without control, I feared I could not tell what would spill out of it. Had he cast a spell on me? My face screwed up and I looked at the door, seriously considering making a run for it. But I turned to his face and saw the arrogant half-smile on his face, and I knew I would not be scared away by this old man and his wiles.

"I am going to find my father," I bellowed. "And I want him to be proud of me for once and make him admit he has a son instead of pretending he doesn't. I want to do deeds he cannot deny and show him I am as much a man as he is. You might burn charcoal, but that is not who you are."

"And who am I then?" came the last challenge. I would only be allowed one chance at this answer, but I needed no more than that.

"The runes all over your house, but no pedestal to sit *seiðr*. A raven doing your bidding. A house protected from a troll by little more than your reputation." I paused before my conclusion. "You are a *galdramaðr*."

A man whose magic was *galdr* rather than *seiðr*. Chanting, runes, more that sort of thing than the summoning of spirits I had seen Huld capable of. But let's call him a wizard, as that's a fair term to use.

Ketill nodded ever so slightly as he took a long draught of ale. He held it so long I almost thought he had forgotten to swallow. Only this time he was concentrating not on me but on the smoke of the hearth fire, which formed up into the image of an eight-legged horse. The smoke horse galloped and then dissipated into the air as it passed me.

"I know the old runes," said Ketill. "For all the good they have done. There is more desire for charcoal than that kind of wisdom."

"What kind of wisdom is that?"

"Painful. Too much for a fragile thing like you to endure, anyway."

"I think you are wrong," I said without thinking. What was I doing? "I would learn the runes as well as I know languages. As well as I know poetry or the lyre or my sling. There is nothing you can teach I cannot learn."

The words were out of my mouth before I could stop myself. Some contrarian compulsion in me was at work, and I knew not how to stop it. And like volunteering for a ship's crew, I was committed.

"To teach the runes as magic is not easy, nor to learn them. Runes are secrets, and with good reason. What do you intend to give in payment?"

I had little to give. My share of treasure was small, maybe not even worth offering. I had my knife, no doubt redundant for a man living out in the woods. And I had my necklace of bones, a gift from my foster mother I did not wish to part with.

"What do you want?" I asked, thinking this was the clever answer.

"What I want is meaningless," said Ketill.

"Then what am I supposed to offer?"

Ketill paused. "Go back to your comfortable hall, boy, and think about it on the way. Think about what knowledge costs. Odin got it twice. What did he give for it? Payment is not for me to receive, but for you to lose. When you have a better answer, come back and give it."

Odin technically got it three times if you count him stealing the mead of poetry, but that was not what Ketill meant. He meant the other two times, once at Mimir's Spring, and once at the trunk of Yggdrasil itself. At the former, he ripped out his eye and gave it as a sacrifice. At the latter, he gave his life, spear-pierced and hanging for nine nights.

"The raven will show you the way back," he added.

The visit was over, and I had hardly realized it was coming to an end. Struggling for an appropriate way to excuse myself, I stood up, thanked him for his hospitality, and turned to go.

The fresh air outside the hut filled my lungs full to bursting. The smoke must have made it even stuffier in there than I had imagined, is what I supposed. But the sounds of the forest were all around me instead of silent, and somehow the trees did not seem so pressed together. Daylight peeked through their tops and hinted at a clear day in the late afternoon. The forest seemed to be working with me rather than against me now.

And then something hit the top of my head and oozed through my hair. It was partly liquid, partly solid. On instinct, I reached up to touch it and then examine what it was, even though I knew what it was before my hand got there. The raven that had led me to Ketill's house glided down to perch above the door in the same spot as when he had ushered me in.

"I don't belong to anyone," said the raven. I stared at it dumbfounded until it continued. "You referred to me as his raven. But I am not his! I am nobody's!"

"So you took a shit in my hair?"

"Ha ha ha!" said the raven, or as close to that as ravens can laugh. "I did! Do you think you will remember who I belong to now?"

"I will remember," I said, looking for leaves or bark or anything to wipe it out of my hair.

It occurred to me that most descriptions of Odin cast him wearing either a hood or a wide-brimmed hat. It made sense for anyone spending that much time around ravens.

"Good boy," said the raven. "I suppose, then, you won't need a number two!" He laughed again, longer and harder this time. I found some dry dirt to rub through my hair, which was better than the bird's oversized turd. It was about as effective as it sounds.

"You have a terrible sense of humor," I said.

"Haha!" croaked the raven, more amused by this than was reasonable. I sighed and nodded my readiness to the bird, who I took to be smiling. "All right then! Follow me."

The forest churned as I walked away from Ketill's hut. It was as if every root and rock were gears in one incomprehensible machine grinding to lock the way back as I exited. It was subtle at first. I startled when I thought I saw movement, then panicked for a moment when I thought I was going insane. The raven's call brought my sense of direction back around, and I increased my pace to make certain I did not lose sight of him.

Which way we went I know not. I can only say it was not the way I came. The flat, birch-studded forest soon gave way to a lusher, greener scene with hills and rocks. The changing landscape and the twisting sensation made me feel as though I was walking outward on a spinning top. At least, I hoped I was walking outward.

A great, sinewy oak was the first thing I saw that seemed familiar, although I still did not entirely trust my senses. I put a hand on the thing to feel the reassurance of its solidity.

"Not bad," said the raven, perched a few feet above me.

"What is not bad?" I asked by reflex, but immediately wondering why I would invite the bird to taunt me more.

"A tough walk, that," said the raven. "I've seen tougher men do worse. You didn't even vomit. Maybe the *landvættir* like you. But now the difficult part is done, so you need to walk alone."

A single wing pointed me in the right direction through the rest of the treeline to open fields and hills. Doubtless, I would be able to see where I was going at the next hilltop or two. The nearer to town I got, the more dangerous it would become.

"It should be an easy walk," I said. "I will likely have those Rus as escorts as soon as they see me. And from there, maybe I am done walking for good."

The raven flapped his wings and cawed loudly. "Well said! Well said!" There was a note of approval rather than of derision in his laughter now though. "Ketill intends you to walk much farther! Otherwise, he would not have sent me with you. I know—I can deliver a message to the king's hall about your great journey! Surely your friends will come down to walk with you right away!"

"And if the Rus hear your story at the same time, won't they also 'come down to walk with me' as well?"

The raven's eyes widened in deep thought. "I suppose they will," he said. "And then many can walk together until there is a great meeting." The bird's excitement increased with every syllable.

"And there will be a feast for ravens," I muttered under my breath, recounting that overused poetic trope to describe the result of a battle. The ensuing fight would be short, I thought, but to a carrion bird, a body is a body. Makes no difference how long or well the fallen fought—they taste the same either way.

"And there will be a feast for ravens!" the raven cried in triumph. "A feast for me! Hurrah!" And off he flew, ostensibly to do me a favor but really to start a fight. The happiest raven in the world.

Of kennings for killing a lot of men, 'to make a feast for ravens' or 'set a table for eagles' or some variant thereof, appeared at least twenty times in every saga I knew.

Kennings provide a variety of ways to describe a thing. We liked them for style, but needed them for alliteration in the poetry, since all good poetry is built on alliteration and not on annoying end-rhyme. 'Blood' could be 'wound-rain' or 'sword-paint.' A kenning for sword was 'Heimdall's head,' and for head was 'Heimdall's sword,' affixing, as I saw it, the god's propensity to use his mind in a fight.

Then again, the ram was Heimdall's animal stand-in. It could be he instead had an affinity for pulling enemies in close and head-butting them to death.

With so much variety available for creation, from the poetic to the absurd, one wonders why my people got so fixed on using this 'feast for ravens' kenning for battle all the time. I won't try to answer that here. But my experience with that murder-inducing bird made me wonder if ravens were so associated with Odin because they were troublemakers like him. Perhaps the ravens were not just feasting but causing those feasts in the first place.

I set out in the direction of the hall and hoped I was not about to be part of that feast. It was a pleasant walk. The sun shone down with just enough warmth to be comfortable. A light breeze whispered in my ear every few minutes. I could smell the lavender from the near side of the hill to my right.

I walked and took my time, the first time I could recall taking my time. It made me think of my foster parents and how quick I had been to get away from them and chase the excitement of my father's life. Perhaps he enjoyed it, the constant moving, the constant unknowns, the constant fighting. The other men seemed to, but they were better at fighting than me. Every thought made me long for the comfort of my home, and then I stopped.

I was not home. I was wandering. I did not have my home, I had the *Sea Squirrel*. I did not have my foster father, but I had the crew who would afford me some measure of protection. I did not have my foster mother to tell me the stories of my ancestors, but I had found a reclusive *galdramaðr*. And he had offered to teach me, if only I found something to give up, to sacrifice. At that, I realized my right hand had moved to the necklace my foster mother had given me for protection.

I had been protected all my life. Partly from my father's life, partly from my father himself. But that was no longer my life. Avoiding danger could not be the whole of what I knew as I continued my journey. The necklace inspired me with love and protection but held me back to a life I was no longer living.

For better or worse, I had chosen to follow my father, only as a skald. And I needed to learn what Ketill could teach me, whatever the cost. The thought chilled me as much for its content as for knowing it was the truth.

Too late, too late, I thought, as seven figures wearing conical helmets crested the hill in front of me.

CHAPTER 24

A FEAST FOR RAVENS

I COULD SENSE TWO THINGS THAT BODED ILL RIGHT AWAY: THEY were not dressed as Danes or Norsemen. And Haldor would not have sent that many men to find me. These were the Rus I knew from having been chased by them, and a few friends with them. The knives they had carried before were still there, but only as backups. These men carried axes and spears, and one had an arrow nocked on his bow. A bit much to fight someone like me, I thought, but dead is dead. My eyes would not taste any different to the ravens either way.

They took their time coming down the hill when they saw me, fanning out to prevent me from changing direction. The only way out was back to the forest, and I wondered if I could outrun them again. Perhaps, but not if an arrow caught me. Going back to the forest seemed like a delay of the inevitable, but I did not see another option until the raven glided into view. Something about the presence of the bird stilled my feet.

Seconds later, I heard the hoofbeats of a horse coming fast behind those men. The Rus deferred to two riders and made way.

Gudbrand cut a nastier figure in full armor than I had seen that morning. His mail shirt was there, but a heavier second layer of mail hung down across his chest and back over a thick cut of leather that went halfway down his arms. His helm too had mail hanging off it to protect his lower face and the back of his neck. The smile and bright eyes from this morning were now metal eye sockets that took no heed of the armed men around him.

His horse panted but kept his discipline despite the exertion. That was a warhorse with a familiar rider. Gudbrand had a shield slung over his back, favoring the atgeir in his hand. A king's staller might carry any weapon he wanted, even a good sword, expensive as that would be. Gudbrand pivoted his mount to give the Rus a good look at his weapon in case they had never seen it before. A heavy hewing spear, not a common weapon. It was a blade on a stick, and that much more imposing from a man on horseback.

Kari rode the second horse and came up to me straight away, dismounting to get a better look. He had that expression of concern he always had, the look that kept his shoulders so tight. But he smiled when saw me and seemed to relax a bit.

"Did you get lost?"

"I was in the forest," I said. "I made a survey of some trees, but a bird distracted me so I had lunch with a wizard. Then I walked back, but I think he fed me some bad mushrooms."

"So the raven spoke true."

"I don't know what he said. I think he likes to start fights."

"The two of you have something in common then," said Kari, eyeing each of the seven Rus in turn. "I have fought before. I will fight again. If it is because of a foul-mouthed raven, then I will have a new story."

Still on horseback, Gudbrand was asking the Rus some pointed questions. It sounded as though he was getting about half their attention. They came in closer and after a dismissive gesture from the supposed leader of that gang, Gudbrand retorted wordlessly by slapping the flat of his atgeir on the man's shoulder and repeating what he had just said.

The argument continued, but there was no further dismissiveness.

Meanwhile, Kari stretched and did silly exercises to rotate his limbs much as Magnus had done before fighting Halfdan's *berserkir*. The chronic tension he radiated at what seemed like every moment was gone.

Kari would later explain to me that it was only the anticipation that bothered him. Anticipation was a killer. Time to fight always came as a relief because it was an end to anticipation and indecisiveness. If you were thinking about a spear coming at your chest, it was hard to concentrate or go about mundane things. But if a spear is really coming at your chest, you just step aside and kill the man who threw the spear. What's scary about that?

None of the spears were ready to be directed at Kari's chest yet. The Rus were still arguing with Gudbrand. The details of the conversation were getting complicated, so Kari and I listened.

"Seven men in full gear to kill one with just a knife!" said Gudbrand with a mocking gesture. "This is embarrassing for you, Vladimir, don't you think?"

"He told such a good story," countered the Rus with a shrug. "It was about cutting down an entire army of my folk by just one man. So one with a knife, if he just has to fight seven . . . why not? Good story then. Besides, we had four, and no big weapons, and he ran away. His choice to fight now. Maybe he runs away again."

"Maybe he ran to where a friend would meet him," said Kari. "If Ansgar's running determines the odds, here they are. I have as much right to fight with him as you against."

"Is good, is good!" chanted Vladimir, with the others following. "Two against seven is fine. We accept."

"Likewise for me," added Gudbrand. "And what's that?" He stopped as if he'd just caught the sound of a stalking predator. Slowly he put his hand to his ear, then leaned forward and shushed Vladimir from making any noise.

We waited. I held my breath. The point of uncertainty came and passed, and the points of confusion and then awkwardness followed in that order. Then Gudbrand continued: "My horse says he fights for the skald also. So: Four against seven."

The Rus cried foul. This was not right. This was not what they had come for. They had a plan to arm themselves to the teeth and murder a gangly pretend-warrior. This was supposed to be easy and instead was much too close to even odds. Could Gudbrand not see they were in the right here, and he was acting as an agent of cosmic unfairness? It was enough to drive a man to drink.

Gudbrand, or rather Gudbrand's horse, was very sorry indeed, they were told. But what else could he do? He served the king, and the king would be very unhappy if the skald were killed. He would lose the one who could speak to the Franks and play the lyre. And also lose whatever flattering stories the skald might tell on later trips. Who would want to go without such things? It made sense to ensure he was not killed.

"I am not talking to your horse," countered Vladimir, his grip tightening on his spear. "And there is no point to fighting the king's staller. If we lose, we are dead. If we win, we are dead. This is a private matter. We are here, still talking. Being very reasonable. But you, Gudbrand, you are not being reasonable. You butt in and prevent this from resolution."

"Resolve it the king's way then," said Gudbrand, who trotted his horse over near me and spoke in a slower cadence. "He sees the value in the skald taking his stories elsewhere, to spread word-fame. Why don't you make a friend of him and ply him for such favorable stories about yourselves?"

The change in position was perfect. It looked like Gudbrand was repositioning himself nearer to me and Kari for the upcoming fight. Anyone facing his direction would have thought the same, that he intended to create, and fight from, a single front.

Anyone facing the Rus from our position would have noticed something else.

A solitary figure had crested the hill behind the Rus. It came on with the speed of a very fat man running full tilt, though this figure was not fat whatsoever. The strange sideways, limping, hate-stuttering gait it ran with defied explanation. Kraki was wearing pants, thank the gods, though no shirt, because he rarely did. Skin so pale you could use it to light your way on a moonless night tracked a steady procession over the grass, eyes wide and fixed, mouth an open, frothing grin.

Gudbrand was not moving towards me as much as away from the danger. I think he would have talked as long as it took to avoid any killing, but Kraki's appearance would end the conversation.

"Eh?" said Vladimir, scrunching up his face and making it clear nothing would be called off. "He is not friend. He is enemy. We silence enemies and make clear that others who would be enemies will also fall silent. It is the only way."

The other Rus nodded in agreement as if Vladimir had just clarified for a confused Gudbrand that the sky was blue and the grass was green.

"In that case," said Kari, speaking more quickly now as Kraki drew nearer, "are you willing to fight a friend of Ansgar's in his stead before you fight him? It would mean Gudbrand was not part of the fighting."

"Yes! Yes!" Vladimir and his men cheered. Finally, someone was seeing reason!

Kraki approached the man with the bow standing at the back of the group. He was close now, but they had no chance of hearing him over their cheers. Distracted by the fight they thought they were about to fight against Kari alone, they had their minds set on an easy victory.

"Very good," said Kari, "because there he is, and I do not think he intends to negotiate."

In the intervening second between the end of Kari's statement and the beginning of Vladimir's comprehension, the bowman let out a quarter to a half of a scream. Kraki's bone club came down on his skull, sending the man's head straight down through his own asshole.

I told you that would happen.

We stepped back, both to remain good to Kari's word and to stay out of Kraki's way. Gudbrand turned and trotted away as well, shouting that he approved this as an honorable fight. I did step back, but half of me wanted a better view, and the other half to hide somewhere safe.

Kraki had not stopped to deliver that initial blow. He hit the man on the move, and then was moving to the next before that body hit the ground. There was no time for the group to form up even if they had the training or discipline to do so. There is a big difference between a melee fight and what happens on a larger scale when it's shield wall against shield wall. Six men against one are far better off getting shoulder to shoulder and lowering their spears together than trying to fight separately.

Had they known to do that, I still think they had no chance.

Kraki charged the next man with a low, laughing growl. Foam flew from his mouth as he made a single pivot to gain the inside of the man's spear shaft, and he drove the spike at the bottom of his club up through the man's neck and into the roof of his mouth.

It left Kraki flanked on both sides by men with axes who closed in fast. But again, Kraki never stopped moving as he delivered that attack or any other. He drove the dying man's body backwards into another spearman, one not expecting to be rushed by the dying body of his friend. The man crossed his spear and shoved back, which is when I swear I thought I heard a guttural "A – HA!" from Kraki.

Kraki let go of his club and used the other man's momentum to take the spear away. As the body fell, he swung the butt of the spear down into a loud, wet crunch against the spearman's knee, then continued the motion as he turned and drove the point into the chest of one of the men who had just tried to flank him.

The second axeman gaped, and in gaping he lost the fraction of a second Kraki needed to close the distance between them. Still holding the butt of the spear while the tip stuck in the other man's chest, Kraki took a wide grip on the handle and shoved the axeman hard, staggering him back. In the next instant, the speartip was free of the first man's chest and slicing open the next man's throat. Kraki dropped the thing as if it were beneath him.

Fighting is almost never done with clean blows that end men's lives quickly. Men with slashed throats charge forward and kill their attackers, and men with even worse wounds continue fighting for what may seem like an age. A man's blood running free of him does not kill him until a great deal of it has spilled. And when the battle lust is on you, pain is a mere abstract concept. So do not think Kraki brutal so much as possessing an efficiency only a century of education in warfare could impart.

Two healthy men remained, along with one whose knee was destroyed. But Vladimir and his ally could no longer stand shoulder to shoulder to improve their chances, as there was a madman with a spear between them. Kraki turned to take notice that he was no longer assailed on all sides at this point and paced between them, daring one or the other to try for a better position.

Seeing the desperation of their situation, Vladimir's last healthy ally planned to salvage some measure of victory. If he was going to die then at least he would complete their mission, or he must have thought so as he hurled his spear square at my chest.

I saw the whole movement unfold, in a trance, wondering to myself if that was what he was doing as he took the stance. Even thinking it, even watching the grim curvature of the spear sail through the air with deadly accuracy, I still stood hypnotized and unmoving.

The spear began its downward arc. A well-aimed throw, a heart-throw for sure. I was still watching it as if outside myself, watching the scene play out until a dark blur shocked me out of my reverie.

Kari leaped at the spear, right arm fully extended as if to knock it away. This was no desperate attempt to forestall that attack, however. Kari caught the spear only feet from its intended destination, landed on one foot to shift his grip, and winged it back at its rightful owner in one fluid motion.

The Rus who had thrown the spear was now the one standing still in disbelief. He became a full believer shortly, however, when his own spear punched through the center of his chest. He took a few steps to halt his momentum, grasped the shaft, and toppled forward. The butt of the spear stuck fast in the grass for a moment, holding his body suspended briefly before it fell to the side.

Kraki made no reaction to the failed attack and threw his bloody spear in a lazy arc in Vladimir's direction. In his final mistake, Vladimir attended to the spear instead of the onrushing figure of Kraki, whose real attack was coming from another source. He slipped by Vladimir's distracted speartip and grabbed the shaft to pull the Rus further off balance and into arm's reach. Vladimir reached for his knife, but it was too late: Kraki's fist was already deployed, and he punched the Rus in the throat with his right while holding the man's skull with his left. Over and over, as the sounds of Vladimir's shuddering throat turned from gasping to wheezing to spluttering.

I will say this for Vladimir: With no counterattack he could make, he stood holding that spear for longer than I could have, taking one blow after another. He looked relieved when he finally fell.

I thought of saying something and started to speak, but Kari grabbed my shoulder and shook his head. One man was left alive. Actually, three men were left alive. As I described, taking a major wound seldom kills a man outright. He can still fight and flail for the most part, or in these cases writhe on the ground. The man with the crushed knee flailed on the ground. The man who had taken the spear into his chest was trying to crawl but failing. And the man who stood next to Vladimir, who subsequently took the spear through his guts, was also failing to crawl away.

Kraki took notice of the man clutching at the spear in him and moved on. He and the other spear-wounded Rus would be dead soon, but Kraki had unfinished business. He retrieved his bone club from the throat it was shoved into, taking more effort to extricate it than I thought would be necessary. Heedless of the blood that painted its handle, Kraki took it up and approached the man with the destroyed knee.

The man was shouting pleas for why he would be more useful alive. He had his hands up in a pathetic defense when Kraki approached, but they did no good.

Kraki brought the club down on the top of his head, and that was the end of him. He dispatched the two still groaning soon after.

"That didn't take very long," said Kari. "Are you tired yet?"

Kraki didn't hear or was ignoring Kari. Instead of answering, he busied himself with pulling the bodies into a circle.

Gudbrand looked from Kraki to Kari and back. "Is this normal?" he asked.

"There's nothing normal about him or anything he does," said Kari.

Gudbrand reigned his horse in and turned toward the bodies. "Others will want to claim the bodies," he added. "It would be better if nothing else . . . happened to them."

"Thor's beard, man, he's just arranging the position of the corpses. He's not going to mutilate them."

"Says who?" said Kraki without looking up.

"We will not let him desecrate the bodies," Kari shouted, as much for Kraki as for Gudbrand. "You can ride back if you like, we won't keep you. Kraki is about to fall asleep. We'll get him back to the hall."

"You won't take . . . ahhhhhhh" Kraki yawned and fell into a sitting position with his back to Vladimir's corpse. He was asleep before he could finish his thought in the middle of a circle of seven corpses. His mouth disappeared into his beard, but still curled into a smile, Kraki cradled the gore-painted club across his chest. His legs splayed out at an angle as if he had fallen asleep drunk.

The contrast of peaceful bliss with the evidence of extreme violence terrified me. It must have had a similar effect on Gudbrand because he rode away without another word.

"What do we do now?" I asked Kari. "Just let him sleep?"

"He will sleep for a little while now regardless of what we do," said Kari. "Who knows how he'll be when he wakes up. Maybe satisfied. Maybe unhappy that he only killed seven."

A loud flapping distracted me from our conversation. It was the raven from Ketill's house. He landed on the chest of the man nearest me and hopped onto his head. I didn't want carrion birds bothering Kraki while he slept, so I shooed him away and nearly had to kick him given his reluctance to abandon the body.

"What do you think you're doing?" demanded the indignant bird. "I'm here to eat that man's eyeballs. Were you going to do that?"

"Of course not."

"Then leave me to it! A feast for ravens! Hurrah!"

"A feast for ravens later," I said. "Our friend is sleeping. You can have at the corpses once we've gone."

"What?" squawked the bird in disbelief. "But I told all my friends!" And indeed, more ravens glided down. This was no defeated army, but seven dead men had enough soft parts to make a few meals for them.

"Promised too much, did you?" I asked. "We could clear off early, but why would I do that for the bird that shit on my head."

This brought a quizzical look from Kari, but it was not time for explanations.

The raven fanned his wings and opened his beak in soundless aggravation. "I won't shit on your head again," he offered, after a moment.

"Not good enough. If you want your friends to feast here and now, I want something more valuable. I want you to teach me how to find my way to and from Ketill's house on my own."

"Agreed, I will show you the way whenever you have the need," replied the raven too quickly.

I paused and said nothing, but only for effect. At the first look of confusion from the raven, I said in a low, clear voice "That is not what I asked from you."

The raven paused to gain time thinking whether to play dumb but must have thought better of it. "No good," said the raven. "Dangerous that way."

"Dangerous because I won't need to rely on you and you have less leverage," I said.

"No! Well, yes. But no!"

"I think this bird wants to become Kraki's pet," interrupted Kari. "We should bring him back to the hall with us and see what he wants from it."

"I am no one's pet!" screeched the indignant raven. "You can't say your friend set a table for ravens and then shoo the ravens from the table! We will spread the word of your friend's battle-stinginess."

"He is sleeping, but if he hears of what you just said"—Kari slowed and lowered his voice—"he is likely to eat you. Odin's birds or not. You saw what he is."

"This is the worst table for ravens ever!"

"Hold your tongue," I said. "Here is maybe a solution to satisfy us both. You will teach me to find my way, as I said. Swear to that, and to favorable stories about our friend, and we leave you and your friends to the feast. Agreed?"

The raven made a phony balk at the offer, but I knew that to be nothing but posturing to not seem too eager. "Perhaps—"

"No counter-offers."

"All right," said the raven. "I so swear. But I do not have the time for teaching right now, I have a feast to host. I will find you at dawn tomorrow, at the hall, and teach you then. For what it is worth."

"Do not be late," I said.

Kari had the look of a man who, not having any idea what was going on, was relieved to hear that whatever had been going on was over. On to practical matters, he chided me for having nothing more than a knife to defend myself with. Reminding him I had my sling did not assuage his criticism.

"Your seax is fine as a tool and a weapon, but it should not be your only one. That one has an axe," he said, indicating the man who had almost skewered me. "He liked to throw his weapons away, so he won't mind if you take his axe for yourself."

I nodded. It was not a weapon I knew how to use well, but I would look less vulnerable walking around with an axe on my hip. The face of the edge of this one was nearly flat, but the toe curved up at the top into a reasonable stabbing horn.

A flutter of black feathers followed. The raven's friends had indeed come for the feast, and their approval rang out all around us in low, hoarse caws. It is a fine thing to hear, a raven's song, and still brings to mind poetry, the mountains, and the open land to discover whenever I hear it. Ravensong on a battlefield changes a bit. It is still recognizable, but the gurgling sounds of gore being gulped mingle with the songs. With that sound behind us, Kari and I draped Kraki over the remaining horse and left the birds to their feast.

"When you tell that story," said Kari, only speaking once we had crested the hill and started down again, "will it be about how one slaughtered his way through some hapless fools, or how four fought against seven and how those Rus fought honorably?"

I blinked my confusion. The Rus had intended to surround a fatigued, nearly unarmed man of no fighting skill with seven men. And then I was to lie about how many of us fought them?

"You don't understand, do you?" asked Kari.

"I do not."

"There are still Rus in the city. Do you want to have your initial mistake linger for all time, or have done with it?"

"I thought I was done with it," I admitted. "But you mean I should flatter the memory of those men so their friends and families do not look to avenge them."

"Yes. Only a fool would take revenge on a skald immortalizing the bravery of his friends. It is also a bit of misdirection. Focus on Gudbrand and his horse and armor. They will take that as the major threat without knowing Kraki is more than an ornery cook."

"Kraki is a *berserkr*!" I said.

"If you say so," said Kari. "Anyone can call himself such. The ones who do are probably not much more than big and stupid, used to fighting weaklings. You saw twelve calling themselves such before. How did they fare?"

There was no comparison to the twelve *berserkir* Magnus had killed. I knew *berserkir* from many stories and thought I had seen the first of them in that fight, but I remembered Haldor's subtle warning at the time: That Magnus was not our *berserkr*. He had killed those twelve because they were pretenders. Big, gruff, posturing—a man good at killing does not need to make such big displays.

And by contrast, there was Kraki. Slumped over a horse's back and still the scariest thing I had seen in my life. Tall, but not big. Gruff and seeming not right in the head. Never posturing or giving any indication of the real demon inside him. He did not care how others reacted. Maybe did not even know how to care about such a thing. That was the difference between a man calling himself a *berserkr* and a man who really was.

"Finnr says you should have seen him when he was younger and quicker," added Kari.

That was a comment to give any witness pause. I just saw Kraki kill six men almost entirely because he was so agile.

"The older and slower version is quite quick enough," I said. "And is there not a problem with your plan? Kraki killed those men with no help from any of us. What if he's unhappy the flattery is not directed his way?"

"He will not care about not getting more fame from your story. He knows how well he fights, he might even find it boring at this point. He will understand what you are doing as soon as he hears the story, and I think he will like it. It is his kind of humor."

"Ironic?"

"Violent."

No arguing with that.

The sun was low in the sky as we walked. Kraki's slumbering form hung over the saddle while Kari guided the horse. I had begun the day with no enemies, free rein to safely come and go, and the good feeling of solid earth under my feet. The day was not over, but I had made enemies quickly and gotten seven men killed. I had negotiated with a wizard and his—I mean *a*—raven, and committed myself to learning *galdr*, which required me to give something up.

I was supposed to help burn charcoal and still needed to learn something about fighting but had managed to avoid my responsibilities entirely. I wondered if spending too much time running around the forest and trying to not be eviscerated counted as 'going where others would not go' as Heimdall had described in my dream.

Kari's advice was good, and I took it. In town, I told a story about how four of us had just barely defeated Vladimir and his men with the advantage of a horseman and higher ground. I mentioned Ketill on purpose but said nothing of his involvement, making just enough of an implication that he may have cast a spell on the Rus to make them slow. It was meant to seem vague and mysterious to get people to insert their own interpretations and add to the story.

It worked. By the next day, they were talking about how the whole place had risen up in our defense. Animals of the forest had come to fight alongside us and witches had cursed the Rus from afar. They had bravely carried on despite all setbacks and then fought like men against terrible odds.

And I gave Kari the name that would stick. The man had saved my life with an impressive spear-catch and not even expected thanks in exchange. He was Kari Swifthand from that day forward.

I wondered if the ravens would spin a different tale from what they had seen. Like what actually happened. I decided it was of no concern. People would believe the story they wanted to believe, and I had given everyone a narrative with something they could nod their heads at in knowing satisfaction that it confirmed what they already believed. Besides, ravens were known to trade in gossip and rumor when truth was in short supply. That was more the province of squirrels, but a raven has to do what a raven has to do.

Still, it left me an unclean feeling only alcohol helped me forget. I had crafted knowing lies about what had happened and why to honor men who deserved none. It was the antithesis of my profession and exactly the kind of lies we're not supposed to tell. It was for good reason—to avoid further bloodshed—but that did not assuage my revulsion.

Haldor explained what had gone on in my absence once we had returned Kraki's snoring form to a peaceful corner in the hall. Fanya had returned to tell Gudbrand about my being chased out of town and into the forest. Being familiar with Vladimir causing trouble in general and not trusting any of the Rus to rein him in, Gudbrand had informed Haldor and hinted he should have the crew of the *Sea Squirrel* do something about it.

Then Haldor told me Huld had advised him to stay out of the forest. Her reasoning: Either I was coming out of that forest on my own, or I was not, and there was probably no finding me while I was still lost anyway. No point in sending anyone after me.

Fanya went into the forest and had not returned. No idea if she had heard Huld's advice.

Only when a raven (I could guess which one) flew into town screaming about a feast did anyone have an idea where I was. Haldor's telling was they didn't want to make a show of sending a large group.

Kraki was among the first to hear the news and never gave Haldor an answer about what he was doing. Just disappeared and then reappeared when we brought him back. He got there late only because he had no horse.

In listening to our true recounting, Haldor nodded in approval about the story Kari had me tell.

I bedded down on my pile of straw early that night. Mental exhaustion had me as soon as our evening meal, and I bowed out before anyone could ask for entertainment. The next morning would bring the raven, if he was as good as his word, and they all are. But I had exposure to much and little to show for it, with more to learn the only certainty.

I fingered the necklace of bones from my foster mother again, thinking of my home, thinking of the familiar and the safe. And I knew that whatever the raven's route back to Ketill, I would need to throw the protection of that necklace into the fire. Heimdall had told me to go where others would not, and that was not compatible with comfort and protection.

Fingering that necklace as I sat back against a support beam, I closed my eyes that night uncertain how to guide my fate. As if I had the ability to do such a thing.

CHAPTER 25

A WOLF OF BEES

STANDING JUST OUTSIDE THE LONGHOUSE IN THE PRE-DAWN twilight, I could still see my breath move in white, wispy clouds. The morning chill was getting less chilly though. Dew covered the grass in happy homage to the warming weather. Soon the sun would break through and make the rest of the day a great contrast to the cold of early morning. In air that chilly and light that dim, I was alone as far as I could see, unbothered by complaints or expectations. Expectations never seemed to be far off, making me grateful for the brief moments of peace when I had only my thoughts to bother me.

I spotted the raven when he was not far off, still before dawn. He came down in a flurry of feathers and talons to stand on the ground before me. He was annoyed, and made that annoyance plain. I took this as his natural disposition though, and so thought little of it. Perhaps he had expected to find me still sleeping at the early hour. I was awake before others, as usual, and already pondering possibilities, already outside enjoying the morning air.

One thing I wanted to know from the raven was his name. I thought he was playing a joke when he told me.

"I am Humor."

"Oh," I said, surprised. "I thought it might be 'Hunger' or 'Instigation' or somesuch."

"Good enough!" croaked Humor. "Now you can stop looking at me like an idiot."

"I do not think you are an idiot," I said. "Yet."

Humor flapped his wings in either a gesture of approval or in mock clapping to make fun of me. Almost everything he did left itself open to one interpretation as easily as another, this being only one early example. It was a bad joke for sure, but Humor loved bad jokes as much as making fun of people. Humor, I suppose now, is as varied as the minds of people.

"That was a very good joke," said Humor. "It made me laugh. It is likely to make others laugh as well. You should tell it next time you are performing. I think . . ." and he continued at length and I tried to let him burn out the commentary by ignoring him. Eventually, he ran out of ways to say the same thing.

"You can turn that ability to misunderstand into a valuable—" but Humor was cut off mid-sentence.

"I think I fed some ravens yesterday," said Kraki, too loud not to demand our attention and too slow to be all he would say. Had he been up early and on the other side of the hall, or just very quiet in coming out? Either way, he was not quiet now. "Well, what do the ravens have to say about that?"

Kraki was looking at the bird, and I noted that might give me time to run. You may note there was no reason for me to run and that in fact, this man had just saved my life by putting himself in danger. It was not practicality that drove my urge to get away, just terror of the man I had seen turn into a killing machine. That and recalling the glee with which he had done it.

"A good feast, but I've had better," replied Humor.

"Doubtless that," said Kraki. "But the king has held a peace in Denmark for some years now. When was the last time you saw that many dead men in one place?" Kraki shook it off but did not wait for an answer. The next statement was addressed to me. "I heard your tale of it, skald. It was poorly done."

The words stuck in me like knives and I could not help myself.

"That story was part of the plan!" I croaked in disbelief. "Even Kari said—"

"Kari Swifthand!" he said, shaking his head as he turned around and stepped towards me. Apparently he did not approve of the byname. "You are soft. We had to save you because you are soft and then you had to save yourself again by telling that story."

"This is good," said Humor. "I thought I was just coming to get the skald, but now I have gossip to share! Sweet, sweet gossip!" He took to the air and rose high enough to be out of Kraki's reach. It was a wise decision to do so before he shouted "Kraki *likes soft men!*"

The old man bristled with anger at his inability to pull down Humor and throttle him. His teeth and fists clenched and his eyes reddened until widening in sudden realization. In an instant, he was reaching to the ground and hurling a rock into the air.

Humor was wise to this possibility before it happened though, and swooped out of the rock's trajectory while singing "Kraki *spends all his time with soft men! He must like them a lot! When he isn't among men who are hard! Ahahahahahahaha!*"

Humor flapped to gain height and glided in a circle around the hall's roof. Kraki reached for another rock but did not throw it as the bird was just out of range. Instead, his angry gaze fell on me.

He said nothing. I felt the blood drain from my face as all manner of unpleasant implications filled my imagination. The look was enough to stir a fear and move me to action.

"Humor, bring me to your master as you were tasked! And quit your insults if you do not wish to be renamed Parsimony." That name was probably a stretch for a raven, but this was all for Kraki to hear. It was the first part I knew would get his attention.

"I belong to no man, skald," shouted Humor. "Check your hair to be reminded if you must."

"But you are an oathbreaker if you spend your time as such instead of taking me to Ketill," I said. "And here is the man who gave a feast to you and your friends. You repay gifts with insults, is maybe what we should say of the ravens of Lejre. How would your friends enjoy that?"

Humor stared at me from his perch. Ravens have no facial expressions to read, but it was obvious he was weighing options. Finally, he decided and said, "You Sea-Norse are no fun at all. I will stick to the forest. But no secrets did I promise the humorless, nor that the journey would be easy."

"No argument," I said, realizing I had an excuse to both get away from Kraki and position the bird where I wanted him. "To the hall then. We will eat before we go."

Kraki growled at me. "So you found a wizard. To what end?"

I swallowed and decided I should start walking away as I answered or risk never being able to walk away.

"He knows things, and I have questions," I said. My hand must have gone to my new acquisition from the previous day given my sense of danger. Even unarmed, Kraki made fun of me for it.

"And that axe—is that for questions?"

I wanted to be away from there faster than I could walk. "That depends on the answers," I said, wondering what I even meant by that. It elicited a full, throaty laugh from Kraki that stayed with me even after he turned toward other business. Humor took to my shoulder and bade me lead the way.

The hall was filled with the smells of fire and food and the sounds of washing and murmuring. Magnus yawned and stretched while Kari buried his head in a washbowl. Haldor spooned porridge into a bowl and sat down on a bench across from Ulf. I did the same.

The king sat on his high seat, away from all but the queen. Those two sat speaking quietly, and I was grateful to have the attention of neither.

"That is not what I eat," said the raven, eyeing my breakfast.

"No eyeballs served here," I said, as if I was going to share in the first place. "If you don't wish to eat, don't eat." I could smell the grains that had been turned into pulpy mush and the salt that had been added for flavor. The morning meal was not much, but at least Ragnvald was generous with the additions. A little salt pork was also out, and even honey to sweeten the porridge. My stomach rumbled. I knew I needed a bowl before setting out.

"Are you the keeper of the bird, or is the bird your keeper?" said Ulf.

Waking up early was a natural inclination, but I was glad of it since it usually kept me away from Ulf. I was uncertain around him, even more uncertain than I usually was, which was saying something. Whatever impression you might have, I felt safe around Huld, who had beaten me senseless and most recently yanked my hair and hissed in my ear. Ulf, by contrast, always met me with a smile and a genial word, but I felt the need to guard against his sideways comments.

"Caw!" said the raven, mocking the comment. "I knew you had a dwarven smith, but here is a professional blade polisher!" Whatever that meant.

Some of the men chuckled, more than at Ulf's joke. His eyes narrowed and his lips thinned, preparing a response, but it was cut off as the raven turned his attention to Haldor. "And look at this great warrior! What a wolf of bees you are to eat that much honey at once!"

Haldor snarled at the bird but kept his seat.

"Pay no heed to that thing," said Ragnvald, breaking away for a moment from his conversation with Alfhild. "We have ravens about with more comportment. That one takes his cues from a charcoal burner in the forest. We do some business with him. He is not quite right. Neither is his raven."

Alfhild nodded. "Wise words, my husband."

Humor squawked angrily at yet another implication he was owned. I just about started squawking at how the king could fail to notice he was being patronized.

Yes, the charcoal burner in the forest. Not the dangerous wizard even a murderous troll was afraid to cross paths with. The king knew very little of the truth about his realm, it seemed to me. I exchanged glances with Humor, and in silence we agreed to say nothing to contradict him.

"Question, skald," said Haldor, who beckoned me sit across from him. "All the crew can fight, and all the crew can do something in addition to fighting." I looked sideways to the source of a loud fart and saw Svein scratching his belly. "Almost all the crew can do something in addition to fighting," Haldor amended.

"I have many skills," I said, unable to recall any just as I sat down. I resolved to answer Haldor's question and be off as soon as possible.

"Everyone fights, including you. And that means training. Every day. But training begins and you are nowhere to be found until we hear word you started a fight. Explain yourself."

"Other than you have been starting fights, he means," added Utstein from down the other end of the table. He was seated across from his brother, already engrossed in a game of *hnefatafl* while they ate. Utstein was playing the attacker again. His black pieces were still in their starting positions at the edges of the board, so no advantage had yet been taken.

"I noticed you two take a lot of breaks from training," growled Haldor. "Maybe we train you harder to make up for it."

"Hard training makes for hard men," said Innstein, moving a piece without looking up.

"If hard men are what you like, so much the better," added Utstein.

"Hard to see how that makes a profit though," finished Innstein.

"Ha!" whispered the raven into my ear. "You should stick with those two. I like them."

Haldor ground his porridge overlong with his spoon while staring hard at the brothers. They ignored it and if anything slowed the progress they were making with both the game and their food. Haldor turned his attention back to me with no less rancor in his gaze than if he had continued staring at those two trying his patience.

"The charcoal burner out in the forest," I said. "He is no charcoal burner. Or I mean, he does that for payment and to be mostly left alone. But he is a powerful wizard—a *galdramaðr*, and an old one at that. The Rus would not go near him. Even the troll avoids him. Here is something truly unique, and I need to find out more. He said he would even teach me magic."

Ulf harrumphed at that idea and shook his head. "What magic is that? Paying to have someone cursed?"

"He asked no payment," I said, electing not to mention the part about giving something up. Perhaps Ketill had meant I had to give up some money and I had been too dense to realize it. The question kindled a suspicion in me, held back only by an instinct to say less than was necessary in that company. "And we discussed no curses."

"What did you discuss then?"

"Runes," I said, intending to be terse. But Ketill's words came back to me. What did knowledge cost Odin? Not money or treasure, those were not even considerations. "And what it cost Odin to learn. He was challenging me."

"Well," said Ulf, "it might be a poor look not to meet such a challenge." He traded looks with Haldor, who was not having a good morning. Not a chance would he have approved of my running around a forest with a wizard instead of learning to fight. But Ulf thought it a good idea; that was in my favor. Perhaps he was giving me a bit more leeway after our previous inter-actions.

"Every man has a job," said Haldor after a long pause. "And every man follows our rules. You heard those two,"—nodding in the direction of the brothers—"they want more money. More treasure. And we could do that quickly if we raided and took people to be sold as thralls. But they know we have a rule against that, so you know what they don't do?" The giant man leaned in, head cocked, and beckoned me to do the same. "They don't even think it," he whispered. "Or their heads would be our ship's prow."

"Dramatic," said Utstein.

"Also quite temporary," added Innstein. "Unless you enjoy the smell."

Haldor's eyes were red as he tossed his empty bowl aside and rose. He was being serious, and the 'Steins were not, and the skald was acting like a jackass. He looked close to doing more than talking to resolve all that.

I tried to swallow but my mouth had gone dry. This was a gentle warning, the only kind that could signify danger if I did not heed it. I nodded, wondering what this had to do with me, but dared not move otherwise.

"The wizard who burns charcoal," said Haldor, his eyes softening. "We don't need a wizard. But the dwarf needs to forge a sword, if this prophecy is true, and he needs charcoal to fire his forge. See to the charcoal, then."

I nodded, taking that as a suggestion I might very likely consider doing.

"But as for the *galdramaðr*," said Haldor, "you should be wary. Their ways are strange. We do not rely on spirits for strength. Only on ourselves, and each other. Understand?"

Spirits! He was thinking of *seiðr*, not the runic nature of *galdr*. I nodded and would obey, thinking I knew better than he.

I did not. I would not fully understand Haldor or his rules until much later.

CHAPTER 26

HUMOR IS A RELATIVE THING

"You do it kind of—" Humor paused, eyeing the others still in the hall. He froze, spun around on one foot, and then struck a pose as he hopped onto the other. His beak pointed away from me while he held his wings, one forward and one back. "Kind of like that!"

Still on one foot, he looked as if he were imitating a running man mid-stride. Or at least as much as he could imitate it, being a raven.

My patience was no longer thin—it had worn all the way through by the end of the meal. I had assumed the bird would tell me directions and I would follow those directions. It was nothing so straightforward as that. Humor had begun by admonishing me against following directions too rote. It was a feel, a pull, an instinct, he had said, again advising that I should not go alone.

I had little idea why I was trying to find this old wizard myself other than I wanted him to teach me some esoteric lore only he knew. What would that accomplish? Nothing, I supposed. Other than I wanted knowledge like other men wanted gold.

And why demand to go alone? Selfishness or practicality, depending on how charitable you want to describe it. If I let Humor lead me, I would be in his debt, and I would need to repay it. Debts are to be avoided when possible.

This was a debt I could avoid. Or I could if the damned bird would stop giving me such evasive answers.

I had thought bringing the bird into the hall and letting the others see I was favored by it was a good idea. The plan, as plans do, had not gone as planned. The bird had all manner of explanations for finding one's way through the forest, each as unlikely as the rest.

"Did you just do a little dance?" I asked. "It looked like you did a little dance, then could not remember what to do next, so you froze in place."

"So what if I did? You remember my name, don't you?"

"Oh, well, then let me try—" But I did not try to do what Humor had done. I instead gained two steps closer before I lunged at the bird and grabbed his throat.

Perhaps it had been only a few minutes, but it felt as though Humor had been 'instructing' me how to find Ketill for an hour. I had been duped into a series of foolish acts in front of several interested crewmembers and a few of the king's ladies. Even some of the thralls were laughing. It had begun with closing my eyes and kneeling, trying to focus on 'seeing without my eyes.' I had sniffed like a dog, tasted dirt, and eventually would be made to do a little dance. I would have no more of it.

"*Tell me where the old man is!*" I screamed into the bird's face.

"The skald is coming unhinged," said Innstein, otherwise engrossed in a game of *hnefatafl*.

Utstein shrugged and made a counter-move.

Humor croaked as if I were strangling him, which I was not. Or maybe I was, but I was not about to believe him. So in my left hand I held the flailing raven and with my right I slipped the knot of my sling onto one of his legs and held the other end. Then I loosened my grip so he could breathe.

It was a ruse, and he squirmed out of my left hand, flapping wildly. I let him go and heard a squawk of triumph as he flapped.

Humor's escape to the air was short-lived. He flew a few feet and then I jerked him out of the air and back into my grip.

I squeezed harder. He made the same sounds, hoping for some relief, but I continued the pressure and saw the fear in his eyes. He tried to say something but could not. All I could think was this thing was making fun of me when it was supposed to be aiding me, and that I'd had enough with being made fun of. I stared back at him with the world falling away. It was murder on my mind, thinking nothing of Ketill or anyone else.

"Is that going to be your first kill?" asked Kari, in between draining his cup. "Will that be the first of all or just the first of this trip?"

His tone was matter of fact, caring little one way or the other. But the question brought me back to my senses, and as Humor gasped for air I realized I did not want to be known as Ansgar Ravensbane. The other birds would never let me hear the end of it.

I turned Humor upside-down and held him by his feet. With great and dramatic effort, he breathed again and called for help.

"You owe me," I said, striding out of the hall. An idea had occurred. I just needed a reasonable co-conspirator.

"That—well—but wait!"

There was a lot of pecking and flapping as I strode down the hill to Finnr's forge. It was a lively walk and drew a fair amount of attention due to the noise, but I would not be deterred and I could not think of anyone else.

The dwarf greeted me as I opened the ramshackle door to the forge. I responded with some terseness. It was not Finnr I needed.

"*I need you to hold this for me,*" I said to Ulfberht.

"*Bad luck to eat them,*" replied Ulfberht. "*Also, I don't think they taste very good.*" He took Humor by the legs, though. Too gently at first, so I wrapped my sling tighter around his feet.

"What are we doing in a forge?" demanded Humor. "I can tell you this is not the way to find that old man, I can tell you that. And I am going to need to fly at some point."

I explained in Frankish that Humor had guided me from a wizard's hidden home out of the forest, but that I had secured a promise to be taught how to find my way there and back on my own. I then explained how the bird was failing in this task. I handed Ulfberht my axe, made my request, and bound Humor's feet with my sling before handing him over.

Then came my own ruse.

"*I need you to keep him bound,*" I said, "*until tomorrow at noon. You can let him go then. But don't tell him that.*"

"*What do I tell him?*"

"*That his life is tied to mine now. I will return by noon tomorrow, or you will chop off his head.*"

"What are you saying?" asked the bird.

Ulfberht looked at Humor. His Norse was probably not good enough for a witty quip. He accomplished one anyway with a smile and a wink.

"I am going to the forest by myself," I said. "And I intend to find Ketill. And after I have spoken with him, I intend to find my way out. I will do this all by noon tomorrow, and you will tell me how."

"But I should really be with you when you try to—"

"And when I am back tomorrow, I will find Ulfberht here, and I will unbind you, and you will do as you please. But if I am not back by noon, you will have a problem. And your problem will be that Ulfberht will cut your head off and make a charm out of your skull."

Humor did not believe me for the first few seconds. Then he did. A more useful explanation began soon after.

"You can—you can follow the signs in the wood!"

"What signs? The trees will point me to Ketill?" I asked.

"No. Well, maybe. Sometimes. But probably not, *it's more like*," gulped the raven, seeing the blade flash mid-sentence. "It's more like you have to watch and listen. Take me, for example: If you used my beak as a direction, you would just go in the direction I was standing. But you might catch a glimpse of my shadow out of the corner of your eye, and maybe it suddenly went the opposite direction it should be. Or maybe it looked like I was flying with the wind, but the wind was blowing against me."

"You will not be there, as I have made clear."

"Or something else! Something different from what's expected. You have to pay attention to details. Those differences are the hints. If the forest accepts you and you follow the hints it gives you, it will bring you to Ketill."

"What if I fail to see the hints?"

"Then maybe you get lost and turn into a tree. You should take me with you! It's dangerous out there!"

"Has the troll ever been seen by daylight?" I asked.

If Humor's face could have scrunched up, it would have.

"I will take that as a 'no.'"

I had little worry of encountering Lejre's troll while the sun was out. Such things were the moon's minions, at least often enough that I was not concerned about it. Most such things had a great deal of power at night, but were so sensitive to the sun it might turn them to stone.

Regardless of my confidence, it did make more sense to take Humor with me. But I didn't want to return a favor. More than that, I was young and had never found learning a new thing to be that difficult. I didn't even want to bring Ulfberht with me right away, because it might distract the wizard, and I was impatient to learn.

My limbs had a restless energy I had never known as I left the forge. My steps were light and quick and effortless. I smiled, and pretty girls in town smiled back and giggled. When I reached the edge of the forest I stopped and thought I might compose a poem for such an important occasion. But I could not wait, and so instead I looked back, took a deep breath, and stepped in.

I could bring Ulfberht next time. This time I had something to prove, even if only to myself.

Chapter 27

The Blade Polisher

When I marched off to the forest, I was looking for things out of the ordinary. Everything familiar seemed new and interesting, and potentially a sign. I was not running and not following this time, but exploring as I followed the raven's directions. Look for the hints.

The sight of three naked witches was somewhat of a distraction to noticing the forest's hints.

I hadn't gotten very far in the first place, and it wasn't the witches I saw first. A dark figure stood further down the general path I was headed in, cloaked and hiding behind a tree. All I could make out was the outline of a man hunched over at first. His attention was decidedly toward the river, and I was too far out of his peripheral vision for him to notice me.

My first thought was to remain silent and not be noticed. I had no idea who this was or why he seemed to be hiding when no one was around. Troll or not, there were still outlaws and other bandits who might rob me. Discretion, I decided, would be the only part of valor in this case.

Hiding is just a matter of remaining still and using your surroundings. Watching is a little different because it requires a vantage point. That requires movement, the primary sign to others that you exist.

I was good at both. To investigate, I made my way back to stay out of sight while getting a better look at this watcher. I took a circuitous route around to go behind him and find a spot in the dense underbrush even further down the same path. Then I lay flat on the earth, peeking through stems while thick green leaves covered me.

I had picked a lucky spot and needed to move little to see what was going on. Then I had wished I had walked on by. The man was masturbating. And it was Ulf!

I looked away and grimaced. No un-seeing that.

Ulf's attention was fixed squarely on the river. Not on the river itself though. That was when I saw what he was watching.

Three naked handmaidens bathing was a startling sight. Valborg leaned back and floated away belly-up on the water without effort, her body stretched out and relaxed. Aldis swam further out, her golden hair disappearing with the rest of her down into the deepest part of the calm water. She came up and found a lone rock to sit on, glistening in the sunlight.

There was Fanya on the bank, washing in knee-deep water. Her body shimmered in the sunlight and, if not made plain already, affected me more than I wanted to admit. My heart was on fire while my guts froze. She was the most beautiful thing I had ever seen, a goddess if I had ever known what one might look like, and I sat entranced.

Their voices carried over the water like sweet birdsong. They were at ease and joked with one another. Those sweet smiles melted my soul, and had I not been hiding my presence, I would likely have done anything they had asked.

I won't lie and say I didn't want to look. I did want to. And I looked. And then I looked away, ashamed. And then I thought: What sorts of things did witches do to men who spied on them while bathing?

I was well hidden, but paralyzed. I couldn't move to get away without alerting either the witches or Ulf. Or both, which would be the worst of all outcomes. It would not matter that I had happened upon the place by chance, and I shuddered to think of my fate given a wrong move. How long my trance lasted I could not say. I was in a daze and only came out of it with the sound of light rustling while Ulf backed away from his hiding place.

He was finished and removing himself from the scene. He was also about to realize he was being watched if he came my way, and would likely be none too happy about it.

Ulf backed away from his vantage point with slow, lithe movements. He stopped as Fanya turned back toward the bank, looking up but apparently seeing nothing. Then he continued moving away when her attention was turned again toward the river. To keep out of sight, he was moving my way, his exit strategy taking him perhaps a dozen feet past where I lay.

As he moved out of sight of anyone on the river's bank, Ulf yawned the yawn of a contented man. He walked by me without noticing and meandered his way back the way I had come, back towards the city. His slow gait had me holding my breath overlong so I would only let it out when he was far enough away to not hear me.

When I did breathe again, my chest heaved and my mind raced as to what I should do. I did not want to overtake him in the forest and need to explain our intersection, nor did I want to wait for the witches to leave that place. For the time being, I thought, I will remain hidden and think of a plan.

As I watched the last view of Ulf fade away into the forest, I mastered my breathing and calmed myself. Whatever I did, it would be better to leave that place right away. I held off to wait for some sound of indication from the bank it might be safe. But I heard no more voices and, in my head alone, cursed the lull in conversation.

This continued for a longer time than I was comfortable with. Just at the dim edge of my awareness was silence. Not the silence of quiet, the silence of stalking. Having exercised patience enough already I turned myself back to see what was happening.

I noticed the red hair first, and then the pale skin. "Hello, skald," said Fanya. "Does the forest floor prove a fine bed?" She wore a wry smile and nothing else. Her visage froze me, body and mind. "Shall I call my sisters over?" she asked, half-leaning on her spear.

"I, uh, I meant no harm," I said, knowing I had nothing more intelligent to say and still cursing the foolish statement.

"Of course not. If you had, I would have known. You are not in your element, skulking in the woods or trying the water for any favors. What should I do with you, do you think?"

She had my fate in her hands and knew it. My only comfort was to read playfulness in her smile rather than contempt.

"Nothing?" I asked. "Nothing is a safe choice. It leaves all manner of options available for later. Yes, I think nothing is the best decision right now."

Fanya threw her head back and covered her mouth. At first, I thought she would burst out laughing and my embarrassment would be multiplied by her sisters. Then I could see she intended to remain quiet but was genuinely amused by my predicament.

"But I have caught a little skald!" she said. "Tell me, little skald, why should I let you go? I know. If you answer me a question truly, you may go and I will not speak of your presence. Is that agreed? For that, and a verse. You are a skald after all."

I nodded.

"Good. Then tell me the name of that man who spied on us. And why he was sent."

My eyes widened. She had found me, but she also knew Ulf had been there? And that he had been polishing his spear from behind a tree?

"His name is Ulf, but I do not know why he was sent, or even if he was. How do you know he was sent?"

"Of course he was not sent," she said. "That part was to test you. If he had been sent for any real purpose, he would have watched us for something other than making a maid of his right hand."

I stared, still disbelieving and half-expecting to be run through at any moment.

"You answered my question truly, but it was not difficult. Perhaps I can take that verse another time when you can catch your breath, but only if you answer another question for me."

The stuttering gibberish that came out of me next is not worth recounting, but was at least recognizable as 'Yes.'

"Where are you going in the forest?"

"Why do you care?" I shot back automatically and stood up.

What an interesting question to ask! I was of no consequence to Fanya that I knew of. Ketill neither, unless some game I knew nothing of was afoot. Able to identify two snooping people without paying any attention, but not able to scry a path to Ketill's house. The forest chose its friends, indeed.

"I have been about my own business," I continued. "I needed to find the charcoal burner."

"The charcoal burner."

"We need more charcoal in town."

"That makes sense. Did you find him?"

"I did."

"And?"

"And you are out of questions," I said, turning around.

"You still owe me a verse!"

I had intended to give it later, but her tone had changed. Gone was the pure practicality, the joy in seeing me squirm. She wanted to hear me speak a verse. How can a skald say no to that?

> "Few friends
>   found in this forest
> spare a man
>   the spear's point.
> Hospitality
>   helps the skald
> watching in the woods,
>   wandering to and fro."

I thought it was good at the time. Writing it down from memory punctuates now how utterly mediocre it was. But I smiled at her then as I walked away and she smiled back. It made me feel confident, that random stumbling into success which I then attributed to skill.

It was like I knew what I was doing, and was even good at it. There is no feeling more dangerous.

CHAPTER 28

FIRST AMONG LESSONS

BRIMMING WITH CONFIDENCE, I PLUNGED DEEPER INTO THE forest. There were no markers or points of reference. The forest was ever-changing and thus could guide or confuse its inhabitants as it wished. The trick, or the only way to navigate it, was to behave, pay attention, and follow the suggestions it provided.

It was a forest. No shroud of tentacled branches or roots coalesced to point my way. No birds sang in voices I could suddenly understand as if they spoke my language. The wind did not whistle in any particular direction. There were trees and rocks and dirt. It was quiet and shady.

I had no idea where to go, and some of my contagious energy left me with the realization that my course was not as obvious as expected. So I walked on, trying to observe, trying to be patient.

To my senses, I never changed direction and continued walking in a straight line. That was likely impossible, but I had no other course to take. What direction was the forest giving me? I could not read any of its signs, if they even existed. Eventually I stopped to look all around me, and realized I was entirely lost.

Then I started to see signs, and the forest got weird.

I came upon a small, circular clearing and saw a fox sitting at its outskirts. It looked at me and rose to all fours. Then it let out a high-pitched 'Yip' and bounded to the middle of the clearing. There was another fox, and it came out to greet its friend. The two met in the middle, sat down, and stared at me for several seconds.

"So . . . so what is the sign?"

The foxes then ran off in opposite directions, to my left and right.

Was I supposed to follow one? I could not follow both. Was there a hidden meaning? Five minutes passed with nothing further happening.

"I just want to find my way to Ketill's house," I said to nothing in particular. "The *galdramaðr?* He knows things I want to know."

Ten minutes passed with nothing more happening. I moved forward into the clearing and heard a rustling sound at the clearing's edge. Behind a large tree were two rabbits engaged in energetic copulation. The male looked me in the eye and, I swear, winked at me.

Stepping away from the sex rabbits, I felt my shoe find a surprise I swore had not been there before. It was that feeling of putting your heel down in soft, slippery mud. And you are going to look, you have to. But you know before you look it was not mud, your mind just wants it desperately to be mud rather than what it is.

Judging from its size, the dung pile had to be from a bear.

This was indirectly confirmed by a growl from behind me. The bear was standing on its hind legs. It was taller than me, with considerably more bulk. It looked at me in appraisal, deciding whether I was worth snacking on or not. Like the foxes and the rabbit, the bear had only a moment's interest. It went down to all fours and walked away.

I decided to go in the opposite direction of the bear and worry about wiping my shoe off later.

The next minutes I spent paying a good deal less attention to what the forest was telling me and more attention to what I was stepping on. I wanted as much distance as possible between myself and that clearing, so I put my head down and plunged deeper into the forest.

I know it was deeper because the treetops got higher and the shade got darker. I was so lost I wondered if the forest had decided to repay my joke on Humor with a cruel jest of its own.

A flicker of bright colors caught my eye. Just a hint of them, and then the color was gone. I watched another moment and it reappeared. The kingfisher had perched on a branch just above me, copper-breasted, the blue of its back so bright it seemed to glow. The hand-sized bird eyed me sideways, showing off its sword-like beak.

Once it had my attention, I wondered if it would speak to me.

No such luck, I thought, and shook my head. Then sudden realization took me: I was trading stares with a bird that was rarely seen by humans. Kingfishers kept themselves hidden much of the time, watching for prey in the river from on high. Despite their bright colors, it was rare to see one, and even rarer that it be social.

"Are you a sign from the forest?" I asked.

The kingfisher chirped.

Ravens talk, of course. How else would Odin know what was happening in Midgard than to get his information from story-mongering ravens? And perhaps the odd eagle or squirrel, not that those usually have anything to say worth hearing. Eagles are imperious assholes who think and talk only of themselves. Squirrels prefer rumor and gossip to the stories that ravens traffick in, and value style more than substance. The less truth to the gossip or insult while hanging on to the barest shred of truth as its basis, the more valuable these were.

But of other animals speech was unexpected. Except maybe dragons, and they tended to end conversations by eating the conversant. It was only because I was expecting the unexpected that I inquired.

Unsurprisingly, there was no answer from the kingfisher.

Or rather, no speech. He was still staring at me when I decided this had to be a sign to follow.

So follow I did. Soon the forest floor was a path and the bird flapped from branches on one side to the other. It chirped as it led me on, flying just ahead of me. I increased my pace. Soon I was running. The faster I went, the more excited this kingfisher became until it stopped and waited for me on top of a boulder.

"Where to now?" I asked, pausing to think. Maybe the bird required a verse. No, verses were for people. Sometimes for ravens, but this bird had no human speech. "I know. You need a name."

Though wild, there are some animals I came to favor in my travels and some I disliked. Kingfishers always intrigued me. I saw one hunting once as I sat quietly on a riverbank. It hovered still, patiently watching, until it dove down and skewered a fish with its weapon-like beak.

"Brandhofdi, I name you," I said. Sword-headed. Maybe he was Heimdall's bird.

The kingfisher chirped at a higher pitch and flapped its wings. Then it flew off, away from any path, and out of my sight.

Ahead of me, in the direction Brandhofdi had flown, was thick greenery going up a hill. It took me some time to find my way through, but the reward was immediate. As I cleared the last of the thick bushes, Ketill's hut lay only a few dozen strides in front of me. I could already smell his cookfire burning.

I almost let myself in before realizing I should wipe my shoe off first. No sense making a name for myself as Ansgar Shitheel.

It was in the middle of cleaning off my shoe that Ketill emerged. Holding the side of the doorway for support with one hand, he swayed in a stupor. With the other hand he held the light from his eyes, even though he was still standing in the shade.

"It is early to be drinking," I said.

"Drinking is never early for a wizard, nor is it late. A wizard drinks precisely when he means to. Now, where is the bird?"

"I left him in Lejre," I said. "I wanted to find my way here on my own. Or did he not tell you he agreed to help me do that?"

Ketill stared at me as if suspicious. "And you trusted him to tell you rightly?"

"I bound him and left him with a friend. I told him if I did not return by noon the next day that my friend would kill him."

"Well," said Ketill, stepping back inside, "I suppose I will have less company in the future then."

I followed the old man in through the still-open door, and closed it behind me. The openness of the forest had given me a sense of wanderlust, but as the door closed, I could feel my world constrict. Ketill's house was dark and smelled of smoke and spilled ale. I hoped learning would mostly be outside.

"I only told Humor that," I said. "He does not understand languages other than Norse, or at least he did not seem to know what I said to my friend in Frankish. I left instructions, yes, but they were for him to release Humor at noon tomorrow."

"Hmmm?" said Ketill, filling a horn with more ale.

He gestured at a ceramic cup for me to help myself with. I had to accept or it would insult his hospitality, but I considered abstaining all the same when I saw that dirty vessel. No sense in walking through the mysteries of the forest only to quit now, though. I blew what seemed like ten years of dust out of the thing, sneezed, and poured myself some ale.

"Everything I have done lately has run me into unexpected problems, so I could not be sure I would return by dark. But Humor will not know this until later, and I told my friend to play the part of the would-be executioner up until that point."

Ketill drained his horn as I said this, his eyes fixed upon me, and let out a cleansing belch after. He stared straight ahead then, and I wondered if he had become confused and drifted off. After a moment he smiled and laughed a little, then a little more. Soon he guffawed so hard he doubled over, at pains to laugh as hard as he meant to and hold on to the table for support.

"So!" he exclaimed among the laughter. "So you played a hideous joke—on Humor? *Ha!*"

It had been entirely practical at the time, but now that I thought about it, I laughed as well.

"We will have to congratulate him on his bravery when he arrives!" he said. Finally, I had done something right.

I told Ketill about my journey through the forest. I was most interested in the meaning of the foxes, rabbits, and bear. He waved off the topic as unimportant.

"That raven is not the only thing with a sense of humor," he said.

"The kingfisher did not appear to be playing a joke on me," I said.

This part of the story was far more interesting to Ketill. He let me describe it fully without interruption, then nodded while I expressed how grateful I was to that bird.

"More grateful to the kingfisher than to the raven?" he asked.

"The raven shit on my head and only traded what he knew for a favor," I said. "The kingfisher brought me to a new and interesting place without compensation."

"Oh, did it!" said Ketill, giving an evil grin. "How certain you are. Let me ask you then: If the kingfisher asked a favor in return now, would you be bound to do it?"

I nearly blurted out 'No,' but caught myself. Considering the question, I realized at once the answer was unclear. "Possibly," I said. "It would not bind me to do just anything, but I could not just refuse."

"You are in its debt, then."

"It would need to start talking first!" I said. "Why does it matter?"

"The kingfisher did something for you, now what do you owe?"

"How is that the point? I thought the point was you would teach me magic."

"Do you know why I am asking the questions?"

Because you are a crazy old man? I bit back. "No."

Ketill took a long draught of ale and wiped the drippings from his beard before continuing. He spoke slowly this time, a contrast to the rapid questions just before. "Why would I help you gain the power of the runes if you cannot even grasp such a simple dynamic?"

The question hit me as if Svein had taken his massive fist and rammed it into my stomach. All this time I had assumed I could learn anything new, and it was merely a matter of access to knowledge. It had never occurred to me that I might not be able to grasp certain things, or that any conception was beyond me. The realization that it was filled me with dread. I was grateful for the fire coloring the room because I was certain I had turned red with embarrassment.

Ketill was not confused or off-topic. He was razor-sharp and had honed in on my inadequacy. He was also the first man to ever tell me, among the many criticisms I had otherwise endured, that I was less intelligent than I thought I was.

"I have learned difficult things before," I said.

Not often. In fact, not much in recent memory, unless you called my recent failings learning. But memory farther back reminded me it could be done.

When I was much younger, perhaps nine or ten, Halstein was instructing me in Latin during one of our long ski trips to trade for supplies. I had gone from a quick study to the language not coming along well by the last day.

"I can't do this," I had said, concluding that if something did not come naturally, easily, and with little frustration, that it was better left for other pursuits.

I told my foster father this, and he listened in the same sage silence characteristic of him hearing other grave news. When we returned home, I was surprised to see him walk in and shut the door behind him.

I pounded on the door. "Let me in! A storm is coming!"

Which it was. It was Dafvik in winter, and we had arrived back just ahead of more wind and snow.

"Life is too difficult for you," he had said. "You said so yourself. Go off into the snow, then. You will find the result natural. And easy. And it will give you little frustration."

I wailed in horror, equally at the danger of being left outside and at not getting my way after giving a reasonable explanation as to why I should.

I heard the door being reinforced from the other side. He replied in Latin that I must complete my lessons to get in. Else I could continue with my decision to quit, but would I please go elsewhere if that were the case.

"But I don't know how to do what you want me to dooooooooooo," I had cried.

"Yes you do," he had said smoothly in Latin. "But you do not like doing it because it is difficult for you. So you think you cannot do it."

Halstein's voice came back to me as clear as that day.

"What you can learn has nothing to do with how easy it is when you begin. All things can be learned. Patience and discipline over time are how you learn; we need to kill this impulse only to do what is easy for you.

"Now finish your lesson."

I was so angry! I knew he was right, and that made me even angrier. I took off away from the house in protest of everything and got five, perhaps even six steps before the cold wind hit me. There was no way I intended to die out there. Freezing to death might be even more unpleasant than learning Latin.

Returning to the door, I announced my intentions, using my skis and sleeping fur to construct a temporary wind-break behind me.

"I am trying to keep warm while I learn your stupid language!" I shouted back at him when asked what I was doing.

And in that gap caught between the freezing weather and the warmth and security in the house is where I learned that most elusive of secrets: Learning is work, and work is a choice.

Also that Latin is a language with too many cases, but mostly that learning is a choice.

Hours later, and with fresh snow falling on me, I finished my lesson. I never complained about easy things to learn or difficult things to learn again. That memory came back so clear I thought I could smell the hot stew waiting for me when Halstein let me back in.

I realized I had drifted off, my eyes closed.

Ketill stared at me, expressionless. Perhaps he sensed the force of what had come back to me and was waiting for its expression. So I told him.

"I do not know why you are asking me those questions," I said. "But what

I can learn has nothing to do with how easily I grasp something right away. All things can be learned."

Ketill's eyes, even the bad one, opened wider than I thought they physically could. He burst into hacking laughter and pounded his thigh with his fist. It was minutes before he was ready to speak again, some of that time spent recovering from the exertion. Was he making fun of me? Was my most formative early experience a joke to him? Had I said what he needed to hear?

I could not tell, but there was nothing to be done about it. I pondered the long walk back to the hall at Lejre if I had to leave with nothing. It would be a frustrating walk, but I would live, and I would find some other way to be useful to the crew.

"Then you already know the first lesson. Now show me what you are willing to give up," said Ketill after a long delay. "Then maybe I teach the second lesson."

CHAPTER 29

WILL AND INTELLECT

There is nothing so refreshing as deciding to do something and marching off with new intentions. There is little more difficult than to follow through and do it.

"Will and intellect," said the wizard.

"Which one is this teaching?" I asked, slinking back against the tree trunk.

Ketill smiled and loosed. I pitched forward and down at first, but I marked the arrow coming at a higher speed than I had anticipated. I stumbled and, fearing I had no other way left to dodge, let my feet out from under me to slam straight down. The arrow thudded into the tree and buzzed sideways from its fishtailed flight.

Ketill might be a skilled archer while sober. I wondered if I would live long enough to find out.

"Back against the tree," he said.

I had struck off from Lejre feeling on top of the world. I believed I had conquered the forest and won a battle of wits against a wizard. I had gotten what I wanted and I could do anything. Now I wondered if I could quit without cowardice.

But quitting now would be the definition of cowardice. I would be *argr*, unmanly. Soft, cowardly, useless, my honor as scarred as if I let random *jǫtnar* use my backside for their pleasure every nine nights.

And I would have gone through the initial ritual, the one Ketill performed in his hut, for nothing.

It had been a short and simple ceremony, to my surprise. When he mentioned it, I expected to have to find some forest beast to sacrifice. Instead, he took the cauldron off the flame and made the fire very hot. He asked me what I was willing to sacrifice of myself. It was as I expected, and I handed over the necklace of bones given to me by my foster mother.

It was no light offering; Taika was the only person in the world I fully loved, trusted, or felt comfortable around. Though I did not understand the necklace's protection, I had little doubt that it protected me. She had not explained fully, and I had not needed her to. It reminded me of safety and understanding. Both of which I wished for more of as I learned magic by dodging arrows.

"What is the test?" I shouted. "You could have killed me there."

"So could your last sea voyage have. So could those Rus. Many things can kill you. You will learn better with your mouth shut." Ketill nocked and drew again, his aim wavering left to right like a man who could barely see me. Which, I supposed, he barely could. "What are you worried about an old man for?" He loosed again and the arrow came dead center at me, its ugly flight my only saving grace.

There was no room to fall and no way I could leap over it. I took one step without thinking and pivoted hard, the arrowhead scratching the front of my tunic as it flew by. Still turning, I had lost my balance and let all my weight sink into my heel as I threw my chest backwards. There was no recovering from that position, and I fell with as much grace as I could manage.

"Will and intellect!"

I had landed badly and scraped my left arm even through my shirt. The impact onto the hard earth reverberated straight to my right shoulder. The arrows had come with no explanation unless you count 'Stand in front of that tree' as an explanation as to what I was to do. I had to avoid the arrows somehow.

Ketill was still nocking the next arrow when I snatched it out of his hand and broke it over my knee. He gawked at me. There were six more arrows in his quiver. I grabbed them all and tried to break them over my knee all at once and failed.

"Do you need some help with that?"

Enraged, I slammed the arrows down a second time. The arrows did not break, but I bruised my leg. Even more furious now, I put three of the arrows in my teeth, broke the other three over my knee, and then finished off the rest.

"Well," said Ketill. "What did you learn?"

I stared at him with total incomprehension, my chest heaving. The whole scene had made no sense. It was as if he wanted to play with my fear and watch for amusing reactions. But it had been a lesson, somehow. I had no idea until I considered the tree.

Yes, the tree. When I stood there, my first thought had been about remaining stoic and still. Then I had rejected that in favor of not being pierced with arrows. That had worked but had not solved my problem. So I said the following:

"When given two choices, choose a third way."

Ketill furrowed his brow and leaned on his bow. "Hmmph," he said. "That is one lesson, just not today's lesson."

"What was today's lesson then?"

"It was will and intellect!" he shouted. "Did you not hear me every other time? Bah." He threw me the bow and turned away. Shuffling side to side more than forward, he threw up his arms. "How you solve the problem is up to you. It depends on what you understand and what you are willing to try. You could stand on the other side of the tree and claim that was the front. That would show an understanding of where the threat came from and a simple reinterpretation of what 'front' meant. You could come up and take the bow and unstring it. That would show a reinterpretation of how far in front. Or you could break all my arrows."

"That's what I did!"

"That was the worst solution! I have never even considered that solution, it is so pointless! The kind that only works once, and worse, the kind that breaks all my damned arrows! Now you need to go back into town for replacements!"

"But I thought I needed to stay here to learn," I said, thinking I had caught the man in a contradiction.

"Yes, you are supposed to study here and not be off on unnecessary errands, fool. That is why this solution is so bad! Your overall intent and your immediate actions are at odds. If what you desire as an outcome and what you do contradict each other, you will fail. In many things, not just using the runes for magic. But especially that!"

"So why even shoot arrows at me at all? Better to be out of range completely."

"That was the other part of the lesson, and now I have to explain that as well?"

The old man shook his head. I had riled him up, gotten him angry in a way he was only beginning to remember. I will admit to enjoying it a bit, as long as you know I find that part embarrassing to admit to. He pulled on his beard, his eye wide as if casting about for the right explanation.

"Think you can cast a spell about fire because you heard about it?" he finally asked. "You have never been burned, so you do not truly understand it."

"I have felt a fire's heat before," I huffed.

"You know the warmth and good intent of a hearth!" he shouted back. "Of fire, you know nothing. You have been nearby to arrows and death as well, but you did not know them. Now you know how an arrow flies from the other end and the closeness of its bite. You will need to get closer, much closer," he said, his breath hot in my ear, "to more dangerous things than arrows to learn rune magic, boy. That closeness is the only way to learn. Close to pain. Close to death. Far away is the mundane where coalbiters find comfort."

"What is next then?" I said. "I am shot with an arrow and bleed and try to not die?"

All I had wanted to do was find the wizard and learn magic. Now I had found him and started learning, all I wanted to do was get away from him.

"No. We are done for now. What is next is you go to a fletcher in town and return here when you have replaced all the arrows you broke. And what's this?"

Humor swooped overhead and perched over Ketill's doorway.

"Caw!" he said, apparently too angry for human speech.

"It is not yet noon," I said. "Did you slip your bindings?"

"I brought you a present, skald," said Humor, almost sounding like he meant it.

The sound of someone crashing through the bushes was not far behind.

"Ulfberht?"

The youth was making his way through the greenery, albeit without much grace. Finally he won free and dusted the leaves off his tunic.

"*Hello,*" he said, catching his breath. "*I was going to wait, but I was worried and the bird promised to take me here and some of the people in town, well, nobody was sure—"*

Ketill snarled. He did not like something about what he was hearing.

"Slow down," I said. Then switching to Frankish to make it easier on him I continued, *"What did you tell the raven?"*

"I offered to free him instead of killing him," he said. *"But only if he swore to take me to you."*

"But why? You could have just let him go!"

"Because!" shouted Ulfberht, eyeing me, Ketill, and Humor in turn. *"People were missing this morning. People in the town. I could not sit around and do nothing!"*

I turned toward Ketill. "He says people are missing from the town."

"I know what he said," growled the wizard. "Unless you are one of the missing, it is foolish that he would come here."

"You know Frankish?" I said. I shook my head, realizing I knew the answer to that question already. "Nevermind. It is not foolish he would come here, just unexpected. You hate burning charcoal but you need to do it to trade for food and supplies. Here is a charcoal burner. He can work here while you teach me, to the benefit of us both."

"Oh, you mean to extend the hospitality of my house to others?" said Ketill. "Perhaps this will more be more efficient in destroying my property."

Humor cawed. "Things have gone well in my absence, it seems! I told you it would have been better to bring me with you."

He was wrong on that count. Ulfberht had taken my plan and improved upon it. Now I did not need to make a separate trip to bring him here, but I was still free of a debt to the raven.

"You've done very well," I said. *"This is Ketill, the wizard."*

"Good day to you," Ulfberht said to Ketill.

"Is it?" barked Ketill, and disappeared into his house.

CHAPTER 30

PURITY IS WEAKNESS

Dusk fell soon after I made my way into the open past the forest's edge. There had been just enough light left in the day to find my way into town. Tromping around in the dark of night was a hazard, and I had not even considered the drink-stealing troll might be about.

Did that thing even exist? I had heard about it but none of us had seen it nor evidence of its thirsty presence. The whole endeavor seemed set up to disappoint seekers of word-fame.

I was no such seeker though. I sought wisdom and new stories. As harrowing as it was learning from Ketill with arrows flying at my face, it was nothing I had not asked for. He said it would be difficult, and it was. I had nothing to complain about. And as such, the endeavor was working out quite well for me.

Perhaps I would even encounter Fanya while traveling through the woods again. Working out quite well, indeed.

The guards standing behind the palisades at the south gate were ready to close up as I approached. They let me through, paying me little attention. The eyes of those guarding the wall looked beyond me, farther out among the farmlands. As the gate closed behind me, I realized I was already in good company.

"You're late," said Innstein.

Both 'Steins stared at me, arms crossed.

"I was not aware I had some place to be," I said.

"The queen sees it another way," said Utstein. "Wanted to account for everyone, and you were the only one not accounted for. Haldor had us come down here to see if you arrived by dark."

"It seems I am right on time then," I said, falling in step with them to return to the hall without delay. "It is not dark, so I must be early, even."

"We've been standing here for hours," said Innstein. "I hope your dealings with the wizard were worth all that boredom."

"I learned much!"

"Oh!" they both said at once, and stopped in their tracks.

"What spells did you learn?" asked Innstein. "Can you blunt your enemies' weapons?"

"Of course not, that would be unbelievably advanced!"

"Can you curry the favor of a beautiful woman?" asked Utstein.

Fanya hadn't run me through with her spear, so I supposed I had done just that. Answering yes would have required a much longer story though, and one whose details I did not wish to share.

"No," I said, preferring that to the embarrassment an explanation would surely bring me. "I have had only a day to speak to the man, and part of that was spent convincing him to teach me at all. I do not have all Odin's spells memorized. None, in fact."

That gave them pause. Only for a few seconds, however.

"You should learn to speak to the dead first," said Innstein.

"No, first he should learn to calm the seas," said Utstein. "What do we need of the dead other than to not join them?"

"We need to know what they know, because we make them dead so often!" said Innstein. "The sea we have ridden for many years without trouble. But remember when we fought Jarl Ivar and you killed his last man? Then there was nobody to tell us where he had hidden his treasure. Just a bunch of confused thralls who didn't know where it was. We would be rich right now if we had been able to talk to the dead then."

"You said we could ask the thralls in the first place! And what if the dead tell us to go hang ourselves? I would rather take my chances on the sea with words to keep it calm than assume we never run into weather."

The debate raged as I continued walking, leaving the brothers to their argument. They caught up as I was close to the hall, still arguing. A red-eyed goshawk stared down at me from the roofline and *ack-ack-ack*ed at me, spreading its wings. That stopped me for a moment, as I thought I might need to duck again, but the bird remained where it was.

"Friend of yours?" asked Utstein. "From the forest?"

"Yes and no," I said. "Or yes and I don't know. High Pants is Hrolf's hawk, so I would take him to be a friend of ours."

"We might need as many of those as we can find," said Innstein.

We entered the longhouse together, the argument between the brothers forgotten. There were plenty of other arguments to be had inside.

"There is no evidence of this," said Gudbrand.

I could hear him before I could see him in the press of people surrounding the high seats for the king and queen.

"Evidence or not," said Ragnvald, "there is still judgment to be exercised, and I will thank you not to question my wife's judgment."

I pushed in through those standing quickly enough to see Gudbrand bow his head and take a step back. He was level with the rest of the crowd, standing next to Hrolf, the king's nephew. The high seats had hard men crowded behind them. Beigadh and Hromund behind the king, and Frothi Stupid-Hair behind the queen.

All three champions looked as though they were grinding solid rock into dust with their teeth.

Alfhild smiled. "Let us not chastise the staller," she said, in a tone sounding very much like she was enjoying his chastisement. "He has spent all day investigating and found very little."

"I think that is our point," said Hrolf, putting a hand to the staller's shoulder. "To condemn this woman without knowledge—"

"But that is *my* point," said Alfhild, tone noticeably icier. "To leave no evidence is the very mark of such witchcraft. And what did those who searched tell us?" She glared at Haldor. "Speak, if you would, and tell us all once more what you found."

Ulf stepped forward. If there was a time for him to act as *þulr*, now was it.

"My queen," he began, "all search parties reported to me, and I think I may best describe what has happened. Most found nothing of any note. No tracks were found outside the farmhouse where Bosi and his family disappeared from. Therefore, no definite direction could be determined to search in. However, the closer our parties searched to the fens, the more they reported being . . . unable to continue searching."

"And this inability," said Alfhild, "what was its nature?"

Ulf cleared his throat. "Those who went in the direction of the fens reported being led in circles," he said.

Murmurs bubbled up from the crowd.

"The forest changed, they said," continued Ulf, louder now, "and as they thought they approached the fens each time, it brought them, unknowing, back to where they had started instead."

Murmurs turned into gasps and worried conversations. In that din, Alfhild rose from her seat all of a sudden, and the hall quieted. The pale smile was gone, replaced by a look of deadly earnestness.

"What is that but the work of a witch?" she demanded. "And this Huld—"

I had covered my mouth to hold in the guffaw, and partially succeeded. I coughed to try to play off the reaction, but Alfhild's eyes were already on me.

"This Huld did not offer prophecy or other service on her arrival here. She is unknown, and her parentage is unknown, though I smell a strange and impure breeding in her. What else would take people and leave no trace? What else might turn around searchers in the forest and confuse them? The evidence it is her is that there is none to examine, and that she herself is gone from here."

Murmurs bubbled up again. These murmurs were of assent, though. Among those from the city and the surrounding farms who had gathered in the hall, most seemed to believe in Alfhild's narrative.

"She saved our lives," I shouted. "Out on the water, she called the wind for us, and we outsailed the Midgard Serpent because of it."

The resulting looks were not unfamiliar to a skald of any experience. Confusion mixed with accusation. An ironic combination given confusion should lead to inquiry and not to a pointed finger. We didn't have a good expression for this in my time. In modern parlance it would be 'don't confuse me with the facts.'

"I recall a different telling," said Alfhild. "Did your captain not pull his pants down and simply bash the thing in the head with his penis?"

That got a few chuckles. That was the story as I told it. She was stealing my audience. I knew she was the queen, but it still made me angry.

"I'm not saying that didn't happen," I said, stepping forward and reclaiming the chuckles for myself. "But she came with us from Fretborg, not from the fens, the obvious source of troubles."

"Now our troubles are added to," said Alfhild. "Unless this witch is one of yours, Haldor! Was she a mere passenger, or does she wear your armring as one of your own?"

Haldor stood arms crossed, chest out. His expression conveyed neither pleasure nor displeasure, only that he was there. "She does not," he said.

"And this skald of yours," continued Alfhild, "the one with different stories about how you got here, what of him? I notice he narrates entertainingly, but this is not a subject for entertaining. Does he wear your armring?"

Murmurs rose again in anticipation of the answer. Alfhild was winning, by a lot. I had challenged her, and I was failing. Was I trying to convince the crowd? To belittle her position with humor? I was unfocused and a rhetorical mess, while she hammered me over and over.

"He does not," said Haldor, who could not but let that hammer fall. Then with much greater emphasis, and in a most clearly defiant tone, he added, "*Yet.*"

Haldor was a man of few words. He let his *þulr* speak for him most of the time. Some thought Haldor simple, perhaps. But Haldor was not simple, he simply knew the power behind words when fewer were used.

Especially when those words amounted to sticking his neck out for a crewmate. I flushed red at that, while the crowd looked to Alfhild for a response. They were disappointed, I think, when the king rose and made his disapproval clear.

"There has been enough talk on this subject!" said Ragnvald. He had attempted a shout and accomplished something between a shout and a squeak. "Whatever experience with such a woman, she may appear to explain herself to me, or continue to draw suspicion! Now the discussion is over, and I will not delay hospitality any longer, either to my guests or myself!"

At least I could agree with him about it being time to eat. I was starving. Magnus intercepted me before I could find my way to the food, however.

"Well done," said Magnus, shouldering me and cocking his head in indication I should follow him. "That's from Haldor, not me. I could have done with more jokes." He walked us away from the crush of people around the stew cauldrons and to a quiet corner of the hall where Haldor met us.

"Tell me of the wizard," said Haldor.

There was much to tell if I gave a full accounting. I settled for telling him the outcome, that Ketill had agreed to teach me, and that Ulfberht was there to burn charcoal for Finnr.

"Good," said Haldor, nodding, "that's good. Go back to the wizard then, and learn what you can from him."

"What about Huld?" I asked.

"What about her?"

"Should I look for her?"

Haldor shook his head and lowered his voice. "If you see her, tell her not to come back. It's plain to see she has done nothing but help us, but that has not stopped rumors from spreading that she goes out to summon malevolent spirits at night. Word has gone against her here, and I doubt we can protect her. Better she moves on. Maybe find shelter with your wizard."

I doubted either Ketill or Huld would find that situation to their liking. I nodded anyway, thankful Haldor could at least see the situation for what it was.

"Now get yourself a bowl, and get out of here," said Haldor. "There has been enough of politics for one evening."

"Go where?" I asked. If I was not to stay in the longhouse, I was uncertain where to go. It was dark by then and I would not want to attempt going back to Ketill's house until morning.

Haldor addressed Magnus. "Get an extra bowl and cup and get him to Finnr. Perhaps some stew and ale will sate the dwarf."

"Is he unwell?" I asked.

"He is furious," said Haldor. "His friend is accused of absurd things, and he can do nothing about it. But you spoke up for her, so that is something."

Magnus and I collected the extra food and drink and headed toward the forge. He was interested in more details of my journey, so I filled him in on the way down. It was a short journey, but as I began telling it I realized how full of adventure it was and how much I wanted to talk about it. I left out nothing. Magnus was a friend I could trust in.

"Perhaps the wizard can lead us to the fens without being turned around!" said Magnus. "Then we can end this ridiculous business."

I couldn't blame him for his impatience. We had been promised a troll hunt, but instead encountered court intrigue and a bunch of ugly Rus.

"I will ask," I said, "but if the prophecy is right, Finnr must finish the sword first. Well, if the interpretation of the prophecy is right."

"Bah!" said Magnus as we knocked and entered the forge. "Finnr! We brought dinner from the hall."

The dwarf sat at a small table, scratching the head of a lazy, white forest cat curled up and purring by him. The cat's eyes went from half-open to wide before it stretched and jumped down. Finnr nodded slightly as Magnus put the bowl and cup down, and then Magnus backed out as he had come.

"May I join you here for the night?" I asked.

"Is this a joke?" asked Finnr. "This cup is empty."

Ymir's bones! Magnus was trustworthy with what I told him, but apparently apt to drink another person's ale if not watched close enough.

I offered my own cup, but Finnr waved it away.

"Why would you join me here rather than stay in the Glorious Longhouse for Glorious People?" asked the dwarf. Finnr poked at the stew.

"I think Haldor wanted me away from that place for the time being," I said. "I argued with the queen."

Still chewing, he raised his hands and brought them down hard on the table. "Well? About what? And did you win?"

"I spoke up for Huld," I said. "But no, I did not win. The queen is clever, and I was unprepared."

Finnr eyed me immediately as I mentioned Huld's name. He was quiet for a moment after my answer, then beckoned me sit at the same table and pull out a stool to sit down. He asked for more details about what was said, and I relaxed a bit and ate my stew.

Though I had no good news to give, Finnr's mood seemed to improve as I spoke.

"Huld would counsel against antagonism of the queen," he said. "But she would secretly think well of you for having antagonized her."

"Haldor suggested maybe she take refuge with the wizard," I said, shaking my head. "Hard to imagine either one living with anyone else."

"Ah yes! The wizard. Did you see Ulfberht before you left him?"

"I did. Ulfberht did well to strike that bargain with the raven. The wizard is . . . cantankerous. That is an understatement. Ketill did not appear to like that Ulfberht was Frankish."

"Hmmph. He will learn to like it if the boy burns charcoal for him. I will need a lot just to begin the smelting process."

"You make your own steel?"

"Of course I do. Why do you think dwarven weapons are so good? I can't use the slag they have around here."

Halstein could pattern-weld a blade like no smith I had ever heard of. But even he lamented it was often just making the best of the ingredients he had rather than making the best steel in the first place. Take different steel ingots, maybe of middling quality if you were lucky, and fold them over and over again until the two were intertwined, and you would improve the strength and sharpness of the blade.

The result from that process was good, but nowhere near as good as the swords he had made in Miklagard when he still traveled. As far east as that was, the finest steel came from still further beyond there. So good, it took the name of where you could find most of it for sale.

"You can make Damascus steel?" I asked.

"Don't know what that is," said Finnr in between bites. "Don't care what that is. I make crucible steel, and better than any of those fools selling their wares on the Silk Road. I need a good, soft steel for the core of the blade and good, hard steel for the edges. Can't find either of those around here, so I need to make them."

I gasped. Damascus steel, crucible steel, whatever you called it, those ingots were rarer than gold and often more valuable. Few made their way into the north or anywhere near us, and only kings could afford them, let alone their smithing into fine weapons. And Finnr could just make them—and make them better! We would be rich!

My left hand was palm down on the table. Finnr slammed one of his fists on top of it. Hard.

I coughed and waved with my right hand. The pain coursing through my left was excruciating.

"That was the dragon sickness taking you," he said. "Are you back to your senses?"

I was too busy sucking in air to make a response. Hundreds of years of swinging a hammer had turned Finnr's fists into rocks. His arms were not the ropy muscle Haldor sported, but the blow felt as if it had a boulder behind it.

"Your hand is fine," said Finnr. "I only tapped it enough to get your attention."

I shook my hand as if that would dissipate the pain. "Well, you got it! What was that about? What dragon sickness?"

"I could see your eyes turning red as gold. Like Fafnir, you would pile up a mound of gold and it would turn you. There is nothing more burdensome to carry than a desire for money, and you were thinking about how much money you could have with a dwarf to make you valuable things. I plied that trade once, to make myself rich, and never will again. It turns people into monsters."

"Why are you trying to make the sword so good then?"

"Because I was called to! Because it is for a quest. But most of all"—and the dwarf threw his hands down on the table—"because I want to. That is the only good reason to craft anything. And the only way to guide the intent of the creation. I know well enough how to do it, but weapons made for profit alone are a disgrace. There is a burden in that much knowledge, and the burden requires wisdom in equal measure. I make weapons for reasons I deem good, not to accumulate a treasure hoard like some lindworm."

Still breathing heavily, I got up and found the nearest anvil in the forge. Fearing another blow from the dwarf if I messed his forge about, I left the random bits of whatever he had put on top of it and put my hand on the anvil's side. It was cold to the touch, and just what I was hoping for.

"Maybe more than just a tap," said Finnr.

I let my hand rest a bit longer on the anvil, taking in the balm of cold steel, and caught my breath. Who signed up for all these dangerous conversations with wizards and dwarves?

Oh yes, I had.

"Fafnir was a dwarf before he was a dragon," I said. "You were after gold too, but you are still a dwarf."

Finnr drew his pants away from his waist and looked down. "Still am."

I ignored the jest, and the potential implication there were no female dwarves. "Don't be so stubborn. There must be a story about your plying of that trade for profit. Why do it? What did you make? And why did you stop?"

The dwarf considered my questions for a moment. "Because I am a wanderer by nature and thought to make a fortune above ground in my travels, the best crucible steel you will ever encounter, and . . ." He stopped, real hesitation halting even his terse answers. "And because a youngling from far away, not still a boy but not yet a man, killed a bunch of people with a hammer." He stopped and crossed his arms for effect. "The end."

"There is more to that story," I said.

The dwarf wrung his stony hands and inhaled deeply. "I will tell you a story," he said. "Or remind you of one, if you've heard it. Freya was traveling one day, and she spied the work of four dwarves. A necklace of gold, the finest torc she had ever seen. She knew right away she had to have it.

"But the dwarves would not accept the offered payment. They wanted a night with Freya each, to do as they pleased with her. And so she lay with them, and gained her necklace. The golden torc of legend. The *Brísingamen*.

"And so she had what she most wanted. She lay in bed all day looking at the necklace, stroking it. Gold has a way of working into one's mind that way. That is why her necklace, her most prized possession, became a slave collar. It made her miserable, yet it made her want it more at the same time. Only with great difficulty did she break that addiction."

"That is not how I have heard the story," I said. "I heard Loki stole it from her at Odin's behest, and she did Odin's bidding to get it back."

Finnr shrugged. "As you like. I sought gold myself, once. If the story is not true, the part about gold worming its way into your mind rings true to me. As does the story of Fafnir losing himself over his treasure and turning into a monster."

"But you did not lose yourself. Even in Fretborg. The queen seemed to shower you with gold and gems, unless she was lying."

"She was not. All the wealth of that place was sucked into her obsession, and she took from her people and took and took. She channeled it all to me for the making of stupid trinkets."

"They must be worth a fortune though," I said, partly to myself. "Shouldn't she be rich?"

Finnr shook his head. "She would not part with a one of them. The lindworm forsakes not its gold, even if that lindworm is a human."

"Pity we did not liberate them for her."

"You would not want them," said Finnr, more strident for just a moment. "I hammer steel. I make weapons. I craft for a reason, and that reason is in my heart. The jewelry Gulldis had me making did not flow from the same place. Those pieces are not cursed outright, not like the sword Tyrfing was cursed. But every hammer stroke that went into them had behind it the bitter ill luck I felt for being in that place, and the boredom of forming gold. Ill luck went into those pieces, and ill luck will come of them."

"Forming gold is boring?" I asked. "I suppose it doesn't require the same kind of hammering that steel does."

"More to it than that. Those wanting gold want it pure—want red gold. Steel is a different thing entirely. Its quality comes from subtle changes, small introductions of other things. See that pile on the worktable?" He pointed to a small bowl with a yellowish powder. "Smell it."

I sniffed the substance and recoiled. "This is like rotten eggs!"

Finnr grinned. "It's one of the things I have been collecting to be layered with the metal in a crucible before smelting. You would not know it from the smell, but the small amounts of that and a few others I add make all the difference."

"These random bits?" I asked, gesturing at the different colored stones and powders, more evident on a table nearby. "I wouldn't have guessed it. I thought you would want a purer metal for forging."

"Purity, ha!" laughed the dwarf. "There is an alchemy to it. Dwarves are closer to the earth and the stone. I can smell the right concoction sure as your nose can tell savory broth from water. There is nothing 'pure' about the makings of a good blade, or else there would be no getting steel from iron. You would get a blade out of an ingot of pure iron, and it would take a good edge, but it would be fragile. There is little value in purity for a durable thing. Purity is weakness."

Chapter 31

A Good Skalding

As much as I needed to get back to Ketill for lessons and Ulfberht to make sure the wizard didn't flay him alive, I decided to wait for sixty arrows. I figured it would buy me some good graces after the disaster that had been 'will and intellect.' I also knew it would take longer, and give me some time to breathe before wading back into Ketill's lessons.

Wanting to learn and wanting to do the things necessary to learn are sometimes at odds, like when the latter involves near-death experiences.

Gudbrand introduced me to a good fletcher named Flosi. Flosi was a craftsman of many things, though he did not mind being called a fletcher. I could have made the arrows myself, but they would not have been nearly as good. Sometimes it is better to be self-reliant, but sometimes it is better to rely less on pride and more on the skill of others.

I made a fast friend with Flosi. He seemed older than Gudbrand by a few years and grayer by about a decade, his beard grown long and trimmed to a tight V pointing to the center of his chest. He wore a wary expression at my presence until Gudbrand made it clear he vouched for me. The wariness faded after that, but he was no less alert.

His house was large enough to be for a whole family, but no such signs were evident inside. Much of it was occupied by tools of one sort or another, much of the rest with half- and mostly-finished things. Arrows, bows, mast heads, bowls and cups, wooden and ceramic statues from knee to neck-high.

He was a maker of many things. More important, he was someone I could trust, or else Gudbrand would not have introduced me.

I told him what I needed and he shook his head a bit, demanding to see the broken arrows. I showed them with more than a little guilt.

"Very exacting," Flosi said. "Some people will take any arrows, but I remember making these years ago. A little longer than usual, spine a bit stiffer, point a bit heavier. These are for an experienced archer pulling a heavy bow."

I gulped down the statement *for a drunk archer pulling a heavy bow.*

"I remember the customer as well," continued Flosi. "He is not an easy man to deal with."

At that I nodded vigorously.

Flosi grinned and asked a fair price without haggling. I paid him, and he told me to come back in a few days.

So for a few days, I figured, I could wait and rest in Ragnvald's hall. Maybe figure out how to avoid the daily training sessions. When I returned there, Haldor already had that covered.

"I am sending you into the forest," he told me. "You've walked it to a good end several times now, so you'll go with Hemming and see if the two of you alone can't find something the larger groups are missing."

So I was roped into the never-ending search for the troll, which I was not entirely convinced existed. I was more concerned about getting those arrows back to Ketill. And then not getting shot with any soon after. But Haldor had made a command, and his commands were not to be ignored.

Besides that though, I was feeling more like part of the crew. For Haldor to say I had no arm ring *yet*—well, that was no small thing. I couldn't let the man down when I knew he believed in me.

Hemming and I set out straight away. I didn't like the man much after our first foray together, but his woodcraft was without peer. If there was a print in the dirt, Hemming knew what made it. If there was scat or marks left on trees, Hemming knew what made them. If the smallest leaf was disturbed, he saw it well before I did.

What Hemming could not know was why the signs he picked up kept leading us back to our starting points. He could tell it was the *landvættir* at work, as could I. Eventually I could even pick up their scent, the subtlest hint of floral aroma when no flowers were nearby. We differed only on what it meant.

"The spirits are playing with us," Hemming said with a snarl.

I don't know why I thought he was wrong, but my instinct said no. My instinct told me the *landvættir* were very much on our side. Hence the magic in the grove. Hence my survival in the forest. Perhaps not instinct then, as much as how they had treated me. But I did not think the spirits, though they did have a sense of humor, were playing with us.

My sense was they were protecting us.

We ventured out during daylight only, and returned each day to fill our bellies with meat and ale in Ragnvald's hall. Inga was brewing again, with Nanthild's help, and for all that ale, the troll had not shown itself.

According to the queen, it was because the troll was afraid of Haldor. According to Haldor, it was because there was no getting away from prophecy. And the prophecy indicated Finnr's sword had to be forged before that fight would take place.

I was more interested in stories than in prophecies. The nights I was back, my stories were well received. I was used to Magnus' heckling by then, which Leif joined in with. His brother Ingolf shook his head every time he spoke, but speak he did. I disliked Leif's outbursts at first. They broke up the rhythm of my tellings and distracted both me and my audience.

By the third night though, I had grown used to them, even worked them into my act. Leif was willing to play the fool a bit, and it lightened the mood when I played along.

Days later, I could delay no longer. I packed heavy for the trip and headed back to Ketill's house. It's not easy to carry five dozen arrows, even less so when laid down with extra food. But I figured the more I brought, the less Ulfberht and I would dip into Ketill's stores, and maybe the less irritable the wizard would be.

The forest felt more familiar as I walked it. Certainly more familiar than when we had been searching. I could never quite discern what direction Ketill's house was from the city. Though I would leave through the south gate and walk east, I only ever came upon his house after feeling completely lost.

Ulfberht was, thankfully, still alive when I arrived. He was even speaking Norse a little better than when I had left him.

"I think he hates me," were the first words Ulfberht said upon my return.

"He doesn't hate you," I said, which was a big assumption. "He doesn't like anyone."

"He said he would teach me to speak Norse if it killed me," Ulfberht continued, "that the sound of my language made him want to strangle me with my own intestines."

I'm making Ulfberht's speech a little clearer than it was, but that was the gist.

"His mood will improve when I show him these," I said, tapping some of the arrows.

Ulfberht shrugged and went back to work as Ketill stumbled out of his house.

"Ah, the skald returns!" he slurred. "Why were you gone for a week?"

"Five days is not a week," I said, a bit disgusted at his demeanor. "You are drunk."

"And so would you be," he said. The old wizard leaned heavily on a staff as he walked out to meet me. He snatched the arrows, all three quivers worth, and turned back around. "Fetch water. Split the wood in the back. Get the boy started on burning charcoal. Come back with something more interesting to say." He stumbled a little as he marched back into his hut.

It took days of quiet work and patience to get the wizard to warm up, and even more days after that to get him to warm up to Ulfberht. The old man was a drunk old crank, but beyond that, he did not like Franks, though he would not say why.

When his attitude softened, he claimed it was due to the young man's willingness to work diligently at burning charcoal, relieving him of much work. Being Ketill, he also provided some barbed comments about how well Ulfberht followed directions in pointed contrast to my approach.

All that was accurate. It was also a lie as far as his affinity for the young Frank.

Ketill's attitude did not change because of Ulfberht's diligence, it changed after he heard the young man's story. I asked Ulfberht to tell me how he and Nanthild had come to Denmark one day. I did so knowing I was within earshot of the raven and I was losing out on trading the information.

Where the siblings were from, Ulfberht could no longer say. Every winter for the last four had seen them in another place. This last had been in Ragnvald's hall. The year before that they wintered rough amongst the sea-borne slavers who would eventually sell them to Ragnvald.

The year before that had been marginally safer and more comfortable in the hall of the Frisian king Radbod. They would have stayed had he not died and his men fled. Radbod had them work as servants but did not treat them as property, according to Ulfberht.

The year before that they had been taken as apostates when their father died fighting Charles the Hammer in Frankland.

That escape from the Hammer's men was the scene of Nanthild's near-rape and Ulfberht's fire-setting. I was curious to know more about how this came about, but I soon realized I did not want to make Ulfberht tell the truth of it. Ulfberht's story was coherent, timely, and detailed. He even told me how the sea smelled when some of Radbod's old allies decided to try their fortune elsewhere along with some of the thralls in his household.

But about the scene with his sister and the burning house, the story's coherence broke down. Ulfberht missed details and then filled them in when I noticed the gaps. Even so, his telling of this part, the most harrowing part, was the least emotional.

I knew he was creating that part of the story as he went, but it was my guess as to the real story that kept me silent. What really happened was likely a deal more brutal than he wanted to let on. No doubt he played a part in saving his sister, then and in helping the both of them find their way to begging from a Frisian trading ship. But he did not set that fire. That must have been Nanthild, and that was more likely for revenge than for practicality.

"It is good you took care of your sister," I said, hoping for more information. "Women are fragile things."

Ulfberht reared back in shock and took the bait. "No, you don't understand," he said. "She is the one—" and cut himself short. "I hunted and kept us fed on the road. At least enough until we found shelter. But for fighting, she is the stronger."

I knew from just the past few months that sometimes it was not easy to identify the most dangerous fighter from looking at him. Or her, as it happened. I did not press any further.

Humor brought all of this to Ketill, as I knew he would. It is an easy thing to dislike a person as long as you don't know their story, and a much harder thing when you know that story. In stories, we can see ourselves, at least in part. I had brought the old man ten times the number of arrows he had before, and that had done nothing to lift his spirits. Ulfberht had followed every direction and worked hard, and that too had failed to make his mood less foul. The story changed things. A new beginning for an old wizard.

A new understanding came over me as well. Here was the power of stories

—not just because they were told in verse. The meter of the verse mattered in the story's execution, but it had to be in tune with the heart of the narrative. There was a grand lesson there, a lesson for a skald, and I was beginning to grasp its shape and scale.

Just beginning. I had much yet to learn about my craft, and even more about others.

Chapter 32

Sitting Out

Things settled in for the summer. So much so that I forgot about the troll. Ragnvald treated us well and was happy to have more champions in his hall. Our crew was happy to be fed and rewarded, more or less. If any were impatient for another fight, they did not say so.

I was more interested in Ketill's teachings, and spent more of my time with him than in the hall. Ulfberht burned charcoal, albeit with a bit of help from me at times, while I was set upon more mundane but less sooty tasks. Fetching water, chopping and splitting wood, gathering food. Make the fire, boil the water, cook and eat the food, go to sleep, repeat.

Meanwhile, I would practice drawing the old runic alphabet in the dirt, practice chanting the runes, and answer Ketill's questions about rune interpretations.

It was not as I had hoped, thinking I would learn spells and cast them within days. I was often bored. But at least no more arrows came sailing at my head.

Chance encounters with Fanya buoyed me through that boredom. Every time I went through the forest was an opportunity to see her. Whether it was traveling or just doing chores for Ketill, she might pop out at any time and surprise me, and I could never predict when that might be. I had some decent woodcraft, certainly not as good as Hemming but good enough to have kept me alive when on all those previous delivery runs. Not good enough to detect this woman sneaking up on me.

I gawped stupidly at her at first, but gained some confidence with repetition. Those interactions were what I woke up looking forward to and bedded down hoping for.

That woman played in my imagination far more than any rune magic did. Fetching water, I would often find myself ambushed. It was her game to see if she could surprise me. It was weeks before I noticed her sneaking up on me. After that, her woodcraft redoubled and I neither heard nor saw until the butt of her spear was gently nudging my ass in a playful statement of *I win again*.

"You should be more careful, skald," Fanya said one of those times. "What if I had wanted your life?"

You could have it then, I choked back. I was not ready with a witty response. I had practiced innumerable lines of memorable verse, but I could not remember any of them. Though fully clothed, Fanya was no less beautiful, and I was no more articulate than when I had been lying on a riverbank with a spear pointed at my chest.

And then she was gone just as quick as she had appeared, darting away and disappearing behind a large tree. No sign of her left but for her faint scent, and after a few seconds I wondered if I had imagined even that.

Such were our meetings.

That was how I knew Fanya, mysterious and unattainable, usually no more than a few sentences of conversation. I think she preferred it that way, and yet at the same time enjoyed my company from time to time. Brief as each encounter would be, every nagging errand suggested the possibility of her presence and that mischievous smile. So I went forth for each task set to me by Ketill, playing that it was an inconvenience while I grinned inside.

She made most sport of me on my delivery trips back to Lejre to deliver charcoal. I had a clear direction to go in and was too overloaded to give chase or respond other than to tell her stories when she requested them.

Those were my happiest days. I hated manual labor but loved seeking Fanya's presence hidden somewhere in the forest. I could not understand the point of Ketill's lessons, especially those involving the identification and gathering of roots, mushrooms, and the like. But soon my sense of constant discovery became stronger. Those errands too became a pleasure when I approached them as searching for hidden things rather than doing work.

Not that I was a most diligent student or chopper of wood. I would take breaks often and in taking breaks I would daydream about Fanya. In daydreaming, I sometimes came back from my reverie to see my own wood grown large. No one saw that, as far as I knew, but I set up for my lonely tasks a bit farther away from potentially prying eyes after that.

Though I might suggest our encounters were all awkward flirting, we shared more intimate thoughts often. She was a Dane by birth, an unwanted daughter who had become her own keeper early on. Forests in many places had been her home, and there she was content and safe. Magic she would sometimes hint at but gave only vague references to what or how.

Seiðr was a flexible type of magic and could accomplish much. To divine the future or make a blessing or curse were only a few things possible. But I knew what lay in that topic of conversation: Alfhild and her would-be sacrifices were not likely to go well in conversation. So I played along with Fanya's secrecy, both in her past and regarding her teacher, and I mostly asked her about the forest.

It seemed to me she could have been sworn to the Brotherhood if she had been born a man. Or perhaps she could in any case. Our rules did not prohibit women from joining that I knew of. One more cast-off child relying on her might and main to make her way in the world would be welcome. Certainly of more use than a skald who could not fight and only sometimes sang poetry to a good end.

It had been some time since I told stories just for the pleasure of it and it felt good to revisit that joy. Fanya loved hearing tales of the *Æsir*, of heroes and monsters. Not just for the stories, which could vary in telling depending on which side of a mountain you grew up on. She could read the undercurrents of those stories, feel the thematic eddies that blew as I told them.

Our conversations took twists and turns, meandering like a happy stream eager to explore its way down a mountain. What other things we talked about are lost to the mists of my memory. But there was one I remember very well.

"What is the difference between a hero and a monster?" she asked once as I was headed to Lejre.

I thought for a moment. "A hero fights for us, and a monster fights for them."

"Who is us and who is them?" she countered. "It seems to me there is no difference at all. Which side you happen to be on does not change the nature of the hero, or monster."

"There is order and chaos," I said, sweating under one load of charcoal in a huge backpack and another dragged behind me in Ketill's small cart. It was well into summer by then, and hot even in the forest. "The *Æsir* bring order to Midgard. The *jǫtnar* and Loki's spawn would tear it apart."

"Perhaps that is because the *Æsir* are monsters."

"The fire *jǫtunn* Surt would burn the world given his chance, rather than rule a world intact," I said, too abrupt in my manner. "But I do not wish to argue. Odin is a treacherous one. If he is an example to use for wisdom, it is as much to show us bad examples as good."

Fanya said little for a long time and could not contain a deep blush. I felt embarrassed, as if I had spoken out of turn and made a fool of myself. Her smile heightened my fear she would leave at my rude comment, but her response was even worse: "Would that we all had wisdom enough to know the bad examples from the good before we became them."

One curse of poets is the keenest possible awareness of when we are outwitted. The witless do not have this problem.

Balancing out such a curse, poets are not half-bad at changing subjects.

"How is it you manage in such a way through the forest?" I asked. "Only Hemming rivals you in remaining unseen."

"Unheard is the more important," she said, happy as I was to leave the previous subject behind. "Walk unheard and no one looks to see you."

"Moving that slow, how do you get to where you're going?"

Fanya threw her head back and laughed. "You are quite the fast mover, skald! No wonder you miss so much. For all your travels did you never practice *útiseta*?"

Útiseta was something Taika had tried to teach me and I had resisted. It meant 'sitting out,' and was a way to talk to spirits without all the coercion inherent to *seiðr*. As far as I could tell it consisted of sitting around being bored, no spirits to speak of. The only wisdom in that was having your mind wander off somewhere because you were so bored, and therefore magically finding something useful to do. Preferably somewhere warm and safe.

"It did not agree with me," I offered. "And I think if spirits want to talk to me, they already have plenty of opportunities."

"'It is not something to agree or disagree. I can show you right now."

"It is the middle of a sunny day and you want to sit around?"

"And the conditions are perfect. Here." She sat down, patting the ground beside her. "Leave the charcoal for now. Sit down. Take a slow breath. Then tell me what you see."

I did as she asked. "Catmint," I said, with bored matter-of-factness. "And bees."

"Are they flying?"

"Of course. They are going from flower to flower."

"Breathe then, and be silent. If you can wait and be still, I will show you something. No summoning, although if you are quiet and peaceful enough, sometimes a cat will appear. I like to think she is one of Freya's."

With the hot blood of insecurity pulsing through me, it felt like coercion. Certainly, no *drengr* would acquiesce to such things. Sitting down and being silent. Hel's dragon! I should have been telling her what to do, said one voice in my head.

Yet even as that voice shouted, my body ignored it, took a quiet seat, and breathed.

I saw the forest, and it was nothing more or less than I had seen before. Trees all around. A canopy of leaves punctured by the light here and there. Dirt. Rocks. Flowers. What of it? Was I supposed to see something more?

Perhaps a squirrel collecting gossip was skulking on a branch, I thought, and there I slowed down. I slowed my breathing, slowed my looking. Squirrels blend into the branches and those practiced spies would know enough not to give away their position. I scanned every curve of every tree, moving my eyes whenever possible and shifting my head slow and steady. I could not see anything suspicious.

Closing my eyes, I opened my ears to notice the noises around me rather than letting them blend into the background. The sound of the forest was of softness, a gentle nature reaching out, even looking for my approval. Then the soft hum stilled just a bit, only noticeable for its absence.

Something was behind that hum. Something was conspicuous in its silence. I began to sweat, my heart beating faster and faster.

The silence played upon my mind not like an absence, but like the presence of a stalking predator.

Fanya's hand on mine brought me out of that reverie. I managed to still my tongue despite my great surprise. Sensing my sudden unease, Fanya put one finger to her lips and then bade me crawl forward a few feet with her. There at the edge of the catmint, she pointed at one flower.

Not a flower, I realized, just a leaf. I shrugged, a leaf with a bee on it.

Again she pointed, and with some reluctance, I looked closer. The bee was curled up, sleeping. Half a dozen others had done the same.

"The forest has many voices and even more secrets," whispered Fanya. "But you must remain still to see them."

I was not much for remaining still. My mind had kept me out of danger by constantly moving for about twenty years. For a few brief moments, I felt the stillness. It did not last long before I remembered how I had misspoken earlier on the trip.

Anxiety returned, and the bees woke and flew away.

When I looked back, Fanya was gone.

CHAPTER 33

THE WIZARD'S ART

"Do not worry, skald, you are maybe less stupid than most," said Ketill. "Or some, at least."

Such were the compliments to which I was becoming accustomed under Ketill's tutelage. We sat in his house, the smoke and heat of his cooking fire making the summer afternoon almost unbearable. It would have been more pleasant to speak outside in the shade and fresh air, but it was not to be.

Ketill was cooking, and in cooking, he was hot as well. He just wore far fewer clothes than I did to compensate for the heat. And by fewer, I mean none. I tried to focus on the conversation, but you know what happens when you think *don't look down* over and over is you end up looking down.

Well, nobody said learning rune magic would be easy.

More weeks had gone by with what seemed to me to be very little progress. I could speak the names of the runes. I could chant their sounds. I could recognize their carvings. And I could recall their most obvious associations for spellcraft.

And after that, things had broken down. I was stuck on some of the less obvious meanings each rune might take in a spell.

Stuck until my conversation with Fanya. The conversation about perspective.

"So now you understand how the same rune can mean two things that seem at odds," said Ketill. "I have been trying to bore this lesson into your skull for some time. What was it that turned for you, that now you say you understand?"

"I was thinking about *þurisaz*," I said. "We call that rune *þurs* now, and use the same letter in the newer alphabet. But a *þurs* is a monster, might as well be a *jǫtunn*. Yet you said it was also Thor's rune, and he is the enemy of *jǫtnar*."

"Yes?" said Ketill, impatient.

I shook my head, realizing I had not said all. "So how can the same rune stand for both *jǫtnar* and their sworn enemy? Because it is a matter of perspective. Who is to say who is the monster and who is the hero?"

Fanya had asked such an obvious question about heroes and monsters, and I hadn't even considered the potential for double meanings. A man could be both a hero and a monster, and I could weave him a description of that duality with poetry. Only because I knew my language inside and out, knew how to use kennings and heiti, and knew how to bring forth my real intent with alliteration and context.

I felt like a fool after speaking to Fanya with such arrogance. There had been much wisdom in her simple question "*Who is us and who is them?*"

Enough wisdom that I could see the runes from a different perspective.

Ketill sighed. "You are closer," he said, and shrugged. "Close enough for explanation, I suppose. And the explanation is this: They are all monsters, one way or another. But they are not all heroes. It is the former that is universal, not the latter."

I nodded, more because Ketill wanted me to than for the explanation. What a deep-seated cynic the old wizard was!

"How is it a storyteller such as yourself found this lesson so difficult?" he continued. "All it requires is taking the perspective of another."

"Perhaps I had not yet encountered another perspective worth taking," I said.

Ketill eyed me suspiciously. "Hmph!" he finally said, and continued as he rooted through a wooden chest in a forgotten corner of the place. "Well. Now you know something, but you do not know how to use it yet. That only takes the rest of your life. But I will tell you a little more today. You will like it."

Turning back to me, he handed over a small knife and sheath.

"This is yours now," he said. "It was intended for a friend of mine long ago. Some of your antics remind me of him, so I think it is only right."

It was a tiny thing with a single edge like my seax, but the blade was no longer than my thumb. The small tip and sharpness of the blade said much about the smith's skill. The handle was polished antler, rubbed smooth and then carved with a crisscrossing pattern. I hefted it and felt the weight balance well, even for a small knife. It had no guard, but the handle rolled inward as it approached the blade.

"For carving," he said, and sat down.

There was no denying the weight of such a gift and the confidence it spoke of. Yet at the same time, there very much would be denial of any possible emotional content in the giving or the receiving. We were men, after all, and men in the north were not supposed to express emotions other than by turning red or breaking things.

And in an environment of such stupidity, it seemed only appropriate to ask a stupid question.

"Why did you not give it to him if you were friends?"

"He blew himself up. Carved the wrong runes, it seems."

"What runes were those?" I asked, wanting to note a combination to avoid.

"He was not there to answer such a question."

"What was he trying to do that he blew himself up then?" I asked, and regretted it immediately.

Ketill affixed me with a stony stare that told of danger in my immediate future. He said nothing at first, but still, his demeanor was so changed from the subject's mention that it was clear I'd touched a nerve.

"That is a story," he said, as I realized he had stopped blinking some moments ago. "Not one for you to trade. Not one for you to know. Even the raven does not know that story, though I am certain he would kill for it. You have his carving knife now, given freely. Whatever story that knife carves, it will be told by you and not by him and not by me."

I could tell I had angered him. He was not the old doddering drunk living in the forest in that moment. Here was the timeless, deathless, murderous wizard who staked skulls around his house so that no one would be foolish enough to come near. A smell of magic rose in the air, neither subtle nor floral like that of the *landvættir*. This was the smell of hot iron and the sense something was about to burst forth.

That sense was telling me Ketill could speak spells as well as carve them, and that he was barely containing himself from the release of some destruction few men might ever see. His good eye held me as if with shackles. I struggled to avoid a shudder as I saw, slowly and with great effort, his lazy eye roll back into focus to track me.

"Thank you for the knife," I said, finally finding the words a reasonable person would have spoken in the first place.

Ketill nodded and rose from his seat. He grimaced, perhaps from bad knees, perhaps from biting back the rage. "You have more work to do now that you have the knife. You'll practice carving the runes, just the alphabet," he continued, handing me a bunch of wooden staves. "That is all. Just carve them and return when you are finished."

"Is carving the entire alphabet how I can cast spells?"

"Of course not!" spat Ketill, frustration returning to his voice.

"But carving is how you cast spells, is it not?"

The wizard shut his eyes and took a few deep breaths. I was pushing my luck again, but a sense tingled in the back of my brain telling me it was a good time to do so. Granted I almost always have that sense tingling in the back of my brain, but what can I say? I am a lucky skald.

"You can cast them that way, yes," he said, sitting down by the fire again and stirring the pot. "There are many ways to do it. Some spells of healing you might carve on a sick person's bed. Or on their door. You might carve a spell into a cup or etch it into a sword. You will do this all later."

"What if I have nothing at hand to carve onto?" I asked.

Grumbling that he was again made to stand, Ketill returned to the chest he had gotten the knife and staves out of, and produced a semi-circular disc of wood. Birch, if I knew my wood, which I did.

"See this disc?" he said. "You will carry many of these. Different woods, different purposes. Given this disc, what would you say about the runes you might carve on it?"

He had me there as my mind went blank. How should I know what runes would work with birch? And then I realized what an easy question it had been.

"I think *berkano* would often be a rune I choose," I said. "It's primary meaning is 'birch,' and here is birch wood. So that rune would be particularly powerful on such a disc?"

Ketill nodded. "It will become more complicated than that, but at least you understand this much. When you understand more, then you would carve a combination of them onto such a thing, and seal it with an offering."

That sounded dangerously close to the sacrifice Haldor had forbade.

"What sort of offering?" I asked.

"Depends on the spell," said Ketill. "To execute the intent and cast the spell requires sealing the carving. Investing in it. Fusing with it for a time. That is when your will flows into the carving. For a mild spell, saliva might do. For a spell involving hospitality, perhaps good ale. Mead or wine are better. For a spell of urgent or grand intent, you must seal the carving with blood. If you misunderstand or your will is weak, you will get a different effect than intended. And unintended effects are never good."

Like blowing myself up.

"How do I begin—"

"No more questions!" barked the wizard. "You have had enough questions to last a lifetime. You will not learn by asking but by doing, so go forth and do! Carve the runes on each side of each stave. Do not return until you have done so, and do not rush the carving. You must carve rightly, or you will not be prepared for the next step."

That was two people telling me I moved too fast. I almost considered listening to them.

CHAPTER 34

THE GIFT OF FAILURE

I RUSHED THE CARVINGS.

Ketill could tell I had not taken my time. It was only one day later, but I had reasoned they were only carvings. How long could I reasonably take? They had been done in a matter of minutes. It was not the first time the wizard yelled at me, and it would not be the last.

At least I did not try to cast any spells. Fear of blowing myself up kept me from that temptation.

I so wished to see Fanya, to tell her what an epiphany I'd had from our conversation. I thought she might share my excitement. She was nowhere to be found, so I was alone with my wood.

Simple alphabet carving was more difficult than I had assumed. Ketill pointed out where different runes were ill-formed, or the cuts were not the right depth, or the size changed as the alphabet went on. Uniformity was important, as was repetition.

"Why did you carve *opala* with those little wings?" said Ketill, not waiting for an answer in this case. "That is not what I taught—do not carve it that way. It is wrong, and something about that particular wrongness makes it foul."

Uniformity then. My mind was wandering instead of focusing as I carved, according to Ketill. A spell was not cast the instant it was sealed in blood. The entirety of the process, from even conceiving the intent of the spell to the carving itself, all had an effect. And that is why I had to concentrate on not just what I carved but how.

A week later I found a quiet spot to work near some catmint. It was not the place Fanya had me sit *útiseta* and I could not close my eyes, but it seemed appropriate enough. My mind quieted, I carved, and I improved. I could feel the staves giving more easily under my knife as I considered each rune's shape and nature.

I returned to Ketill's house after that long day out in the forest. The wizard was outside when I approached, loosing arrows into a berm nearby. A rotten log was his target. The arrows were tightly grouped around the same fist-sized spot.

Less drunk than usual, it seemed to me. I took it as a good sign that he was practicing archery for one, and wearing clothes for another.

"Took your time," said Ketill, loosing as one eye turned to me. Despite looking away, the arrow found the mark as well as the others.

"Whether that made any difference is what I wonder," I said.

Ketill reviewed these staves and almost complimented me again. I took this as permission to ask more questions.

"If I carved *fehu : hagalaz*, wouldn't that be *cattle : falling from the sky*?" I asked.

"It could be."

"It seems to me there has been no cattle falling from the sky," I said, uncertain after Ketill's terse response.

"Do you think you could will such a spell to happen?" he asked.

"Yes. Well, why not?" I was very willful at the time, hence the confidence.

"And as far as your intellect goes," continued Ketill, "is it your understanding that cattle might fall from the sky?"

"Not . . . yet?"

"Will *and* intellect," said the wizard. "Not *or*. You know very well cattle don't fall from the sky."

"What would be the result of such a spell then?"

The wizard shrugged. "If I cast it, it would be something very different in mind to make it work. A man's wealth collapsing in on him, perhaps, taking *fehu* to mean wealth in general. A pointless curse."

"Why pointless?"

"Because wealth collapsing in on a man is likely to happen on its own, if it is likely to happen at all. Better to try spells with more immediate effects when you need them than invest yourself in longstanding curses."

"What if I wanted to make a curse look like a blessing?" I asked.

"Why do that?" he demanded.

"Well," I began, less sure of myself than even a second prior, "it seems to me some of rune magic is like poetry. And in poetry we love double meanings. Maybe unclear which meaning is intended, or, even better, both meanings at once. Sometimes a poet will say such a verse and I can hear the irony behind it."

Ketill lowered his bow and took a hard look at me. What was on his mind during these looks, I could never tell. I was so often stumbling into areas I knew nothing about, and to him everything was so obvious. Whether he thought me a bumbling fool or an intrepid pathfinder at any time was unclear.

"Your will must be clear when you carve," he said. "Your intellect must sort out those other meanings and your will must reject those you do not intend. Will is more than intent. A divided meaning between two at once would be . . ." He shook his head. "This is far too complicated to be a concern right now. You need to carve well."

I gestured at the staves. "Do I not?"

"You do *not*," he replied. "You have got the basic forms well enough, but carving is much more. You will need many discs to carve on now. Ash, yew, birch, elm, oak. See which ones work best for you."

"The entire alphabet on discs?" I asked.

Ketill shook his head as he went to retrieve his arrows. "Of course not. There is little space for that, and not the carving you must do. Next you are carving spells."

I stopped dead, mouth open, unbelieving. Spells, finally!

"You just won't cast any."

My mouth hit the ground. The emotional back and forth of sensing accomplishment and disappointment was trying my nerves.

"You will conceive spells and carve them, but not seal them. Some will be of my assignment and some of your creation. You will take . . ." He stared upward, considering. "You will take nine at a time and return when you are finished. Then you will explain your thoughts and I will tell you why they are all wrong." The wizard pulled his last arrow from the rotten trunk and turned back to me, grinning. "Just at first."

"I will begin making the discs then," I said.

I turned and started to stalk off. Ketill had knowledge I wanted, but he was the least encouraging, most excruciating instructor I had ever encountered. How much I missed the few words of praise Halstein would give when I finished a lesson in Latin or Greek. How much I would have given for Taika's easy smile as I named plants we found in the forest.

The feeling was beginning to grate on me. So much so that even I was surprised.

Between my tone and manner, and probably both, Ketill seemed to sense it.

"Perhaps an errand less apt to draw such criticisms first," said Ketill. "An errand for yourself. You will need a pouch for the discs, so go kill something with that sling of yours and take its skin. You will need something small, but not too small. This will be yours entirely, nothing inherited from me. Go off then, and see what the forest offers you."

CHAPTER 35

BEAVER? HARDLY KNEW HER

THE FOREST OFFERED ME AN OTTER, WHICH I REFUSED.

Bad luck to kill an otter, especially with a stone. There's a story about you might even recognize once I tell it. Grieving kinsmen and cursed gold and a man turning into a dragon and the dragon eating people.

It is a good story. It's really the story of Sigurd the Dragon Slayer, but almost all Norse stories begin at least a generation before the hero is born. Instead of beginning with Sigurd, it begins with a bunch of people he is not even related to. In fact, unlike Sigurd, they are all dwarves.

These were three brothers, Ottar, Regin, and Fafnir, and their father Hreidmar. We begin with Ottar, who could transform himself into an otter, hence the name. He did this and probably enjoyed the swimming and fresh salmon a great deal.

Then Loki, the betrayer of the gods, crushed his skull with a rock.

Loki hadn't betrayed anyone quite yet. Well, depending on the chronology of events you believe in, he may already have cut off Sif's hair, stolen Freya's necklace, and aided in the kidnapping of Idunn, for a few. But in this case, he had not meant to cause any Asgard-shaking mischief. Like me, Loki had just seen an otter and an opportunity for a nice pelt.

And he got that pelt, showing it to his traveling companions Odin and Hoenir. The three came to Hreidmar's house looking for hospitality. Hreidmar gladly took them in. Then Loki offered the otter pelt as a gift, which

Hreidmar recognized right away as the skin of his dead son. This did not go over well.

Upon learning they had just offered Hreidmar the skin of his own son, Loki had to pay weregild for the killing. Should he find enough gold to cover the pelt entirely, that would be enough compensation. And he found it! Through a series of tricks and threats, he acquired just enough gold, with a magic ring covering the last whisker. The debt was paid, and the gods were off.

Except that treasure was cursed. Not just the ring that covered the last whisker, but all of it. Maybe the curse didn't matter to someone like Loki, who was already rotten. That gold would overtake anyone with greed and turn them. This was the dragon sickness Finnr had described. You don't turn into a dragon all at once. There are plenty of bad decisions between the beginning of the sickness and any such turning.

First Fafnir killed his father, Hreidmar, to keep the gold to himself. He shut his brother Regin right out of the inheritance. Then, over a period of years, Fafnir's body became as corrupted as his mind, and he turned into a dragon. Not a big, incredible flying dragon like Nidhogg, the dragon of Hel. Just your run of the mill lindworm, more slithery and snake-like with its long body and stubby claws, and no wings.

Fafnir slept on his hoard and only ventured out from it to eat people once in a while. Regin obviously thought this was unfair, so he sent his foster son Sigurd to kill Fafnir and thus regain that gold.

Finally, we get to the protagonist!

Regin was no lindworm, but that treasure had turned his thoughts just as much as Fafnir. He planned to have Sigurd kill Fafnir, and then kill Sigurd, his own foster son, later.

Regin's plan was half successful. Sigurd hid in the ground and stabbed Fafnir through the heart as he crawled over, won the treasure, and ate the dragon's heart. Dragon's blood is an unpredictable thing, however. Even the taste of it gave Sigurd the ability to understand the speech of birds, not just ravens who can speak and trade stories.

Sigurd was quite interested to hear the birds discussing Regin's plan.

How these random birds knew the dwarf's plan to kill Sigurd is not explained in any version I ever heard. Maybe birds are just that much smarter than the rest of us.

Armed with this knowledge from the birds, Sigurd killed Regin before Regin could kill Sigurd.

Then begins an even longer, even more sensational story about hurt feelings, kinslaying, and thoughtfully assessing situations to consistently make bad decisions. In that order. We call that the story of the Volsungs, the most famous and most stupid family in the history of Midgard.

So when the forest offered me an otter I could kill with a stone, I remembered that chain of events Loki had set off by killing an otter and I refused the offering. I suppose sometimes an otter is just an otter, but even I wasn't willing to push my luck quite that far. More of that sense of humor the *land-vættir* have, or maybe a test. Spirits are never very explanatory.

I kept looking and I found a beaver. No stories about beavers being bad luck to kill, at least none I knew of. I let fly a stone and hit him full in the side of the head. Then I had what the forest had offered me.

That beaver's body was no easy thing to fetch. I had hit him squarely in the side of the head to make an instant kill. Not quite as instant but not far behind, its body fell sideways into the river and began to drift down with the current.

Then came a series of awkward missteps as I tried to retrieve the carcass. Frustrating for me, comical for anyone watching, if anyone was.

I ran down the bank and found myself blocked and needing to backtrack. So I did that and thought I would go further along to cut off the dead beaver's escape, but decided against this because I might lose sight of it. I ran back to where I had slung the stone, took off my belt, pack, and shirt, and dove into the river after it.

The current was gentle, just as it had been that first day I saw Fanya in all her glory. I swam out easily and grabbed hold of the beaver with one hand. I had swum against currents before, just never with a single arm. The exertion to get there felt good, and I decided to try swimming back with a stroke modified for one arm. The exercise was refreshing after days or weeks of little else but walking and menial errands.

I emerged from the water panting but with more energy than usual. It was when I started wringing the water out of my hair I noticed Fanya.

She was standing up the bank and just inside the shade of the forest, smiling at me. A hand to her lips as she looked down seemed to speak of embarrassment for my being half-undressed. Her manner was different in that way, more playing the shy girl than I had ever seen before.

Something was up (take that to mean what you will) and she beckoned me to follow her.

There was a warmth growing inside me and a numbness in my limbs as if I were in a dream. A really, really good dream. I stumbled my way up after her. A foot disappeared behind a tree and I followed it, but found only air as I turned the corner.

Quiet as a cat, she had snuck around from behind and gently caressed my shoulder. I turned to see her so radiant she glowed.

The palm on my chest was gentle, but the feeling it produced shot through the rest of me such that I gasped. My head swam, the anticipation bubbling through my entire body and making the world's sights and sounds a blur. Still, it was unmistakably Fanya, her flowing red hair and glowing green eyes melting me with desire.

She was through playing games. My fear of what came next punctuated the dumb lust I felt at that moment.

Then I was on my back. Someone had taken off my pants. Was it me? I couldn't tell. I didn't care.

Fanya stood over me and lifted her skirt, teasing me with a few peeks beneath. I lay there motionless, my limbs heavy with pleasure, and she descended upon me. She moaned as I felt her enshroud me and she pulled my hands to her breasts.

What a wonderful feeling that was. It was almost so overwhelming I hardly noticed the black blur in the tree above us. I saw it, it was nothing, and I went back to giving in to Fanya. Then the black blur spoke, and in a voice clear and loud enough to cut through my ecstasy. And this is what it said:

> "Buried in the bush
> > a new beaver in his britches;
> water instead of wind.
>
> The skald plays
> > another's skin game.
> Now that story stops.
> Now that picture is pierced.
> Now that bust is burst!"

What did he mean, '*water instead of wind . . .*'

I blinked. The world unblurred and my senses returned to normal, the dreamy tenor of everything evaporating in seconds. I blinked again, and again, and wondered if I was going insane.

Fanya was no longer Fanya. It was Queen Alfhild astride me, her voice encouraging me in time with every gyration of her hips. Her eyes were not closed in ecstasy but rolled back in boredom. Coming out of my stunned state, I heard the tone of irony in her moans.

Humor stared down at me wondering what I was about to do.

I stared back at him wondering what I should do. I wanted to throw her off me, but assaulting a queen was generally a bad idea.

Humor shrugged.

The queen noticed my sudden lack of enthusiasm and stopped her gyrations. "You picky little man," she said, her voice with all the warmth of a frozen lake. "Must it really be the redheaded bitch?"

"You sounded so enthused, I had to respond accordingly," I said.

No doubt, Queen Alfhild was beautiful. Her face was carved as of marble and the curves of her body were those any man would wish on his wife. But her face! Perfect features could not mask the disgust it held. Her voice was like acid, every gesture she made contemptuous. She had beauty, but so maligned it with an inherent ugliness she could never truly be called beautiful.

The queen hissed at me as she rose and darted away behind that same tree. When I got up and looked around, there was no trace of her.

"Well done," said Humor. "Or perhaps, well not done. Which is it, anyway?"

"Never you mind," I said.

I lay there propped on my elbows, wondering what had just happened. Or rather, why it had just happened. I did not wish to ask Ketill, but Humor would no doubt tell him the story. Ymir's bones! Nothing to do but get that over with then. I just needed to get dressed again, and then a parting thought occurred to me.

"Humor?" I asked as the raven fluttered his wings. "Do you know where I left my beaver?"

He did.

CHAPTER 36

GALDRALAG

The gods do not help you forget things. That is what alcohol is for, and why it is so much more important than faith.

I pondered this as I returned to the river's edge and let the sun embrace me, the energy welling up as I walked out of the shade. Some experiences leave one with the feeling of great and insightful change. The experience I'd just had made me want to wash off and have a drink.

It gave me a new appreciation for Ketill's constant drunkenness. Maybe the old man was that much wiser than the rest of us.

But I had expectations levied upon me, and those were by my own choice. So I was working instead of drinking ale. Skinning the beaver was a good distraction from being alone with my thoughts.

A better distraction was Ulfberht when he showed up. He was so covered with soot, he looked like he had just crawled through a fire giant's tunnel.

"Had enough charcoal burning for today?" I asked.

"It is as much as I can fit in his cart," said Ulfberht, his Norse having improved. "And more."

He flung off his clothes as if never wanting to see them again and waded into the cool river. I knew the feeling. Between the smoke from the long, slow burning to make charcoal and then the clouds of dust kicked up by hacking the finished bits into uniform pieces, you would almost want to breathe the water in to clean yourself out.

The dirty feeling of it wasn't the worst though. That was the waiting. Charcoal is just partially burned wood, but burned in a controlled way. It took a long time and during long times of waiting, I would be distracted. And distraction is no better for a charcoal burner than for a baker. Fouling up a batch meant starting the hated process over, and that was the worst of it.

Ulfberht had more patience for it than I had. More patience indeed than I had for anything in those days. But he had his work to do and I had mine. The simple task of getting an animal skin had become a conversation I dreaded having with the wizard. It would happen sooner or later, and so I bade Ulfberht goodbye and returned to Ketill to tell him what had happened.

It was a serious conversation with serious questions, and somehow he expected me to respond with answers. The question of why Queen Alfhild would bother seducing me in the first place was not answered. Any time I was tempted to conclude she had found me irresistible, I reminded myself of her eyes rolling in dismissiveness rather than pleasure, and her moans a mockery. Only when I was under her glamour did her facade fool my senses. Otherwise, she had been disinterested, perhaps even disgusted. Disgusted with me, or with herself?

The wizard poured me a drink when I returned and bade me sit in his house. It was still stiflingly hot and smoky, but at least he had ale. It was time for a long drink.

"So tell me," he said.

I interrupted him, wiping my mouth with one hand and holding the cup out for more ale with the other. To his credit, he did not hesitate to fill it. I was three cups in when he spoke again.

"Tell me of this encounter you had."

He wanted to know every detail. As for commenting on it, he offered little other than reassurance that I was not the fool I thought myself to be. Or not in this case. It was Ketill, after all. The one observation he did offer was about Humor's verse being done well. It was the meter of magic spells, or *galdralag*.

"I thought that was just a meter to describe magic," I said. "Like in Odin's rune song. He tells us about eighteen spells he knows, but never how to cast them. At least not in any version I ever heard."

"*Galdralag* is the meter of magic, to describe it and to weave it. Like your other poetry, but there are more subtleties in speaking such spells than adding an extra line with a few alliterating syllables. The raven knows it well."

I had so many more questions.

"What kind of magic did Alfhild use? What could I carve onto a charm to counter Alfhild's magic in the future? Could a carved charm counter *seiðr*? Would I need to carve the runes right onto myself? Why did she even do it?"

This was all much more complicated than I ever thought it would be, and the wizard had few answers.

"She used *seiðr*, of course," was one answer. "Not that it matters whatsoever. You would not disperse the spirits she trapped to do her bidding with a simple talisman."

"Was she trying to get one of those spirits inside me?"

"It sounds more like she wanted to get something out of you," said Ketill. "And those spirits doing her bidding may have already gotten inside you. Was it a spell to change her appearance, or only your senses?" The wizard shrugged. "A good verse by the raven, though. Poetry is often the best of counterspells."

"Why do you not instruct me in *galdralag* then?"

"Because you already know it. Was that not how you stopped that sacrifice?"

"I used a different verse form."

"Ah, you were not instructed on the intellect. But it was close, and your will cast it forward. There is some magic in all poetry, as you should already know."

"I suppose. I thought it was not very strong though. Good for influencing or inspiring, maybe."

"You can do more than that. Perhaps I have assumed too much . . ." The old man's voice trailed off into a whisper. "You know *ljóðaháttr?*"

"The meter of wisdom? Of course." I used it when I wanted to make a point rather than tell a story. "I used it to insult Halfdan the Toothless. And also later, when some of the men wanted to throw Huld overboard but I wanted them to listen."

"That is the basis of *galdralag*, you only add a line or two. Or three, depending."

"Depending on what?"

"Depending on the feel of it. You are the skald, you will learn by doing. But the thing is, there is more than alliteration in those extra lines. There is repetition, and the saying of the same thing in different ways, as if you are surrounding an idea and forcing it to happen."

"You mean like 'the bust is burst'?"

Ketill laughed. "He is Humor, after all."

At least the wizard approved of taking the beaver. In a week, I had a fine bag made from its skin to carry my carvings in. Ketill had me stay at night to keep up on errands and rune study. As Ulfberht had to carry charcoal back to town anyway, he also carried word of my progress back to Haldor.

Fine with me, as it meant I did not need to explain my, um, meeting with the queen. I was uncertain how to handle seeing her next. Better to stay away and focus on learning.

Expecting to carve runes with any skill given all the necessary tools is like having an axe and assuming this is all you need to build a house. It is what you need to get the job done, but getting the job done requires something more than just the will to do it. It requires knowledge of subtle meanings and esoteric allusions.

Will and intellect, the lesson of every day. And it was not that day I started to get anything else right.

Nor was it the next.

More weeks passed. My frustration grew, both with the wizard and with myself. I missed telling stories in the hall and drinking ale with the crew. I did not see any sign of Fanya or hear news of the troll. Those things were out of my control, so I focused on what I could do. And as far as Ketill was concerned, I could do his chores and I could carve runes for practice.

Now I knew poetry better than I had even before, but there was no way for me to use it. I was stuck trying to carve spells, and failing almost all the time.

"Some of your combinations are acceptable, but the way you understand them is wrong," Ketill told me, in one of his gentler corrections. "You cannot stumble into a spell and cast it by accident and have it turn out well. Those castings go awry—you would be lucky to get no effect."

"Why do I keep carving new discs and then carving the discs wrong and then throwing them in the fire then? I could just draw the runes in the dirt and wipe the wrong attempts away."

"You could," said Ketill, who hid nothing of his own rising frustration. "But you would be nearby bothering me. I would need to attend to you constantly as if you were an invalid. You need to go do your work and not expect praise for every effort you make. More important is you need to go away and not bother me for most of the day."

"I wonder what it is you are doing all day that I should not disturb you."

Ketill looked at me with something between the end of patience and the beginning of every look I had ever received from Kraki.

"Yes, you wonder," he growled, tugging at his beard. "I need to think. Do some of that if you can manage it."

"I—"

"*Elsewhere.*"

Sometimes I forgot Ketill's limits. Faced with the ability to live a comfortable life in Lejre, he had instead chosen to live away from its inhabitants. Not only away, but hidden from them so no one could find him even if looking. Unless he wanted them to. His tolerance for loud-mouthed company would have been much like my tolerance for sea travel and fermented shark. I would tolerate them to avoid dying, but not for any other reasons.

Something deep inside me growled its displeasure. I understood the old man, yes, but I did not like thinking of myself as rotten shark meat.

So I set out for a suitable spot to practice feeling not at all good about practicing. Humor was nowhere to be seen or heard, which was good. I didn't need that bird distracting me. Carving required ever-increasing concentration, making it doubly disappointing when I learned all that effort had been in poor attempts.

I knew the forest well enough by now that I could sense the direction it would give me. There was little need to mark my path or even intend a specific course, so I headed away from Ketill's hut and let whatever intent was guiding me show me a path.

Wherever I was going, it was away. And when I came back, it would be towards. North, South, East, and West did not seem to have the same meaning when the forest was involved. The geography itself appeared to shift. I had gotten used to it by then and accepted the guidance as offered.

That day's guidance led me to an unfamiliar place. It was a small clearing from which nothing could be discerned. Only birch trees and some groundcover stretched on as far as I could see. In the middle of the clearing there was a stump cut from a tree much thicker than those grown around it. A bright green layer of moss looked to soften its surface, making it an inviting seat to take. This was the kind of sign I had come to take as a suggestion from the forest to sit.

So I sat.

No ravens or kingfishers. No rabbits or foxes or bears. Only the soft sound of the wind kept me company. I had questions to work out, and the one that nagged at me most was a spell I could use for protection against my senses being so easily confounded. It was difficult enough to figure out what was going on around me without my eyes and ears telling me the wrong things. Besides, if it aided my senses, perhaps I could begin to hear Fanya sneaking up on me.

Nauthiz meant 'need,' and so if another rune meant 'protection' then I could use the two in combination. No runes meant 'protection,' at least in a straightforward way. I could carve the combination *nauðiz : þurisaz* for 'need the protection of Thor,' but maybe that would be 'protection *from* Thor,' as in protection from a lightning storm. Also, I could see Thor becoming annoyed at constant calls for his protection.

Maybe *dagaz* for 'day' or 'light' instead, the intent to illuminate what was around me in my perception. Yes, I thought, *nauðiz : dagaz*, and I carved that onto a disc to show Ketill later.

Having finished that carving, I had another thought. Must I carve the runes in sequence? And must I carve them all upright? If I carved *nauðiz* upside-down, would that mean to have an excess of something? That was not my intent for this spell, but I wondered at the possibilities.

The idea I had was not to turn the runes but to combine them. Carving them in sequence would limit the interpretation to the order left to right, but if I carved *nauðiz* as my need inside a *dagaz* rune, I could take that as illumi-nation of my need, whatever it might be. Would that type of carving work at all? Or could it be something terrible unleashed? I carved it all the same, intent on asking Ketill many questions, and then readied another disc to carve.

So many questions. These were not the first. For certain they were not the only ones I wanted to ask the old wizard. But his patience was thin and his temper was mighty. I chose my questions carefully those days.

That was on my mind as I pulled another disc from my pouch, this time paying attention to the wood. It was ash, *askr* in my language. The word could mean ash the tree or a small ship. Or a spear of ash. Were the other meanings of the word more important, or was it more important that ash was strong and unyielding compared to yew and elm?

My blade fell from the disc. I still had no idea how this worked, even after weeks of practice. I knew how language worked and what turned language into poetry. I knew how to work in themes and underlying ideas. That was because I could hear it and feel it and be inspired by it myself. This runic language was something else—a code rather than poetry, and meant for whose consumption?

I could not feel my way through it. When I did feel as though I was getting somewhere, I found I was farther afield than before. I was lost, in over my head, biting off more than I could chew. Pick your metaphor, that was where my mind was at. It left me in a foul state of mind.

"Has your wood gotten the better of you?"

I was startled at the sound of Fanya's voice. She stood behind me half-leaning on her spear. Sunlight filtered through the trees and caught her hair so that it shone like fire as she smiled.

"A man is worth little who cannot control his wood," she said. "Such a scowl!" she continued, smirking at the jest and then disappointed when I did not respond in kind.

I cannot fault her for my ill feelings now. But then? Then my mind went immediately to how she had disappeared for so many weeks. Weeks when I was struggling, when a kind word would have meant a great deal. Her absence felt like abandonment, and her sudden reappearance like I was a fun plaything only. But that was hardly all.

Frustration was from more than failing to make progress at rune carving. However much a relief it had been to have a drink (several drinks) after the episode with Alfhild, that relief had been temporary. I was hurt at being deceived, frustrated it had not been Fanya after all, and angry I had not been warned.

Was a simple warning from Fanya a reasonable expectation? Only if she valued me over her queen, which seemed foolish. Foolish or not, I was jealous that Alfhild had Fanya's loyalty and I did not. All those emotions meant I was indeed scowling instead of smiling.

Had I been a simple man with simple inclinations, life would not always have felt so complicated. And it felt very complicated at that time, made more so by Fanya's presence which I never knew how to take. She was there and gone in a flash most of the time, more exciting for the tease and uncertainty. But did she return my feelings? It was unthinkable to ask, and so I remained brooding on my stump.

In a better mood, I might conjure a verse or make witty wordplay with her, but I was worn down and raw. And I wanted something I could make sense of.

"What does Alfhild want with my seed?" I asked, omitting the queen's title on purpose. Fanya's smile vanished and she hefted her spear, pacing back and forth in front of me.

"Most men would not complain about such interest," she stated in a thin voice.

"Perhaps most men are under her spell," I said. "I remember that state. I followed a picture of beauty as it bid me. But I remember what I woke to when that spell broke, handmaiden. It was disgust and I have never seen anything so ugly. I have enjoyed our games but I cannot play today. So tell me: What does she want?"

"Do you not care what I want?" she shouted, rounding on me. "Disgust and dismissal, why do you even give her a thought then?"

"I tire of mysteries," I said, my voice rising. "What do you have but more of them?"

We stood staring into each other's eyes, the tension thick with pride holding back dams of unspoken desire. Nothing more did either of us want, I now think, than to have those dams break open to one another. Yet neither of us could be the first to yield. So we watched, each hoping to find a crack in the other and thus a reason to give in. But both of us were strong and weak and afraid in all the right ways for neither dam to give way.

The only way to win such a contest is by not speaking first. Or if speaking, to act as if no contest ever existed. A bit like the rope-pulling game. Either dominate your opponent or, in the height of his pull, let go of the rope and walk away ceding the victory but causing him to fall on his ass.

"Perhaps you should go where you are wanted then, and put your mysteries away," Fanya said, dropping the proverbial rope on me.

She turned and set off at a light jog and disappeared behind a tree.

She was gone, I thought. I felt her absence in a more profound way than I thought I could feel an absence. One thing her visit had changed in me was my blood was up. I was done being sad and avoidant and careful of everything around me, and I marched off with clear intent.

That wizard was going to start answering questions, whatever his damned mood might be.

CHAPTER 37

SHITSTORM

I SLAMMED THE DISCS ONTO THE TABLE LIKE A TRIUMPHANT gambler showing off how much he had to bet.

"What do you think of these?" I asked, waiting for Ketill to rage at me so I could rage back.

"You were gone for some time," answered Ketill. "Was this all the wood involved in your private machinations?"

Had Humor been there to report on my argument with Fanya? Every move I made might be watched and relayed, it seemed.

"I was working on that spell of protection against the kind of glamour Alfhild used on me," I said, taking a page from Ketill and ignoring most of what he said. "I thought about a lot of possibilities that might work, but they did not feel right. This feels right to me. Is it—"

"A bind rune?!" Ketill did not shout it, but the surprise in his voice was evident. "I did not teach you this. Where did you get this idea?" He flipped the disc over so I could see it. It was the version where I had carved a rune within a rune instead of in sequence as he had instructed.

I shrugged. "I was experimenting. It occurred to me that inverting a rune for *need* might then turn it into *obligation* or somesuch. But that did not help with the spell I was trying to create, so I thought about other manipulations I might make to the way they were carved. *Need light* seemed too literal, as if you needed a torch lit in the dead of night. I need something to make my senses accurate against magic, not against darkness. So I thought that *light* within *need* could imply an inside light, something that sees through an illusion."

Ketill looked at me, then at the disc. He pulled at his long gray beard, looked at me, and looked back at the disc. "This is too advanced for you," he said. "Interesting though."

"I am glad you find it so interesting," I said, my voice rising. "Now how do I cast a rune spell to protect me from witches?" I was near shouting with frustration by the end. All that consideration and Ketill taking an obvious interest, but he was being very reticent about my experiments.

Ketill growled. Not at me in particular, just a low, guttural uncertainty that was out of character for him. He looked about the hut and fixed on what seemed to me as random objects, giving a dismissive expression after each one. "Hmm," he hmmed, as if that was some answer, and as if pulling on his beard while he hmmed it made it that much more sage advice.

"Aha!" he finally concluded. "Sit down, and I will get some ale."

Why he would not want me to pour the ale, I had no idea. I had done something and still could not tell if it was good or bad.

"If I sit down will you explain what is going on? I have had enough of mysteries for the day."

"Ha! You are a strange one indeed. You understand some things too far, and other things not far enough," he said as I sat down. He was fiddling with the containers and tossing some, hopefully the filthy ones, aside as he rummaged through a box. "That can cause difficulties."

"Difficulties as big as serving ale?"

"Patience!" he shouted, without looking up. "I would ask you to tell me about your encounter. *Which* encounter, you might ask. You know the *witch* of which I speak. You wanted her, but you did not have her. Correct?"

So the raven had been watching me.

"I hope this is a large serving of ale," I said as Ketill continued to mess about with his back to me.

"Aha! It is, but that does not matter much." Ketill turned around with a horn in each hand. Apparently it was a special occasion. He looked from one to the other and back, then dipped the first one into the barrel, poured its contents into the second, and handed it to me. Then he dipped the first one again and kept it for himself, raising it in a toast.

I returned the toast with less enthusiasm, and we drank deep.

"So you had the curiosity and the courage to go off by yourself and try carving experimental spells. But a beautiful woman you are in love with appears, and you are afraid to do anything about it. Most men would have this reversed. Or, if not reversed, most men would hobble back with blue balls, considering how to bed the woman rather than demanding explanations on esoteric rune lore."

"Is there a point to this or are you just shooting me with insults rather than arrows now?"

"You mistake my meaning. You have learned so much, your mind takes new knowledge and turns it over in a hundred ways. And you want to know more, always more. But I told you there was will as well as intellect in magic! Do you think there is no magic inherent to love or lust?"

"So if I bed a witch, then I can cast spells?"

Ketill choked on his ale. "You are not listening! If you want to control magic, you need to understand it."

"But I understand what the runes mean!"

"You do not." His voice was flat and the animated charm in him vanished. "You memorized what I told you they mean. You do not know them any more than a sober man knows drunkenness or a living man knows death."

"So I would know better if I got drunk and died?"

"Yes," he said, and meant it. "You just described Odin's life and death and life after death when he found the runes and brought them back. Why do you think the stories say all he consumes is wine? Why do you think he hung there, spear-pierced, for nine nights? Recall his description:

> *I took up the runes—*
>> *Screaming I took them—*
> *And then I fell from there.*

"That is the wisest of the *Æsir*, the Hel-blind, the Father of the Slain. Willing to put himself through something that made even him scream, just so he could learn. And that is how you will learn if you can manage it. Most cannot. They like the idea of learning and that contents them enough they don't actually do it. Odin warns us too much wisdom is a prescription for unhappiness, and he knows it first-hand."

"You have had me carving runes this whole time. It has not made me scream yet."

"Yes, quite," he said, draining and refilling his horn. "That was my mistake, to have you occupied in such a way. Now I see you carving bind runes out of boredom given too much knowledge and not enough application."

"What do you mean by application?" I asked, excited. "You mean you want me to cast basic spells first? Will you show me how?"

"No and no. You have the basis as far as knowledge goes, but you lack the experiences that would let you mold it."

"A man should have room to make mistakes," I said. "Otherwise all he learns is avoiding mistakes. My foster father told me that, and it served well enough in learning languages."

"You are making plenty of mistakes!" said the wizard. "Yet you are not maimed or dead. Do not think you can demand the safety of making mistakes and immediate results both in the same breath."

With a great effort, I held my horn and thereby prevented myself from throwing my hands in the air with frustration. It would have been unseemly to react so, even if the old man kept talking around the point and not getting to it.

Without further direction, I was adrift like a boat in open water. But as I would learn over and over in my later years, the passing on of knowledge is a strange thing. It is done poorly if lectured directly, but often the more subtle attempts go unnoticed. How then to teach the ignorant?

"Have you ever shit your brains out?" asked Ketill.

"I may have retained them," I said.

He continued as if not hearing me. "I know a very effective spell for affecting the insides of your enemies to their great detriment. People talk about making swords sharp and spears fly far. Ha! If you want to break a shield wall, evacuate the bowels of its front line all at once! You skalds do not like to write poems about that sort of thing being true, but it is. It is the same as all the other spells though, so you cannot cast it effectively if you have, yourself, never shit your brains out."

"Pity I have missed such an experience."

"Oh but you can do that tomorrow."

"What? Shit my brains out?"

"Of course! Then you can cast the same spell. Your first spell: the shit-stormer."

"I do not believe such a storm is brewing," I said, patting my midsection.

Ketill laughed that slow, self-satisfied laugh. "It is though. I cast it on you already. The runes are carved into your horn, and the ale has carried that spell down to your belly at this point." Fear or spell, my stomach lurched at the statement. Even Ketill heard the grind of my intestines. "Then again, maybe it will not take until tomorrow. I am old, after all, and I shit my brains out with some regularity only to scoop them up and put them back in. Wisdom grows with suffering and power grows with wisdom. My spell may be more potent for that." He downed the rest of his ale. "Good luck."

My insides growled as if inhabited by the Midgard Serpent, and by then it was clearly more than fear at work inside me.

"Hel's dragon!" I said. "You crazy old man! I'm going to shit my brains out now!"

"Haha! Yes you are," said Ketill. "But not here. Get back to the city and shit where it already stinks. Otherwise, the forest may stop liking you so much."

Likely you have experienced a sudden need to empty your bowels. Perhaps you have taken it upon yourself to run long distances without stopping. I had known both, but never at the same time. I do not recommend combining them.

Out I flew from that place, clutching my midsection as if to keep it from bursting forth. I could feel it bubble and hear it groan, whatever worked its ill intent inside me. What I would not have given for a witch and her herbs just then. Perhaps if I had offered a poem of my love for Fanya and a flower or two, that would have stayed her wrath and I might have called upon her for health.

Those thoughts distracted me for some minutes as I plunged through the forest before my guts wrenched my mind to more bowelly matters. I broke air for twice as long as I ever had and felt some relief. Partly in the release of pressure, and partly because it was only air. So far.

I pressed on, my will focused on 'away' even more powerfully than it had been earlier in the day when Ketill had near chased me out.

The forest responded. My footfalls were easy and sure, with no branches or rocks or exposed roots to hinder me. But the warning of that evil wizard was still with me, and I did not wish to lose favor with the *landvættir* by splattering bowels and brains all over the forest floor.

I mean regular defecation, silent or silent-ish and soon buried, that's one thing. But what I was eager to expel would be angry sounding and splash with a suddenness that could easily be taken as an insult. Perhaps the forest had a sense of humor, I thought as I looked up at the treetops for the raven. He was not there, and I hoped the forest had a sense of humor without Humor himself.

So I kept running. And breathing. And just in case the spirit of the forest was confused about the intent of the farting man running through its woods, I shouted my situation to the leaves, to the rocks, to the animals that might listen. There was no ill intent on my part, I wanted to make it clear. Just get me past the treeline to a place I could safely expel the evil inside me, preferably a place with a lot of broad leaves around.

The path I found was one unfamiliar to me, though that was no surprise. My need must have been clear because I was soon out of the forest and into open greenery. I looked at the unfamiliar hill that sloped gently upward abutting the nearby fens and saw a lone linden tree at its apex.

Flowers on the tree were blooming. I could smell the soft aroma as I approached. It seemed to me the forest had extended its will just beyond the treeline or else directed me near to the fens. The fens smelled foul already, but I was not about to venture into them and risk my safety if Gudbrand was right about what lurked in them. Hearing my need, the forest had offered me a path to a linden tree, a tree we knew otherwise as perfect for making shields. It was the poetic gesture of a true friend.

Not yet to the point of inadvertent expulsion, I made my way up the hill, untying my pants as I went. The warm afternoon was giving way to evening by then, and I hoped the cursed liquid I had drunk would not keep me until nightfall. Ketill had intended I shit my brains out, but how long would that take? And the spell worked quite a bit faster than he had intended. Would it literally be my brains then? Would that be the end of Ansgar Styrgrimsson?

What stories would they tell of my death if they found such a corpse?

A pang of pain tore back my attention to the present. It was near time, I knew, but I was not so desperate I could not undress. I tore off my shoes and socks and pants and laid my belt and weapons along with my pouch beside the clothing, all well away from the spot I had chosen. Thinking twice, I removed my long shirt as well.

I chose a low-hanging branch with many leaves, thinking that would be enough. Then I stopped and hacked down another equally leafy branch. I would take no chances.

There was a joint between two large roots as they met the trunk that I was able to position my feet outside of with some support. That would give me at least a bit of a splash shield. If it worked, I swore I would forever love linden trees and never mistreat them. I squatted facing the fens as I offered this small prayer, not to anything in particular yet to anything that would listen.

Great shooting pains went through my body and whatever mild discomfort I had heretofore experienced became great, wracking spasms. Lightning coursed through me. Liquid fury erupted from my arse at high velocity. The impact made a mockery of the splash shield I had scouted out. My only comfort was the support of the tree as I rocked back while my legs shot straight out in front of me. I tried to push myself up the trunk to get away from it, and that was my last thought before I passed out.

It was not a long time. Perhaps only a few minutes. I awoke face down, thankfully in nothing but dirt and grass. As I uprighted myself, I looked behind me to see the tree and the unholy fecal altar I had carved into it. I closed my eyes and shook my head as if to not retain the image. But I could not but look again, and I sighed a sad sigh as the light caught the steam floating upward. At least this was nothing anyone had seen, I thought.

"Mmmmmmmm" said the stupid, low rumble of a voice behind me.

I thought it might be Humor, because who would be more appropriate to appear at such a point? But it was not Humor.

The owner of the voice was one I did not recognize but knew as soon as I saw. The huge frame towered three heads above me, half again as broad. The skin showed an oily slick sheen painted over pale flesh. Not a similar pale to my skin, this had a sickly green tint to it. And yet I knew it was not sick, that this was the natural and healthy pallor of the thing, sickening though I found it.

It turned out Lejre's troll could be out in the daylight after all.

CHAPTER 38

THAT WITCH DOES NOT KILL ME

EVEN IF I COULD HAVE REACHED MY WEAPONS IN TIME, THEY were small and this thing was huge.

Even with an adequate weapon, I would not have trusted my skill to use it effectively.

The troll looked at me with one good eye and one bulbous and red. It pointed back in the direction of the fens, though if I could read anything in that face, it was confusion. I spent less time thinking about that than about how the hideous teeth pointed in every different possible direction with no two going the same way.

It breathed in great wheezing gasps through its mouth and smacked its lips. To this day that hideous memory comes back to me when I am around open-mouth chewers. Trolls, all of them.

A single step forward indicated knock-knees, but still a huge length of stride. I put up a placating hand and it paused, now more confused. Could I distract it? Could I buy myself time?

No, I decided. So I ran.

Howls of a type I never heard before or since answered after me along with great, loping steps. I ran away from the forest and towards the city. The opposite direction I had run when pursued by angry Rus. This time more complicated because I had to run through the crops rather than over them.

I began a series of new calculations: How far away were the nearest

Danes? How many were there? How close would I need to get for them to intervene? How fast could the troll run after me?

And would my insides explode again while I was trying to run? I thought they had cleared out completely, but my legs were not my own as under normal circumstances. My right foot was still asleep and my ass burned as if Surt the fire giant had kissed it with a touch of his sword.

I slowed for just a moment as my breath nearly left my control. The thought of that horrible face full of horrible teeth bore me on again, faster than before.

I chanced a look back and saw the thing had gained no ground. Every strange, lanky movement shouted its intention to embrace me and eat my face. I was not at full stride and could still put further ground between us, and this was my only comfort. This thing that slunk through the night might be able to crack my bones like twigs, but it had practiced the art of waiting until night had darkened the sky and ale had dulled men's senses. It was unused to running down sober prey through an uneven field full of vegetables.

A smile broke across my face as I thought this and it made me bold. Another wordless cry from the thing behind me tore that boldness down and stomped on its head. I jumped forward several paces for no reason other than I wanted to be as far from it as possible.

It was then I noticed the two figures walking the path up from the sea. Perhaps they had gone down to check on the *Sea Squirrel*, as shipwrights are wont to do. Or maybe they had spied easy gambling to win in Roskilde. Innstein and Utstein were enjoying a laugh about something until my piercing, incoherent screech got their attention.

They yelled back, though I could not hear over my heart beating a drum in my ears. But they shook their weapons and cheered, and Innstein lifted his horn to sound it. Utstein meanwhile pointed his spear at the thing in challenge, but still it kept after me.

I could not lead it to battle with but two of my crewmates. Even six might not be enough. I also could not run forever. What to do?

I had the sudden urge to climb a tree, and then recalled the ineffectiveness of doing so last time I had run for my life. Who knew if the troll could climb trees, or just rip them out of the ground. No, that would not solve my problem. I had to get to a place where I could go but could not be followed.

An image of a high cliff overlooking water came to mind. That would not save me—there were no inland cliffs I knew of nearby. Only a slow-moving river. And I had it! Whatever this thing looked like, it did not look like a swimmer. I swerved south towards the city at an impossible angle, making the troll think it (it was a he, but if you saw what I saw you would say 'it' as well) could cut me off.

The troll committed to my misdirection and howled when it saw the mistake as I cut a path north. The sudden adjustment back in my direction was a massive over-commitment its frame was not meant to handle. I wondered if the rigid, awkward design of that body had caused it to roll an ankle. In any case, I gained some ground, and I knew where I was going.

That was almost enough to keep me safe.

I scanned the riverbank for a place to jump straight into the deeper water and avoid slowly wading out. A fallen tree trunk did the job even better. I dove in and soon I was being carried away. Only when I swam enough to find myself in the middle of the water did I look back to see my pursuer stomping on the ground at the water's edge.

The water was cold, but my smugness warmed me, and I took comfort in the healing balm on my still-burning bottom. My mind wandered from the immediate threat and I floated on my back to relax and consider my next step. While I floated down towards Roskilde, I felt briefly guilty that people there would be drinking the water.

Animals must do far worse in this river all the time, I decided, and felt better.

Then again, how much of that sort of water had I drunk?

Such were my thoughts as let the river carry me. I floated a long time, confident I had gotten the better of that troll. When I was probably most of the way to Roskilde, I felt a tug.

Had I brushed against an otter or angered some large fish? I flipped around to float upright in the water, slowly buoyed by the current. I felt nothing, my feet suspended well above the bottom.

Nothing until a hand grasped my left ankle and dragged me beneath the surface, the water enveloping me in a cold, wet cocoon. Through the water, with sky bright above, then through a tunnel too deep and too long to seem real.

How Alfhild pulled me through that dense murk or for how long, I couldn't say. It felt like being pulled through water, through rock, through the boundaries of Midgard. I had no control over myself in that watery place.

I came to again and realized I was coughing. I lay shivering on bare rock, desperate to catch my breath and to expel the water inside me at the same time. It felt as though I had been under water a very long time.

Valborg pressed her hand to my chest, and at that, I spluttered up a bit more water and could breathe again. Alfhild stood behind her, looking bored and wet.

"Get up," Valborg demanded as she covered the wet queen with a cloak.

"Is that a reference," I said through quickly numbing lips, "to my lack of pants?"

Valborg smiled and kicked me in the ribs. Lucky for me, witches, while dangerous magical creatures capable of ruining men's minds and visiting all manner of illusory and elemental horrors on them, are terrible at kicking.

I winced to fake a pain that might satisfy her. Content sufficient punishment had been meted out, she withdrew.

Cold water splashed at my side as I coughed again. We were in an underground cave somewhere the water had tunneled through but did not fully flood. That had been the route in, but I could also see a dry tunnel beyond, where Valborg must have entered through.

"Bring him and keep him sound of body," Alfhild told Valborg. The queen made her exit into the tunnel and left us behind. Alfhild looked to be in a hurry to get somewhere as she disappeared into the darkness.

My phony wincing bought me time to think, but not much. It was easy to conclude I was to be brought somewhere else. What my fate would be there, I could not say, nor where we would go.

Foxfire sprouted here and there where thick tree roots had delved deep into the earth and rock. The light of that fungus glowing along the walls bathed us in blue and green hues. I could see well enough, at least where the tunnel did not curve around. But there was little room to maneuver, and I had little enough to maneuver with, having left my weapons safely out of the way of Ketill's lesson.

I could grab a rock and try my luck at overpowering Valborg . . . and go where after that? The way I had come was a water demon's highway, not a route for a mere man to swim through. The other way would lead to the unknown. I had to wait, and catch my breath, and choose a better place and time.

A placating hand held off further kicks as I rose. "Poems for you and the queen," I stammered. "On your beauty and wit and guile. How about that? But they might take some time. Perhaps you could lead me away from this place, and I could find some pants." Contrary to common belief, it is very difficult to compose poetry with no pants on.

"You need no pants where I bring you," said Valborg. I raised an eyebrow at that and she got her inadvertent joke, kicking me again at the realization. "And the poetry the Mother demands is of a less verbal sort."

I considered what the queen wanted with me and could not imagine it would be much different than what she had wanted me for in the forest. Was that such a bad thing? Arguable, but whatever came after that could not be pleasant for me. I had to escape.

"The queen chose a softer bed last time," I said, standing up. "Are you full of haste, or is it jealousy that drives your anger?"

"Better than the likes of you have come into these caves," Valborg spat, her head arched forward in fury. "We have seen greater than you, and we will see greater yet. Now walk!"

She slapped the back of my knee with her wand. Wand or staff, it was a solid if short piece of hardwood with a small iron fitting at the top. I half-buckled and started shuffling forward, compliant with just enough defiance to make it known and not enough to get another whack.

"So cocky, skald," said Valborg. "But you react to my wand just as any other man." She smiled at her control over me as she led a path through that place.

"I am just as any other man," I said. "It seems you cannot get enough of my attention even with my betters about. I wonder: Did you even know what to do when heroes roamed Lejre's hills? Or did you quit the sun-washed world to curl up in this cave and gossip with the other girls?"

Only the wand answered, a sharp sensation of heat in its wake. The blow made my back spasm and I stumbled forward, cutting my foot on a rock. I resolved to stop speaking. She might need to deliver me alive, but not necessarily in excellent condition.

So I walked. The cave was not warm on that walk, and so it was around that time I began my true appreciation for pants. I walked on one foot that froze and the other that burned from its cut and tried to use the time to think my way out.

It is difficult to make those thoughts materialize while being marched away naked, though. How long I walked was difficult to say. My foot began to throb at an even pace. My thoughts could never get very far past a few seconds of consideration before they returned to the distraction of my pained foot.

"Why does the queen want me so much?" I demanded, more out of frustration than a brilliant plan to extricate myself.

"Why why why," said Valborg. "You attach so much meaning to that question. What does it matter? To receive such royal attention is an honor and makes you a lucky man, even if you are a bit of a boy."

"Perhaps I could make my own choices about whose attention I have."

"Oh, skald," she said, focusing the latter word as if speaking to a dumb animal. "You are such a little man. You want little things and you think little thoughts when you could be so much more. She can smell it on you. So can the wizard, but I wager he has said nothing of that, has he?"

As the words were forming to ask what she meant, we heard something that stopped both of us.

The caves began to whisper and then to wail, and a deep, sonorous voice from far away carried its message clear. There was pain in it, and humiliation, and a plea. It begged for comfort at the same time as forgiveness for failure. Surprise and shock and nowhere else to go were evident in cries coming from elsewhere in that cave, and I did not want to meet their owner.

I had met him once already, and I did not like his face. Or any of the rest of him. That troll was in agony. The sounds made me want to be in that cave even less, if that was possible.

As I listened more closely, my awareness soon discovered it was not the only new and surprising sound in the cave. Valborg stopped and was doing her best (not good enough) to conceal her fear. What could that mean, I wondered? And could I use it to get away?

I remember being on the cusp of saying something biting and witty that would throw the witch off and allow me to keep her distracted. It slipped my mind when Valborg jabbed me with the end of her wand again. Poetry lost to the ages, that, as Valborg demanded a faster pace.

Complaining did little to slow us down other than the pauses for being whacked with her wand, so I tried to ignore the deep ache in my foot and carried on.

As the tunnel widened, I realized we had gone from solid rock to a man-made tunnel system. The tunnel we were in opened up to a central area with multiple rooms. Though the light was low, the dim luminescence of different colors in the rooms was visible enough.

The wailing had grown tired and quieter. I started to make out the other voices nearby.

"He has bled much already," I could hear Aldis saying. "He will need more care."

Sped on by curiosity, I crept toward that conversation. Low light was enough to show me shadows moving in one of the rooms. I headed that way and stopped at the corner of the entryway as Valborg raced to catch me.

"Where is your sister?" demanded Alfhild.

"Fanya is—" Aldis paced over to a table full of vials and materials, and in doing so saw me standing there. She eyed me with evil intent and curled her lip. Whatever insult she was loading, she took too long.

". . . is anywhere but in this cave full of batshit and gloom?" I finished for her. "Most people are anywhere but here. Because this cave is full of batshit and gloom."

"You will show respect to the Mother!" shouted Valborg as she prepared another swat with her wand. I raised my arm to parry it. I was not done dealing insults. I had not even made a wordplay on her use of the title 'mother' yet.

"Queen of the worst place I have ever seen, and I have been to Fretborg. What a pathetic life to live here. No wonder Fanya is somewhere el—" and then she stomped on my injured foot.

It had her desired effect. I yowled and went down, not much in control of my body, and held my foot. As if that would make it less painful.

"I thought I was supposed to be of sound body when she returned," I said from the ground. "She meant for you to heal my foot, not make it worse." The reinterpretation of Alfhild's words was not at all what Valborg wanted to hear, but the possibility that was what she had meant stopped her in mid-thought. If I could get the gash in my foot healed, I could run again, and if I could run again, I had a chance.

I could see the steam from the stew in Valborg's brain cooking the different possibilities. Her face contorted, relaxed, and then turned into a sneering smile. "I can stop that bleeding," she said. "It will not be pleasant."

"Do it," said Alfhild. Then turning to Aldis, "It will be some time before we return."

I was about to make some reply when Valborg waved her wand in a series of ritualized motions and drew it slowly across my wound, singeing my foot. Pain blasted through me, threatening to send every limb into spasm while instead freezing my muscles in place. When it was done, my foot was steaming and blistered along the line of the cut. But the wound was no longer bleeding, even if the cure had been so much more painful than the injury.

"Take care of that one," Alfhild said, looking to Aldis. "He is soft, and I want him healthy when I return." Then turning to Valborg, "Come."

"Yes, Mother." Aldis bowed low and kept her eyes down as Alfhild strode quickly away and Valborg followed.

The soft green glow of Aldis' staff illuminated the harshness in her face. It was a heftier thing than Valborg's wand for sure, straight but gnarled wood taller than she was. I resolved to find out what these different implements meant, Valborg's wand, Aldis' staff, Fanya's spear, as soon as I was done avoiding torture and death.

When Alfhild was out of sight, Aldis was on her feet and squaring up to my prostrate form as if to challenge me. "Get up," she said, smiling.

It seemed to me the situation was likely to involve my refusal to get up, followed by a beating for refusing to get up, and then my inevitable getting up. It also seemed to me that to skip that second undesirable step I would probably need to skip the first. Still, something seemed wrong with just taking such a simple command and I did not want to get up or do much of anything else.

The queen would squeeze me dry of any worth she saw, whatever it was, and Humor was not around to help me this time. So I complied. Or tried to. That burn on my foot was quite a bit more noticeable than the cut alone had been, and I stumbled back down and knocked my head against an outcropping of rock wall.

"My foot hurts," was one of the last thoughts I recall, followed closely by something about investing in a good helmet. Then everything went black.

CHAPTER 39

WHOEVER KILLS MONSTERS

I passed out for a bit. It seemed like the prudent thing to do. A good helmet definitely would have been a good investment early on.

When I came to I was sitting back on straw bedding, my injured foot raised on a chair. A thin wool blanket covered my more sensitive bits. There was a poultice on my foot, which throbbed with pain but seemed to be better for what Aldis had administered. It was certainly an improvement on the cut I had given myself and the burn from Valborg.

An array of ingredients, dry and liquid, were spread about on the ground near a second chair. A single source of light glowed somewhere outside my small room. The light's position shifted as I heard movement.

I rose and tested my weight on the injured foot, looked around, hopped a few times to test my foot further. I had no idea where I would be stumbling in the dark if I chose to run. But I could run. Not comfortably, but I could do it. And that meant I needed a way to see and a means of guidance. Either that or wait to be used up and then discarded. Or worse, used up and then used in some awful ritual where the main ingredient would be my screams.

A torch would do me for light, but I hadn't seen any yet. Some glowing fungi in the tunnels, a glowing wand, not much else. Maybe if I had Aldis' staff. Hel's dragon, I thought. I might need to fight my way out. It made me wish I had taken Thor's advice and learned how to do that.

There were no good options. There were not even any pants—I had to settle for tying that blanket around my waist as my only clothing. So when I heard that troll groan and Aldis say something soothing in response, it seemed to me my situation had not gotten any worse. At least now there was something interesting to investigate. I rose and hobbled away from my straw seat.

I left the small room I had woken in and made for another room, larger and better lit. Each step became a little easier as I approached the source of the noise and peered in.

The troll lay on the ground in the middle of the room, its head lolling from side to side in a stupor. Aldis was fast at work with an unguent in one hand and her staff in the other. The healing salve applied, she then stood up and whispered a series of syllables I could not make out. It was all applied to a massive wound on the troll's right side. Not his arm, because there was no arm anymore. This was an irregular wound, a tear rather than a cut from a blade wound. Hand, arm, and shoulder had come away and now the broken wreckage of it steamed under the magic of her staff.

Staring over his broken body was a carved wooden statue of a boar atop a dais. No ordinary boar. The open jaw sported two sets of massive tusks, bigger than any on a wild hog I'd ever seen. The ridge along its back was carved to show three rows of bristles, each one long and sharp as an arrow. A pitiless expression looked over the troll, who turned away from the thing.

The troll winced and whined. I could not blame him since something had ripped his arm off. I shuddered to think what could have done such damage against that much bulk. A few more moans and Aldis assured the thing she was done in a low, soothing voice. She then took a vial of liquid nearby and dabbed her fingers in it before rubbing them on the smoking meat that was the troll's stump. The moans trailed off into sniffles, and, I thought, crying?

Hel's dragon, I mouthed silently to myself. I will admit it was exciting to discover such a conspiracy. But discovery and explanation are two very different things, as I was learning first-hand. I shook my head as I tried to form a narrative for what I knew, but every attempt I made seemed as illogical as the next.

Alfhild and the other witches used the troll to steal alcohol and thereby make the men of Lejre more sober and frustrated. The troll was the true king of Denmark and cursed by Ragnvald. Just as likely: The witches kept a pet troll to keep vermin away because they couldn't find a suitable cat instead.

I realized I was wrong on at least one point when a vibrating ball of fur and muscle rubbed up against my leg. The witches had indeed found a suitable cat. Or maybe the cat had found them, as I remembered this one curled up at Finnr's forge so many weeks ago. This cat found me to its liking as it purred and then let out a satisfied meow.

Too late, I realized I had lingered overmuch watching Aldis' ministrations and pondering the meaning of all the insanity happening around me. Aldis stopped and turned her attention towards the cat, which was rubbing up against something just around the corner of the room's opening.

That something was me. Should have been looking for a way out, but I was transfixed by things I did not understand. I wondered if running was a better option than fighting. Neither was a good idea. I was a terrible fighter and had no idea where I might run to. This was a point in my life where I learned an important life skill.

When you don't know what you're doing: Stall.

I picked up the cat which came willingly into my arms. A heavy beast with a thick white coat, more suited to snowy forest than humid cave tunnels. The warm vibration of the cat's purr comforted me for some reason. Perhaps it was the most familiar thing to me in that cave. In the low light, I thought I saw its eyes flash in brief at mine. It must have been a trick, I thought, as they were the round pupils of a person rather than a cat. I had no time to ponder that observation further though.

"What did you see?" demanded Aldis as she rounded the corner.

"I found this cat," I said, changing the subject. "What is his name?"

"Get back to your straw bed, little man," growled the witch.

"That is an awfully long name," I said, without the slightest hint of confidence but without the slightest hint of knowing how else to proceed.

The top of her staff glowed in an ominous green. This was not going well.

And then a curious thing happened: The cat hissed at her. Not a casual or fearful hiss from seeing a dog two houses away. It was long and loud and had more challenge to it than mere distaste. Even I felt a shudder when I heard that thing's battle-grumble.

Aldis snarled back and leveled her staff. Whether this was to threaten me or the cat, I could not tell. To act without thinking first was rare for me. I did not understand how to do it very well. But I did it. And I threw the angry cat over Aldis' staff and right into that witch's face.

The cat did not protest. In fact, I could swear his intention was for me to toss him in the first place. Eyes ablaze, teeth and claws aimed right at her eyes, the cat dove through the air with the same battle glee I had seen from Kraki as he charged down that hill to have the pleasure of fighting one against seven. The cat attached himself to Aldis' scalp via multiple jagged edges and screamed with fury.

In understandable confusion, Aldis dropped her staff and tried like mad to get a hold of the cat with both hands. He was a slippery one though, despite two thick coats of fur and about thirty pounds of muscle. Grabbing a front paw in each hand, Aldis began to lift him away. Too late though—he kicked off her forearm and struck like an adder with his teeth to bite her hard on the nose.

Aldis yelped. The cat bounded away with a meow that echoed off the nearby walls like maniacal laughter. Knowing full well what I intended, I grabbed Aldis' staff.

"See what magic you can get out of that, manling," she said, wiping away the blood that seeped out of a hole in one nostril. "And then bow to me unless you want every moment until the queen returns to be agony!"

She was right. I held the staff and thought thoughts about lightning and storms and chaos, and it was just a staff. If she disarmed me I was done for, a world of pain for who knew how long. And I was neither prepared nor armed for a protracted fight. I had a stick.

Aldis reached behind her hip and drew a knife. Not the kind with a cheap, gleaming blade. This blade was as subdued as the ambient light around it, reflecting just enough to show its razor edge.

She began to circle to my right, testing the ground with her feet. Maybe she was looking for the cat as well, now ready with a weapon she could use against it with greater effect. She smiled and her teeth shone white in the darkness.

Then it was my turn to hold the menacing staff out, only in my hands it was not very menacing. The rings at its top jingled, mocking my inability to harness the staff's power. I stepped back for greater separation between us, but to what end other than a delay of the inevitable? Aldis was not stronger than I was but knew how to handle her weapons with greater skill, and that would be the end of me.

I needed to stall again and introduce something unexpected into the fight. The cat had been perfect at the time. If only I had a bag to pull angry cats out of, I could survive. Probably. But no such bag was forthcoming, and the one cat was gone from my sight. And I was vulnerable out in the open.

Feinting a forward thrust, I forced Aldis back a step as she reacted, then I bolted straight for the room with the troll. Yes, it was a confined space and probably a bad idea. But it had something she would need to step around and that might give me an opening. It was only one among many bad ideas I could choose from, and I chose that one.

The troll lay unmoving, its huge bulk laying across half the room. In front of it were some of the vials and tools Aldis had been using. I grabbed a handful of the glass containers and stepped behind the troll, next to the hideous boar statue.

"Are you threatening to drink that, or throw it at me?" asked Aldis, smirking from the doorway.

"I am not sure," I said, the words coming before my brain could catch them. I had three vials in my fist and had indeed considered both ideas. "Which one should I drink?" I asked with a sudden idea to play the witch.

The knife danced in Aldis' fingers. No small blade, but she moved it up and down with a grace only the very practiced would have. "Try the red one," she said, leaning against the doorway. "Yes, the red one. It could save me plenty of time I would have spent carving small bits of you away. Alfhild needs you whole, but only in a few places."

I unplugged the vial's cork with my teeth and held the open container over the mouth of the troll. The smile vanished from Aldis' face in an instant and I knew I had the answer I needed.

"Toss your knife over here," I said.

"And then what? You stupid manling! You have no idea how to get out of here even if I left you alone."

"Give up the knife and I will leave without further argument," I said, hoping that somehow sounded like a fair deal. "You were healing this . . . thing, and I slipped away."

"This . . . thing? You have no idea. And you cannot leave, you will never find your way out even if you can find a way to see in the darkness. Toss my staff over here and I might let you keep your ears. The queen has a use for you for now, but it need not be pleasant. She will take what she needs and when she is done, we will use your parts for our rituals. Keep this up and we will remove them slowly when it comes time."

Two sounds in quick succession ended the argument. One was the cat's meow, which drew Aldis' attention to her side. The other followed shortly thereafter, a hard, dull thud.

Aldis lurched forward in shock, then staggered back and fell over, the world no longer stable for her. She cursed under her breath, but either dizziness or an inability to focus prevented her from standing up. Her voice began to trail off as her labored breathing became heavier. Her head lolled back and forth in an effort to remain conscious, but finally she stopped trying to talk.

Fanya stepped into the room, her spear going from inert to a dull blue at its head as she entered. The cat walked in at her heel and nuzzled her calf with a purr, but she did not look down. We locked eyes and neither of us could look away, much like when we had seen each other in the forest last, only this time I had no pants.

"I would not remove your parts," she said.

I exhaled, realizing I had been holding my breath for far too long. We kept staring into each other's eyes the way only two very young, very dumb people can do.

It eventually occurred to me it might be my time to say something, though as you might expect, it was not "Thank you for saving my life," which might have been appropriate, but "What rituals were they going to use my parts for?" instead.

Fanya shook her head. "I don't know. Your seed first, and then something else."

Back to my senses a bit, I managed a 'thank you' at last. She smiled and nodded. Perhaps she even blushed in the shadows as I did. "Was it to summon more like this troll?"

"No, it is—I mean, he is not what you think. And I do not think it was for more summoning. She has done that already, from the Ironwood. Monsters of many types. We found them for her, and her spells have kept them hidden."

The troll who was not a troll groaned, low and pain-filled. His head flopped over and he blinked, then shut his eyes again. I could not tell if he had seen me or was blind at this point.

"And witches," I added, regretting it immediately. Fanya's lip curled. "I beg your pardon, I do not know your ways. You saved me from being carved into bits. But you have two sisters and a mother—"

"She is not my mother," Fanya said. "She is *the* Mother. Or she claims that title as teacher and protector. She took us in. You could never understand, but —" Fanya looked away then. Her eyes said she might cry, but her jaw was set strong, and no other part of her body betrayed the emotion she had cut off an instant before it was expressed.

What Fanya did not say let me intuit much of her story. She and her sisters were not meant to be *vǫlur* as Huld had been. Huld, if cynical, intended to serve her community at large with lore and potions and visions as requested. And in all likelihood, without any thanks. But the knowledge she had, and perhaps with added magic I knew nothing of, could be turned against those same communities in rage against mistreatment. Or for personal gain.

In Queen Alfhild's case, who could say? But she did not keep her Daughters around to see and interpret visions, and they were not learning to serve anyone but their Mother. It was a tight bond of loyalty with a deep hostility to those outside it.

I wondered what Fanya's early life was like before finding Alfhild. I decided this was not the time to ask.

"She is powerful," I said, to let Fanya finish without divulging more.

"Yes, very. You have no idea. I helped her. I was supposed to—"

"Kill me," rasped the troll. Fanya and I both turned toward him to see his chest heave and shudder. "Kill me," he said again, this time interrupted by a fit of coughing.

He was injured beyond just his arm being torn off. He held his right side with his left hand. Through those enormous sausage fingers, I could see at least two ribs broken. A closer look at his face showed the cuts and bruises of a pummeling, not one cut from a hard punch but a pulverizing from repeated blows. One large gash bloomed up from below his chin and up to his eye. It had begun to bleed again, and it smelled like that awful mix of rotten blood with other fluids never meant to touch the open air.

The single arm left to him reached out with a single finger extended in my direction. "You," he hissed. The great, rock-smashing arm retracted with care not to jostle the rest of his body. Even that gesture looked difficult for him now.

"Me? Why me?"

He closed his eyes and shook his head. I looked at Fanya and saw sadness in her eyes, but firmness as well.

"Why me?" I asked, now directing the question to her.

Holding her spear, her posture strong and steady, Fanya closed her eyes. "Will you deny his last wish?" she asked. Opening her eyes, she changed the subject again before I could accuse her of changing the subject. "Alfhild wanted me to bring you back here. She assured me she would not harm you, and that is why I was suspicious. And you—you incorrigible man!" She looked away and shook her head, breathing in gasps. As she mastered herself, she continued in a quieter voice, "Could you not find one soft word in the forest? Now here we are, and neither of us can go back. You will kill Olgram, Alfhild's son, and I will help you escape this place."

Well, at least we know Olgram's name now that he has about two minutes left to live.

By this time I was cultivating a hostile disinterest to any idea delaying me in going straight back to the hall at Lejre and drinking as much ale as I could stomach. So my next thoughts were: Need to get out. To get out, need to kill Alfhild's son here. To kill him . . . Shit, how do I kill him? Not likely with the staff in my hands.

Fanya was blunt in her suggestion: "Use a rock."

"You have a knife on your hip. How about that instead?"

"He is hard against steel. He will suffer longer if you do not act. Use a rock."

This was not the idea I wanted to go with, but it was the only idea in sight that would get me out of that place and back to drinking ale. There was indeed a good head-splitting rock in the corner of that room. It was as big as my head and flat at the top, but the shape angled sharply in one corner. I flicked the old candles off the thing and tested my grip. In a real fight: Near useless. Against an unmoving, suicidal whatever-Olgram-was: Perfect.

I knelt by Olgram and he smiled a dull smile, rolling his head to look back at me. "Let us understand each other: I want this done as quick as possible," I said. The flat stone below his head would be just as lethal a part of the setup.

He chuckled, adding, "I as well," and I realized the stupidity of my last comment. Still, he knew my intent.

The first blow skidded off his skull to my right as if I had clanged stone on steel, and he grunted his displeasure. I had altered the angle of the rock as I brought it down and made a mess of things. Fanya held her arms and winced.

The second blow was square, but by the gods, his skull was so thick I only cracked it. Blood pulsed from his forehead and into his wide-open, unseeing eyes as he smiled at me. I could not believe the force of the second blow failed to smash his skull completely. A great sense of urgency took me to finish the job, lest I cause more pain than I might prevent.

"Thank you," he whispered as I recovered my position. I scrambled to lift the rock once more, and, leaning back just a little bit further, I readied the rock to come down in an even wider arc. At that moment, the height of tension before I sprang down again, Olgram spoke his final word before the lip of my rock careened through his skull and into his brain, splattering me with dark red and bits of bone. It was a word I heard as the rock came down but was not fully aware of what I'd heard until just after.

"Cousin," he said.

Crack. I stared at the body knowing what would come next.

The death throes took hold, and for a few horrid moments, his limbs would be animated as if trying to escape from something there was no escaping. This is the part you never hear included in tales of adventure and fighting. And maybe I left it out of the other deaths before and will leave it out of the deaths after in my story.

But not this one. This one begged me for his execution, thanked me during my inability to give him a quick death, and then called me kin as I brought the death blow down on him. And now I was watching his massive body twitch and convulse. So much I had to move away, lest I be pounded with one of those massive limbs. Fanya also took a few steps back. Soon it was done, though the scene would replay in my mind many times over.

Olgram's final word echoed through me like an unshakeable spirit. Was that the raving of a skull-cracked monster about to die? If so, why did he not rave? It was a simple statement, a whisper of connection that made no sense. Confusion took me then, and I looked at my bloody hands. Were they even mine? How could I be certain? Perhaps they belonged to Olgram's cousin. Nothing made sense.

"Ansgar!" said Fanya. I slowly came to realize this was the fifth or sixth time she had shouted straight into my face. I heard her like a drowning man might hear the shouts of his comrades still on a ship, and then my senses surfaced and I came to. "We have to go!" She turned with a bag slung across her back but I grabbed her arm and pulled her back to me.

It was not a romantic gesture. I was shocked to numbness by what had just occurred. I could sense the import of something, like an animal sensing an earthquake. But unlike the animal, I had no inkling of what was coming other than a foreboding of a great unknown I did not, maybe could not, understand. So I grabbed her arm and pulled. I would demand some answers, and I would have them *now*.

Maybe Fanya saw the rawness in my face and took that vulnerability a different way. She dropped her spear, turned, and embraced me in a kiss I was not expecting or ready for. She poured herself into me, and, expecting reciprocation, backed away at my surprise. I was taken entirely unaware (you will find I often am by women if you keep reading) and reacted accordingly. Realizing my massive folly, I pursued her lips as she drew them away. Our timing off for what must have been a full minute at least, we found each other comfortably in each other's arms at last. Still kissing awkwardly, but now pleasantly.

"What in Jotunheim is going on here?" I asked, with my heart racing but still just as confused.

"We have to get back to your crew," she said. "We have to warn them."

"Warn them of what?"

"Olgram was to take the place of the king with Alfhild still the queen. Without Olgram, she will move her armies immediately. She does not intend to usurp the throne so much as destroy the king and his influence. Your friends are in danger. The whole city is in danger!"

"In danger of what? What armies?" I asked, every statement bringing up new and more disturbing questions.

"One is her army of men, outlaws found throughout the land led by her Rus," she said, "but that is not the one to be feared. An army of monsters remains at her command. Were you not listening? Things from the Ironwood! Wargs and dragons, trolls of all types. Loki's distant spawn. She has been summoning them, binding them to her purpose, and hiding them. What do you think she left her dying son for, other than to burn Lejre and everyone in it?"

Chapter 40

Answers and Other Confusion

"What are we supposed to do against an army like that?" I asked as we sped through the maze of caves. Running away seemed like the best course of action.

"Fight them!" she shouted back to me, urging me to go faster.

"I can hardly keep up as it is," I said, intending for more but stopping to suck my teeth as my injured foot found a rock. It was better than it had been as a prisoner, but still sore.

Showing pain would not just be shame now. It would be shame in front of my beloved, the only woman I had ever kissed and therefore the woman I then assumed I would marry and make babies with.

This army from the darkest of dark realms—led by a witch not bent so much on victory as destruction—was merely a delay in that process.

"Are you hurt?" There was genuine concern in her face as blue light sparking from her spear flickered off the walls.

"I am fine, keep going," I huffed.

She did not wait for a second answer before her lithe form sprang forth again. Every way that woman moved was a marvel to me and it was all I could do to keep my mind off stopping right there to kiss her again.

"What does Olgram's death have to do with attacking now?" I asked. "She left him to be cared for."

"She knows," said Fanya. "She saw his injuries. Even if Aldis could have saved his life, he would be useless to her. Not an heir, not a warrior."

"Surely no one would have accepted a troll as king! She would have been better off claiming it herself."

Fanya shot me a look of disappointment. "He was no troll. Men are more apt to accept a man in charge, even if only for the appearance of it. And who could have challenged Olgram after the fact? The arrival of you lot changed things."

"She left Aldis more to watch me than to save him then."

"You have value to her, and he no longer did. He never did follow directions very well, and now she has something more powerful to draw upon. Besides, the whole city is likely to be drunk and distracted right now."

The murk at the end of the tunnel was a welcome sight. Up and up we ran towards what had to be the main entrance. I was so glad to see the outside again I forgot my aches and pains. We emerged into a misty nowhere, one small and dry island in a bog. I had overtaken Fanya for a few moments in my excitement and then had to pause. This was not a place that favored me as the forest around Ketill's house did. I would not find my way out without a guide.

"What is this she draws upon?"

"A sacrifice," said Fanya. "One of your friends. I do not know which one, but she stole him away to be kept with her army. She is powerful enough without spilling such blood. With it . . ."

"Hel's dragon!" I said shaking my head. "When was this?"

"A week ago. You have been away, and I . . . have been hiding from her." Fanya shook her head in a violent spasm. "This way," she said, showing me small stepping stones with each stride. She bounded away, finding a dry path among the bubbling wetness.

I was able to keep up until I saw the first body.

It had been there many months, probably over a year, just under the shallow surface of a green pool. The champion's mail shirt was rent, as was most of his face. A broken shield lay nearby. I imagined that had been the first casualty before Olgram broke the man's body for it to lie in such a twisted state. Many champions had come to find Olgram, none had returned. I wondered how many other shallow pools nearby held such scenes. Fanya noted my slowing and saw my reaction.

"Men who came to test their glory," said Fanya without sympathy. "And their rewards." She turned then, and I followed in silence for a while.

"What rewards was Lambi seeking?" I asked. "Just a brewer as I heard it."

"He meant no harm. Alfhild offered him gold while he was alone on the road. He was to brew for Olgram and bring it to us. Alfhild wanted to end Olgram's distraction of stealing alcohol in town. Lambi refused."

"So Olgram did kill him then?"

"I don't think so. He was good at avoiding his mother. It was more likely one of her hidden things from the Ironwood."

So here was a troll meant to be a king, and strong enough to best every champion sent after him. Yet here were the only marks of violence left by him. In town, his crime had been theft only. This struck me as strange, and I had to ask as we continued.

"Why did he steal all the decent drink?"

"He had quite a thirst," said Fanya with a laugh. "And he could smell it fermenting from miles away. But it was never what he was directed to do by his mother. He was supposed to kill the king's nephew Hrolf, or the staller at least. I watched over him once to report back, and he would not offer violence to anyone not attacking him. I lied to Alfhild about it. I suppose my betrayal is longstanding."

"So he was a friendly troll?"

"I told you he was no troll!" she said with no small irritation. "Alfhild conceived him and birthed him in secret, telling us only that one of the *Æsir* had come to her bed one night."

"How does a woman keep a pregnancy secret?"

Fanya looked at me as if her eyebrows would come off her head. "How much do you think you men notice?" she asked. "It was twenty years ago. The king could have been gone fighting at the time. And in the case that he was present, it bears mentioning this king is neither perceptive nor thoughtful."

"I noticed that. And it was the queen who had us going on that errand for the right steel to create the right sword that would be the only weapon capable of killing Olgram. The king seemed . . . preoccupied."

"That fool would be preoccupied with anything that flattered him!" The anger in her voice hammered my ears even in the open air.

Seeing my discomfort, she cut short what would otherwise have been a longer tirade. I could hear her panting not from the running but from the fury directed at the king. Another subject to avoid, I noted, especially as I needed to know more pressing things.

"It was Alfhild who encouraged most of the fighting men to go off and raid, and Alfhild who hired the Rus to replace them," I said, seeing the whole picture come into focus. "And she never laid all her hopes on one plan, so she gathered an army."

"Two armies," Fanya reminded me. "She let the king take the credit for hiring the Rus, and with every boast he believed more in their loyalty."

"But they will fight for Alfhild."

"They will. The king has few allies to fight for him now." What little daylight entered the fens pierced the trees in rays rather than a muted glow. The air of the bog-stink was still preferable to the stale air in that prison. "Tradesmen in the city. Farmers come to do business. Some are accomplished fighters, but many others sailed away in the warm weather. He has his champions and the staller. And your friends."

"And you," I added.

Fanya blushed. It would only be later I would realize how little value she had felt and how great an effect a kind word might have. Not poetry or verse of any kind, but merely to tell a truth usually left unsaid. But she knew as little how to react to that unexpected consideration as I did to her first kiss, and we had ground to cover. If only that damned raven would show himself, I could surely wing our warning to the hall. "Humor!" I called. But he was nowhere to be seen.

A roar from the cat spun me around. If not for that, I would not have noticed the creature padding silently alongside us. His voice now seeking to add his name to the warriors who would stand and fight the Ironwood rabble. I could not add him yet though, as I was missing a most key piece of information.

"What is your cat's name?"

"Hmm?" Fanya looked confused. "Oh, the cat. I never thought of her as mine. Or anyone's. She was just there sometimes, I assumed she followed me to the tunnels from the forest. We never gave her a name."

A she-cat then. I had made an unjust assumption.

"Her fury bought me an advantage when I threw her into Aldis' face." It was a simple restatement of what happened but earned me an incredulous backward glance from Fanya as we made our way through the greenery. "I had nothing else to throw at the time. And you should have seen him. I mean her.

No doubt that was what she wanted me to do. A *berserkr* rage came over her when Aldis threatened me."

"So the cat was bear-shirted or bare-shirted?" asked Fanya, noting the play on '*berserkr*.'

Perhaps she was cat-shirted, and from there derived her rage at all living things, as cats hate them all.

"I hope you can use weapons other than slings and cats."

"I have words, and, uh, runes," I said, with less enthusiasm than I meant to muster. "But if this cat is so willing to stand and fight, she needs a name." I turned toward the cat, looking even bigger than I knew her to be. She looked at me and licked her lips in hunger. Only a living piece of food would do for this one. "I know your name, tearer of faces: You are Rota."

Rota let out a triumphant meow and bounded past us, too eager to allow slow humans to delay battle. I wished I had half her fighting spirit.

We cleared the fens and found open ground soon enough, and there I was by several degrees more comfortable. Fanya fanned her nose at a terrible smell and looked over to see a befouled linden tree just off our direct path back to Lejre.

"Goat's breath and cat piss!" she exclaimed, holding her nose, although it was far worse than either of those smells.

I made a face and offered no insight as to how that might have happened. Admitting to the tree's befouling would be too embarrassing. But I would be found out if I tried to retrieve my clothes or weapons. A difficult choice: Prepare for a battle with witches and trolls or charge into the same with my pride intact but wearing nothing.

I did not want to be associated with that mess on the linden tree. So I did what any self-respecting young man would do when faced with a tough decision. I put my clothes on, grabbed my things, and played ignorant in the face of clear evidence.

Fanya was suspicious. That much I would pay to be clothed again and have my weapons back. Now I really could use runes, sort of, by carving them onto the discs. It felt good to be wearing real clothing again.

On we ran to the main path to Lejre, approximating part of my recent run from Olgram. Had he been trying to catch me? I wondered if he had just wanted to talk to me. But no, if Alfhild had sent him to bring me back, that would have been his mission.

The images of his dead body thrashing about came back and I had to physically shake my head to be rid of them.

We spoke little more on our way to the south gate of the city. Perhaps Fanya was saving her breath. I knew I had more questions but could think of none. My mind was bent towards how we would fight witches and trolls and Rus all together. At least one witch had been disabled well enough by a sharp blow to the back of the head. Perhaps she had died of that blow—in our haste, neither of us had checked.

Kraki had made short work of seven Rus by himself. And somehow, someone had beaten Olgram and ripped off his arm. Now if we could get the witches to turn around and be bashed in the head, the Rus to all fight Kraki, and the arm-ripper to fight the trolls, maybe a few well-placed stones from my sling would be more than we would even need.

Of course, it wouldn't work out that way. It never works out as planned, and that was not a plan even by very loose standards. We would need more, much more. A few more ships full of seasoned warriors, to begin with. A wizard would be most helpful, assuming he could do more than criticize my carving.

This gave me an idea for a spell that could be used as a fiery missile to be launched at our enemies. I turned some variations on this over in my mind, then considered how Ketill would reject each one. Circumstances were different than practicing in the forest, however. If I'm about to be eaten by some unnamed thing from another realm, what's the problem with flubbing a spell such that I blow myself up? It might even be preferable my way.

At least I would die with my pants on, I thought. Later on in life, I thought the opposite might be preferable, and now I am undecided. Wearing pants is also sort of a precursor to credibility though, which was the first challenge we faced.

"Gudbrand!" I shouted. The king's staller stood well beyond the path we intended to take, but his bright mail shirt glinted beneath his light cloak and made him easy to recognize. He turned at my shout. "An attack is coming!"

How many things have I already related in this story that I did and then right away wished I had not done? This was another where I spoke without thinking. Gudbrand was talking to two tall, scruffy-looking men, weapons sheathed, manner relaxed. I had just given him information he did not yet understand the extent of. The two others might, though.

One of the men was loosely fur-clad, looking more like a man who wished to show off his hunting skills than keep his back warm. The other was shorter and wore wool and leather more like my clothing, but with a different and unrecognizable flair. He tensed and stroked a well-groomed mustache grown out longer than the rest of his beard while his scraggle-faced companion stayed comfortable. The hunter looked on in mild confusion mixed with mild disinterest, a look I was used to by then.

But I was not disinterested. I was very interested in closing the space between us as quickly as possible.

"Shit!" I barked, realizing I had just put two Rus on notice, leaving Gudbrand vulnerable.

He remained relaxed and gave no indication he understood the hostile nature of his companions. Furrowing his brow, he called loud and slow back to me and turned his back to both of them.

"Ansgar, where have you been?" Gudbrand sidestepped, leaving my line of sight to the Rus unimpeded.

They shifted uneasily, as if each was uncertain whether it was time to attack. But attack they would, I was certain, and before Fanya or I could get close enough to help.

"The 'Steins were ready to raise an army to follow you!" Gudbrand continued, the only one who did not seem to see what was about to happen.

He spread his arms wide in a grand gesture uncharacteristic of him, or what I knew of him. Then I saw what he intended, and in that same instant, it all seemed to happen at once.

He spread his arms wide, opening his cloak with his left arm. He let it out like a large, red wing while his head faced me and his eyes watched the ground. The day was nearly done, and shadows were long.

The fur-clad Rus took that bait, drew his axe, and came at the staller with a blow aimed at Gudbrand's head.

He took too long to ready it. Gudbrand's cloak had concealed the movement of his right arm, which drew a long seax from his belt. He let the attacker get close, then turned and buried the long weapon hilt-deep into the Rus' throat, pressing right up against his surprised face. The movement was so certain and swift, Mustache stood gawping for a moment before he realized what had happened.

Gudbrand already had the first man's axe out of his hands and then kicked him in the midsection to push him away. The man staggered and clutched at the long seax while his friend drew his own long knife.

The weapon was not even fully deployed by the time Gudbrand threw the purloined axe into the man's face. It did not cleave bone, as the blade was over-rotated to make contact. Even so, the top of the axehead crashed into the man's mouth with a crack that sounded like broken teeth. The man held his weapon firm but was driven back several steps. He regained his footing, dropped his hand from his broken mouth to pick up the axe, and smiled a bloody smile at the now-weaponless Gudbrand.

I don't know why he thought Gudbrand would be unarmed at that point. Axe and knife were standard, no matter where one went. Unlike most, the staller did not make a show of his weapons until he intended to use them. Out from his back, Gudbrand drew his axe, one with Arrow-Odd's sigil on it.

Mustache's smile did not fade when he saw Gudbrand was still armed, but I knew it was a brave face. For a long moment, the two men squared off, doing little other than circling and staring into each other's faces.

I stopped short, uncertain whether my presence would do any good or provide an unneeded distraction. Also, I was afraid of being caught up in real fighting. My latest hand-to-hand combat had been my best showing, and that had only been a draw even with a maniac cat for an ally.

Something was happening to Mustache. I thought he was losing his nerve at first, but that was not the case. His eyes widened and his bloody lips curled into a series of twitchy snarls, and then he looked at his knife. Or rather, his hand.

It was smoking.

The knife itself changed color from dull gray to red hot. Frantic, the man looked about him, fixing his gaze on Fanya who stood a few paces behind me. He pointed an accusing finger at her and shouted something I interpreted as mentioning a witch. He circled back around to try charging her while avoiding Gudbrand, but the staller pressed the attack and refused to let him pass.

Out of allies, weapons, and options, the man lunged at Gudbrand. He took the axe blow to his left temple, the low thud accompanied by a crunch that spoke of no need for another strike. The man's expression went limp in the same instant, and the knife attack never fell. His hand continued smoking as he lay on the ground.

Gudbrand put his weapon away, ignoring both me and Fanya, and walked over to the still form of the man with the knife in his throat. "I hope you do not mind if I take back my last gift," he said. "It seems I will soon need to be generous with such offerings."

The man was too dead by then to argue about it.

"How did you know they would attack you?" I asked.

"They had become strangely inquisitive for some time," he said. "And then I watched the shadow of this one." He cleaned his blade on the dead man's clothing, then looked up at me and smiled. "I have known something was afoot all day and have been on my guard for the unexpected. The first thing I heard today was a story about an insane man running around naked just outside the city. Was that you?"

"I was only running because the troll—" At this point, Fanya had joined us. "I was only running because I thought he was chasing me."

"And why do you say you thought he was chasing you rather than he was chasing you?"

"He did not mean me harm. I think. He intended to bring me back to Queen Alfhild."

"And why were you naked?"

"Because I could not stop to put my clothes on when he appeared and started chasing me!"

The statement broke Gudbrand's bemused expression, and he sneered in both disgust and surprise. "Why would this troll be taking anything to the queen?"

"He was her son! She conceived and birthed him in secret and intended to have him become king."

Gudbrand ran his gnarled fingers through his hair as if to clear away something from his mind. "That is three whys deep and all I have for it is more confusion. You, handmaiden," he said, turning to Fanya, "the queen is missing, yet here you stand with the skald. What do you have to say about all these goings-on?"

"I say you need to muster all the warriors you can," said Fanya. "There is an attack coming. And if you are ready for the unexpected, you should be ready for the unthinkable, because it will attack this city and soon."

"Why the unthinkable?" The staller shrugged. "I fully expect the queen to take those Rus and attack us. With so few good warriors left to the king, she may even win."

"She has more than men of Midgard under her banner. Denizens of the

Ironwood are assembled in the forest nearby, hidden from view by her magic. She has built up a secret army for years now."

"That is powerful *seiðr* to hide such an army."

"She has that and more."

Gudbrand grimaced and shook his head. "But you return with the skald, whom we had thought lost to a terrible fate. And I saw that man's hand burn on his knife—that was your doing. You fight for the rest of us, or else I am a fool. Why?"

"She would burn the city and all those in it," Fanya said, her chest heaving with the difficulty of the answer. "I would not."

For a people favoring such direct speech, we had quite the penchant for statements pregnant with implication. Fanya would fight for those she cared about. She was fighting for me. No doubt my face went red as Gudbrand's cloak, and perhaps seeing this is why he accepted her answer such as it was.

"I like her answers better than yours," he said to me. "Men of Midgard and creatures from the Ironwood, you say? I think they all have bones that break and blood that spills, so I am as ready for them as I might be. I will do what I can to muster the city. Get yourselves to the hall and ready your comrades. Only Haldor has had any fighting to do, and the rest are spoiling for glory."

"There has been fighting already?" I asked. "I thought the Rus had not yet made clear their allegiance."

"Not Rus, young skald. He fought the troll who was not a troll. Pummeled it and then ripped away an entire arm while in a grapple. He's hanging the arm from the ceiling. Since they couldn't find the wounded thing to finish it, they are celebrating. I will rally the city. Get to the hall and ready them for battle before they get more drunk than they already must be."

Chapter 41

Twilight

"So the troll is more than one troll?" asked Ulf.

The entire crew of the *Sea Squirrel* had crowded around me almost the moment I opened the doors to the hall. Questions had come one after another with no pause for me to answer them. The first among them had been from the 'Steins, who peppered me with more and more absurd questions until Kari and Ulf had interrupted.

Others in the hall gathered around to hear what was going on. More than a dozen men crowded right around us, asking questions or cheering and offering ale. Gudbrand had been right to urge us on quickly. The heavy breathing of so many not-quite-drunk-but-definitely-not-sober men drowned out even the smell of the hearth fire. That and the lingering effects of foot and head injuries and Ketill's spell left me nauseous and aggravated.

I tried to explain what was going on, and that was when Svein pushed forward to clear a way for Ulf. Questions only from the *þulr*, but sometimes questions are just statements in disguise.

"The troll is dead," I answered. "And it was just him, and he wasn't really a troll as he meant no harm. But there are trolls, and other things."

"You saw them?"

"No, well not I, but Fanya—"

"And we should take the word of the queen's handmaiden?" Ulf shook his head and turned to Fanya with a condescending tone. "Tell me, where is this army hidden?"

Fanya bridled at the implication her warning might be a ruse. "I cannot provide details only the queen knows," said Fanya, staring Ulf down. "But if you intend to face your enemies unarmed and unprepared, they will owe you a favor after you are dead."

"We all die eventually," retorted Ulf, rolling his eyes. "Living like a fool is not what I desire."

It was about damned time when Haldor Skullplitter made his presence known, moving Ulf and Svein aside with more vigor than perhaps they took nicely.

"Make way for the king," Haldor growled, dragging the supposed ruler of Denmark behind him.

Haldor's sense of simmering urgency was still not as much as I had hoped for, but it was at least a great contrast to the reactions of the other men. He would bring the other men around, but bit by bit rather than all at once.

"The troll," he boomed, silencing the room. He looked me in the eye and did the same with Fanya, letting a deliberate and heavy silence reign. "Explain. Slowly."

Fanya began but I cut her off. Still too hot from Ulf's accusations, I needed her to seem rational otherwise these fools would dismiss her and listen only to me. Listening only to me on matters of war was ill-advised, and so I needed her to be credible to a suspicious audience.

I, however, could seem as insane as I wanted. It would be surprising to no one the unwarlike skald had lost his nerve a bit.

"Dead! Very dead! He was disarmed, and he took badly to the new look. In league with the queen though. And the Rus! Gudbrand just killed two who attacked him in town and there are more and they are joining up and they are going to kill everyone—that's the queen's goal now, to kill everyone, not just the king!"

"This is the skald's version of 'slowly,'" quipped Ulf as he cuffed Svein's shoulder.

Svein chuckle-snorted and shook his head.

"Where is my sworn brother Leif?" demanded Ingolf. His voice did not cast out and rumble the room as Haldor's did, but rather quieted the room to make it all the clearer.

"Alfhild took one of the men," said Fanya. "If he disappeared about a week ago, it must be him."

"We searched the forest for days," said Ingolf. The more even his voice held, the more I could hear the homicidal anger behind it threatening to burst. "We found no sign of him and nothing of any such army of monsters."

"And did you find yourself always going away from the fens and often returning to where you began, thinking you had come a long ways?" asked Fanya. She did not wait for a reply. "Alfhild hid them with her magic. Cursed the *landvættir* to do her bidding and lead anyone in the forest away from them."

"That is a powerful witch then," said Ingolf. "You would have us believe you now go against her?"

"I had a brother as well," said Fanya. "His name was Olgram and he was no troll. I called him my brother, if not by blood. She left him to die when she had no more use for him. I see her clearly now."

Ingolf crossed his arms and nodded. Leif was his sworn brother, not his brother by birth. I could see the anger and understanding both swirling in his mind as he considered Fanya's words. "We saw the thing Haldor fought," he said. "If he was no troll, what was he?"

"He was the queen's son. She kept him secret before and after his birth," she said shifting her attention to the king.

The king shifted in what he supposed would be dismissal but to me looked like he was nervous. I wondered if he was about to deny the possibility of the thing, that he would have known if she had been pregnant. A difficult thing to say though, given his time away and her penchant for locking herself away from him. He went a different route to defend his honor.

"I suppose she hid this child from me with magic as well then," said Ragnvald.

"That is unknown to me. It was before she found me and I know only what little she said about it. But I do believe he was her son, and I know she intended to have him inherit your wealth and power while she ruled through him."

"You knew him well then?" said the king. "And who his father was?"

"One of the *Æsir*, she claimed, but that hardly matters now. He is dead, and she now has no reason to delay."

"Well, Haldor," said Ragnvald, "you did kill it after all. I thought not finding the thing meant it would heal and come back."

"No, he died when—" said Fanya, almost outing me before I interrupted her.

"He died of his wounds," I said, with considerable energy. I did not know why at the time, but I did not wish to relate my part in ending Olgram's suffering. "He had an arm ripped off and it would not stop bleeding. That was not even his only injury. I heard him accept his death." All true.

Fanya eyed me with some confusion but did not contradict me. My part in things involved a troll calling me family, and I was not ready to tell that part of the story.

It was a dirty thing, to tell that bit without my part made clear. Ulf whispered into Svein's ear—I was sure he knew me for a liar. I did kill Olgram, even if he had asked for me to do so. I rationalized it as not wanting to seem as if I was stealing Haldor's glory, and that the truth was Haldor had killed him. I did nothing more than speed him along. Still, there was something about telling it that way against my nature, and I could not shake that feeling.

"Haldor Skullsplitter! Haldor Trollslayer!" roared Svein.

A great cheer erupted from the other men, including the king. Cheers of congratulations, of triumph, of shared glory echoed throughout the hall. Horns were raised and clanked and emptied as if the deed had just occurred.

Someone had pressed a cup into my hand as I looked about me, thinking I was taking in the scene. But I was not taking in the scene, because the scene had taken me in already. I joined the cheering and the drinking before I even realized what I was doing, and only Fanya's pleading expression to stop being a fool brought me back around.

"Stop drinking!" I shouted, embarrassed I had so quickly forgotten my errand. "Stop stop STOP!"

The room went silent. "Is your cup empty, little brother?" asked Svein, to much laughter.

"You can have some of mine," added Ulf, offering up his horn to continue the joke.

Before I could speak again, and before I could stop her, Fanya's spear collided with Ulf's horn and knocked it away.

This brought even louder cheering and laughter all around. Except from Ulf. He was not hurt, but his pride was punctured, and I saw him seethe inside. It was the same look he had after watching Fanya bathe in the forest that day. It was the look of a hungry wolf catching sight of prey.

I felt both jealousy and fear when I saw it.

"Goat's breath and cat piss! Is this how you prepare for battle?" Fanya screamed at them all. "So impressed with the deeds of another man you would try to claim them as your own?"

Ragnvald gasped at Fanya's brazen calling out of every man in the hall. Men held Ulf back while the king raged as only a man not involved in a fight can rage. Amid the confusion, one unrecognized man slipped from my sight towards the entrance. Unrecognized because I only saw the trail of his cloak on the way out. I cast about looking: There was the crew, all those I have named and some I have not. The king. Fanya. That king's champions.

Only two champions. Frothi was gone.

"You can try me next," said Svein, patting the axe at his side. "Otherwise, where is the battle? Though that is not much of a deed, fighting a woman. I would prefer the hordes you mentioned. Glory enough for the rest of us, if they exist."

I heard the sound of wood on wood clanking at the entrance and looked over to see the doors close. The light of the day had gone dim, and it had turned from sunset to dusk. Little light was left to creep in through the cracks of the doorway at any rate, but when I looked closer, I noticed I saw nothing beyond. It had gotten darker faster than I thought, it seemed.

"They do not exist!" roared the king. "I am the king of Denmark! Do you think such an army could exist under my nose without my knowing it? No one acts as such without my permission, lest they feel my wrath." He pointed to the great arm hoisted above the middle of the room and added "See what comes of such rebellion! My wife would not dare!"

I don't recall everything the king said in that bit of monologue. It was so damned long, nobody could remember it all without a drink of memory-ale first. The key bits about claiming status as if it were armor against his enemies, about his incredulity at Fanya's warning, and about his implication that Haldor's great fighting skill and strength was somehow a reflection of his leadership. I believe I got all the ideas if not all the words.

During this long polemic, a smell began to rise. Nothing to take notice of at first, though slightly unexpected. Then more. Until at last, every man in the hall was sniffing at the strange resiny odor and the distinct change in temperature they had only begun to register.

They looked around, and so did I, and I cursed my idiot self for ignoring the man who had left the hall. I suspected he had a stupid haircut under that cloak and hood, but that was just a guess.

Not at all a guess was that the smell of smoke had overpowered the smell of bad breath, and that little wisps of smoke were sneaking in through the walls.

"The door!" shouted Haldor, pointing at Magnus as the closest man.

Magnus pushed it with one hand, then two, then took three steps back and charged it, hitting it hard with his shoulder. "Blocked from the outside!" he said.

The hall had become very warm all of a sudden. Kari put his palm to one wall, then withdrew it immediately. He moved further down to try another spot. And another, and another, as realization rose hand in hand with panic around the hall.

"Well?" said Haldor, knowing Kari would take his meaning.

Kari turned and shook his head. "It is hot. All of it." He stopped feeling along the wall and turned to the rest of us. "I think the entire hall is burning outside."

CHAPTER 42

BEAR

ENDURANCE OF EXTREME PAIN IS A WELL-HELD CHARACTERISTIC among my people. Also affinity for risk, stoicism in the face of overwhelming odds, and blonde hair. I've seen two men face down an army by themselves. I've seen a foot cleaved halfway through between the first two toes being cleaned out by a healer while the owner of said foot showed no reaction to the pain other than a sweaty brow. My father had continued fighting after taking an arrow through his balls.

Out of those traits, I got the blonde hair only. Not very helpful in battle, especially when you need to figure a way through burning oak walls just to get to the fight in the first place.

With every bit of ignorance possible about the depths of my incompetence in war, Fanya looked at me with encouragement and hope.

"I do not know what the *galdramaðr* taught you," she said, "but if you know magic that can help us, now is the time to carve your runes."

The shouting broke out all at once. Utstein and Innstein wanted to know what kind of spell I would cast and if it was a sure thing. Ulf just wanted to know what the direction would be so that he could get well out of the way whatever I decided to do, not concealing his lack of confidence. The king suggested I summon some creature, the bigger the better, heedless that this was an absurd idea. Even if summoning worked the way he thought it did, such a creature would probably eat him.

That stupid king! Who could tell if Queen Alfhild had brought such hostility to the land there? Perhaps she had merely turned hostile given the constant company of her imbecile husband. We had no word in my language for 'entitlement,' the same way you might use it. A strong man felt entitled to what he could take, but that was the difference: The king did not take but believed he should be given, and that the giving should be accomplished by others who would receive the great gift of his presence for a time. So he treated his wife, and so he had treated his kingdom. Now his wife would burn him alive, and who knew if his kingdom would be able to stop her.

Well, we would try.

If I could clear the front entrance or breach a wall, that would save us from the fire. Having learned runes from a wizard most of the summer, I was the only one with any working knowledge of how to carve them. Which is to say, not a very strong working knowledge at all, and a rapidly diminishing ability to focus.

"GATHER 'ROUND," bellowed Haldor above both the burning outside and the commotion inside. I recognized the magic inherent to voices, as had happened in the grove. Haldor's was the voice of command, and there was no need for him to repeat himself. We would listen, we would do as we were bidden, and we would do so without hesitation.

"Listen," he said, knowing he did not need to, even to the king. "The hall burns outside, and the door is blocked. We are not yet roasted, so gather your weapons and your courage. Kari, find the weakest part of the walls if we need to break through ourselves. Ulf and Kraki, see what you can find to help us batter our way through somewhere. I will speak with the skald."

"Surely you would have me assess the witch and whether we can trust her," said Ulf.

"You had time enough to assess me while I bathed in the river that day," Fanya shot back at him. "Haldor said to gather up your courage. It may take you longer than others to find yours."

Ulf's pride would demand redress later for that insult. Assuming we didn't all burn alive in that hall.

"Go," said Haldor, and turned to me as Kari put himself between Ulf and Fanya. My culture had a great deal of pithiness that might otherwise be expressed with very many words. In this case, some of those words might be *Ulf, shut your mouth and do not even think about responding to the insult that woman just gave you. I will tolerate no word or act that is not directly in service of getting us out of this hall. Go.*

Ulf went, his face a snarl.

The men moved, some with purpose but others with the timid rapidity of a mouse uncertain if it was heard. Haldor noticed the hesitation before addressing me, and his voice raised to a roar above the din.

"The rest of you lie down and gather the dirt over top of yourselves if you are so ready to let your fate be dictated." This raised the hackles of the mouse-movers, and they did not ignore it. "Otherwise, ready your armor. They will have men ready for us. We will need a shield wall as soon as we are outside. For those unstricken by terror, there will be a great deal of killing to do."

"More for the real warriors among us," Svein called back as he tossed a heavy oak table over his shoulder.

The two behemoths were not friends, but the interplay between them was what the crew needed. Fear evaporated like a mist in the morning sun of well-led purpose.

"Skald," Haldor said, turning to both me and Fanya. His voice resonated like a call to a final battle.

My hair stood on end, and I straightened, realizing I had become lazy in my posture.

Haldor lowered his voice. "We must break through and soon. Find a suitable part of the wall and blast a hole through it."

'Blast a hole through it' sounded suspiciously like the fate of Ketill's friend who 'blew himself up.' Right.

Ironically, I thought I wanted fire for that, and I knew where I wanted it to be. But how to control the intensity, the duration, and the size of the flame? Carve certain runes bigger? Deeper? I might very well cook us all with too much force or encourage the existing fire just enough to hasten the flames threatening to engulf us. This is where rune carving gets tricky.

So I wanted fire: Was that *kauna* (torch) or *sowilo* (the sun)? Maybe both could be light or both could be heat depending on the other runes carved with them, or maybe not. If I wanted to direct fire as if from a dragon's mouth, was that *uruz* (strength) or maybe *raiðo* (journey) indicating I wanted it to go somewhere?

The reading of *sowilo* would usually have to do with the fertility or cyclical aspect of the sun, not its heat. But then, a torch is lit for light, not to be thrown at an enemy. Usually. My study of the magical properties of runes was elementary. And, as Ketill would likely attest, almost always wrong. I suddenly wished I had paid more heed to previous mistakes so that I might avoid one in a crisis. Will and intellect, will and intellect.

My intellect was at that point telling me that my will was not doing so well, and I found in myself the urge to lower expectations. Perhaps something indirect and subtle that Haldor would understand as my concern for those around me more than fear of failure.

"I have no idea how to do that," I said.

"No one has any idea how to do that," echoed Fanya with naked admonishment. I thought this was directed at Haldor, but she was staring at me. "Not until they do it. We did not do the carving you do, but I know the runes. Well enough to know it is almost always just what you make of it, so try something!"

Out of the corner of my eye, I noticed Utstein and Innstein exchange unsatisfied looks. Their first impulse would be to bet on my success, but there's nothing to be gained by betting on dying. Too hard to collect the winnings, even if you get favorable odds.

"Why not break through with a ram?" I asked.

Haldor shook his head. "It will take too long, especially with the tools we have. These walls are thick so—"

Something, or rather somethings, called out above us in the rafters in high-pitched screeches. It was part taunt, part celebration, all reveling in its own ugliness. If they were once human, as some lore said, or if they were their own race of deplorable things full of hate, I could not say. Elves are just about any magical being, some benign, some helpful. Some ugly and apt to skin you alive. These were a small and ugly lot with sharp teeth. You would probably call them 'goblins,' so goblins they will be.

My ears came near to splitting before I could cover them against their high-pitched cries.

Those goblins were probably not much in a straight fight, but this was no straight fight. Perched comfortably above, they flung darts at us while we scrambled for shields.

Haldor grabbed me and threw me bodily across the space of the open hall to get me to cover. I crashed into Ulf, knocking both of us to the ground.

In his next movement, Haldor unhooked his shield and covered himself and Fanya. "Protect the skald!" shouted Haldor. "He is our way out!" He turned back to Fanya, but what he said, I could not hear.

Around us the smoke and crackle of fire, above us cackling little demons. The men ran to and fro, dodging what the goblins threw and trying to take aim with their own weapons.

Utstein wielded two shields to protect himself and his brother at all angles. I blinked, and one shield dropped for a fraction of a second. Innstein's arm lit out in a sideways motion to send his axe spinning at a goblin above.

It squealed in surprise as its leg was severed and it fell, the thud of hitting the ground ending its cries. A chorus of the dead goblin's brethren cried out in horrid voices and rained darts on the 'Steins, but they had already moved to take refuge under a table.

"How are you getting us out of here?" demanded Ulf.

"Galdr!" I shouted into his face. I hoped my answer was not as ironic in real life as it was in my head.

Ulf's shield came up to stop a dart that collided with the boss and bounced off. Their weapons were made of slate and their craftsmanship was atrocious, but our position put us at great disadvantage. And I did not want to find out whether those points were coated with poison.

"Am I supposed to believe that?" said an incredulous Ulf.

"Are you supposed to believe you will get out of here some other way?"

Ulf looked at the entrance starting to glow orange, then up into the rafters where at least ten more goblins were visible. Then he looked at the walls, where smoke was seeping inside even lower than it had been before.

"Shit," he said, realizing he was just about out of potential things to believe in.

Haldor had moved Fanya away from the attackers at the back of the hall. The ceiling at the front was lower and more difficult to negotiate, but the front of the hall was noticeably hotter by then. He beckoned the brothers out with him, and they formed a wall of three shields, then shouted for the others to join them. The king sprinted for their protection, tripped, and crawled the rest of the way behind the wall's protection.

Ulf moved to go, but I stopped him. "Haldor is causing a distraction to draw attention from us," I said. "Try to stay hidden and let me work here."

A spell of concussive force without fire would have been preferable but was even less clear to me how to carve. A fiery explosion would be a bit easier, assuming it exploded after I threw the disc at a weak part of the wall and not before. It might still bring the ceiling down on us, but I reassured myself that most of the men would prefer to die violently rather than from breathing too much smoke.

I settled on '*fehu : sowilo : uruz*,' which I intended as 'wealth : of the sun : charging like an aurochs through this stupid wall.' That last bit was especially suspect. I thought about using *þurisaz* or *tīwaz* to call on Thor or Tyr to break down the wall. But *þurisaz* could just as likely refer to a *jǫtunn* as to Thor, and Tyr's best-known feat involved sacrificing his hand. I was hoping more for a 'smash things' aspect than an 'I don't mind losing body parts' aspect.

My heart pounded. The room became a blur. Breathing was becoming difficult. There was no time to think, yet I had to get it right.

I drew my small carving knife and a wooden disc from my pouch, realizing that I already had the knife out and hadn't considered the type of wood to carve on. Maybe ash? That was *askr* in my language. Close enough to actual ashes, or *aska*, I wanted to reduce the walls to? That seemed appropriate. But not really, because *askr* is masculine and *aska* is feminine, and—

Ulf slapped me in the head. "Not the time for overthinking!"

Trembling, I smiled and let out a nervous laugh.

"Battle glee for the first time, eh?" asked Ulf. "I knew you were a virgin."

The *þulr* grinned and held his shield firm as another dart thunked off the boss. He was insulting me, but only to get my head straight. Or, mostly to get my head straight. It worked enough that the room came into focus again.

When I looked up, a makeshift shield wall to fend off the goblin weapons was fully formed. There was no melee to prepare for unless those goblins decided on a suicide charge. At three or four feet tall each, they would not have lasted long on the ground, and so still the missiles flew and thumped upon wooden shields.

To Hel with the choice of wood. I grabbed the first disc I could. Turned out it was ash. I shrugged and muttered curses to no one in particular.

I carved the runes into the ash disc, enlarging the third to indicate my intent to break through a wall. The disc was just a bit smaller than my palm, a purposeful bit of design. This kind of casting would not be satisfied with a simple carving and strategic placement. Sweat, spit, or mead would not suffice to activate a carving of this violence. This would require blood.

That shield wall had become a shield house, complete with a ceiling. Inside I saw Fanya sitting on her shins, hands grasping her spear, which poked out through a break in the shields above. She was chanting again, louder this time than when she had cast her spells against the Rus. Whatever it was, it was long and unintelligible.

I tried to focus on carving. My head ached from an abrupt pressure I had no source for and took that to be part of whatever Fanya was doing. Ulf's face told me he could feel it as well, but for me, it was a crushing weight I could not think through.

"Come on!" yelled Ulf as he slapped the side of my head. This did not help. I was not holding my hands to my temples in reverie but as a desperate attempt to stave off the agony.

The slap nearly deafened me. I could still hear muted sounds, but even those were cut off for a moment as I wretched. Nothing came out—I had neglected a morning meal, and the witches' hospitality had not included any food. I was becoming ill from all the exertion and the dehydration.

Holding myself inches off the ground, I thought this was where I would die. And then the pressure lifted with a great *whoosh*. My headache was still there, but it felt more like Humor pecking at the back of my head than someone driving a knife through it. That pressure change was not just in my head, however. It was Fanya's doing, and the change from one area of the hall to the other rocked us all bodily.

About half the goblins were knocked off their perches by the gust. Haldor pointed with Silence, and three pairs of warriors hurtled towards those unlucky elves. Axe and seax worked quickly on those that had fallen. Their comrades fled through the holes in the roof from whence they came.

I had dropped the ash disc when I was dry heaving. I found it soon enough and continued the carving. Almost done, just smoothing some of the lines when Kari came to me. The shield wall had dissolved, and the men were again looking to do anything but wait. Heat baked my lungs while the acrid smoke threatened to do us all in before much longer.

"Can you get us out of this hall?" he asked.

"I will need to throw it at one of the walls. Which one?"

Kari called to Haldor, who had the men form up again. I advised another shield wall in case my spell went awry. Hopefully, it would protect them from fiery wood splinters if I blew myself up. There, away from the shields and facing a wall on the long side, I prepared my spell.

I slowed my breathing so as to not slip and slice open any major blood vessels. Before this, I had had trouble removing so much as a splinter. My entire life, I had cringed from pain, shrank in its presence, and sought any way possible to avoid it. Near to retching a second time, I mastered myself. "No," I whispered.

Placing the disc into my knife hand, I sliced my left hand crossways before pressing the disc back into my bloody palm. If only my carving was good, I knew the will was there. I knew it as soon as I held up my open palm. In that moment, I embraced the pain, welcomed the injury as an undeniable part of my being. I held it, savored it. The pain was good. It was right.

Sweat dripped from my nose as I pressed the disc hard into my palm. Panting from exhaustion and pain, I could barely stand up. But I had to stand to throw the disc, and so I steadied myself. I heard my name called as my arm moved back, but I paid no heed as I let the thing fly.

Time slowed down for me, and I saw the disc spinning end over end as it hurtled toward the wall. A dim awareness that I should seek cover grasped at my mind but found little purchase there even as a shield came up from behind to cover my right side. Before the shield obscured my vision, I caught a final glimpse of the disc. Blood on one side. Runes carved on the other.

The blood needs to cover the carved runes for the thing to work. Half delirious, I had bled onto the wrong side. There was no spell, only a bloody piece of wood thumping against the wall, to no effect.

Whoever had brought the shield up shoved me down and crouched beneath the shield for protection. On my knees, unable to fight, useless to my comrades, an embarrassment to my family, Kari held his shield firm against an incoming javelin. It bit his shield and more, driving through the wood and piercing his arm.

Other shields crowded around us as more goblins with bigger weapons poured through. Haldor shouted something to reform and adjust to the attack. The hall was hot now, and the ceiling shed cinders and ash in fist-sized pieces. Smoke shrouded our midst in pillowy white wisps.

My head pounding, I attempted to stand and failed, not unlike my spell that could not work because I had bloodied the wrong side of a piece of wood. The utter frustration was infuriating, but my body would not respond as I wished.

With great effort, I stood and reached for my sling but could not grip it. Like my hand was not made to slip the leather onto one of my fingers.

The others nearest me were looking in my direction now, eyes wide. What were Innstein and Utstein so surprised about? Why was Fanya shouting at them to cut off my belt? A half step forward, and then another, and I felt myself falling forward onto my hands.

But they were not my own hands anymore. Pain ripped through me the likes of which I have never otherwise known, paralyzing me in body and mind. I could not hear. I could not see.

If Ketill had demanded I understand the essence of each rune, what I felt then was the essence of blood—its taste, its smell, its sound. The feeling seeped in through my cut hand and ran through my arm and down my spine.

It was as if something had entered the cut in my hand and taken hold of my shape, expanding it from the inside outward. It grew even as it condensed and hardened. I could feel it enveloping my mind, covering the shame and insecurity, burning them away as my body changed.

My fangs curled up and over my lips. Claws dug inches into the hard earth beneath them. Fur like a million threads of armor thrust through my skin. And I could smell my enemy. I could smell everything.

My *hamr*, my very shape, had changed. I was no longer the swooning skald of the *Sea Squirrel*. I was the great white bear of the north. My roar at the end of the change stilled the room as I stood on my hind legs and towered twice over even Haldor and Svein.

The men had all given a wide berth by now, but I did not look to them. The goblins froze, eyes wide and almost level with mine while still in the rafters. There was no relief from the ceasing of pain, only the desire to bring that pain to battle. I read the goblins' expressions and tasted their fear like it was sweetrolls. They fled a second time as I took in their smell.

They smelled like something I had to kill. Not to stalk, not to hunt, not to eat. But to rend and stomp and make it cease to exist because its presence in this world was an affront to mine. That smell was like a horn announcing the arrival of the frenzy.

I smelled more of them outside the main entrance where they had gathered. So I charged it.

Splinters of thick oaken boards and posts exploded in all directions. Smoke trailed each fiery piece of wood like comets in the night sky. The goblins were already scattering. Only Valborg, her wand cast into a magical torch, stood before me.

She would have screamed if that first blind leap had not landed my two thousand pounds or so on top of her.

Behind me the crew of the *Sea Squirrel*, a witch, and a useless king with a useful retinue made quick exit of the flame-engulfed hall.

I flung Valborg's body aside, the first affront to no longer offend me, and looked down into the city. Our battle was not the only one occurring at that moment.

Two contingents clashed down the hill. One uniform and disciplined, the other a mishmash of sizes and positions. Men and women in the city had formed a shield wall against Alfhild's mercenaries, or a wall of whatever they could find as many were missing actual shields.

Sometimes there is a great deal of poetry in few words. At my full height, I felt the warm blood drip down my fur while I roared a single note. It was to challenge, to announce, to oppose. And to affirm Haldor's earlier comment in the clearest, simplest voice:

There was indeed a great deal of killing to do.

CHAPTER 43

MIGHT AND MAIN

I OUTPACED MY FRIENDS IN GREAT, LOPING STRIDES AS I PLUNGED down the hill and into the fray. Smoke from burning buildings hung low like a mist of Muspelheim.

I could see a few smaller skirmishes detached from the main shield walls now clashing ahead of me. Four Rus had broken off from supporting their shield wall to surround two small figures waving spears at them. Inga, it seemed, had traded in her spoon for something more substantial. She stood back to back with another woman, smaller but helmeted and surer of her weapon's grip than Inga was.

The women both screamed and pointed their spears at me as I charged. And why not? They would not know me for Ansgar the Skald.

Meanwhile, my chest-sized paws reached out for a Rus warrior each and pulled them down. Claws pierced the mail of one, and he screamed. The other I grabbed fully by the face so he had not the luxury of saying anything. I slammed the two bodies into each other over and over until I was satisfied their friends would not be able to tell where one man ended and the other began.

But it was not enough. It would never be enough. Not enough destruction. Not enough blood.

An arrow found its mark in the neck of one of the surprised Rus. Out of the smoke-filled night, Flosi nocked another arrow as he ran toward the fray.

A shadow to my left leaped forward following the twang of a bowshot. Though Flosi was fast on the move, the king's nephew Hrolf raced faster. Shield half-cloven and on fire, the young warrior hewed down that last detached foeman before pulling the women back behind him. Broken shield up, sword back and ready to strike, the skinny nephew of Denmark's coalbiter king set himself ready to face me alone.

Standing at full height, I extended my forelegs and dropped the two bodies that had become one in a gory salute to the warrior.

He did not take this as the intended peace offering, and instead readied to strike while Flosi drew for a shot at my face.

"Stop!" cried Nanthild, pulling the young Hrolf back. I almost did not recognize her with the helmet on.

Hrolf gaped in surprise but held back.

"This is no enemy," said Nanthild, stepping forward.

I dropped to all fours and leaned to meet her nose to nose. What visage such a muzzle would have been, snarling and drooling, big enough to bite a man's head full off, disturbed her not. Such contrast to the young woman's pale, pretty face must have seemed the greatest incongruity. But not to me, and not to her. There was an unseen thing about, a quality unrecognized other than by those with the experience.

I knew then what Ulfberht had meant when he told me 'She is the stronger.' This was not the *berserkr's* rage, nor whatever magic was on me then. But I could smell it on her, the fury. The cold-striking battle mind of that woman had been earned with blood. She would temper it with more still.

I turned, eyes wide and maniacal, and fixed on the Rus shield wall. Only the edge was visible among the dense smoke, but that flank threatened to envelop the remaining Danes.

That flank angered me. The Rus angered me. I remembered something vaguely about being attacked by many Rus. The thought of being surrounded by them now seemed a great opportunity. So I headed for where they were thickest.

I took my time with them. Paws batted back shields and broke bodies. Claws shredded mail and tore the soft flesh beneath. Teeth crunched skulls through steel helmets. One warrior, thinking a close-in attack against my belly to be wise, dove in under me, knife in hand. I dropped my full weight and crushed him.

The Rus, so recently confident of overwhelming the surprised townsfolk, hardened their faces against a real enemy. They were no fair-weather fighters. A few shouts, and they re-formed their line to end this new menace while holding the original line. Soon I was surrounded by spears just out of my reach.

Come on! I thought, and roared my frustration. But come on they would not, as they bided their time and waited for openings to make quick thrusts and hop back out of reach.

"Shield wall!" called the unmistakable voice of Haldor Skullsplitter. The men of the *Sea Squirrel* knew on instinct how to form up. They had taken their time getting down that hill, those poor two-legged slowpokes. But there they were, shields packed on one another and moving as a single armored line. Haldor and Svein waited to shatter shields with their axes. Between them stood a grinning Magnus, his long seax looking for stray enemy hamstrings.

They rolled into the Rus flank in a wave of crashing steel and splintering wood. To their credit, those Rus held even during that confusion. Innstein and Utstein held the end of the line, joining the crew's ranks with the group of townspeople.

Shields pushed back and spears licked out or came flying at my head as the Rus line re-formed yet again. Always a wall of spearpoints dogged me until, in my fury, I snatched the end of one into my teeth. The owner of that spear pulled back, just as I hoped he would. With such a hard grip on his weapon, he came flying forward when I set my hind legs and yanked him back towards me. Then he was down, and half a dozen others readied for my charge.

My fur was like heavy chain armor against those paltry weapons. Some found their way through to flesh, but could not score a deep injury. Perhaps there was a weak point, but I would find that if and when it became impor-tant. In battle, there is always the element of the unexpected, even when things look as predictable as that moment.

Nanthild the Raven Feeder delivered the next unpredictable thing: She thrust a long axe forward and hooked the heel of its blade into the throat of one of those preparing for me to charge. In half a moment, the man was clutching at his neck while the man next to him took Nanthild's next blow between his teeth.

An arrow shot out of the misty smoke and found a third, and by then I was indeed charging.

We put an end to those spearmen, and I found myself just outside the trapped Rus contingent. There, to complete the encirclement of the enemy, was Hrolf. He attacked the Rus rear himself, his lithe form dancing aside of each stoke and countering with his own.

"I see my house burning," laughed the king's nephew between slashes. "Where will you fine fellows find a bed tonight? I hope shelter beneath my sword will be sufficient hospitality."

At that, he stabbed one man who had overcommitted in his attack. In a second smooth motion, he claimed the dying man's shield and dodged his way to Nanthild's side.

I found my feet in that bear's body and began sweeping away the spears that had so vexed me before. Then I turned toward the deepest pit of the wedge where the Rus were assailed on two sides. No hammer and anvil this; it was mortar and pestle as I ground into those hardy men while the shield walls of the Danes and the *Sea Squirrel* men held in an unpierceable reverse wedge.

The Rus sounded retreat. I wanted to tell them what a good and yet irrelevant idea that was.

With a shout, Ragnvald's picked champions were released from the shield wall and fought alongside Hrolf. Three swords slashed out over and over, the moonlight glinting off their blades enough to light the scene. Hromund and Beigadh settled scores longstanding with the mercenaries then. Ragnvald's champions did not fight for gold. They cut more than purses as they unmanned one after another. The survivors broke and scattered in the concealing smoke and ruins while I finished my own fight and remembered to breathe.

That first fight was over. Inga stood a few steps behind, shaking as she looked for more enemies. Nanthild's hands were reddened but steady.

Madness came over me in waves and receded almost as quickly. A hunger had hold of me. More blood, more violence. Where would it be next?

"There is a body in your teeth," said Nanthild.

Indeed, I had almost completely bitten through the midsection of the thing. Must have lost track. I dropped the lifeless form and spit out loose mail links after it.

Dimly I heard Haldor speak with Hrolf. What a waste of time! I needed only a direction. Something about the north gate. Of course! The host hidden in the forest would seek entry there. The fools would find me there too if they ever finished their endless talking about one contingent here under Hrolf and another under Gudbrand. I had no patience for strategy, but Nanthild's hand stilled me.

The young woman had appropriated a mail shirt and shield off the dead. Both were stained red with the mark of a recent owner. Her helmet was of a Norse style. She must have picked it up from a fallen ally. Porcelain as her features were, no delicate expression stared out from those iron eye sockets.

"You are too hasty," she said. "And others will also think you an enemy if you arrive alone."

This was taking too long. Where was the fighting? I growled my discontent and shook my head. Others turned our way. Some balked at the sight, and I felt their faith fade as fear returned to their eyes.

"*Hold, demon!*" shouted the young woman in her native language. "*If it was my summons you answer, you are late in arriving. Where were you when I had no weapons to fight with or armor to protect me? Where were you when I was weak and called for help? If tonight is your answer to summons long ago, I demand more than a brash surge forward to a quick death!*"

Arms spread with shield and spear, she called that challenge, no less brave than when the king's nephew had faced me. Was she indeed a shieldmaiden now, or a valkyrie eager to spill as much blood as I, the bear?

The blood rage ran through me in red waves. She could see it, I was certain, as I could see it in her. Her presence was not controlling but steadying, and I poured every pulse of energy into a vessel inside me. I could control it, build it, set it free bit by bit. Now was not the time. Soon, though.

I lowered myself and let her climb onto my back. Kraki approached, the only other person willing to come very close. Long, thin lines of red revealed cuts he had taken already. Splatters indicated spray from the blood of enemies he had smashed to pieces with his club.

"To the south gate then," he said, club restless in his hands.

So we strode off shoulder to shoulder, the *berserkr* and the bear and the shieldmaiden. Haldor heartened the men and set those fleetest of foot to guard our advance from surprise attack.

The king found his voice for what that was worth. He seemed to enjoy hearing it.

"With Thor's blessing," called out the king to his people, "with that blessing we go on to battle!"

Those two fine champions held fast to his side, but I imagined them wishing to take up closer with his nephew instead.

"That's a fine thing, uncle," said Hrolf. "Though I think I find more comfort in good guests than in gods tonight."

"You forget yourself, boy!" cried the king, less in anger than in concern. "And you know not what we face! Where is that witch? If she spoke true, we face a fight of more than mercenaries ahead. Of dread beasts and dark things, as if we did not have enough with just one troll. I will reward our guests greatly, no doubt, but mortal strength cannot withstand the strength of such fiends unless divine power should intervene."

Finding new energy in his piety, the king rose his voice to a shout and raised his shining sword as he spoke to all those around. "That favor alone stands between us and victory, Hrolf, and we have it! We have it!"

The crew of the *Sea Squirrel* continued in silence, though you could hear their thoughts rage if you knew how to listen. I craned my neck to see the king's nephew exchange a look with Haldor.

Our captain gave no reply nor changed his expression. No look of surprise or judgment at Ragnvald's words. No recognition of value as guest or commander, hero or monster. The king was as outside Haldor's calculations as the gods. He would not deny the king's existence but would give it no authority, no offering or sacrifice.

And that is when I understood Haldor's rule: That men (and women, especially considering the one who had saved me and the blood-soaked one seated on my back) did not increase themselves by deferring to more powerful beings, but found only diminishment there. And in that diminished state, there was no way forward but to beg for more favor until death. Haldor's rule was there to leave us unto ourselves, and in that naked state create the might and main to rely on later.

Gaze fixed, Haldor banged the side of Silence on his shield boss twice and lowered his weapon.

We walked a few paces more, and up came Silence again. Kari strode just behind, sweat beading on his brow, barely able to hold his shield, but joined our captain.

Gorm Tin-Whisker, who had found us in the fray, had no shield but thumped his spear on his helmet. Bang bang.

A few paces more, and again Haldor raised Silence to crash louder and louder against his shield. Nearly all were joining. They knew what was unspoken.

Bang bang. Might and main.

The core I controlled inside me swirled and circled with each undulation. Waves crashed on inside and threatened to burst forth as I growled my discontent. I wanted blood, the hot blood that pulsed out of a still-living body. I wanted Alfhild's screams. I wanted to find Frothi and climb up through his insides and chew my way out.

"*Steady, demon,*" said Nanthild, sensing my state. "*Soon, but not before.*"

It was indeed not much longer before the south gate came into view. All attention lay on what scuffled just beyond that border. Terrified townspeople gripped their spears and trembled at each terrible thump against the gate while men with drawn faces looked down from the palisades and tried to sound brave. Limbs climbed, clambered, and cracked at the line of pointed timbers we called city walls. Claws and wings, armor and weapons clinked under the moon with night fully upon us.

One warrior looking over the edge turned to shout a warning that another push was coming. In that call, his voice cracked, and I saw the spears of those on the ground wince. Still the Spear-Danes held their ground. They knew fear, but would face it standing steady.

Striding past the front lines on his horse was Gudbrand, as the staller was the only one I knew to fight on horseback. Hearing the same thing I had, he found a voice to counter that near-despair.

"Get those shields to the front!" he shouted, gesturing with his atgeir at where to stand. "Keep a path in the middle open to reinforce the gate! They cannot get in so easily as they think. Let them fall on your spears if they do!"

It was no false confidence. Men and women dressed for battle ran forward with stout beams to brace the gate. Warriors atop the gate hacked downwards at unseen limbs. Whatever Alfhild had in store, it would face no few weapons opposed.

"What in nine realms?!" said Gudbrand as I approached. "Spears!"

The Danes obeyed as I came down the middle path Gudbrand himself had ordered. The shock of that great white beast did their nerves no favors, but Nanthild shouted for calm.

Kraki spread his arms, bone club in hand, and strode towards Gudbrand. "You know me!" shouted the ancient warrior turned awful cook.

Gudbrand never wanted for a mail shirt, and tonight he wore two in layers. The staller whirled his weapon on his mount, an old hand both with horse and atgeir even so heavily armored. He was not convinced.

"Are you mad? There are monsters on the other side of that gate, and what is this with you?"

"Monsters on this side of the gate!" cried the cook. "And the king," he muttered with less enthusiasm, "if that matters."

Ragnvald was soon at the forefront and had important shouting to do. 'Do this' and 'Do that' were what most of it consisted of. Hard to deny a man dressed in purple and wielding an ornate sword as a king. Who else can afford either of those things? It was to little effect, though. Impressive impressions are good for when people are standing around doing little or nothing.

"This is well reinforced," said Ragnvald. "Get some of those men to drop their spears and find bows! And get a fire brigade going!"

"Those things will get through soon!" shouted the staller, incredulous. "We need every spear on the ground, not blind shooting of arrows over the wall or to waste time splashing in water!"

The rest of those with us had made it clear they intended to reinforce the existing Danish lines. Haldor and Hrolf directed their men, both in support of Gudbrand's tactics.

No shield wall for a bear, however. I leaned down to drop Nanthild and pointed to the shield wall with my nose. Her eyes would not leave mine.

I growled as best I could to convey my meaning. Once. Twice. Then a roar that blew back the loose strands of her hair unheld by her helmet. I could not make her blink.

"*Do not forget me in the fighting,*" she said in response, a gentle hand to my giant muzzle. Only then did she leave me to join the group under Hrolf's command.

That was when we heard the screaming.

CHAPTER 44

SACRIFICE

THE KING STOPPED ARGUING. THE GUARDS ON THE PALISADE stepped back. Howls ripped through the night, and the air took on the smell of clotted blood and rot.

I padded up the earthworks on the side of the gate and peered over. Ingolf broke ranks and came to look as well, standing by my side, along with some of the others.

A man, naked but for the greasy drawings on his flesh, rose upside-down just beyond the gate. His hands and feet were bound by writhing, slithering shadow that flickered in the low light of the fires. I saw he had not been merely painted, but carved on with runes like one of my wooden discs. The runes on him glowed green here and there, faded, and then others came alight. With each new pattern he let fly with fresh, hoarse cries, wordless and yet telling all.

"Leif!" shouted Ingolf.

In such a state, I had recognized neither the man nor his voice. The raving in pain told of a man whose mind was blasted beyond healing. It had little resemblance to the man I knew as Ingolf's sworn brother.

Suspended by nothing, held in place by nothing, Leif hung there trapped and desperate to see his life end while the Danes gasped. Up then rose Alfhild, slow but certain while we stood transfixed. The moonlight shone pale on her face as she smiled at us and addressed the lot as one.

345

I will not repeat her words. They were vile and, worse, they were in *galdralag*. She cut Leif's throat and spilled his life into a bowl as we stood impotent behind the still-shut gate. That witch would make the most of Leif's sacrifice. Three spells she cast with that life, three spells as a haze like smoke or mist poured over our walls. Over and over, she repeated the same things in different words, like weaving a pattern layer after layer. The sounds of a hundred horrid creatures chirped, growled, and squealed on the other side.

The king nearly despaired at the sounds, his sword drooping. I saw him hunch and hide, old and enfeebled by Alfhild's sorcery as much as by her betrayal. His champions held him fast, however, and would not allow him to fall to his knees.

"No time for the timid," shouted Beigadh over the awful din.

"Swordplay is not for the soft-hearted," added Hromund.

Kraki's gaze was fixed on the witch. Quick as his crotchety body would carry him, he scaled that wall while Beigadh and Hromund comforted the king. Not one of them noticed the hooded figure descend from the top of the gate. I thought this guard was trying to get away, but his movements were not so desperate or fearful. Then I realized what I was seeing all in one instant.

Frothi knocked away the supports and opened the gate just wide enough to fit before I was after him. That traitor, the one who locked us all in to have us burned alive, that witch's lackey! He was just out of reach, so close to my claws as I thudded back, the opening not big enough for my bulk. I grabbed the gate door and heaved it open before returning to all fours to charge.

The boar hit me like Haldor's fist careening through the pallid face of a priest. I went down hard and with a solid gash from one of its tusks on the way.

On it charged, that huge troll Alfhild had conjured. It found a weak spot in part of the shield wall and scattered the warriors there, throwing one high in the air with its great tusks.

So I saw from my dizzied position on the ground while warriors poured around me and through the gate. Mail-clad men with heavy spears and torches rushed forward heedless of the huge bear, and others with axes hewed away the gate's hinges so that it could not be closed. Among those getting through were vile things Fanya had warned about. Wargs and dragons, trolls of all types, Loki's distant spawn, she had said.

Many were man or woman-shaped, but no longer man or woman. Their jaws hung open too wide and their teeth too like needles while too-long arms swung wide looking for unwary enemies. Others with faces divided into two hideous grins, one eye looking up and the other down, stumbled as if just now finding their balance on backward-facing limbs.

Whatever they were, they were all trolls to me. Some looked like dead trees or mounds of earth come to life. Others charged forward on four legs, bigger and more monstrous than mere animals, though none were as massive as that troll of a boar.

A warg leaped over my prostrate form, or tried to. Not all my balance was back after that hit from the boar, but just enough to hook claws into that big wolf-thing's haunches and fling it back bodily into the onrushing others. I rose to my full height and bade the battle begin again. No more holding back what sought release inside me. What carnage ensued as every onrushing spear and claw then turned on me was unexpected to Alfhild's allies. Feral cries made the music of murder in front of that gate; claws cut through heavy armor and thick hide while teeth crunched their bones.

Some toothy monster, too used to taking unaware victims under cover of darkness, came forward. Whether to try its fame on the great bear or incapable of such thoughts, I did not try to ascertain after the thing bit me near the elbow. A few of those teeth got past the armor of my fur and pricked more than my pride when they sank home. I could feel the injury but not the pain. There was no pain. All was rage.

I grabbed the back of the thing's head to tear it from my arm and held it aloft for those others not yet joined to see. And when I knew they could see, when I knew they had just readied themselves to attack, I ripped that thing's head off and let them get a look, a good look, at what they had in store.

Hromund the Hard and Beigadh the Bold kept their king between them and gave no ground to man nor troll. Their blades flashed faster than the eye could track. Their pommels cracked skulls and teeth. Many a forgotten outlaw and unnamed thing fell thinking they had found easy prey outside a shield wall's protection.

In the midst of his champions' hewing, King Ragnvald regained himself from the coals he had too long chewed upon. He would not stand by while demons destroyed what he presided over. He had no wind, being old and unmoving for so long, but he knew how to fight. Timing picked between the parries of his champions, his sword licked out to sever limb and head alike.

On toward the Danes came Kraki and Ingolf, heedless of the horde's danger and looking for no shield wall's shelter. They had not come for the king's aid, however, and fought through the fray and unto the gate. As I dashed left and then right in a killing frenzy, they held that area and barred entrance by more enemies, whatever their shape or size.

This, I came to realize in my blood rage-addled brain, was not their intention either.

"That's quite the skin change, skald!" cackled Kraki. Gleefully he bashed brains in, and no shield could hold under the blows from his bone club. "But whatever your shape or his, we will not leave Leif as someone's sacrifice."

Ingolf had done away with his shield and wielded his axe with both hands. If Kraki's fighting was aggressive and brutish, Ingolf's was cold and calculating. Not one movement of that man was wasted on anything unnecessary. The spear of one foeman I thought would pierce his heart, but Ingolf slipped inside the weapon's range and sliced the man's throat open with a push-cut of his blade. As the man staggered, he grabbed the spear for himself and threw it into the chest of some hunchbacked thing with knife-long claws.

Leif still hung suspended in mid-air when we reached him. His last blood dripped onto the ground after Alfhild had drained him of the better part of it. His glassy eyes stared at nothing. Kraki held off further attacks from the front, facing back into the city while I took the rear and scattered whatever fiends Alfhild still sent forward. No amount of tugging by his sworn brother could bring Leif down to earth, to Ingolf's great frustration.

I turned my attention back to the body. Ansgar the Skald might have devised some rune magic to counter Alfhild's binding there. Ketill, certainly, could have undone such work. But I had no hands or equipment to work with. Even my weight would not lower the body when I wrapped my forelegs around it, and I had to return to fending off our rear with no progress. We were being swarmed. Soon there would be nothing but to continue fighting rather than to let Ingolf return that body to his brothers in arms.

A warg dove in to bite me on the ass, if you can believe that. I heard its back break as I slammed it into the ground.

I looked back to Lief then. A loose circle of spears had formed around us, and they were closing in. I could break through, even clear enough way for Kraki and Ingolf. But that would be to leave Leif. Perhaps it was the bear's shape that killed my caution, I can't claim to have had that kind of courage, but there was no choice involved. We would not abandon Leif's body, and I roared my defiance at any fool spearmen who would come closer.

They laughed. Somewhere out in the darkness, Alfhild sat cackling, her voice taunting us in an eerie timbre. All the brute strength of the bear could not bring that body down, but I was more than the bear. The skald was still inside, seeing the battle from deep down. And while the bear roared, the skald whispered an idea.

I still wonder what it looked like, a giant bear jumping as high as his hind legs will leap. Being the bear, I could not very well see myself do it. But I did see the shadowy bindings around Leif's ankles, and with one outstretched claw, I dug deep into those bonds. They withered and broke when I pierced them, and Ingolf caught his sworn brother's body as it fell.

The ranks around us swelled with spears. Our enemies had turned, as if by Alfhild's will, from the city back against us. Whether to deal with the great bear or merely to prevent the small victory of retrieving our friend's body, who knows. It was a mistake.

"Swine array!" called Haldor. On through the wall's open wound, he and Svein charged at the head of a tight wedge as men of the *Sea Squirrel* made their counterattack. They led with their shields and drove those spearmen back before they could turn in the right direction. Warriors turned and slipped or dropped. Svein stomped on the head of one as the wedge rolled into and over their front line.

Weapons caught up amongst the crush of men, and those left standing against Haldor's wedge found little room to swing. The wedge was not deep on either side, but it had done the intended thing. The enemy ranks were not just pushed back, they were parted.

Through that opening came Magnus, low and fast, a long seax in each hand. One attack was not even finished before the next began in a series of lightning slashes. Faster than they could react, even faster than most of them could see, Magnus was slitting throats and slicing hamstrings. Over his head sailed one of Kari's javelins to take its target in the chest.

The enemy line at the gate reeled from the shock. It was cleaved in two, men and monsters alike pushed backwards.

Ragnvald bade his champions leave his side then and sent them to reinforce Haldor's wedge. Those two needed no encouragement.

"Frothi!" called Beigadh after stabbing one man through the throat. "Did you earn so much gold by selling your ass that you need none earned with your sword arm?"

Hromund bashed the man in front of him with his shield buttressed by his sword pommel, breaking the man's nose. "Perhaps he has changed professions," he added, following the shield hit with a downward rake of his blade across the man's exposed throat. "Perhaps he needs more oil now."

"Ha! My sword is well oiled! Do you hear me, Frothi? Come test my sword!"

Realizing he had taken the metaphor further than intended, Beigadh laughed at his own joke, and Hromund joined him. They continued to call for their former friend as they hacked down hapless warriors in front of them.

"Now this way!" Ragnvald beckoned to us.

First went Kraki, whose club beat back an attempt by those outlaws to reform and come around a flank. Ingolf slipped through and back to the city, slashing blades of his crewmen keeping enemies at bay.

Slowly I rumbled in behind Ingolf and swiped at any men who got too near him. Back fell the brothers and Magnus through the gap, and there I stalled. Why retreat? It was as good a killing ground as any, and Haldor's men were already arrayed next to me. There would be little chance for further incursions against both shield wall and bear.

It was the moment I locked eyes with the king and saw his sword rise and his expression fall that I knew I also must fall back. I knew but could not reach him. Down came his sword against the boar's charge, but not in time. That troll's tusks tore the king nearly in two.

On it ran, and I ran after it.

Thick bristles shot out from its hoary mane, most finding their marks amongst the Danish line. Mail and helmets and shields they pierced, though the troll itself kept away from the massed spears Hrolf and his men set against it.

At the king's final battle cry, the lines lost their discipline. Even Gudbrand's commands could no longer be heard above the clamor of shouts and roars and the clang of steel on steel. Fires ate at nearby buildings, the smoke making it as hard to see as it was to hear.

Some rushed to Ragnvald's body despite the danger. He had squandered much loyalty before, but still stood steadfast with death charging at him on sharpened hooves. I supposed that counted for something.

The staller brought his horse around what was left of his shield wall, and I could see the boar oblige him from across the field. I was not about to let that collision happen, however. The staller had never done me other than a good turn, and I owed that shrieking pig-god a deal of pain.

The boar went at Gudbrand and saw me coming at his side about halfway there, turning away well in time from both horse and bear. Hrolf saw the scene playing out and concentrated his spears. That swine found it more difficult to get away than he had thought and rounded on me rather than rush headlong into that many Danes.

I was running at my full speed when we collided, turning only to avoid those tusks. But I had him. Had him caught in my claws, and so we tumbled together end over end through the shouts and smoke and into the fire of what used to be some rich merchant's house.

No more knock-down and running away; there we tore at each other in earnest, trading a dozen swipes, each of which could have killed a man on their own. Flaming timbers crashed around us and burned my coat black with soot. We scratched at each other with wild, feral ferocity. The squealing mass slashed at me with its tusks, but I sunk one set of claws deep into its snout and twisted the thing over. He gored my paw but that was all he could manage before retreating.

I smelled bacon as he ran headlong through the next flaming wall, and it was too delicious a thing not to follow.

I would kill Alfhild's demon and devour him. Through the next wall I followed, not nearly so thick as those in Ragnvald's hall. Through smoke-filled streets we ran, half the buildings in the city aflame.

In those streets and through one, then two, then a third building, that great boar turned for his final confrontation. Huge, gleaming tusks threatened against blackened, bloodied claws, and I saw both my enemy and myself. No pretense, just monster against monster.

I was the *Sea Squirrel*'s monster, and Alfhild's champion was a poor antagonist. I would make them wish they still had that barrier to keep me away, to keep them safe.

A growl, low and smug, rumbled from my core as I pulled down their monster and dragged it outside. Screaming, it thrashed with sharp hooves to squirm away, but I had dug into him deep and did not let go.

As it squealed, I plunged my paw deep into its underbelly and ripped out its entrails in defiance of whatever spirits were watching and all who could hear. And when I knew they could all hear, every outlaw, every troll that had come to Alfhild's bidding, I screamed in the bear's voice the tone of *nauðiz*, of need, of hunger. I eviscerated their oversized pig-god. What was next?

What was next was I should have been watching my flank. Instead of being ready for it, the lindworm's strike took me off my feet, and I was suddenly fighting both surprised and on the ground. My hide was tough, but I still bled as long fangs sank into my flesh.

I could tell this was no poisonous serpent monster. The teeth were wrong, and it did not retreat after the first strike. It had hit me hard and coiled around me as we fought on the ground. The arms (legs? who cares) were of little danger to me, little appendages for crawling were not its main weapons. It was a constrictor, and the danger to me was not breathing well enough to keep fighting.

So we rolled and tumbled, sometimes over a hapless warg or man, both of us trying to attack and defend at the same time. Every time the lindworm bit me, it was in danger of having its face ripped off or worse. But any time I tried to stretch towards the head, the serpent was better positioned to squeeze the guts out of me. It must have been a terrible thing to watch as two huge monsters tore at each other on the battlefield, though not as terrible as having your ribcage crushed and your face chewed on by a fifty-foot dragon.

Giving as good as I got as far as drawing blood was a losing proposition in that fight. I realized this too late. My breath was too shallow, and my vision began to blur. Ignoring the pain, I made a desperate grasp for the monster's head to end the fight there, but it craned its neck back to put it just out of reach. I was going to fail, and tonight failure meant death.

I saw the javelin first and the rope it was attached to next. Kari was on a fishing expedition and had pierced the thing in the back of the neck. The dragon screamed, a small sound compared to Jormungand's but still recognizable with that monster, and it jerked backwards and thrashed at Kari. He was fast, but its tail was faster, and Kari took a blow so hard, it bent his neck over backwards with a loud crack.

Kari fell, and I could do nothing. The lindworm held fast and smiled at me before preparing a strike to my face.

The strike never came. The rope pulled taut and snapped the dragon's head back. Haldor Skullplitter held the line with both hands. The two glared at each other as I fought to breathe. Down, down, down moved the monster's head as Haldor pulled, took in the slack, and pulled some more. Still, I could barely breathe from the tight coils as man and monster drew ever closer.

Silence sat unready in Haldor's belt while the serpent's weapons were fully deployed. Any part of its body could be lethal. I wanted to yell a warning to Haldor that his opponent would give in suddenly and strike, but he was waiting for it.

The body of the serpent uncoiled from me to strike with speed I could barely register. I flopped forward, my body unwilling to do the bidding of my brain for the moment other than gasp for air.

Haldor had no intention of drawing his axe before the thing struck— there was already a perfectly good javelin right there in its neck. So when the lindworm's attack missed, and the rest of its body attempted to coil around Haldor, it found only air.

He was already on its back, climbing up its scales like a mountain goat on a fjord cliff while the thing tried to thrash him off. Once high enough, he grabbed the javelin embedded in the back of its neck while it writhed high in the air.

One image fixed in my mind will never fade: Haldor, his face of cool fury, holding onto the javelin with his left hand, raising Silence high with his right, his teeth and eyes gleaming in the firelight to contrast his beard stained black with the blood of unnamed things. He buried the spike of the axe deep into that serpent's skull, and there it fell. Its thudding to the ground announced the death of another of Alfhild's champions.

The serpent's body shuddered as I shed its coils. Breathing again took some getting used to, but that was not the worst of it. My vision unblurred and I saw Kari Swifthand, his body still. I would have blood for that man's life, however much blood I would have had otherwise.

"Back to the gate," said Haldor as he saw his friend's fate. Mourning that man would come later, though little did we all know then how much we would come to miss his counsel.

We were scattered in those loose streets, hardly able to see for the dark and the smoke. I had been lucky Haldor and Kari had found me in time, but there seemed little else to do. A fat troll with a nose like an onion and a mouth like a serving bowl rolled out nearby with a child in each fist. They squirmed and kicked at the thing's massive buck teeth to avoid being swallowed whole. I had hardly seen it before Kraki was there, pounding its skull into the earth.

Ulf appeared, panting from exhaustion, his knife hand bloodied. According to him, the Danish lines had dispersed as some were pushed back by the boar, and some broke ranks to fight the fires consuming their homes. What fighting was left was isolated and in small groups.

"Something is strange," said Ulf, and at this, Haldor turned his full attention to the man. "I killed a man early on and watched him wither from the knife in his guts. He had something written on his neck."

"It is strange what they paint themselves with, but what of it?" asked Haldor.

"I just fought a man with the same markings. He fell too, but . . ." Ulf shook his head. "The look in his eye. It seemed to me I was fighting the same man!"

"A fog of war," said Kraki, wiping the gore off his club. "The night will play tricks on the mind. I have seen much worse than a man thinking he fought the same enemy twice."

Ulf shook his head and staggered as if hit in the head but said nothing further. Kraki was the most experienced among us, a veteran of more battles he had forgotten than the others had ever fought. Still, something about Ulf's description raised my hackles, and I growled and sniffed the air for danger.

It smelled like the dead.

"Back to the gate!" commanded Haldor. "Rally to Hrolf!" He had seen what I only began to surmise as Alfhild's second spell after her summoning, the one that could wait. Its evidence turned a corner ahead of a billowing gray cloud, the bright of the moon reflecting off their eyes and pallid skin.

It was a group of disfigured Rus warriors. Helmets halved, cloaks dyed crimson with caked blood, shields shorn where they still existed. A short one was missing his mail shirt and much of his throat. It was the same group we had fought at the foot of the hill. Ahead of them marched a giant boar, eyes glazed, intestines dragging behind it.

All around us, from misshapen troll to nameless mercenary, our fallen enemies began to rise and reach for their weapons.

CHAPTER 45

HELBLIND-SIDED

"THIS BATTLE WOULD HAVE MADE FOR QUITE A SONG," HALDOR said as he Silenced a rushing warg. "But only with a skald to sing it."

I grabbed the nearest foeman with a spear and bit off his lower jaw, leaving him to scream with half a mouth. The dead might rise, but they could still feel pain. No words followed, but Haldor knew my next roar's meaning. I would not quit the battlefield, and we would live on in the lasting horror inflicted upon our enemies.

Haldor smiled and the brothers banged their shields in approval. We fought back to back then, determined to destroy everything in sight.

Innstein and Utstein, who I had thought of as jokesters we kept just to repair the ship, fought like one man was using two bodies. Svein shouted with every great blow he brought down. The sound of Kraki's club came down on our enemies like thunder. Silence rang against armor and bone, trails of blood following its flight through the air.

Horns had sounded from the area at the gate to call us back and regroup. Most did, as far as I could tell, though that area itself was no haven. How many of our enemies had fallen there only to rise again? It mattered little. The Danes needed something to rally to, and they listened to the call of Gudbrand's horn. Ragnvald's sword, heavy for the aged king, found its way to Hrolf's hands where it sang a new song in the night air.

We would be worn down at some point; it was only a matter of time. As long as dead men got up to take their places back in the shield wall and the other monsters Alfhild had summoned rose again and again, they had only to wait until we were exhausted. Svein was already shouting less with every strike. I had lost track of Magnus, and who knew where Ingolf had gone with Leif's body. Whatever had become of the dwarf, and where was Fanya?

Torches scattered among the battlefield and fires of houses nearby lit a dim scene. My vantage point at full height showed me more than others, but still, I could not spy the queen. The boar was stuck, or one of its hooves was. It struggled with something in the ground and dug at it with its snout and tusks.

Two claws of a huge black and white badger reached up, and up, and up, as if from a very long way down, and took hold of that great snout. The badger dragged itself up to take a bite straight out of the boar's septum, cried out in triumph, and disappeared back into the earth. The ground around it parted as the thing burrowed with unnatural speed.

Some of the Rus tried to stab at the bulges in the ground but missed. The badger shot out of the earth like a crossbow bolt at the leg of one man, who swung his spear too broadly and hit his own allies. The badger growled and chattered as it dove back into the earth and out again, sowing chaos among the enemy ranks.

"Hold your ground, bear," boomed the staller's voice. "Here is where we stand, if you stand with us. I will meet that boar charge for charge myself."

A raven flew low, or low for a raven with any sense. It croaked in a low, hoarse voice at nothing in particular, just a bird taking a look at several meals in its near future. I wondered if the bird could see Alfhild, and if the bird was Humor or a harbinger of something else. I looked back to where he had flown in from, and there were new figures to the battle.

"HA!" shouted Hrolf. "The north gate is not overrun, and they return to our aid!"

It sent a cheer up among the warriors, or those at least that could not see very well. The city's north gate was not overrun, but neither were the few men guarding it able to fight their way forward without casualties.

That was no tight formation or fresh set of sword-arms. Most limped or helped others. There was Flosi at the front, another arrow nocked and one of the few no worse for wear. He stayed by Inga, who used her spear to steady herself and the one she carried. Worse, they would soon run right into that boar and its entourage.

Out of that shuffling mass, one figure with a gait no more graceful than the others pushed its way forward. It wore a heavy cloak and hood, bow in hand. I knew that bow, and I knew that drunken shuffle, but what I had not yet seen for all my time with Ketill was how dangerous he was. Beckoning forward another figure, he drew one arrow lazily back. His aim lolled up and down, left and right, finding little balance. Finally, he loosed with a great swish of air to puff his beard forward.

The old man craned his head forward after loosing as if to see what effect an arrow would have on a living thing. His expression told me he was hoping for something awful.

Ketill's arrow pierced that boar's bacon and glowed. Or part of it glowed as the runes carved into the shaft shone as if on fire. A simple carving, *jera* inverted and then *gebo*. Molten fire seemed to light those carvings bit by bit. My mind was half on tearing the head off a large Rus with a large axe and half on deciphering that carving. Well, *gebo* meant 'gift,' so that was easy, but the inverted—

That was as far as my mind got when the boar exploded in a hail of meat and bone.

The force of it splattered the surrounding Rus with gore and knocked half a dozen down. To my further surprise, they were not getting up. There was no fire, no smoke, but the sound stilled the battlefield for just a moment as everyone's heart jumped and then settled as they collectively stole glances in that direction.

The boar's legs were attached to nothing, and they fell to the ground in different directions.

"AHA! It worked," said the wizard as he demanded a second arrow from the figure next to him. "Keep carving that," he demanded. Ulfberht's face was white with terror, his face a mask of misery. Still, he drew another arrow and carved what he was told, perhaps the only one of Ketill's charges with that unique ability to follow a simple direction.

The raven passed us overhead, speaking a verse this time. Said Humor:

> "Weary warriors
>   wonder aloud at
> fell deeds of
>   fallen fiends.
> That evening rider

> will rob you of life
> if she stops that wasted
> wizard's stinging!"

Winged things I had hardly noticed converged on the raven. Bats maybe, and things with necks too long to be bats but just as hideous to look on. I roared to warn the raven, but my call did no favors. Humor dodged the first two, swooping out of the way easily, only to find something bigger coming head-on.

It was a vulture, or vulture-sized, beak as big as Humor's head. My eyes went wide as the raven did not attempt to avoid this one.

The quick, high-pitched *ack-ack-ack-ack* came too late for the vulture to turn. High Pants tore through the larger bird like a javelin and came out its other side splattered in gore. Humor flapped away laughing as his former pursuers scattered. That was some good hawk.

Hrolf's lines were still hard-pressed on all sides, but that man knew what stood between his warriors and victory. "Skullsplitter," he called out, "take your men and protect that wizard! We will meet you in the middle."

I was loathe to leave the fighting right around us, but it had to be done. It would be a close thing even if Hrolf's lines did not collapse. From somewhere unseen, Alfhild's angry screech reverberated. At that, her minions massed in one direction: Towards Ketill.

Three killers, however, had already left our ranks before Hrolf could even voice his command. Innstein and Utstein tried to outrace one another to get there first while Nanthild followed. How many times had she fought alongside her brother already? Neither pair of siblings would be easily parted.

Spearmen, axemen, trolls, wargs, misshapen things I had no name for came at me to slow my own advance. I took their limbs if they stayed partly out of range and took their heads otherwise. Haldor did the same, cleaving deep into one enemy after another. We piled body parts in pools of blood. Death and destruction, blood and fury; I was content to continue fighting without another thought. The Bear and the Skullsplitter side by side. One after another our enemies fell, but their numbers were hardly lessened. Only utter dismemberment or Ketill's arrows put them down permanently.

"Push them back!" demanded Haldor, despite their greater numbers.

Ketill's arrows sailed over our heads, accompanied by his drunken chortling. Organized pockets of the enemy attempted to form into makeshift units to attack our protective barrier. Intermittent explosions in their rear ranks always followed soon after. The front ranks arrayed against us began to shudder at those sounds.

Yet still our line lost ground as men faltered. The king's champions had come with us and were fatigued and bleeding, but they fought on. Hromund held his shield to his side with a likely broken arm. Beigadh was half-dazed from a blow that had destroyed his helmet. Hromund wheeled to cover Beigadh despite the injury as they were about to be swarmed by a coordinated attack of human-ish looking trolls. The two champions had almost regained our line when they disappeared behind a wall of dead men.

We could not meet Hrolf's group in the middle. Men in the line staggered and fell to spears or axes or claws. Others rushed in to replace them. Our smaller line around Ketill could hold but for the faltering suddenly upon so many. Ulf took an axe to the boss of his shield he should have shrugged off but instead sent him reeling. Inga had to set down her charge and held her spear steady.

Ulfberht, to the wizard's vocal annoyance, became distracted in his carving and only regained his mind with encouragement from Nanthild. Seeing the line's need for reinforcement, she then gestured and spoke to the brothers keeping watch at Ketill's side. They disliked it but obeyed, leaving the wizard's side to reinforce the line because something was wrong.

Something smelled wrong. It smelled like magic.

Not the kind I had become accustomed to, like the fresh greenery of the forest indicating the presence of *landvættir* in a friendly mood. Not the crisp breeze blowing in off snow-capped pines from my previous travels or the warm welcome of bread baked by my foster mother's hand on my returns. Not the hint of harmony I could conjure when stopping to tell stories and weave a bit of wonder in the minds of my audience. This was a smell from a rotting branch of the same family that had more to do with blood and rust than fresh air.

The smell of Ironwood, from which many of these things had been summoned. The stink of it mixed with the smoke of burning buildings and bodies to make the air so heavy it felt like swimming just to walk around.

Alfhild had spoken three spells with Leif's sacrifice. First a summons, and hence that boar in the face to begin the battle. Raising the dead she had waited to use until much of her force had fallen. Now the final spell, a magical torpor, threatened to drag down the last Danish defenders. Black wisps eddied up from the earth and tugged at our legs. The battlefield was so thick with *seiðr* it was as if we fought in between realms for the right to return to Midgard.

No such arms reached for Kraki, however. The moonglow of his pale skin was left unarmored in all its sagging, wrinkled glory. Alfhild's spell and minions alike recoiled from that figure. Forward he rushed, past our line to fight beside me in the melee, eyes bright with the light of rage. It was a malevolence to double whatever horrors met it, to be the monster that monsters hide in fear of.

In that frantic effort, I lifted a warrior bodily above my head to let all see him thrash, and I pulled him apart by his ribcage.

It was in that effort I had risen up to my full height and saw something more clearly than before. Inga held two spears and passed one to the injured warrior she had held before. Fanya took her spear with one hand and braced herself up on one knee with it. Blood pulsed through the fingers of her other hand. That hand was the only thing holding her guts in.

Whatever spell she was speaking, I could not make it out over my own deafening cries. Up I swiped with great, razor-edged paws one way and then another, clearing whatever foemen I could reach in a blind rage. One warg I slammed into the ground only to lift it and repeat the process over and over until I saw not the warg's brains (although those were there, in multiple places), but the ground itself.

Louder than I could ever be, louder than anything I had ever heard, thunder cracked open the sky while the wind whistled and began to clear the mist of Alfhild's conjuring. The black tendrils dragging us down dwindled. Some withered completely under the lightning.

Thunder crackled in the air. Cloud to cloud strikes lit the sky. And the murk that was Alfhild's conjuring began to retreat against the brightness.

Inga cradled Fanya's face and the two spoke too low for me to hear. Turning around, Inga shouted a plea to anyone listening. "Find the queen!"

It was too obvious after her command—of course Fanya had lit the way to Alfhild. We would need to strike her down or continue fighting through her spells.

Lightning lit a clearer battlefield than before. Hrolf had not joined his group with ours but rather attacked with none but Kraki at his side. The clearing showed his champions still alive. The cook and the new king cut and bludgeoned their way through to Hromund and Beigadh. Pulling those two back in got a great cheer from the Danes, and they pressed harder against the horde as a whole.

Beyond the edge of even the horde pressing Hrolf's far flank, I caught a glimpse not of Alfhild but of something near as good. Out there, her lindworm slithered back, away from the fighting. Only one reason that serpent could be headed away from the fight, and that was to rally to its master.

Lightning struck again, and for a second it was brighter than daylight. Out beyond the gate, there she was, sitting in a tall *seiðr* chair and weaving her magic.

I followed Fanya's wish then and left to bite the heads off of both proverbial and actual snakes. The lindworm had almost crushed me to death before, but it would have no advantage of surprise as I chased it down. It would be a straight fight, and I intended to tear that thing's tongue out through its asshole. I charged forward and through the enemy line. Spears struck at me but fell or snapped under my onrushing form, some of their wielders crushed underfoot.

Dead men exploded around me as thunder boomed above, announcing my race towards the lindworm as if Thor rode to battle at my side.

Gudbrand's horse snorted, and I turned to see he had ridden his mount around the enemy flank. Layers of mail clinked in time with his beast's stride, and through the eyelets of his helmet, I could see his goal. He was charging straight for Alfhild, knowing he had to end her to end the battle.

We attacked from different directions; I pitted my speed against his horse and lost. I closed in on the lindworm, the big serpent too stupid to run from what had become my singular existential purpose. Silhouetted against the fires, I saw Gudbrand's great horse go down from a bolt to its chest. Gudbrand kicked out of his stirrups before the horse stumbled forward and fell, breaking its neck.

Even fully armed and armored, the staller was agile enough to manage a rolling fall and keep his weapon.

The lindworm lay between me and Alfhild. Frothi guarded her other side. He was still reloading his crossbow when Gudbrand thrust the atgeir at his face. Well in time, Frothi abandoned his slow-loading crossbow to take up his sword and shield. That was a fight I wanted very much to see, but I had my own duel.

The lindworm coiled in over itself, readying for a powerful strike. Perhaps it had fought strong warriors before. They likely stopped to circle around it, see how it moved, and made tentative attacks.

I was not in a mood for anything tentative. I wanted to feel its blood stain my fur while it shuddered in agony. I slowed not one bit as I leaped for its head.

Our first fight's outcome I put down to surprise, but I had relied too much on my strength and, consequently, done a good deal of flailing. That would not happen again.

I was so intent it would not happen again that I overshot the thing entirely when it ducked out of my way at the last moment. Moving that much bulk that fast had its disadvantages, one of which was the inability to stop quickly. I soared over the ducking lindworm, if we can call what a serpent does ducking. Steadying myself with all four paws I came to a full stop, and that is the moment the lindworm chose to strike at my face.

Maybe the worm expected me to flinch at that. I was in no mood. Defense at all was not on my mind.

I ducked my own head, forcing the toothy strike low, and turned enough to drive it into my shoulder. This would be where the lindworm expected me to fall backwards.

Instead, I wrapped my paws around the back of its neck and drove the thing belly-down into the ground. The teeth ground through my armored fur and deep into muscle and bone. They tore streaks of pain in my shoulder as the thing tried to wrench free.

A scream from elsewhere on the battlefield pierced my ears like a nearby thunderclap. It hung there a long time, and I roared along with it finally to help drown it out, so loud it was.

The lindworm had not expected me to give up a bite to my shoulder to gain better position. The first few seconds were of wriggling to get free, and then a sense of urgency that it might not be able to. The thing lashed with undeniable force, smashing pylons in the city walls. I dug my claws into its sides just behind the head so that every movement it made tore its own flesh.

The contest of pain versus pain was on, and I looked on it as if watching myself. I was winning, and terror took the thing as I walked up on it with my hind legs, bending its head back, and back, and back. It was trapped in my embrace and could see its own doom.

Rage drove me forward on huge, clawed feet as I thought of Kari Swifthand's broken body. I pushed, and pushed, drove forward until I heard the thing's last sound.

Crack.

No more lindworm, at least for now. Other things were closing in on me, but they stopped short after seeing the fight had finished. I pried the dead thing's clamped jaws off my shoulder but I was not done with it, oh no. That was the first I knew of bloodlust, and I intended to kill that thing until it was dead beyond raising. Once off me, I ripped its lower jaw right off so the tongue lolled out in a testament to its utter defeat.

No sooner had I done this than every unnamable fiend in Alfhild's horde seemed to climb upon me and secure itself with teeth or claws.

Dead things rose around us, far out of Ketill's range. Frothi did not so much rise as refuse to die despite being stuck on the blade of Gudbrand's atgeir. The staller had won the fight but could not disengage to get around Alfhild's last bodyguard. At the point so close to killing the enemy commander, the staller was stuck, and I was mobbed by enemies.

We would make it a feast for ravens indeed, but my injuries were taking a toll and the two of us were just short of being able to press that attack home.

I fought the group amassed around me. Gudbrand planted the butt of his weapon in the ground and raced around his adversary. If only he could reach her in time, he could end the battle.

Alfhild lifted her distaff toward the charging staller, smiling. He would not reach her in time. Still sitting, she rose into the air above her seat, hair and robes floating weightless around her, and pointed her weapon. Though I raged, too many hangers-on prevented me from moving at more than a crawl.

At the last, a final player appeared out of the darkness. No ferocity matched this maniac, not mine or Haldor's or Kraki's. And Gudbrand's cold calculation paled in comparison to this critical timing. Where she came from, I could not say. She was a blur of white out of nowhere anyone had expected a new front.

Rota the cat emerged from the darkness and sped toward Alfhild, unerring and merciless as Odin's spear. The cat took to the air, used the chair as a springboard, and came down on the queen's head. Four taloned paws wrapped fully around her face and teeth tore at her ear while ribbons of blood opened across that smooth skin.

The witch queen dropped to the ground screaming, and the sound of it made me forget I was wounded. She lowered her distaff out of shock and pulled at the cat, stumbling away.

Whatever magic she had relied upon shuddered as if hit in the chest with a forge hammer. Half the contingent I was fighting lost its artificially bestowed life, and the rest I tore apart. I panted from the exertion and eyed my remaining enemies, snatched one into my paws and slammed his head deep into the ground.

Behind us, there was another explosion. Ketill had survived. The wizard was coming, and the wall of unnamed things in front of me was disappearing faster than ale in Svein's drinking horn.

I wanted to feel the crunch of Alfhild's skull between my teeth and taste her blood more than I had ever wanted anything else in my life. I turned toward her, but she was gone.

One moment I had seen her extricate herself from the cat, then I threw down one more warrior and when I looked back, she had evaporated like morning mist. Or whatever would be like morning mist on the night of a fire-lit, smoke-covered battlefield full of the thrice-dead and dying.

I roared my frustration, a thirst that could now not be sated, and intended to charge our enemies yet again and bring the full force of the bear down on them.

That was my intention. I also had half my ribs broken, many hard knocks to my head, and had been bleeding from dozens of wounds. Whatever they tell you about shapeshifting, whatever casual ease it is mentioned with when Loki or Odin do it, know that it takes a toll on you.

So I turned around to face a disintegrating horde of men and things, Gudbrand at my side, took one step, and fell flat on my face.

CHAPTER 46

A WARM UNWELCOME

"THAT WAS A DISAPPOINTMENT," SAID THE ROUGH VOICE.

"Of course it was. We knew that already." The second voice was smoother but not musical. More like wind over a field of grain as it picked up to tell you to get home for the evening. Maybe a bit annoyed at having to call out in the first place.

A third voice joined them, steady and amused. "Only one disappointment I saw. Many things have yet to be decided. The spear of the gods is as much a riddle as a plan."

I opened my eyes to a blurred world. A longhouse, no doubt, though it was difficult to see. Was I in Lejre? No, that hall had burned to the ground. And someone had crashed through one of the walls.

Oh, that had been me. It was coming back to me in slow waves. Memories were vague and indistinct, but the more effort to conjure them I made, the stronger they became.

I had been here before, this hall in Asgard. The first time I had walked in through the door, but this time I came to while lying on the floor. I sat up next to a hearth fire in the middle of the hall.

Savory stew bubbled in a cauldron. Torchlight augmented the cooking fire. The place was impossibly bright for so few flames and I squinted after opening my eyes. The length of the place was just as immense as I remembered, neither end of the hall visible from where I sat.

Once again, three gods argued nearby.

A goddess helped me to my feet. Idunn was just as beautiful as I remembered as she held her hand out to me. I took it, grateful for the help. Her touch was soft and warm, a needful comfort even though I could not quite remember what I needed comfort from. Idunn smiled, a little sadness in her green eyes, not looking at all like she might claw my eyes out for eating one of her apples.

"Many things, yes," said Frey. "A single acorn is just a hope. It is many seeds that make for a good harvest."

"Harvests come and go," said Heimdall. "An oak is unconcerned with passing storms."

"Clear as a snow-covered lake," huffed Thor. "Let me know when you two are done riddling and– O-ho! Here he is again!" He slammed a massive fist on the table, shaking the very foundations of the hall, and pointed an accusing finger at Heimdall. "Some watchman you are!"

My head throbbed, yet the gods were clearer to see this time.

"How he got here, again, is what I would like to know," said Frey. His left hand dropped absently to the hilt of his sword. It was no sword, however, but only a deer antler in his belt.

He traded his sword for a wife who did not want him, I thought, musing on that particular myth.

"After what we have seen, I am not surprised," said Heimdall. As he turned, one misshapen ear showed a wound from claws or teeth.

He lost an ear when he and Loki fought in the form of seals, I remembered, although there were many versions of that story.

Thor reached for his great hammer Mjolnir. "Surprise or no, I will show him out!" As he shouted, a piece of stone showed itself among his thick, red hair.

The whetstone piece stuck in his head from his fight with Hrungnir. A vǫlva nearly removed it, but a distraction caused her to forget her spells, and so it remained stuck fast in his head.

Standing less gobsmacked before the gods this time, it was not just their finery I noticed. They were scarred, or had lost something. All of them.

"That is some hospitality you offer!" The woman's voice cut like a blade of ice and stopped Thor's rage cold. "I remember a time when such a visit would have been a source of congratulations and respect. Perhaps he happens upon the ill-prepared, that he finds them so ungracious!"

"Easy to be prepared with only *one job* to do," said Frey. "Other than not being kidnapped, of course."

"As much as I enjoy the exchange of insults, it is not helpful," said Heimdall. "There are plans to lay, choices to make. Idunn, please escort the visitor away from here."

Her hand on my shoulder was strong but gentle. I turned to see her expression, not at all the rage I remembered from before. "Hush," she whispered before I could say anything, and palmed something into my mouth with her other hand.

Away she led me, down the hall that never seemed to end, where I could see everything but the doors out. Brighter and brighter became that place until I could see nothing, yet my eyes did not sting from it. The only sensation was of floating. Down, always down. And with the sour flavor of apple on the back of my tongue.

CHAPTER 47

WORDS OF HONOR

MY RIBS REBELLED WHEN I TRIED TO SIT UP. I GASPED AND THEN relaxed back on the straw I lay on. A sideways glance was all I could accomplish. The bandages heaped upon me justified the pains I felt crisscrossing my body.

I was in a tent. It muted the bright light outside. A sunny day, one most were probably thankful for. I had no need for bright light, but I did need water. Blinking away the sleep, I found someone had left a cup within easy reach. Thank the gods for that person, whoever she was.

Ketill sat back on a bed of straw on the opposite side of the tent. His face was flushed and soaked with sweat as he stared wide-eyed at me. Was it cold? He was shaking. No, it was not cold, even as he clutched his blanket.

"How did you do it?" shuddered the wizard.

"Do what?" I said, swallowing with some difficulty. Movement was painful. Breathing was painful, and I resolved to only do just enough of it.

"Hel's dragon, boy," said the laid-out wizard, who seemed to find talking no less painful than I did. "The bear! How did you summon the bear?"

A fine question I had no answer for.

"It is good to see you survived," I offered back. "Assuming you are not about to die in this tent."

"My injury is unlike any of yours. The injury was too much drink for too long," he said through chattering teeth. "This is the recovery."

I had heard of this before but never seen it. Halstein had told me about men in their cups from the first of the morning, which Ketill had been, and they often did not stop for fear of what would come if they did. Mad ravings would presage illness and sometimes death.

"How long were you drunk?"

"Oh," he said with bushy eyebrows raised in contemplation, "who can say? Ha, no one. It was before anyone you know would have been born."

"What? How old are you?"

"Old. Too old to remember, even if I cared. I do not. I care how you summoned the bear."

"You know how well I understand the runes. You think I know what I did?"

"I had two days of craving a horn full of mead but without these maddening shakes, and I spoke with your friends. I know a few things you know and a few you do not. So: What were you carving on that disc in the hall? No one could tell me that."

"I was trying to cast a spell. I carved a disc, but . . . I bled on the wrong side before I threw it."

"What spell? Spell to do what?"

"An explosion. I wanted to blast a hole in the wall. Power of the sun, with the aurochs charging. We were desperate. I cut my hand, but too deep, and then I pressed the wrong side of the disc into my palm before I threw it." I examined my left hand, still healing from the gash. I had cut deep but didn't remember having a wounded paw while I was a bear. The injury remained with me as a man, though. "Then I was spent. Tried to get up but couldn't. Kari took a javelin in the arm to save me. And then . . ." And then memories of blood overtook me. Memories of thinking thoughts and feeling emotions that were mine and yet seemed impossible. Had I really felt that strong a craving for violence?

"And then you changed skins."

"How could what I carved have done that?" I had succeeded by accident only, an accident even the wizard could not explain.

Ketill shook his head. "I can't see how it would. And it would not have blasted that wall. Can't blow something up with the power of the sun. That is light. Energy and warmth. Guides your way and keeps away certain things men don't like. Fire in concentrated form? You should have inverted *isaz*. But

I did not teach you inversions, and that still is the wrong way to think about rune carving."

"How do you think about it then?"

"You cannot—" He choked and coughed, too much energy in his voice to handle in his current state. The wizard held up a hand telling me he would live, however, so I waited. Minutes went by before Ketill reasserted control over his breath. "I spoke with the *vǫlva*. She told me about your incitement of Halfdan the Toothless. You already know magic, boy. You keep approaching the runes as if they are different from your poetry. But carving is a kind of poetry just like playing the lyre is a kind of poetry. Just different forms. When you goaded Halfdan into a fight, what did your poem say? 'Halfdan gets angry now'? Of course not. You crafted something that reacted with him to create the effect of him getting angry. Ha, 'shy of shield walls,' and of course he is."

"I don't know about reacting there. Wood does not just crumble. At least did I choose the disc correctly, an ash?"

"No."

"Well, which disc then? And what was it you carved on your arrows— should I have used that?"

"None of the discs! You wanted an effect on the wall, carve runes on the troll-cursed wall! *Laguz* : *kaunan* for roughly 'water ulcer' to make the wall rot, and then break through, among other possibilities. And why would you try to copy my arrows? I used them to deliver a counterspell to what the witch cast on her army."

"How did you know what to carve then?"

"I did not," Ketill snorted. "Not until it worked, at least. What kind of magic Alfhild would use to bring her warriors back from the dead was a guess when I saw them rise. I did not design runes that said 'make the recipient explode.' I considered the witch's most likely spells and carved a subversion of it. *Purge gift*, because most of the ways I could figure her casting that spell involved life as a gift, otherwise she would keep less control over them. Forcing an issue like that generally has some disgusting results. I thought they would just throw up and die. I was rather pleased with the actual result."

"Shit. I don't understand the carving at all."

"It is not your magic. Yet. All things are difficult at the beginning. You have more practice in your art, but do not think you are limited to it. You are capable of more than you think you are."

"My art. So I goaded a stupid jarl into a fight. What else has my art been good for? The men say they need poetic telling of their deeds, but what of it? What they needed was someone who knew how to carve runes onto a wall to weaken it so they would not burn to death."

"Or someone to wear a bear's shirt."

"I do not know how to do that again. Or if I want to. It was more than a skin change. It was—" I stopped short of voicing the thought, recalling Huld's rooftop yawn and the subsequent pair of voices she spoke with. That was the essence of *seiðr*, to let a spirit into you for a time. I shivered in disgust —to be ridden by something else that took up residence inside me was not an experience I wanted to think about. Like inviting a guest into your home, if your home was very, very small and cramped, and your guest was a hundred vipers.

But I didn't know *seiðr*, not even a little, so that could not be it, either.

"Your shape is a fluid thing. But a bear? That is not an easy change." The wizard shuddered again, drawing the blanket tight. He paused for a long time, unable to catch his breath. "What were you thinking about as you cut into your hand for that spell?"

"I was thinking I wish Ketill were here to cast this blasted spell. I was thinking I wish the survival of us all were not on my shoulders. I was thinking . . ." I relaxed in reverie and brought my mind back to those moments, but they were all well before I cut my hand or even carved the runes. The fear of failing my friends had turned into a manic sense of urgency when I thought I was failing Fanya. I did not wish to relate that part and so did not mention it. "I whispered 'No.'"

The wizard considered this for a long time. Conversation outside the tent was audible but indistinct. Outside, people conversed and worked in the waning light of the afternoon. A smell of burned-out buildings that told something of the battle lingered, but it was not the only thing in the air. Freshly sawn wood and stew cooked out in the open mingled there as well. The sounds of hammering and bustling outside told of rebuilding. The battle had happened. Lives would move on because to dwell on the past would be a bit of death every time.

"Difficult to say," said the wizard, chewing over the words as if there were many more he was not yet willing to speak. "Maybe Odin favors you, who knows. But you had better hope it was something other than the Gallows Lord. He takes more than he gives, always."

Ketill did not need to remind me of that. Odin never favored anyone for very long, even kings. Soon enough, they all met with bad ends either by his machinations or by his own hand. That was one faithless god, and he had left me broken and near death if it had been his hand behind it.

"Maybe that is why Ragnvald died," I said. "Put his faith in the gods. Got run over by a demon boar."

"At least he died fighting. Hrolf won the day. For his uncle, there was sadness but also relief a more vigorous man would rule. There was more grief for that witch who turned against the queen."

Here was the bottom of the spiral. Fanya, my love, the only person who wanted to see me so much it hurt, was dead.

"I saw her wounded," I croaked out, determined to not express any emotion in front of another man. I must have known from the time I saw her injuries that she would not survive, but here was proof.

"Yes, her last moments," Ketill continued, as if describing no more than the last moments before sunset on a pleasant day, "her last breaths included some instructions after the invocation. Gudbrand wanted her buried in the fens with great honors and valuable trinkets laid about in her mound. Probably he hoped to count her spirit among the local *dísir*. It made sense."

Thank goodness Ketill knew enough to mention it casually so that I might react in kind and not admit to being so taken with her. To be broken up over the death of a woman would be unmanly, to show it intolerable.

"I missed her burial then."

"You missed her pyre. I said Gudbrand wanted the burial. Inga demanded cremation. Said that was the witch's wish as she lay dying."

"What about the invocation?"

"Not clear. Does it matter?"

Perhaps not. And perhaps showing it mattered to me even if it didn't matter enough to change anything was a mistake. I struggled with how to respond and decided what I thought would be the most Norse response.

"It doesn't matter. Tell me anyway."

"Inga said something about the sky or the air, speaking in a familiar-sounding language but one that did not make sense to her. But I do know what the lightning did that night: It lit the battlefield in a way the fires did not. That was also when wind cleared the air of that noxious vapor pulling at us all. I think that witch showed you where Alfhild hid in a dark corner of the battlefield. And I know there was no indication lightning would be in the sky that night after a cloudless day. She showed us our enemies and turned the tide."

He paused then, after giving quite a lot of information for someone who had just acted as though none of it mattered.

"Did she summon Thor?" I growled in bitter sarcasm.

"Bollocks to Thor, that fat, goat-seducing troll!" spat Ketill, suddenly rising to his feet. "Where was his hammer when men of Midgard needed him? She spent her life casting that spell. It was her own casting, her own expense. Give no credit to gods for that. Coming down to deal out boons based on petitions. We bought victory with sweat and blood, some more than others."

The room rocked as if the ground bent and shifted beneath me. The tent twisted as if curled up by an unseen force. Straw beneath me flew from a gust of wind. The effects made me think I had been knocked hard on the head and then had far too much to drink, but I knew the cause was the wizard's ire. He had just made men and beasts explode not a few days prior and nearly killed me with a careless spell before that. There was power behind his words, so much he did not even realize what he had loosed until it left his lips.

Returning to his seat, Ketill calmed and did not sit so much as fall back down onto his straw bed. The room stopped wobbling and the inexplicable wind ceased.

Huld rushed into the tent, staff raised as if ready for battle.

"Huld?" I croaked.

The old *vǫlva* sneered as she looked around. "What is going on here?"

Ketill shrugged and rubbed his head. He had the look of a man whose everything hurt. "I did not intend to make more work for you."

"Do that again," said Huld, "and I will have less work by half, because that will be the end of you!"

The wizard nodded slowly, his eyes closed.

"Where have you been?" I asked. "How did you come back? I mean, what—"

"Hidden," she said, cutting me off. "When someone speaks up for a friend, a friend remembers. Never you mind the rest."

"But you were gone," I said.

The *vǫlva* hmphed at me and put her hands on her hips. "So like a man," she said. "Something is out of sight, and to you it is gone. Well, I am not gone, am I? If I had really gone, you would be dead and your friend would wish he was dead."

"Who said I don't?" croaked Ketill as he rubbed his temples.

"I will remember that gratitude when I bring tomorrow morning's porridge," said Huld. "Now keep your talking to regular talking if you want to recover. Both of you."

She did not wait for a response before leaving. The tent flaps shut behind her and then it was just me and Ketill again. Both of us feeling worse than when I had woken up.

"We have talked long enough," said Ketill. "The crew awaits your recovery. They want to see the man who became a bear. They think it is a sign Odin is with them. Pity us all if that one-eyed evildoer has taken notice of your tiny ship."

He was asleep within seconds. I regretted demanding so much explanation of him, yet still had questions. Why did that troll call me cousin? Where had Huld gone, and when did she come back? And what had really happened to me?

I pondered this as I rolled alliterations over in my mind, preparing to put on a good show for the crew when it came time. I had slept for three days but would cheerfully shut my eyes again to avoid that responsibility. There was no avoiding it and no sleeping for some time. The question I kept returning to as I scanned the wizard's face, however, was this: How did he know Thor was fat unless he had seen him as I had?

CHAPTER 48

THE CHOICE

"Heel to toe
   hewed Silence,
the heads of unhappy
   harrowed trolls.
The water demon
   weaved her spells.
Her loom unraveled
   under the light.

The wizard's hail
   halted her monsters,
A coming of the tide
   to crush that queen.
Her fiends fell
   by the firelight
When Haldor's Heroes
   hurried down that hill."

I REMEMBER THE END VERSES. THE WHOLE THING WAS LONGER
and paid some homage to the dead. Leif and Kari by name, Ragnvald got a

sidelong mention. Fanya I named first and with a kenning, which seemed only fit. The exact lines I cannot recall. It was a long time ago, and for all the praise I received, it was the loss I felt that stayed with me.

The crew cheered and clasped me on the shoulder and congratulated me until I couldn't take any more. The shoulder pain was hardly the worst of it. That was still the ribs—breathing hurt and talking hurt even more. But I wasn't going to let that stop the verses. I had to speak them, for the fallen, for myself.

Every man had his turn in making it plain how happy he was to have me as a crewmate. They were immortal with such a skald who was obviously favored by Odin. I did not like that explanation, but having no other, I did not argue.

I can't recall the rest of what I had composed for the crew, but only the last stanzas really mattered. It set their blood afire, especially 'Haldor's Heroes.'

I spoke the verses just outside the tent I recovered in, which I intended to go right back to. Just a little skalding, I thought, and that was as much of the world as I could take. Others had other plans, however, and soon I could not disappear quite as easily as I had intended.

Ever one to make a scene about himself, Svein demanded silence for a moment. It was for Haldor's ritual, he said, which was for me, though neither I nor Haldor needed the quiet.

An armring of silver, two axeheads facing away from each other, was my reward. No praise was spoken. No oaths were sworn. The giving of it said all. I was no longer just a hanger-on of the crew. I was one of the Brotherhood. One of Haldor's Heroes.

It was a bittersweet reward, but one I had to fight showing emotion over. The armring was a gift, a symbol, a connection, the same way a child is given a gift along with a name. Assuming the child isn't left to be exposed, of course.

And it was not my only gift. Hrolf also was a ring-slinger that day. I and every other member of the crew received his gift as he recounted something he saw each person do. Though not part of the crew, he gave them also to Nanthild and Ketill.

The implication was clear. Hrolf would be the new king, and he wanted us to remain as his new champions to fill out his hall.

Haldor accepted the ring, but made no comment. It was a great honor, and yet all I wanted was for the attention centered on me to stop. At times like that, only a true friend knows what to do without being asked.

"And who recruited him?" shouted Magnus, already animated beyond all reason. He moved man to man, seeming to ask each question of someone new, yet addressing everyone. "Who found him in the first place? Why, where do you think he would be if not for my intervention? I think maybe a finder's fee is in order—oh don't shake your head, Ulf, how many bear-poets have you recruited to this crew? Haldor! What do you think?!"

"I think there is much work to do," said Haldor. "Get to it."

And with a few parting chuckles, everyone did.

There was an unspoken conspiracy between myself and everyone else. They would pour adulation over me and I would act the humble skald. In truth, they had no idea what to make of me, perhaps even less so now than before. A skald who could not fight but might change into a giant bear made no sense. Should they take it that I was favored by Odin, or that I had learned some strange magic to be suspicious of?

I knew even less than they did on that count. I only knew enough to attribute none of our victory to competence on my part. Leaning on a spear for support, I smiled through my grimaces to show the endurance to physical pain I had developed. They assumed my pain stemmed from still-healing injuries. It was, but not the physical kind, and there seemed to me no healing for it. I suspect only Magnus knew the truth.

Then there were too many things to do for even an injured man to sit idle. I helped with light labor as I could, wandering the city to look for small errands I could accomplish. Really I was looking to speak with my friends without an audience gathered round.

Having helped save my life, Huld would remain with us for our own good. I had this from Magnus, who repeated her many criticisms of the men of the *Sea Squirrel* ad nauseam. We were idiots. We were morons. We created trouble and then pretended to solve problems when it would have been better to have no problems in the first place. Also, Svein was fat and stupid, and Ulf was more concerned about being considered a *drengr* than about being one.

I suspect Magnus may have used Huld's name to level a few criticisms he himself had authored. Then again, nobody disagreed that Svein was fat and stupid.

Ulf congratulated me on a battle well-fought. I saw something of myself in him when he spoke—whatever I saw or heard, it told me of pain and anger seething inside a happy shell outside. Perhaps knowing what it was to become that myself, I could see it in him. His right shoulder drooped from an injury, and something about the way he repeated 'Haldor's Heroes' sounded disapproving. "And what of the young Frank?" he asked as a casual afterthought.

I smiled to hide my confusion.

"I heard you mention the girl, but what about the young man we buried?" said Ulf.

I thought I might vomit. I had not known Ulfberht's fate. The last I saw of him, he was whole.

"We will drink to the memory of his courage," said Innstein, cutting in.

"He sealed the hole in our shield wall when we two became separated," added Utstein, also sounding less like himself than usual.

Perhaps wisely, the *þulr* shrugged and bowed out of the conversation.

"Ulfberht left Ketill's side then?" I asked.

"And drove his spear through the heart of some troll twice his size," said Innstein.

"Had to keep that shield wall intact," said Utstein. "They were trying hard to get through and stop those arrows flying."

Innstein nodded. "Ulfberht fell fighting there. No shield with him, just his spear. A warg grabbed it and pulled him forward and he fell while hanging on. We fought our way forward and thought we dragged him back in time. He bled out trying to stand up and take his place in the shield wall again."

"The battle scream from his sister when she saw him fall," said Utstein, stroking his beard. "And then the terror she brought down on them when she waded into their lines."

The scream. I heard that as I was running—it could have been heard all the way in Uppsala, I thought.

"And hasn't spoken a word since," said Innstein. "We thought she might be angry we had failed her brother. But she just put a hand to our shoulders and nodded once."

The brothers were still smarting from their failure. It was their efforts to appear otherwise that gave it away. Few times had they become separated in battle, they had fought so much side by side or back to back. They would not make such a mistake again, both of them said.

Next time, they said, it would take an army to break their ranks.

Nanthild put her hand to my shoulder and nodded once when I saw her as well. There was no accusation or anger. Her eyes told only of sadness. I wondered when she would speak again.

To my knowledge, she never did.

Nanthild followed Finnr to his forge rather than going back to brewing. The dwarf was no worse for wear, and I noticed the pattern of silver and black on his beard was familiar. It was not until later I remembered the same pattern on that earth-swimming badger during the battle. Finnr was able to change his skin, it seemed.

Only one man that day had a softer attitude than I had known before. Kraki dished out the disgusting rotted shark, as much of the other food stores had burned in the battle. He seemed to fling the portions at his crewmates with less force. He held my gaze for just a fraction of a second longer than expected when congratulating me on a good fight and a good poem. His grip seemed lighter for a moment before squeezing my forearm. As if an ounce of gentleness had snuck into his brain and he had been slow in tamping it back down.

There was more work that day. Also more bad food, but mostly work. I was in no shape for digging or woodworking and was aimless for a time since I had few ways to be useful. I wandered up the hill to see whatever remained of the great hall.

It was not much. I kicked away debris in the ruins, looking for something. Looking for what, I could not say. Just looking. Aimless and unable to do much other than walk slowly, I paced and pretended to investigate things when I felt prying eyes on me.

"If you are looking for the witch who tried to burn us," said Ingolf, "you can save yourself the trouble."

Valborg had died underneath about a ton of fur and muscle when I charged out of the hall. I had not given any thought to her remains.

"Did you burn her body?" I asked. "I can't tell if that would be appropriate or ironic. Perhaps a sea burial to quench her spirit."

"Neither," came the response, to my surprise. "We scoured the whole of this hill, especially where you broke through. There was no body."

A memory from the rush of blood and the explosion of burning wood came to me. Out I charged and landed right on top of that witch. I felt her chest break. Not just a few ribs.

"She could not have survived," I said.

Ingolf shrugged. "A body disappearing from the hill would hardly be the strangest thing to happen that night." I could not disagree. "Leif's body we set on a pyre."

He nodded at me, a serious thing. It would be too much to give his thanks or show his grief. He had the chance to send his sworn brother off because I had brought him down from the hung meat Alfhild had turned him into.

Leif had been flighty, more than a free spirit. At times annoying. He had been a bit like me, I thought. And in exploring, like me, he had been taken and used up for someone else's purpose. No one would forgive Alfhild for that.

I kicked something. It did not have the dry crunch of half-burned debris as most things did in those ruins. Wiping off a layer of ash revealed an almost impossible discovery: My knife and bag of rune carving discs had not been consumed by the fire. As I picked them up and shook off more of the soot it became even clearer that fire had not hurt either one at all. I looked around that spot for what other items must have been left behind when I changed skins, but found nothing.

The evening passed on too slow for my taste. I did not want to perform and had no instrument to play in any case. Sleep would not come easy, and I feared being pulled into another nightmare. Not some hall in Asgard this time but dragged along a dark path where trolls wandered. Watches were set throughout the night, given the gaping holes in the palisade, and I volunteered to give up sleep at night so those working by day could rest. It made sense, and Haldor agreed.

What Haldor had not agreed to was the plan I considered for being alone at that north gate. The aloneness allowed me to drop all pretense as long as I was out of sight. There I let all the shame I felt for failing out, my face in my hands.

My father could take no pride in a son who succeeded by happenstance. The change to the bear happened for reasons even the wizard could not explain. I felt Fanya's absence most of all. How she would have enjoyed the new stillness under the stars—a new calm was over the hills without the same suspicious air from the forests nearby. I had failed her, too, even as she had saved us all.

Facing the crew again with the same false smile seemed too much. Here I was alone, invisible. Lone men disappeared all the time. If I wished for the *landvættir* to have the forest swallow me whole, they would likely oblige. Or I could make my way down to Roskilde, drop into the water at the end of the pier, and kick out as far as my legs would take me until it was too far to come back. The sea never refused such offerings.

Yes, perhaps that was best. A disappearance to rid the crew of its burden and me of my ale-induced mistake in signing on. Should word ever reach him, my father would know only of my last acts in the battle for Lejre. A suitable memory to sustain him. I could live on in memory as one of Haldor's Heroes, even if my real end was to sneak away to stop the awful pain I felt. To the crew, I would just disappear like a spirit in the night, perhaps to bring them good luck later.

"We could tell your ribs hurt when you came out of the tent," said Kraki. Where he had come from or how he had snuck up on me, I had no idea. I turned to see him, half-expecting his amiable tone must be due to him sleep-walking.

"Everything is pain right now," I said, unable to think past speaking unfiltered truth. "I thought you would give me a good shaking when we clasped hands."

"I would not add to your pain. You took it on for the good of your mates. That is not shame. That is honor."

"It should have been you cheered today for honor. You knew what you were doing. I don't even know what happened, much less what to do next."

"Men who fight for cheering after are fools. The dead are the ones who need remembrance. You gave it to them. Is that not what you came for?"

"How much of that loss is my doing? I could have cast the runes correctly. I still can't, but I also can't control whatever it was that happened. I think it unlikely to happen again, in any case."

I stared fixed on a point out over the dark woods where I could discern nothing other than an uncertain expanse. The silence between us was long. I fought to keep my lip from quivering by gripping the side of a crooked post, my ribs aching from the tension throughout my body. Near a breaking point, I thought I might fall forward and never get up again. Or worse, cry.

The moment never came. Kraki's hand came to my shoulder, and a clap of thunder reverberated through my body. It was not the competitive clap of who can hit harder. It was elevation, support.

"We are fighting men," said Kraki. "We bleed together. We are knocked down together. Not our choices." Another long silence, and Kraki's hand fell away. "When we stand up together, then we are brothers. Standing up after defeat is a choice. For whatever reasons."

The staggering gait was audible as Kraki trotted away, no longer trying to conceal his presence and done saying what he had come to say. My gaze went from the unseen horizon to the sky above where stars lit the night. A gentle breeze rustled branches somewhere out there beyond my sight as if to release the tension from the forest. Tension it had too long held under its canopy.

Kraki turned to give me a sidelong glance. "Choose."

I stood there much longer, alone with my thoughts. The bear had left me, the only thing to save my life when I needed a real skill. But the bear left me with memories, with feelings, with memories of feelings. I remembered what must have been a feeling that had been part my mind and part the bear's.

We did what we had come to do, and the monster of Lejre, even if he was not a monster, was dead. It was Olgram's mother who was the concern now. She would regain power any way she could. She would remember our names, as well as the people of Lejre who had humiliated her forces in arms and magic.

I thought of Kari, saving my life once against the Rus, then twice in one night, and fighting on despite his injury. Of Ulfberht, putting himself in danger without a thought, standing firm while mortally wounded. Of Fanya, casting even as she held her own guts in. And I thought of Leif, not fallen in combat but *sacrificed*.

Alfhild would come for us. Haldor's Heroes would come for her first.

Fanya died asking for a pyre, not regretting her choices that caused her to need one. Kari died because even already wounded, he came to my aid and challenged the biggest monster on the battlefield. They had bent their every fiber toward victory without regard for their survival. A suicide would dishonor them, only I did not know how to move forward. I stood paralyzed, the horizon offering relief and an insane old warrior offering . . . what?

That unknown was what tipped my scale. It was the reason for my being who I was and who I would become, and what I would fight to the death over. Curiosity, for better or worse, had landed me all the discomfort that gnawed at my body and mind. But finding hidden things drove me forward as well. I did not yet know my story.

There was one story I had to know without delay, though. And so I ran after Kraki, who turned to me with no change in expression when I caught up.

I asked him: "How did the *Sea Squirrel* get its name?"

It was a good story. Maybe I will tell it someday.

The sun rose by the end of its telling, finishing a recounting I wished would never end. The sun burned away morning fog to reveal a new vista, a new world by then. There was nothing to do but go out into it and create more of my own story.

Coming next in Spear of the Gods Book Two: Rune to Ruin

- How much magic has Ansgar really learned?
- What happens when you go too deep under Midgard where some very unfriendly things live?
- How do you prevent a giant sea monster from swallowing your ship?
- Who wins more bets: Innstein or Utstein?
- What is Huld not telling everyone?

And many more exciting adventures as the *Sea Squirrel* heads into the far north!

About the Author

Gregory Amato made a career of selling his quill as a mercenary writer for many years. He wrote true and important things for newspapers, magazines, academia, and, for over a decade, intelligence analysis for the FBI.

Now, he writes fantasy stories based on the myths and sagas of the vikings. His fiction is often influenced by tales lost to time, usually full of high adventure, and always the sort that makes readers late to dinner.

Outside his time spent spinning yarns about vikings and wizards, he teaches Judo, brews beer, and plays DnD when he gets the chance.

Gregory lives happily with his family in the Pacific Northwest.

Acknowledgments

Like the skald in my story, I did not get to where I was going by myself.

A huge thank you to the many friends and family who supported me along the way. To my wonderful wife CJ. Without your love and encouragement, this book might not have happened. And to author Michael J. Sullivan and Robin Sullivan for your friendship and mentoring.

Thanks to my Alpha Readers Zepheniah Sole and CJ Grimes, who helped me make sure the major thrust of the story was on track, and provided early encouragement. Oh, how the manuscript changed from there!

Thanks to my Beta Readers Angela Marie Howe, Michael Klaas, Ryan Connole, Inga Thornell, and CJ Grimes, who helped me smooth out the narrative. I owe you all big favors.

Thanks to my most ultra-super-generous supporters on Kickstarter: Author Michael J. Sullivan, Ralph A. Iannone, Robert Amato, Dussstyyy, Christian Sledd + Greg Shepherd, Scott Mist, Karen M, IGK, Waldout, Thomas Edward Maguire (aka Tommy), Charles E. Norton III, and Amy Meskill. You guys rock!

I've been engrossed in Norse myths and the history of the people who told them for almost 30 years. I owe a great debt to the hard work and dedication of many philologists, archeologists, and other scholars.

Thank you in particular to Jackson Crawford for patiently answering questions when I thought I knew much more than I did, and for giving me the reading list that took me from motivated consumer to serious student. To Tom Shippey for being a fantastic educator, highly engaging writer, and also coauthor of the Hammer and the Cross series. Best Viking novels ever! To Neil Price for his exhaustive work on Norse mindset and magic. To Carolyne Larrington not just because hers is still the best translation of the Poetic Edda, but also for how she integrates modern media into her work. It is timely, and it is relevant to a vast audience.

You all, and many more, have kept alive stories that might otherwise have been forgotten. This story is based on real myths and beliefs that are not easily pieced together. We only know as much as we do about them because of your work, and this story would not exist without you. You are the real skalds.

Finally, the biggest thanks of all goes to you, the reader. Without you, there would be no Ansgar, no skalds, no need for stories. Thank you for reading!

Major Characters

Aldis – One of Queen Alfhild's three handmaidens.

Alfhild – Married to King Ragnvald of the Danes. Arguably the real wielder of power in Lejre.

Ansgar Styrgrimsson – The narrator and protagonist of the saga. A skald by trade, he gets plenty of good hospitality at the mead halls he visits for telling stories. He uses that good will as he travels, delivering weapons made by his foster father Halstein.

Arrow-Odd – A legendary saga hero. Ansgar's father Styrgrim fought for him 20 years ago against his old enemy, Ogmund.

Beigadh – Danish champion loyal to Ragnvald.

Bolli Mossneck – A vagabond warrior and friend of Ansgar's. An honorable man and a solid fighter. Lets his beard grow freely instead of trimming it.

Fanya – One of Queen Alfhild's three handmaidens. The first one Ansgar meets and, to his mind, the most beautiful woman in Midgard.

Finnr – A dwarf and master weaponsmith. Friend of Kraki Bentley.

Flosi – Fletcher in Lejre. A fair man who knows his archery, and has dealt with Ketill before.

Frey – God associated with good harvests and fertility. Used to have a very nice sword, but traded it for a wife.

Frigg – Wife of Odin, and one of very few people to outsmart him.

Frothi – Danish champion loyal to Alfhild. Keeps a unique weapon nobody else has seen, and a stupid haircut.

Fulla – Frigg's handmaiden. Most well known for bringing disinformation to King Geirroth ahead of Odin's arrival at the king's hall, thus setting the stage for Frigg to win a bet.

Gorm Tin-Whisker – Jarl on the island of Fjon. A friend of Ragnvald's.

Gulldis – "Queen" of Fretborg. Her husband Gansi has been absent a while, leaving her in charge. Likes shiny things.

Gudbrand Shirtless – The Danish king's staller. Ostensibly the keeper of the king's horses, he is more like the king's general problem-solver. Said to wear a chain shirt even when he's bathing. Prefers to fight from horseback—unlike most others—and uses an atgeir (heavy hewing spear). Fought alongside Ansgar's father for Arrow-Odd twenty years ago.

Haldor Skullsplitter – Leader of the Brotherhood, his sworn men and women, and commander of the *Sea Squirrel* crew when it comes to leading on land. A huge warrior, he and his Brothers seek out bounties no one else will take, supposedly all in the pursuit of their everlasting word-fame.

Halfdan the Toothless – Semi-famous viking known for the story that he bit his brother's throat out. Craftier than the story lets on, but not a very honorable man.

Halstein the Smith – Ansgar's grandfather and foster father. A smith of great renown in Midgard, working in the western fjord lands of what is now Norway.

Heimdall – The watchman of the gods, who guards the bridge between Midgard and Asgard. Incredible vision and hearing.

Hemming – The Brotherhood's tracker, trapper, and forward scout. Incredible woodsman, but poor as a warrior. Ill at ease in cities. Doesn't even like to sleep in a longhouse when he can avoid it.

High Pants – A northern goshawk trained by Hrolf. An aggressive, homicidal bird apt to attack things much larger than he is.

Hrolf – King Ragnvald's nephew. Rather tall and skinny, but a good fighter nevertheless. Keeps an aggressive hawk named Highpants.

Hromund – Danish champion loyal to Ragnvald.

Huld – A mysterious *vǫlva* (wise woman) in Fretborg. Disappears often and without warning.

Humor – A raven who frequents Ketill's company.

Idunn – Keeper of the apples of immortality in Asgard.

Inga – Lejre's main brewer after her husband Lambi was killed by Lejre's troll. Distrusts all associated with Ragnvald and Alfhild.

Ingolf – Crewman of the *Sea Squirrel* with his sworn brother, Leif. Serious, stoic, dependable.

Innstein – The Inside Stein. One of the two shipwrights who keep the *Sea Squirrel* seaworthy. Brother of Utstein. A bit shorter than his brother, but faster. Prefers to bet on long odds.

Kari – Haldor's closest advisor. Tall and agile, always tense before battle. Prefers short javelins as his main weapon, which he can throw with uncanny speed and accuracy.

Ketill – Known to residents of Lejre as a charcoal burner who lives deep in the forest nearby. He is more than they think. Also, total alcoholic.

Kraki Bentleg – The elderly captain of the *Sea Squirrel*. Carries a bone club. Never wears armor and usually doesn't even wear a shirt. Despite his advanced age, he is still strong and is hard against steel.

Leif – Crewman of the *Sea Squirrel* with his sworn brother, Ingolf. Silly, awkward, fun.

Magnus the Red – Both Anagar's heckler and the first person to invite him to join the *Sea Squirrel* crew. Short with bright red hair and arms like iron. Not a great fighter in a shield wall but almost without a peer in a melee.

Nanthild – Young Frankish woman kept as a thrall at the Danish court with her brother Ulfberht.

Njord – God of the sea. Supposedly has very pretty feet. Husband to Skadi.

Odin – A god strongly associated with war, sorcery, death, and wisdom. Hung on a tree as a sacrifice to himself in order to gain knowledge. Capricious and fickle, yet charming and wise.

Ogmund (Eythjof's Killer / Tussock) - Generations-long enemy of Arrow-Odd.

Ragnvald – Danish king, with very nice mead hall in Lejre. Alfhild's husband. Old and likely to defer to his wife's wishes.

Silfast – Owner of a mead hall that Ansgar frequents on his travels.

Skadi – Beautiful *jǫtunn* who married Njord. Good to call on if you're skiing or hunting. She prefers the mountains to his seaside home.

Subtlety – A raven who frequents the town of Fretborg.

Styrgrim the Bear – Ansgar's father and a man with a reputation for fighting. Mostly absent during Ansgar's youth and someone he wants to prove himself to.

Svein Helgisson – The biggest man on the crew of the *Sea Squirrel*. Bigger than Haldor and younger, but also fatter and slower. Knows Ansgar from growing up in the same village, where they both hated each other. Good fighter. Dumb as a rock.

Thorgils Thorkelsson – Intended recipient of Ansgar's delivery. He has six sons: Thorkel, Thorstein, Thorlief, Thormod, Thorald, and Thorarin. Also a daughter named Aslaug.

Taika – Ansgar's Sami foster mother and grandmother. Wife of Halstein the Smith. Taught Ansgar some woodcraft and gave him a lot of good advice he ignored.

Ulf – The *Sea Squirrel's þulr* (chief negotiator and diplomat). Formerly chief translator as well, but less so since Ansgar's arrival. Charming when he needs to be.

Ulfberht – Young Frankish man kept as a thrall at the Danish court with his sister, Nanthild.

Utstein – The Outside Stein. One of the two shipwrights who keep the *Sea Squirrel* seaworthy. The outside 'Stein. A bit bigger and stronger than his brother but not quite as fast. Prefers creative ways of getting people to make stupid bets.

Valborg – One of Queen Alfhild's three handmaidens.

Glossary of Old Norse Words

Æsir – Group of gods living in Asgard, including but not limited to Odin and Thor.

argr – Cowardly, weak, unmanly.

berserkr – Literally 'bear-shirt' or 'bare-shirt.' Usually a bully who is overrated in martial ability but howls a lot and wears too many animal skins. Plural: **berserkir**

Brísingamen – The golden torc belonging to the goddess Freya.

dísir – Supernatural female being with its own cult. This is a general term that may refer to a local spirit or spirits, or may refer to valkyries or the goddess Freya. Singular: **dís**

dísablót – Sacrificial ceremony for *dísir*.

draugr – A dead person who returns to harass the living. Usually this person was not well-liked in life. A ghost, but not in the sense of being a spirit, as they are fully corporeal; more like a ghost/zombie/vampire. Plural: **draugar**

drengr – A person of integrity and honor; a stalwart, courageous/brave person; a badass.

fornyrðislag – The meter of stories. A simple but effective poetic format consisting of eight half lines, each with two stresses, where one of the even numbered half lines contain a stress alliterating with the above half line. Example of two half-lines (stresses underlined):
This <u>wr</u>iter's <u>b</u>lood
   <u>b</u>lackens the <u>p</u>age;

fylgja – A female guardian spirit. Not subject to worship like *dísir*, this kind of spirit usually follows families. Plural: **fylgjur**

galdr – Sorcerous incantation, spell, sorcery, magic, song (with magical connotation), charm.

galdralag – The meter of magic. Poetic format with the intent of casting or describing spells. Structure is *ljóðaháttr* with one to two additional long (three stresses, sometimes just two) lines. Example:
This <u>wr</u>iter's <u>b</u>lood
   <u>b</u>lackens the <u>p</u>age;
<u>S</u>ummoning the <u>i</u>nk <u>e</u>lves.
<u>Cr</u>ushing the <u>k</u>eyboard <u>w</u>arriors.
<u>W</u>hispering the <u>u</u>nheard <u>w</u>ords.

galdramaðr – Sorcerer whose chief magical practice involves *galdr* and *galdralag*, focusing on linguistic aspects to cast spells. A wizard.

hamr – Shape, form, or skin.

holmganga – Ritualized duel for settling disputes.

hákarl – Fermented greenland shark. The worst food in the world.

Hávamál – 'Words of the High One.' Wisdom on how to live well delivered in verse, supposedly from Odin himself.

hnefatafl – Board game pre-dating chess, where one player tries to move his king from the center of the board to one of the edges, while the other player tries to capture the king.

hugr – Mind. Related to Odin's raven Huginn.

jǫtunn – Member of a tribe equivalent to the *Æsir*, but antagonistic to them. Frequently translated as 'giant' despite *jǫtnar* being of the same size as *Æsir* most of the time. Some are giant in size, but not all. Plural: **jǫtnar**

landvættir – Land–spirits.

ljóðaháttr – The meter of wisdom. Poetic format consisting of a full line of *fornyrðislag* followed by a third line, where the third line has three stresses (two of which alliterate). Example:

This writer's blood

 blackens the page;

I hope it had an effect.

níð – Scorn or libel so strong, it could lead to the speaker's outlawry.

níðingr – Villain, traitor, truce–breaker; a person worthy of scorn.

níðstǫng – A pole carved detailing a curse against someone.

Ragnarǫk – Series of events leading to the doom of the gods and the end of the world.

seiðr – Sorcery involving spirits used to work spells or for divination. Generally performed by women. Considered 'unmanly' despite Odin being its foremost practitioner. Possibly a victim of post viking–age sources' dislike for such magic.

útiseta – Sitting out in the open air for the sake of sorcery or prophecy, especially at night.

vættir – Spirits or supernatural beings, including but not limited to land-spirits, *dísir*, dwarves, and *jǫtnar*. Singular: **vættr**

vǫlva – A female practitioner of *seiðr*. Prophetess, wise woman, or witch, depending on the intent of the speaker. Plural: **vǫlur**

Yggdrasil – The world tree, probably an ash. Connects all realms such as Midgard, Asgard, Nidavellir, etc.

þulr (thulr) – Member of a court considered as a main speaker. Identical to Old English *thyle*.

þurs (thurs) – Giant, ogre, monster. Carries connotation of malevolence, but not necessarily large size.